NIGHT WORK

Also by Thomas Glavinic, available in English

Carl Haffner's Love of the Draw

NIGHT WORK

THOMAS GLAVINIC

Translated from the German by
John Brownjohn

CANONGATE
Edinburgh · New York · Melbourne

Originally published in 2006 in Germany and Austria by Carl Hanser
Verlag, München, Wien, under the title *Die Arbeit der Nacht*

First published in English in 2008 by
Canongate Books, Ltd. Edinburgh

The publisher acknowledges subsidy from the
Scottish Arts Council towards the production of this book

Scottish
Arts Council

ISBN-10: 1-84767-184-5
ISBN-13: 978-1-84767-184-4

Canongate
841 Broadway
New York, NY 10003

Distributed by Publishers Group West

www.groveatlantic.com

08 09 10 11 12   10 9 8 7 6 5 4 3 2 1

There's no happiness in living,
in bearing one's suffering self through the world.
But being, being is happiness. Being: transforming
oneself into a fountain into which
the universe falls like warm rain.

Milan Kundera, *Immortality*

1

'Good morning!' he called as he entered the kitchen-cum-living-room.

He carried the breakfast things to the table and turned on the TV. He sent Marie a text: *Sleep well? Dreamt about you, then found I was awake. ILU.*

Nothing on the screen but snow. He zapped from ORF to ARD: no picture. He tried ZDF, RTL, 3sat, RAI: snow. The Viennese local channel: snow. CNN: more snow. French-language channel, Turkish-language channel: no reception.

No *Kurier* on the doormat, just an old advertising leaflet he'd been too lazy to remove. Shaking his head, he pulled one of last week's papers from the pile in the hall and went back to his coffee. Made a mental note to cancel his order. They'd already failed to deliver it once last month.

He surveyed the room. The floor was strewn with shirts, trousers and socks, and last night's dirty plates stood beside the sink. The waste bin stank. Jonas pulled a face. He yearned for a few days' sea air. He ought to have gone with Marie, although he disliked visiting relations.

When he went to cut himself another slice of bread the knife slipped and bit deep into his finger.

'Damn! Ah! What the . . .?'

Gritting his teeth, Jonas held his hand under the cold tap until the blood stopped flowing. He examined the wound. He'd cut himself to the bone, but he didn't appear to have damaged a tendon. It didn't hurt, either. There was a neat, gaping slit in his finger, and he could see the bone.

He felt queasy, took some deep breaths.

No one, himself included, had ever seen what he could see. He'd lived with this finger for thirty-five years without ever knowing what it looked like inside. He had no idea what his heart looked like, or his spleen. Not that he'd have been particularly interested in their appearance, far from it. But this bare bone was unquestionably a part of him. A part he'd never seen until now.

By the time he had bandaged up his finger and wiped the table, he'd lost his appetite. He sat down at the computer to check his emails and skim the world news. His browser homepage was set to Yahoo. A server error message appeared instead.

'Damn and blast!'

He still had time, so he dialled the help line. The automated voice listing alternatives didn't answer. He let it ring for a long time.

*

At the bus stop he took the weekend supplement from his briefcase. He hadn't had time to read it before. The morning sun was dazzling. He felt in his jacket pockets, then remembered that his sunglasses were lying on the chest in the hall. He checked to see if Marie had texted him back, opened the paper again and turned to the Style section.

He found it hard to concentrate on the article. Something was puzzling him.

After a while he realised he was reading the same sentence over and over again without taking it in. He clamped the newspaper under his arm and took a few steps along the pavement. When he looked up he saw there was no one else in sight. Not a soul or a car to be seen.

A practical joke was his first thought. Then: it must be a public holiday.

Yes, that would account for it, a public holiday. Telephone engineers took longer to repair a faulty line on public holidays. Buses were more infrequent too. And there were fewer people in the street.

Except that 4 July wasn't a public holiday. Not in Austria, at least.

He walked to the supermarket on the corner. Shut. He rested his forehead against the glass and shaded his eyes with his hands. No one there. So it had to be a public holiday. Or a strike, and he'd missed the announcement.

On his way back to the bus stop he looked round to see if the 39A was turning the corner. It wasn't.

He called Marie's mobile. No reply, not even her recorded message.

He dialled his father's number. He didn't answer either.

He tried the office. No one picked up the phone.

Werner and Anne were both unobtainable.

Bewildered, he replaced the mobile in his breast pocket. At that moment it occurred to him how utterly quiet everything was.

He went back to the flat and turned on the TV again. Snow. He turned on the computer. Server error. He turned on the radio. White noise.

He sat down on the sofa, trying to collect his thoughts. His palms were moist.

He went to the corkboard in the kitchen and consulted a grubby slip of paper Marie had pinned up years ago. It bore the phone number of the sister she was visiting in the north of England. He dialled it. The ringing tone was different from the Austrian one, lower and consisting of two short purring sounds. After listening to it for the tenth time, he hung up.

*

When he went outside again he peered in both directions. He didn't pause on his way to the car, just glanced over his shoulder a couple of times. Then he stood and listened.

Nothing to be heard. No hurrying footsteps, no throat-clearing, not a breath. Nothing.

It was stuffy inside the Toyota. The steering wheel was so hot, he could only touch it with the balls of his thumbs and his bandaged forefinger. He wound the window down.

Nothing to be heard outside.

He turned on the radio. White noise on all stations.

He drove across the deserted Heiligenstädter Brücke, where the traffic was usually nose-to-tail, and along the embankment towards the city centre. He kept an eye open for signs of life, or at least for some indication of what might have happened here, but all he saw were abandoned cars neatly parked as if their owners had merely nipped inside for a moment.

He pinched his thighs, scratched his cheeks.

'Hey! Hello!'

On Franz-Josefs-Kai, driving at over seventy k.p.h. because he felt safer that way, he was flashed by a speed camera. He turned off onto the ring road that separates the centre of Vienna from the rest of the city and upped his speed still more. At Schwarzenbergplatz he debated whether to stop and look in at the office. He sped past the Opera, the Burggarten and the Hofburg doing ninety. At the last moment he braked and drove through the gate into Heldenplatz.

Not a soul in sight.

At a red light he screeched to a halt and killed the engine. Nothing to be heard but metallic pings from under the bonnet. He ran his fingers through his hair and mopped his brow, clasped his hands together and cracked his knuckles.

Something suddenly struck him: there wasn't even a bird to be seen.

*

He skirted the 1st District at high speed until he found himself back in Schwarzenbergplatz. Turning right, he pulled up just beyond the next intersection. Schmidt & Co.'s offices were on the second floor.

He looked in all directions. Stood still and listened. Walked the few metres back to the intersection and peered down the adjoining streets. Parked cars, nothing else.

Shading his eyes, he squinted up at the office windows and called his boss's name. Then he pushed the heavy door open. Cool, stale air wafted to meet him. He blinked, still dazzled by the brightness outside. The lobby was as gloomy, grimy and deserted as ever.

Schmidt & Co. occupied the whole of the second floor, six rooms in all. Jonas toured them one by one. He noticed nothing out of the ordinary. Computer screens on desks with stacks of paper beside them. Walls hung with garish amateur daubs by Anzinger's aunt. Martina's pot plant in its usual place on the window sill. Rubber balls, building bricks and plastic locomotives lying forlornly in the crèche corner installed by Frau Pedersen. His progress was obstructed at every turn by bulky parcels containing the latest consignment of catalogues. The smell hadn't changed either. A blend of wood, cloth and paper. You either got used to it at once or handed in your notice within days.

He went to his desk, booted up his computer and tried to access the Internet.

'This page cannot be displayed. There may be technical problems, or you should check your browser settings.'

He clicked on the address line and typed:

www.orf.at

'This page cannot be displayed.'

www.cnn.com

'This page cannot be displayed.'

www.rtl.de

'This page cannot be displayed. Try the following: Click on "update" or repeat the procedure later.'

The old floorboards creaked beneath his feet as he toured the offices once more, closely scrutinising them for something that hadn't been there on Friday evening. He picked up Martina's phone and dialled a few stored numbers. Answering machines only. He blurted out some incoherent messages followed by his phone number. He had no idea who he was speaking to.

He went to the kitchenette, took a can of lemonade from the fridge and drained it in one.

After the final swallow he swung round abruptly.

No one there.

He removed another can from the fridge without taking his eyes off the door. This time he paused between swallows and listened, but all he could hear was the lemonade fizzing in the can.

Please call me ASAP! Jonas

He stuck the Post-it on Martina's computer screen and hurried to the exit without checking the other offices again. It was a spring lock, so he didn't bother to double lock the door. He ran down the stairs three at a time.

*

For years his father had been living in Rüdigergasse, in the 5th District. Jonas liked the area but had taken an instant dislike to the flat, which was too dark and too overlooked. He loved to look down on the city from above. His father didn't mind passers-by gawping at him in his living room. It'd been like that before and he was used to it. Besides, he'd wanted to make things easier for himself since his wife's death. The flat was a few steps from a supermarket and there was a GP's surgery on the floor above.

On his way into the 5th District, Jonas had an idea: why not make a racket? He honked his horn as if he were in a wedding convoy. The speedo needle quivered on twenty. The engine stuttered.

Some streets he drove along twice. He looked left and right to see if a door or a window opened. It took him almost half an hour to cover the short distance to the flat.

He stood on tiptoe and peered through his father's window. The light was off. So was the TV.

He inspected the street, taking his time. This car's wheels were touching the kerb, that one was parked further out. A bottle protruded from a dustbin, the plastic cover on a bicycle saddle flapped gently in the breeze. He counted the motorbikes and mopeds outside the building. He even tried to memorise the position of the sun. Only then did he get out his duplicate key and open the front door.

'Dad?'

Quickly, he locked the door behind him and turned on the light.

'Dad, are you there?'

He called before he entered every room, trying to make his voice sound deep and forceful. From the lobby he went into the kitchen, then back through the hallway and into the living room. Next, the bedroom. He didn't forget the bathroom and toilet. He even stuck his head into the larder, with its chill smell of fermentation, of apples and cabbage.

His father, an inveterate collector and hoarder who spread butter on mouldy bread and heated up out-of-date tins in a double saucepan, was not there any more.

Like everyone else.

And, like everyone else, he'd left no clue behind. The whole place looked as if he'd just gone out. Even his reading glasses were lying in their usual place on top of the TV.

In the fridge Jonas found a jar of pickled gherkins that still looked edible. There wasn't any bread, but he unearthed a packet of rusks in the kitchen cupboard. They would have to do. He didn't feel like opening the larder door again.

While eating he tried, without much hope, to get a TV channel. He couldn't entirely dismiss the possibility, because it had occurred to him that his father's set was connected to a satellite dish. Perhaps only the cable network was affected, in which case some TV channels should be accessible via satellite.

Snow.

*

In the bedroom his father's old wall clock was steadily beating time. He rubbed his eyes and stretched.

He looked out of the window. Nothing had changed as far as he could tell. The piece of plastic was still flapping in the breeze. None of the cars had moved. The sun was hovering in its accustomed place and seemed to be on course.

Jonas hung his shirt and trousers on a coat hanger. He listened once more for any sound other than that of the clock. Then he slid beneath the bedclothes. They smelt of his father.

*

Semi-darkness. At first, he didn't know where he was.

In the half-sleep that preceded his awakening, the ticking of the clock, a sound familiar to him since his childhood, had lulled him into the false belief that he was in a different place at a different time. He had heard it ticking as a child while lying on the sofa in the living room, where he was meant to take his afternoon rest. He seldom closed his eyes, just daydreamed until his mother came to wake him with a mug of cocoa or an apple.

He turned on the bedside light. Half-past five. He'd slept for over two hours. The street was so narrow and the sun so low in the sky that its rays were illuminating only the upper floors of the buildings across the way. Inside the flat it was like late evening.

He shuffled into the living room in his underpants. It looked as if someone had just left. As if they'd tiptoed out so as not to wake him. He could positively sense that some-one's lingering imprint on the flat.

'Dad?' he called, knowing he wouldn't get an answer.

While dressing he looked out of the window. The piece of plastic. The motorbikes. The bottle in the dustbin.

No change of any kind.

*

Back home he found some tinned food in the kitchen cupboard. While the plate was rotating in the microwave he wondered when he would go to a restaurant again. He watched the countdown on the display. Another sixty seconds. Another thirty, twenty, ten.

He eyed the food, hungry but with no appetite. Covering the plate with some foil, he shoved it aside and went over to the window.

Below him lay the Brigittenauer embankment. His view of the cloudy, softly gurgling waters of the Danube Canal was partly obscured by a row of lush, luminous green trees. Looming up on the far side were the trees that flanked the Heiligenstädter embankment. The two big Ö3 logos on the roof of the radio station continued to revolve as usual on the right of the BMW building. On the skyline the city was bounded by the wooded local mountains: the Hermannskogel, Dreimarkstein and Exelberg. And soaring above the Kahlenberg, where Jan Sobieski had gone into battle against the Turks over three centuries earlier, was the huge television mast.

Jonas surveyed this panorama. It was the view from the flat that had prompted him to rent it two years ago. He used to stand there in the evenings and watch the sun go down behind the mountains, bathing him in its rays until the very last moment.

He checked that the front door was locked, then poured himself a whisky and returned to the window, glass in hand.

There weren't many possible explanations. Some catastrophe was to blame. But if everyone had fled from the threat of an attack by nuclear missiles, why hadn't those missiles landed? In any case, why should anyone take the trouble to waste such expensive technology on an old city that had lost its importance?

An asteroid strike. Jonas had seen films in which kilometre-high tsunamis came surging inland after such an event. Was that what the Viennese had fled from? Had they taken refuge in the Alps? If so, they would have left some trace behind. The authorities couldn't have evacuated a million-and-a-half inhabitants overnight and forgotten about him alone. And all without his noticing.

Maybe he was dreaming. Maybe he'd gone mad.

Mechanically, he took another sip of whisky.

He looked up at the cloudless sky. He didn't believe that extraterrestrials would have spent light years travelling through space, simply to annihilate every Viennese except himself. He didn't believe in any of that stuff.

He extracted his address book from under the phone and dialled every number listed. He called Werner again, likewise Marie's relations in England. He dialled the police, the fire brigade, the emergency services. He tried 911, 160 604, 1503. No emergency services. No taxi. No speaking clock.

Jonas looked through his collection of videos for movies he hadn't yet seen or hadn't seen for a long time. He deposited a stack of comedies in front of the TV and lowered the blinds.

2

Jonas awoke with a sore throat. He felt his forehead. No temperature. He stared up at the ceiling.

After breakfast, having satisfied himself that the TV was still flickering and the street deserted, he sat down beside the phone. Marie didn't answer – neither her mobile, nor her relatives' phone. He couldn't reach anyone else either.

He turned out half the medicine cabinet before he found an aspirin. Leaving it to dissolve, hissing, in a glass of water, he took a shower. He put on some casual clothes. He drained the glass in one gulp.

He looked in both directions as he left the building and came out into the sunlight. He took a few steps, turned his head swiftly. He stopped. Listened. Just the muted lapping of the Danube Canal. He craned his neck and scanned the windows for signs of movement.

Nothing.

Back inside again, he went downstairs to his storage space in the basement. He turned the contents of his toolbox upside down without finding anything suitable. Then he remembered the pipe wrench he'd left beside a stack of old tyres.

*

'Anyone there?'

His voice sounded absurdly feeble in the Westbahnhof's spacious concourse.

Shouldering the pipe wrench, he stomped up the steps to the departure hall. Bureau de change, newsagent, cafés – all were shut.

He went out onto the platforms. Several trains were standing there as if on the point of pulling out. Back to the departure hall, then out onto the platforms once more.

Back again.

Out again.

He jumped aboard the Intercity to Bregenz and searched it carriage by carriage, compartment by compartment. He called out as he entered each stuffy carriage in turn, gripping the pipe wrench tightly. Sometimes he coughed or cleared his throat with the ferocity of a man fifty pounds heavier. He made as much din as possible by banging the wrench against the partitions.

By midday he'd explored every last corner of the station. Every train, every ticket office. The lounge. The restaurant where he'd eaten a few lousy meals, which still reeked of stale fat. The supermarket. The tobacconist's. The News & Books. He'd bashed in windows and glass doors with the pipe wrench, disconnected wailing security alarms and searched a whole series of back rooms. Bread two days old indicated the last time anyone had been there.

The big arrivals and departures board in the middle of the concourse was blank.

The clocks were working.

So were the cash dispensers.

*

At Schwechat Airport he didn't bother to park in the multi-storey and walk all the way back. He left his car right

13

outside the main entrance, in the no-waiting area normally patrolled by policemen and security personnel.

The temperature out here was somewhat cooler than in the city. Flags were fluttering noisily in the breeze. Shading his eyes with one hand, he searched the sky for aircraft. He strained his ears, but all he could hear was the flap-flap of the flags.

With the pipe wrench on his shoulder he strode down some dimly lit passages to the departures level. Menus were stuck in their holders on the tables outside the café. The café was shut, like the restaurant and the pub. The lifts were working, the departure lounges accessible. No flights were listed. The electronic displays were blank.

He combed the entire area. An alarm went off when he passed through a security gate. Repeated blows with the wrench failed to silence it. He peered around uneasily. There was a box on the wall. He pressed several buttons and the wailing finally ceased.

On the arrivals level he sat down at a computer terminal, trying to discover the last time an aircraft had taken off or landed. Either he didn't have the expertise to tackle the problem, or the computer had a fault. No amount of messing around with mouse and keyboard would bring up anything on the screen but meaningless, flickering columns of figures.

He got lost several times before he found the stairs and walked out onto the tarmac.

Most of the aircraft attached to the telescopic walkways belonged to Austrian Airlines. There was a Lauda, a Lufthansa, a Yemeni machine, another from Belgium. Standing further away was an El-Al 727. This plane interested him most. Why was it so far out? Had it been about to take off?

When he reached the plane he crouched down. He looked up at it, breathing heavily, then back at the airport

14

buildings. He felt disappointed. It wasn't anything like as far out as he'd thought. The runway's dimensions had played a trick on him, nor was there any indication that the pilot had been on his way to the take-off point.

Jonas started to shout. He hurled the wrench at a window, first in the cockpit and then in the passenger cabin. When it landed on the tarmac for the eighth or ninth time it broke in half.

He combed every hall, every lounge, every area accessible to him. In the loading bay he made a discovery that galvanised him: dozens of bags and suitcases.

Excitedly, he opened one. Underclothes. Socks. Shirts. Swimming trunks.

Neither this bag nor any of the others contained any clue to what had happened to their owners. There weren't enough to suggest that they belonged to an entire flight. It seemed more probable that they'd either been forgotten or were awaiting collection. They might have come from anywhere, any time. No help at all.

*

He got out at the intersection of Karolinengasse and Mommsengasse. Reaching in through the driver's window, he sounded the horn and looked up at the front of the building as he did so. Not a window opened, not a curtain twitched, even though he hooted continuously.

He didn't bother to press the intercom button. The front door, most of which was glass, yielded to a couple of blows with the remaining half of his wrench. He ducked through the jagged opening and went inside.

Werner's flat was on the first floor. A photograph of a heavily laden yak was pinned to the door beneath the spyhole, and the doormat greeted visitors with a grimy Rolling Stones tongue. He couldn't help remembering how often he'd stood there, bottle of wine in hand, and listened to Werner's approaching footsteps.

He hammered on the door with the remains of his wrench. He couldn't open it – only a crowbar would have forced the lock. He felt in his pockets for something to write with, meaning to leave a message under the spyhole. All he found apart from a pencil was a dirty handkerchief. When he tried to scrawl a few words on the door itself, the lead broke off.

*

On reaching the Südbahnhof he noticed how hungry he was.

In the station concourse he trotted from ticket office to ticket office, shop to shop, smashing the windows with his wrench. He didn't disconnect the security alarms this time. Having broken the window of the bureau de change, he waited to see if its alarm would go off, or if he would have to continue his orgy of destruction. Perhaps some still-surviving guardian of the law would think a heist was in progress and intervene.

To the ear-splitting accompaniment of the security alarms he rode the escalator up to the platforms. Taking his time, he began by exploring platforms 1 to 11 in the east section, where he'd seldom been before. Then he boarded the second escalator.

He also smashed the windows of the shops in the south section. They weren't equipped with burglar alarms, which surprised him. He raided one for a bag of crisps and a can of lemonade, plus a packet of paper handkerchiefs for his runny nose. From the newsagent's he grabbed a stack of newspapers two days old.

Without searching it from end to end, he got into the rear carriage of a train bound for Zagreb. The seat was hot, the compartment stuffy. He yanked the window open and sat down, putting his feet on the seat opposite without removing his shoes.

While mechanically stuffing crisps into his mouth he looked through the newspapers. Not the smallest indication that some exceptional occurrence was imminent. Political squabbles at home, crises abroad, reports of horrors and banalities. The TV pages listed series, talk shows, magazine programmes.

His eyelids drooped.

The muffled, monotonous wail of the security alarms drifted into the compartment.

He swept the papers off his lap. He could afford a brief nap. Only a minute with his eyes closed and the muted strains of the sirens in his ears. Only a minute . . .

He jumped up and rubbed his face hard. He looked for a bolt on the door, then remembered that only sleepers were lockable.

He went out into the corridor.

'Hello? Anyone there?'

He tested one of the curtains with his fingertips. It was so grimy and impregnated with nicotine, he wouldn't have touched it normally. He tugged at it with all his might. There was a ripping sound and he fell over backwards with the length of material in his hand. Using what was left of the pipe wrench, he managed to tear it into several strips. These he used to lash the door handle to the grille of the luggage rack.

Having made a bed out of the six seats, he drained his can of lemonade and lay down.

He felt a bit more cheerful now. Lying there open-eyed with his head resting on his arm, he ran his fingers over the plush upholstery. They encountered a cigarette burn.

He couldn't help thinking of the summer he and some friends had spent touring Europe by train. He'd travelled many thousands of kilometres on a moving bed like this one. From one unfamiliar smell to another. From one happening to the next. From one exciting city to an even more alluring one. Fifteen years ago, it was.

The people he'd slept rough with in parks and railway stations – where were they at this moment?

Where were the people he'd been speaking to only two days ago?

Where was he? In a train. It was uncomfortable. It wasn't going anywhere.

*

He might have slept for half an hour. Some saliva had trickled from the corner of his mouth. Instinctively, he wiped it off the seat with his sleeve. He looked at the door. His makeshift lock was intact. He shut his eyes and listened. No change. The security alarms were wailing exactly as before.

He blew his nose, which was stuffed up with cold and the dust from the compartment. Then he tried to untie the strips of curtain around the door handle. It turned out that he'd done his work too well. He picked at the knots with his fingers, but he was too clumsy and impatient. He tried brute force, but the door wouldn't budge and the knots tightened still more. They were past untying now.

He had no choice but to free himself by violent means. He smashed the window with the wrench. Carefully, he climbed out into the corridor. He glanced back into the compartment, committing the scene to memory in case he should return for some reason.

Then he looted the supermarket.

He filled a wire-mesh basket with drinks and tins of soup, nibbles and bars of chocolate, apples and bananas. He also took meat and sausages. The perishable stuff

18

would soon go off. He didn't dare think when he might get another fresh steak.

He circled his car before getting in, uncertain whether he had parked it at that particular spot.

He peered around. He walked a few steps, then went back to the car.

3

Jonas awoke fully dressed.

He thought he remembered putting on his pyjamas last night. Even if he hadn't, he always wore something comfortable at home. He'd certainly got changed.

Or had he?

In the kitchen he found five empty beer cans. The beer he'd drunk – that he did remember.

After showering he threw some T-shirts and underpants into a bag before undertaking the depressing check of the window, TV and phone. He was hungry, but his appetite had deserted him. He decided to breakfast somewhere on the way. He blew his nose and smeared some ointment on the sore places beneath it. He did without a shave.

The look of the wardrobe puzzled him. Something had changed since yesterday. There seemed to be one jacket too many hanging there. That was impossible, though. Besides, he'd locked the front door. No one else had been here.

He was already standing on the doormat when something impelled him to go back inside. He stared at the hangers in the wardrobe but couldn't put his finger on it.

*

The air was crystal-clear, the sky almost abnormally cloud-less. Despite an occasional puff of wind, the dashboard in his car seemed to be melting. He lowered all the windows and half-heartedly pressed a few buttons on the radio. Nothing emerged but a hiss of static, sometimes louder, sometimes more subdued.

He found his father's flat unchanged. The wall clock was ticking. The tumbler he'd drunk from was standing, half empty, on the table. The bedclothes were rumpled. When he looked out of the window he caught sight of the bicycle with the plastic cover on its saddle. The bottle was protruding from the dustbin. The motorbikes were in their places.

He was about to leave when he thought of the knife.

He didn't have to search for long. His father kept his war souvenirs in the drawer beside the drinks cupboard. His Iron Crosses First and Second Class, his close-combat clasp, his wounded-in-action badge, his Eastern Campaign medal. Jonas knew them all. Often, as a child, he'd watched his father polishing them. An address book, his army paybook, some letters from comrades-in-arms. Three photos showing his father seated in some gloomy rooms with a group of fellow conscripts. The expression on his face was so unfamiliar Jonas couldn't recall ever having seen him look like that. The knife was in there too. He took it.

*

His last visit to Schönbrunn Zoo had been a work outing – a cheerful occasion several years ago. He had a vague recollection of dirty cages and a café where they hadn't been served.

Much had changed since then. The newspapers claimed that Schönbrunn was the finest zoo in Europe. It offered some new sensation every year. A pair of koalas, for example, or other exotic beasts that obliged every Viennese with still-impressionable young children to make a pilgrimage to the zoo. It had never occurred to Jonas to spend his Sundays gazing at the big cats' enclosure or the insectarium. Now, because he wanted to discover whether the animals had vanished as well, he pulled up beside the ticket office and the metal bollards that denied access to cars.

He didn't get out until he'd sounded his horn for a couple of minutes. He stuck the knife in his belt. He also took the wrench with him.

The gravel path crunched beneath his feet. It was a little cooler here than in the city centre. Wind was ruffling the trees that surrounded the zoo, but nothing was stirring inside the fence which, according to a noticeboard, enclosed the giraffe paddock.

His legs refused to carry him beyond a point from which he could still see his car. He couldn't bring himself to turn off down one of the lateral paths. The car was his home, his insurance.

He swung round, gripping the wrench tightly, and stood there with his head down, listening.

Just wind.

The animals had gone.

He sprinted back to the car. No sooner was he behind the wheel than he locked the doors. Only then did he put the wrench and the knife on the passenger seat. He left the windows shut in spite of the heat.

*

He had often driven along the A1. An aunt of his lived in Salzburg, and he'd regularly visited Linz to inspect new ranges of furniture for the firm. The A1 was the motorway he liked least. He preferred the A2 because it led south, towards the sea. The traffic was lighter too.

Without taking his foot off the accelerator, he opened the glove compartment and emptied the contents onto the passenger seat. His sore throat had developed into an increasingly troublesome cold. His forehead was filmed with sweat and the glands in his neck were swollen. His nose was so blocked up he was breathing almost entirely through his mouth. Marie seldom went anywhere without some remedies for minor ailments, but she hadn't left anything in the glove compartment.

The further he got from Vienna, the more often he turned on the radio. Once every frequency had been scanned, he'd turn it off again.

At Grossram service station his hopes were raised by the sight of several parked cars. He sounded his horn. Then he got out, carefully locking the car behind him, and went over to the restaurant entrance. The automatic door hummed open.

'Hello?'

He hesitated. The restaurant stood in the shade of a clump of fir trees. Although the sun was shining, it might have been early evening in the dim interior.

'Anyone there?'

The door closed. He jumped back so as not to be squashed and it opened again.

He fetched the knife from the car. He peered in all directions but could detect nothing unusual. It was just an ordinary motorway service area with cars parked in front of the restaurant and alongside the petrol pumps. People were the only missing feature. People and sounds.

The automatic door glided open again. Its hum, heard a thousand times, seemed suddenly like a message to his subconscious. He walked past the turnstile that separated the shop and cashier's desk from the restaurant and stood among the tables with the knife clutched in his fist.

'What's going on here?' he called, louder than was necessary.

The tables, rows of them covered with white table-cloths, were laid. The self-service counter, which would normally have held soups and sauces, baskets filled with rolls, small bowls of croutons and big bowls of salad, was completely bare.

He discovered the remains of a loaf in the kitchen dresser. It was stale but still edible. He improvised a snack with some sandwich spread from the fridge and ate on his feet, staring at the tiled floor. Back in the restaurant he brewed himself some coffee at the espresso machine. The first cup tasted bitter. The second tasted no better, and it wasn't until he'd made a fourth that he placed the cup on the saucer.

He sat down on the terrace. It was scorching hot. He put up a parasol. The tables were just as unremarkable as those inside. Each had an ashtray, a list of ice creams, a menu card, salt and pepper shakers, toothpicks. They would have looked just the same had he come this way a few days ago.

He looked around him. Not a soul in sight.

After he had spent a while staring at the grey ribbon of the motorway it occurred to him that he'd sat here once before. With Marie. At the very same table, in fact. He recognised it from its position, which gave him a view of a small, secluded vegetable garden. They'd been on their way to their holiday resort in France. They'd breakfasted here.

He jumped up. Perhaps there was something wrong with the phones in Vienna. Perhaps he could call someone from here.

He found a phone at the cash desk. By now he knew the number of Marie's sister in England by heart. The same unfamiliar ringing tone.

No one in Vienna answered either. Not Werner, not the office, not his father.

He took a dozen postcards from a stand. He found some stamps in a folder in a drawer beneath the cash register. He wrote his own address on a card.

The message ran: *Grossram service area, 6 July.*

He stuck a stamp on. There was a postbox beside the entrance. A little notice stated that it was emptied at 3 p.m. No mention of the days of the week, but he posted the card anyway. He took the rest of the cards and the stamps with him.

He was about to unlock his car when he noticed a sports car parked nearby. He went over to it. No ignition key, of course.

*

Jonas left the motorway at the next exit and pulled up outside the first house in the first village he came to. He rang the bell and knocked.

'Hello? Hello!'

The door wasn't locked.

'Anyone there? Hey? Hello!'

He checked all the rooms. Not a living soul. No dog, no canary, not even a fly.

He drove through the village, sounding his horn until he could stand the din no longer. Then he searched the local pub. Nothing.

All the villages he passed in the next couple of hours were off the beaten track. The few houses they consisted of were so dilapidated he wondered if anyone had been living there at all. No chemist's anywhere, let alone a car showroom. He regretted not having left the motorway near some sizeable town. He was lost, from the look of it.

He pulled up on the right, out of habit. It was a while before he found his position on the map. He'd strayed off into the Dunkelstein Forest. It was over twenty minutes' drive to the next motorway access road. He itched to get to it and put on speed again, but he was too tired now.

In the next village, which at least had a grocery store, he made for the most expensive-looking house. It was locked, but the remaining half of his wrench came in useful once more. He smashed a window and climbed in.

In the kitchen he found a packet of aspirin. While one of them was noisily dissolving in a glass of water, he combed the house. It was well furnished in dark wood. Some of the pieces he recognised. They belonged to the Swedish 99 Series, with which he himself had done good business for an entire season. Antlers hung on the walls. The floor was covered in the kind of thick carpets known at the office as 'bug rugs'. None of the decor was cheap, but none of it was tasteful either. Children's toys were lying around.

He returned to the kitchen and downed his aspirin.

Back in the living room he shut his eyes and listened. From the kitchen came the muffled ticking of a clock. Soot dislodged from cracks by the wind came rattling down the chimney. There was a smell of dust, timber and damp cloth.

The stairs creaked underfoot. The bedrooms were on the first floor. The first was obviously a child's. Behind the second door he found a double bed.

He hesitated, but his eyelids were drooping with fatigue. On a sudden impulse, he undressed completely. He drew the dark, heavy curtains and turned on the bedside light, which cast a faint glow. Having satisfied himself that the door was locked, he lay down on the bed. The sheet was soft, the duvet cover of exceptionally fine cotton. Under other circumstances he would have felt good.

He turned out the light.

An alarm clock was ticking almost inaudibly on the bedside table. The pillow smelt of a person Jonas had never met. Wind whistled in the roof space overhead. The sound of the alarm clock was strangely homely.

Darkness engulfed him.

*

He was feeling less muzzy than before. Sitting up, he caught sight of some gilt-framed photos on the chest of drawers. With a handkerchief clamped to his streaming nose, he tottered over to them like a sleepwalker.

One showed a woman of about forty. Although she wasn't smiling, there was a hint of gaiety in her eyes. She didn't look the kind of person who lived in a house like this one.

He wondered what she did for a living. Was she a secretary, or did she own a boutique in one of the larger towns nearby?

The next photo was of a man. Her husband? A bit older, with a greying moustache and dark, piercing eyes. He looked like someone who spent all day driving around on business in a 4WD.

Two fair-haired children. One eight or nine, the other only a few months old. Neither looked particularly bright.

*

The woman's image stayed with him all the way to the motorway. Sporadic thoughts about the house recurred even while he was twiddling the knobs of the radio shortly before Linz. Then he forced himself to concentrate so he didn't overshoot the exit.

He made out the huge factory chimneys from far away. No smoke was rising from them.

He drove into the city without observing the speed limit. He hoped a policeman would stop him, but he quickly realised that something was wrong here too.

There were no pedestrians.

The shops flanking the street were deserted.

Traffic lights turned red, but he waited in vain for other cars to cross his route.

He sounded his horn, gunned the engine and slammed on the brakes. His tyres screamed, sending up a stench of burning rubber. He sounded his horn again: three short, three long, three short. He drove along the same stretch several times. Not a door opened, not a car came his way. The air smelt less unpleasant than it had on his last visit, but it was thundery.

When he pulled up at a chemist's and got out, he wondered why it felt so exceptionally cold. Having suffered from the heat for weeks, he was now shivering. However, this probably owed more to his cold than to the gathering storm.

He smashed the plate glass door of the chemist's and took a packet of aspirin and some throat pastilles from one of the shelves. On the way out he noticed some echinacea and pocketed a small bottle.

It didn't take him long to find a pub whose door was unlocked. He called. There was no response, but he hadn't expected one.

He noticed nothing out of the ordinary in the bar, which reeked of stale tobacco smoke and rancid fat.

He called again.

In the kitchen he put a saucepan of water on the stove and tossed a handful of potatoes into it. He killed time in the bar with a newspaper dated 3 July. People had still been here that day: gravy stains and breadcrumbs on the pages showed that. The newspaper itself was just as unremarkable as those he'd read at the station the day before. Nothing pointed to an event of exceptional magnitude.

He went outside. The first flashes of lightning could be seen. The wind was getting up. Empty cigarette packets and other bits of rubbish went skittering across the street. He tilted his head back and massaged his shoulders, which were stiff after his drive. Black clouds were massing in the sky. A distant rumble. Another flash of lightning. And another.

He was about to go back inside when a crash rang out directly overhead. Without looking round he ran to the car and locked himself in. He withdrew the knife from its sheath. Waited for a few minutes. The windscreen misted over.

He lowered the driver's window.

'What do you want?' he yelled.

Another crash, fainter than before, followed at once by yet another.

'Come out of there!'

Heavy raindrops came pelting down on the bonnet, on the roadway. More rumbling.

He looked up as he ran back to the entrance through the rain, but his view was obstructed by trees. He dashed into the bar, opened the door to the stairs and pounded up them, knife in hand. On the first floor was a long, narrow passage almost devoid of light from outside. He failed to find the switch in his haste.

He came to a door. It wasn't shut. The wind kept banging it against the jamb with monotonous regularity. He pushed it wide open with the knife held out in front of him.

The room was completely bare. There wasn't even any furniture in it. The big casement window was flapping in the wind.

He turned on the spot a couple of times, knife at the ready, then walked to the window. He looked out, glanced back over his shoulder at the room, looked out again. The window was above the entrance and a little to one side.

Just as he withdrew his head a gust of wind blew into the room. The window banged against his arm. He shut it and went downstairs again, still with the knife in his hand.

In the bar he subsided onto a bench. It was a while before his rapid, shallow breathing steadied. He sat staring at the wooden panelling until he remembered the potatoes.

*

The thunderstorm ended just as he laid his knife and fork aside. He left the plate on the table and returned to his car, leaping over muddy puddles on the way.

He drove to the station.

The booking hall and the long, gloomy passage from which flights of steps led to the platforms were as deserted as the forecourt and the platforms themselves. He smashed the window of a kiosk and took a can of lemonade, which he drank at once, dropping the empty can in a litter bin.

He found a postbox on the forecourt. *Linz Station, 6 July*, he wrote on a postcard. After a moment's thought he addressed it to his father.

*

Although Jonas had passed a number of car showrooms, he had something better in mind than an Opel or a Ford. No good opportunity to exchange his rattletrap of a Toyota presented itself until he reached the outskirts of the city, where he at last spotted a dealer offering more than just family saloons.

Jonas was no petrolhead. He'd never gone in for fast cars, but it now seemed absurd to restrict his speed to 160 k.p.h. That meant saying goodbye to his old car. It had cost more than it was worth and held no sentimental associations.

To his surprise, his wrench made no impression on the showroom window behind which the cars awaited their purchasers. He'd never had to deal with safety glass before. He rammed it with the Toyota instead. There was a crash, and splinters came raining down on the bonnet. He backed out again. The hole in the glass was big enough.

He chose a red Alfa Spider. He found the keys on a hook behind the sales desk. It proved harder to locate the key to the only vehicular exit, a pair of big double doors, but he eventually found that too. He went back to the Toyota and cleared out all his belongings.

Before getting in he turned and waved his old car goodbye. He felt foolish a moment later.

A hundred metres from the car showroom he stopped at a service station. The petrol pump worked without any problem. He filled the tank.

On the way to Salzburg he tested the Spider's potential. The acceleration pressed him back into his seat. He put out his hand, meaning to try the radio, but none had been installed. He reached instead for the throat pastilles on the passenger seat.

*

Lying beside the road beyond Wels, as though someone had thrown it away, was a guitar case.

Jonas backed up. He threw stones at the case from a few feet away. He hit it but nothing happened. He kicked it. Eventually he opened it. There was an electric guitar inside. Water had seeped into the case. It had evidently rained hard here too.

He walked around for a while. The grass soaked his trouser legs to the knee. He was near the motorway access road. This spot was probably frequented by hitchhikers, so he shouted and vigorously sounded his horn. He came across discarded beer cans, cigarette ends, condoms. The sodden earth squelched beneath his shoes.

He leant against the passenger door.

Anything might or might not be significant. Perhaps that guitar case had fallen off the roof of a car. Perhaps it had belonged to some person who had vanished at this spot. However and whyever they'd vanished.

*

The sun was going down behind the castle as he passed Salzburg station. He drove across the station square, sounding his horn, then headed for his aunt's flat in Parsch. It took him some time to find the way. He sounded his horn when he finally got to Apothekerhofstrasse. When there was no response he got in again. It was unlikely that he would find anything informative at his aunt's place, so he saved himself the trouble of breaking down the door.

He drove across the border to Freilassing.

No one there.

*

No one.

*

Almost unable to believe it, Jonas drove round the village for an hour. He had secretly assumed that he would come across some human activity on German soil. He'd expected to see soldiers. Possibly tents and refugees – even, perhaps, tanks or people in protective clothing. Civilisation, anyway.

He turned off the engine. Staring at the sign that indicated the route to the motorway for Munich, he drummed on the steering wheel with his fingertips.

How far should he drive?

Using his mobile, he dialled the number of a furniture manufacturer based near Cologne. The phone rang three times, four, five. An answerphone cut in.

*

It was dark by the time he parked in front of Salzburg's Marriott Hotel. He tossed the wrench into his bag and stuck the knife in his belt. Locking the car, he peered in all directions and listened. Not a sound. There had to be some flowering shrubs nearby. He could smell their scent but didn't recognise it.

He stumbled through the revolving door and into the lobby. It was so dark inside he caught his foot in the thick carpet and knocked over an ashtray on a stand.

A shaded lamp was burning on the reception desk. He put his bag down, drew the knife and peered round the gloomy lobby. Without looking, he groped for the main light switch with his free hand.

He blinked.

Once his eyes got used to the light he noticed the stereo system housed in a cabinet beside a wide-screen TV. An empty CD sleeve was lying on the deck. Mozart, of course. He pressed play. It was a while before the first notes rang out.

He took a closer look at the stereo. It was a more expensive system than he himself could ever have afforded, complete with every conceivable extra. The CDs were automatically cleaned. There was also a repeat button. He pressed it and turned up the volume until it made him wince.

He wrote on a slip of paper: *Someone's here. 6 July.* He secured it in a conspicuous position beside the entrance, then wedged the side door open with an armchair so the music could be heard in the street.

He took a random assortment of keys from behind the reception desk, feeling as if the loudspeakers' output would flatten him at any moment. He had never heard anything like it from an ordinary home stereo rig. His heart thudded as if he'd been running, and he felt slightly sick. He was glad when a dozen keys and their tags were jingling in his pocket and he could escape the din.

Using the stairs because he didn't trust the lift, he found a place to sleep on the top floor. It was a suite of three interconnecting rooms and a spacious tiled bathroom with underfloor heating. The music from the lobby was inaudible with the door shut. If he opened it, however, he could tell when the various sections of the orchestra came in.

He locked himself in and ran a bath.

While waiting for the bathtub to fill he turned on the TV. He dialled Marie's mobile again and again, and tried her sister's number for the hundredth time.

He toured the suite, his feet sinking into its oriental carpets. The floorboards beneath them creaked faintly. Once, he probably wouldn't have noticed this, but the unnatural silence of recent days had honed his hearing to such an extent that the slightest sound made him jump.

A bottle of champagne was chilling in the minibar. Although it didn't seem appropriate, he stretched out in the tub with a glass in his hand. He took a sip and shut his eyes. There was a smell of bath salts and essential oils. Foam hissed and crackled around him.

*

Next morning he found his shoes not only one on top of the other but face to face. It reminded him of the way Marie sometimes arranged their mobiles: as if exchanging an armless embrace.

Jonas felt pretty sure he hadn't left his shoes like that.

34

He checked the door. Securely locked.

He regretted not having taken some bread or rolls from the deep-freeze in the hotel kitchen the night before. He found a couple of kiwi fruits. He scooped out their flesh and ate it as he stood by the fruit shelf in the kitchen.

The stereo system was still blasting out through the entire building. Wincing, he hurried to reception. He scribbled his name and mobile number on a slip of paper, together with a request that anyone who found it should call him. This he stuck to the reception desk. Before leaving the hotel he stocked up with paper and sticky tape.

Salzburg, Marriott, 7 July, he wrote on the postcard he dropped in the letterbox outside.

*

At midday he drove through deserted Villach, at half past he sounded his horn in front of Klagenfurt's celebrated Dragon Statue. In both places he wrote postcards and left slips of paper bearing his phone number. He didn't stop to search any buildings.

Several times he pulled up in the middle of large squares where he could get out and stretch his legs in safety, without having to watch his back. He called out. Listened. Stared at the ground.

Thanks to his powerful car and the fact that he didn't have to worry about oncoming traffic, he crossed the Loibl Pass and reached the frontier within a few minutes. The frontier post was deserted, the barrier raised.

He searched the offices and dialled some numbers stored in their phones. Nobody answered. He left a message there too and did the same at the Slovenian frontier post a few hundred metres further on. He filled his tank, stocked up with mineral water and sausage, swallowed an aspirin.

It took him less than half an hour to cover the eighty kilometres to Ljubljana. The place was deserted. So were Domzale, Celje, Slovenska Bistrica and Maribor.

He left messages in English and German everywhere. Posted cards with Slovenian stamps on them. Dialled stored numbers at service stations. Tried the internal communications network at toll gates. Set off alarms and waited a minute or two. Left business cards behind because he'd run out of notepaper from the Marriott.

Just short of the Slovenian–Hungarian border he passed an overturned truck. He braked so sharply he almost lost control of the car. The cab of the truck had come to rest on its side. He had to clamber on top to open the driver's door. The cab was empty.

He examined the nearby area. Skid marks could be seen. The crash barrier was damaged and part of the load – building materials – was lying in the ditch. Everything pointed to a normal accident.

*

Jonas didn't find a soul in Hungary either.

He drove to Zalaegerszeg. From there he took the expressway to Austria and crossed the frontier at Heiligenkreuz. Absurdly, he felt he was back home.

4

The night before he'd left a matchbox propped against the front door the way he'd seen people do it in films. It was still there when he checked in the morning. In exactly the same spot.

Except that the side with the eagle was facing upwards, not the one with the flag.

The door was locked. It was a deadlock. No one could have got in without a duplicate key. Besides, the matchbox was still propped against the door. No one had been there. No one. It was impossible.

But how to account for the matchbox?

*

When he made himself some coffee the milk curdled. He hurled the cup at the wall. It smashed, leaving brown splashes on the wallpaper.

Cautiously, he put the milk bottle to his nose. He winced and pulled a face, then dumped it in the waste bin and poured himself another cup.

He stormed downstairs with the cup in his hand, spilling half its contents. He put it down on the grimy pavement outside the supermarket and kicked the automatic door a couple of times. When it refused to open he picked up a bicycle and flung it at the glass. A few scratches, nothing more.

He used the Spider as a battering ram. There was a crash, and the door disintegrated into a shower of glass. Shelves toppled over like dominoes as he drove to the back of the shop. Coming to a halt in a mound of overturned tins, he went to fetch his cup and took it to the dairy section.

He unscrewed a bottle of milk and sniffed. It smelt iffy, so he tossed it aside. He opened another bottle and flung it after the first. The third smelt passable. He poured some into his cup. No clots.

He leant against a humming freezer cabinet and sipped his coffee with relish.

He wondered how many more such coffees he would drink. Made not with powdered or long-life milk, but with milk yielded by a cow only days ago.

How much more fresh meat? How much more freshly squeezed orange juice?

He took the bottle back upstairs with him. He left the car where it was.

*

After his third cup he tried Marie again. Nothing to be heard but the English ringing tone. He slammed the receiver down.

He hurried downstairs again and checked the postbox. Empty.

He ran himself a bubble bath.

He pulled the dirty dressing off his finger. The cut was healing pretty well – it wouldn't leave much of a scar. He crooked his finger. It didn't hurt.

He got into the bath. His toes protruded from the foam. He fiddled with them, had a shave and cut his nails. Now

and then he darted out of the bathroom, leaving wet footprints on the floor, because he thought he'd heard a noise.

*

At midday he took the scratched and dented Spider on a
tour of the city. He met no one. He sounded his horn at
every intersection, but more for form's sake than anything
else.

He doubted if he would find a crowbar in a normal
DIY store, but that didn't deter him from demolishing the
glass doors of several such establishments with the Spider.
He didn't get out to look for a crowbar. It was an odd
sensation, driving a car along aisles normally frequented
by taciturn men with big hands pushing trolleys and
putting on their reading glasses to squint at price tickets.

I need something more robust, he told himself, having
inspected the front of the Spider after his fourth foray.

He eventually struck lucky in a musty old hardware
store near the Volkstheater. He couldn't help recalling that
Marie had lived near there years ago, when they'd first
met. Engrossed in his memories, he stowed the crowbar in
the car. Just as he slammed the passenger door he heard
a noise behind him. It sounded like two bits of wood
knocking together.

He froze, unable to turn round.

He had the feeling that someone was there. He knew
there wasn't, but the sensation tormented him.

He waited, hunching his shoulders.

Then he swung round. No one there.

*

It took him a while to find a gun shop, but the one in
Lerchenfelder Strasse left nothing to be desired. Rifles of all

kinds stood in racks against the walls, and revolvers and automatics were displayed in glass cases. There were throwing knives, even Ninja throwing stars. Tear-gas sprays for the lady's handbag stood on the counter, and hunting bows and crossbows were hanging in cabinets at the back of the shop. Also on sale were camouflage jackets and protective clothing, gas masks, radio sets and other equipment.

Jonas was familiar with guns. During his national service he'd been offered a choice between doing a normal stint in the army and signing up for fifteen months. In the latter case he could choose which unit to be assigned to after basic training. He hadn't hesitated for an instant. He didn't enjoy marching and would have done anything to avoid the infantry, so he became a driver and later joined an explosives team. He'd spent two months blasting avalanches in the Tyrolean mountains.

He toured the shop. He disliked guns on principle and abhorred loud noises of any kind. In recent years he'd seen in the New Year in a mountain hut with Marie and Werner and Werner's girlfriend Simone. However, there were situations in which the possession of a gun had its advantages. Not just any old gun. The best firearm in the world, at least psychologically, was a pump-action shotgun. Nobody who had heard one being reloaded ever forgot the sound.

*

A bollard-free side street enabled him to drive out across the Prater. The first turning he took brought him to a hot-dog stand. He lit the gas under the hotplate and brushed the surface with oil. When the temperature was right he laid out a row of sausages on it.

With the scent of frying sausages in his nostrils he looked up at the towering, motionless shape of the Big

Wheel nearby. He'd been on it often. The first time as a boy accompanied by his father, who may have been quite as intimidated by the unaccustomed altitude as his son, because it would have been difficult to tell whose hand had squeezed the other's harder. He'd had many rides since then. Sometimes with girlfriends, mostly with colleagues at the exuberant conclusion of a work outing.

The sausages sizzled and smoked as he turned them on the hotplate. He opened a can of beer and drank it with his head tilted back, gazing at the Big Wheel.

On the day Marie landed a job as a flight attendant with Austrian Airlines, Jonas had overcome his reluctance to splash out: he'd rented a gondola for three hours, just for the two of them. Overly romantic gestures weren't his thing. He detested sentimentality, but he felt sure Marie would be thrilled.

A dinner table awaited them, complete with a bottle of champagne in an ice bucket and a long-stemmed red rose in a cut-glass vase. They took their seats, the waiter brought the hors d'oeuvres, bowed and withdrew. An almost imperceptible lurch, and the wheel got under way.

One revolution took twenty minutes. From high above they had a panoramic view of the city, whose traffic lights, street lights and floodlights punctuated the dusk. They drew each other's attention to long-familiar sights, now given fresh appeal by the unaccustomed viewpoint. Jonas topped up their glasses. By the time they reached ground level and the next course was served, Marie's cheeks were glowing.

During a conversation a year later, she made some faintly ironical reference to his romantic streak. Taken aback, he asked what she meant, and she reminded him of their evening on the Big Wheel. That was when he discovered that Marie had as little time as he did for candlelit dinners high above Vienna. She had enthused about the atmosphere to please him, whereas what she'd really longed for was a glass of beer on a bar stool in some pub or other.

He took a bite of sausage. It tasted of nothing. He looked around for some ketchup and mustard.

*

He was surprised to find how relatively easy it was to operate the fairground attractions.

He smashed the window of the ticket office with the butt of his gun, took a handful of chips and seated himself in a go-cart. Nothing happened when he depressed the accelerator. He inserted a chip in the slot. Now it worked. With the shotgun on his lap, his free hand on the steering wheel and his foot down hard, he raced round the track several times, doing his best not to graze the barriers on the bends.

He broke into the ticket office of the old scenic railway. All he had to do then was press a button, and the wooden cars came gliding into position alongside the boarding platform. The trip passed off without incident. He might have been an ordinary customer on an ordinary day.

He hurled spears at balloons, threw rings over statuettes, fired arrows at a target. He spent a short time in the slot-machine arcade, but winning money was no fun.

He surveyed the rows of empty seats on the Flying Carpet. An idea occurred to him. He stripped off his shirt and tied it to one of the seats in the huge swingboat. In the ticket office he found the lever that controlled the motor. He turned it to automatic. The Flying Carpet swung into action. No girlish screams rent the air, as they usually did, and no one but Jonas stood watching.

His shirt was fluttering in the front row. He followed its progress through the air, shading his eyes with his hand.

After three minutes the swingboat came to rest and the safety bars snapped open automatically.

Jonas retrieved his shirt. He wondered if you could speak of a view if there was no one there to admire it. Was a shirt enough to make a view a view?

He opened another can of beer and took it with him into the House of Adventure. A children's attraction. It was quite hard to squeeze between sandbags and cross swaying wooden bridges with the shotgun on his back. He trod on stairs that gave way with a crash, teetered across sloping rooms, blundered along unlit passages. When he hadn't activated some mechanism or other, all was quiet. Now and then a beam would creak beneath his weight.

On reaching the third floor, he stationed himself beside the balustrade overlooking the forecourt.

Nothing was stirring down below.

He drank his beer.

Then he went lurching down a rope walkway in the shape of a spiral staircase.

At the shooting gallery he couldn't resist the air rifle lying on the counter. He took his time aiming. He fired and reloaded. He took aim, fired and reloaded again. Six times the gun spat air, and six times came the almost simultaneous smack of the slug striking home. He examined the target. The result was not unsatisfactory.

He hung up another target and slowly crooked his finger.

He had always fancied that you could die of slowness by prolonging some everyday action indefinitely – to infinity, or, rather, to finality – because you would depart this world while still engaged in that process. A step, a gesture, a wave of the arm, a turn of the head – if you slowed that movement more and more, everything would come to an end, more or less of its own accord.

His finger curled around the trigger. With surprising clarity, he realised that he must long ago have reached, yet failed to reach, the point of release.

Unslinging the shotgun, he cocked it and fired. A gratifyingly loud report rang out. Simultaneously, he felt the weapon kick him in the shoulder.

The target displayed a gaping hole big enough to take a man's fist. Sunlight was twinkling through some other, smaller holes around it.

*

He went for a trip round the Prater on the miniature railway, whose diesel locomotive was simple to operate. The engine puttered, the air smelt of greenery. It was much cooler in the shade of the trees than among the booths in the amusement park. He pulled on his shirt, which he'd tied round his waist after its ride on the Flying Carpet.

At the Heustadlwasser he climbed unsteadily into one of the boats moored there. Tossing the painter onto the landing stage, he pushed off and rowed vigorously until the boatman's hut was out of sight. Then he shipped his oars.

He lay down on his back and drifted. Sunlight flickered through the trees overhead.

*

He awoke with a start.

Blinking in the gloom, he gradually made out the furniture's familiar outlines and realised that he was at home in bed. He wiped his sweaty face on his forearm, threw back the thin linen sheet he slept beneath in summer and went into the bathroom. His nose was blocked up, his throat sore. He drank a glass of water.

Sitting on the edge of the bath, he groped his way back into the nightmare.

He had dreamt of his family. The strange thing was, they were all his own age. He'd spoken to his grandmother, who was seventy when he was born and had died at eighty-eight. In his dream she was thirty-five. Although Jonas had never seen her at that age, he knew it was her. He'd marvelled at her smooth complexion and dark, luxuriant hair.

His grandfather, likewise thirty-five, had also appeared. His mother, his father, his uncle, his aunts – all were his own age.

David, his cousin Stephanie's son, who had celebrated his eleventh birthday last February, sported a moustache and had chill blue eyes.

Paula, another cousin's seventeen-year-old daughter, whom he had bumped into by chance in Mariahilfer Strasse not long ago, glanced at him over her shoulder and said: 'Well?' Her face was older, more expressive and a little careworn. She, too, was thirty-five beyond a doubt. Standing beside her was the baby she'd given birth to last autumn, an aloof-looking thirty-five-year-old man wearing brown gloves.

There was something else as well, some disquieting feature he couldn't put his finger on.

They'd all yammered at him in a language of which he understood only snatches. His dead young grandmother had patted his cheek and muttered 'UMIROM, UMIROM, UMIROM' – at least, that was what it had sounded like to him. Thereafter she merely moved her lips. His father, who resembled his wartime photos, had been jogging along behind her on a treadmill. He hadn't looked at Jonas.

But there was something else.

He sluiced his face in cold water and looked up at the

ceiling. A damp patch had appeared there some months ago, but it hadn't grown any bigger of late.

Going straight back to bed was out of the question. He turned on every light in the flat. And the TV, whose flickering screen he now accepted as normal. He put in a video but killed the sound. It was the highlights of the Berlin Love Parade of 1999, which he'd inadvertently tossed into his trolley at the supermarket.

He blew his nose, then squeezed a throat pastille out of its blister pack. He made himself some tea and sat down on the sofa, cup in hand. Sipping, he watched the gyrations of the young people aboard the floats streaming past the Victory Column at a walking pace. Their half-naked figures twitched in time to inaudible music.

He got up and wandered around. His eye fell on the wardrobe. Again he had the feeling that something was wrong. This time he realised what it was. Hanging inside was a jacket that didn't belong to him. He'd seen it in a shop window some weeks ago, but it was too expensive.

How had it got there?

He put it on. It fitted.

Had he bought it after all? And forgotten it?

Or was it a present from Marie?

He checked the front door. Locked. He rubbed his eyes. His cheeks burnt. The longer he thought about the jacket, the uneasier he felt. He decided to shut it up in the wardrobe for the time being. The explanation would occur to him of its own accord.

He opened the window. The night air was refreshing. He looked down at the Brigittenauer embankment. Once upon a time the night had been filled with the steady hum of passing cars. The silence that now weighed heavy on the street seemed to be trying to drag him down there.

He looked left in the direction of the city centre, where here and there a lighted window could be seen. The heart of

Vienna. History had been made there once, but it had since moved on to other cities. What remained were broad streets, grandiose buildings and monuments. And people who had found it hard to distinguish between past and present.

Now they had gone too.

When he looked straight ahead at the 19th District, he saw a light flickering in a window several hundred metres away. It wasn't a Morse signal, but it might be a message of some kind.

*

He had never known such darkness. A windowless room could be very dark, but it was an acquired, unnatural kind of darkness quite unlike the gloom prevailing here in the street. No stars were twinkling in the sky. The street lights had failed. Cars nudged the kerb like dark mounds. Everything resembled a heavy mass vainly endeavouring to move.

While covering the few yards from the front door to the Spider, he glanced round several times and called out in a deep voice.

He could hear the Danube Canal lapping against the embankment wall.

*

Although he had only a vague idea of the direction in which the building in question lay, he didn't take long to find it. He pulled up three car-lengths away, with his headlights illuminating the entrance. Then he got out, shotgun at the ready.

Crouching down beside the driver's door, he listened intently for a minute. Nothing broke the silence but an occasional puff of wind.

47

He locked the car, leaving the headlights on, and counted the storeys to the lighted window. Then he took the lift to the sixth floor. The passage was in darkness. He felt for a light switch.

Either there wasn't one or he failed to find it.

Holding the shotgun out in front of him, Jonas made his way cautiously along the passage. He kept stopping to listen. There was no sound, no indication of where to look. It wasn't until his eyes had grown accustomed to the gloom that he saw a shaft of light at floor level. It was the door. When he pressed what he took to be the bell, the passage light came on. He screwed up his eyes against the glare and raised his shotgun.

The passage was deserted. An ordinary passage.

He looked at the door, which had no nameplate. Like the building itself, it must have been a good thirty years old. There was no spyhole.

He rang the bell.

No response.

He rang again.

Still nothing.

He hammered on the door with the butt of the shotgun and rattled the handle. The door was unlocked.

'Anyone there?'

He found himself in a kitchen-cum-living-room. Sofa, armchair, glass-topped table, carpet, TV, kitchen units along the back wall. The decor bore a startling resemblance to that of his own flat: parlour palm in the corner, loud-speakers on hooks on either side of the window, herbs in little pots on the radiator, full-length mirror.

He looked at his reflection, holding the shotgun in both hands. Behind him was a sofa that resembled his own, a range of kitchen units like his own. A standard lamp like his. A lampshade like the one at home.

The light was flickering. He wound a tea cloth round

his hand and screwed the bulb in tighter. The flickering stopped.

A loose connection.

He walked round the room, touching things, shifting chairs, tugging at shelves, reading book titles, turning shoes over, removing jackets from the wardrobe. He checked the bathroom and bedroom.

The more closely he looked, the more differences he spotted. The standard lamp was grey, not yellow. The carpet was brown, not red. The armchair was worn and threadbare, like the sofa, the decor universally shabby.

He went from room to room once more, unable to rid himself of the feeling that he'd missed something.

There was nobody here and no indication of when anyone had last been there. It seemed probable that the lights had been on from the first. He hadn't noticed the flickering window before because this was the first time he'd ventured to look out at the city at night.

An unremarkable flat. CDs lying around, washing hanging up, crockery on the draining board, crumpled paper in the waste bin. An entirely unremarkable flat. No hidden message anywhere – unless he'd failed to grasp it.

He wrote his name and mobile number on a notepad and added his address in case the mobile network failed.

From the window he made out a small, glowing rectangle a few hundred metres away.

The light was coming from his own flat.

Was everything where it should be at this moment? His cup on the sofa table? The duvet on the bed? Were the young people dancing silently on their floats?

Or was there nothing there? Not until he returned?

5

In the morning he checked the postbox, then drove to the city centre to look for clues and leave some behind. At lunchtime he broke into a pub and ate something. In the afternoon he went on looking. When evening came he stretched out on the sofa with a beer and watched the Berliners dancing silently. He didn't go to the window.

He explored almost every public building between the ring road and Franz-Josefs-Kai. He combed Vienna's government offices, museums and banks. With the pump-action shotgun in his left hand he made his way across the stage of the Schauspielhaus, along the passages in the Hofburg and past the exhibits in the Museum of Natural History. He walked round the Albertina, the university, the editorial offices of the *Presse* and *Standard*, leaving notes bearing his address and mobile number everywhere he went. It was hot outside, cool and dim inside. Specks of dust floated in shafts of light slanting down through windows. The sound of his footsteps on the stone floors reverberated around the spacious buildings.

Anxious to leave traces of his presence behind, he loaded a handcart with props and trundled them onto the stage of the Burgtheater. He piled them all on top of each other – costumes, plaster statues, TVs, plastic hammers, flags, chairs, swords – and pinned a business card, medal-fashion, to the chest of a dummy soldier.

He visited every hotel on the ring road, dialled stored numbers at the reception desks, called Marie in England. He studied the hotel registers. They listed reservations for the period after 3 July. At one hotel he poured himself a drink at the bar and laid out a slalom course with bottles in the lobby. At another he wrote his name in bold capitals on a flip chart he found in a conference room and set it up in the hotel entrance.

He wrapped the Secession building in so much black sticky tape it might have been mistaken for a work of environmental art by Christo. He sprayed his name and phone number on the tape with a can of bright yellow paint.

In the parliament building he set off an alarm when he passed through the metal-detector gate carrying his gun. In the chamber itself he fired at tables and benches. He stuck one note on the lectern and one on the Speaker's chair.

He checked the Ministry of the Interior, the barracks, the Austrian Radio building. He found his way into the Federal Chancellor's office and left a note on his desk.

He wrote HELP in gigantic black letters on the paving stones in Heldenplatz.

He looked up at the sky.

Not a cloud for days.

All blue.

*

He could hear the alarms sounding even in Südtiroler Platz, hundreds of metres from the Südbahnhof. He stopped at a red light and turned off the engine, climbed onto the roof of the car and sat there with the shotgun across his knees.

He dialled the number of his flat on his mobile and let it ring for a long time.

He turned so the sun was shining on his face. Shutting his eyes, he abandoned himself to its rays. He felt his forehead, nose and cheeks grow hot. There was almost no wind.

He called his own mobile number.

Engaged.

*

The remains of the windows he'd smashed lay untouched on the floor of the ticket office. Nothing seemed to have changed in the last week. The arrivals and departures boards were still blank. The alarms continued to fill the air with their monotonous wailing.

Shotgun at the ready, he boarded the train to Zagreb. His compartment was just as he'd left it. The window in the door was smashed, the door itself still held by strips of curtain and immovable. The 3 July newspapers lay scattered across his makeshift bed of seats beside the lemonade can and the empty packet of crisps.

It was stuffy in there.

Nothing was stirring outside. Another train was standing two platforms away. The intervening tracks were strewn with rubbish of all kinds.

*

Two minutes' work with the crowbar sufficed to open the door of Werner's flat. His bed had been slept in, the bedclothes were thrown back. A towel, obviously used, was lying on the bathroom floor outside the shower cubicle. There was a pile of dirty plates on the draining board in the kitchen. In the living room he found a glass containing dregs of red wine.

What to look for? Jonas didn't even know. He wanted

to find some clue to where everyone had gone, but what sort of clue? Could he find it in a friend's flat?

He wandered around for a while. For the first time in days, he came across familiar objects. He was moved even by something as banal as the leathery smell of Werner's sofa. He'd often sat here in the past, when everything was still as it should be.

He opened the fridge. A lump of cheese, some butter, a carton of long-life milk, some cans of beer and lemonade. Werner hardly ever ate at home. He occasionally sent out for a pizza.

Jonas came across the medication in a drawer.

He had found something important without looking for it. This medication meant that his friend hadn't disappeared of his own free will. Werner wouldn't even have gone down to the cellar to fetch a bottle of wine without his tablets and inhaler.

He remembered now. Werner had called him on the evening of 3 July. They'd chatted for a few minutes and then made a vague arrangement to meet that weekend. It was Werner who had called him.

He pressed the redial button on Werner's phone. His own number came up on the display.

*

In Rüdigergasse he tried to recall how the street had looked on his last visit. He immediately recognised the plastic cover on the bicycle saddle. He saw the bottle protruding from the dustbin. The position of the bikes and mopeds also seemed unaltered.

The postbox: empty.

The flat: unchanged. Every object was where it had been before. His tumbler on the table, the remote on top of the TV. The usual chilly atmosphere, the smell of old man.

The displays on the electronic gadgets glowed green.

The same silence.

The bedsprings creaked ominously as he lay down. He stretched out on his back and folded his hands on his chest. His eyes roamed the bedroom.

He'd known all the objects he could see since his childhood. This had been his parents' bedroom. That portrait of an anonymous young woman had hung opposite the bed. The ticking of the wall clock had accompanied him into sleep. The decor was just as it had been thirty years ago. Only the walls were wrong. Until his mother's death eight years ago, this bed had stood in a flat in the 2nd District. The one he'd grown up in.

He shut his eyes. The wall clock struck half-past. Two deep, resonant notes.

*

Jonas almost drove past the building in Hollandstrasse. The frontage had been repainted and repaired in places. It made a respectable impression.

He prised open the postboxes in the lobby with the crowbar. They yielded with a crash. Masses of junk mail, one or two letters. All the postmarks predated 4 July. Postbox No. 1, which had belonged to his family, and from which he himself had often collected the post, was empty. The subsequent tenants' surname, Kästner, was inscribed on a little plaque dangling inside.

While climbing the stairs to the first floor and making his way along the old, winding corridor, he remembered how, as a boy, he'd been treated to a nameplate of his own by Uncle Reinhard, who'd had it made for him specially. It was attached to the door, and Jonas had proudly showed it off to every visitor. Bearing his first name and surname, it had even hung above the family nameplate.

As he expected, both nameplates had been removed and replaced with that of the Kästner family.

He tried the handle.

The door was unlocked.

He looked around. Resisting an urge to remove his shoes, he tiptoed into the flat.

Hanging in the hall was a sign reading *Welcome!* in childish handwriting. Jonas gave a start. It looked familiar. He peered at it more closely – he even sniffed it, he felt so puzzled – but came to no conclusion.

He toured the familiar rooms with their unfamiliar, incongruous pieces of furniture. Often he came to a halt, folded his arms, and tried to recall what the place had looked like before.

The tiny bedroom he'd moved into at the age of ten, formerly his mother's sewing room, had been turned into a study. The big room that had doubled as his parents' bedroom and the living room was still a bedroom, but atrociously furnished. To his annoyance, it contained a three-piece suite in the lousy '98 series from Holland, which Martina had almost had to force him to sell. The presence of children was indicated by some rubber balls and toy guns in a corner behind the door. The bathroom and toilet were unchanged.

In the toilet, on the wall beside the cistern, he discovered, in childish writing, the phrases: *The fish and I. The fsh.* The 'The' and the 'f' and 'sh' of 'fish' had a line through them.

He remembered it well. He'd written that. But he didn't know why any more. He'd been eight or nine. His father had told him off for scribbling on the wall but had forgotten to wipe it off. Probably because it was in such an inconspicuous place that it had been months before he'd even noticed it.

Jonas walked up and down, leant against doorposts and adopted certain positions, the better to remember. Shutting his eyes, he fingered door handles that felt the same as they had in the old days.

He lay down on a strange bed. Staring up at the ceiling, he felt dizzy. He had often lain in this position, and now, after many years, he was doing so again. He had gone away, the ceiling had stayed put. The ceiling didn't care. It had waited, watching other people's doings. Now he was back. Staring up at the ceiling. As before. The same eyes were looking at the same spot in the ceiling. Time had gone by. Time had broken down.

*

Jonas hesitantly entrusted himself to the lift in the Danube Tower. He dreaded to think what would happen if it got stuck, but he couldn't dispense with technology altogether – that would have tied his hands. So he got in, pressed the button and held his breath.

It was 220 metres to the top of the Danube Tower. When the door of the lift opened again, he was 150 metres above the ground. The observation terrace was at this level. A staircase led up to the café.

He found his bearings there at once and helped himself to a bottle of lemonade. He had often been here with Marie, who loved the view and the odd fact that the café slowly revolved. Jonas had always found this rather weird, but Marie had taken a childish delight in it.

In the control room, you could set how long the café took to complete a single revolution: 26, 40, or 52 minutes. Marie had always managed to persuade the man in charge to set the controls at 26. On one occasion the uniformed technician had taken such a fancy to her that he'd started telling stories just to keep her there.

Jonas's presence didn't seem to bother him. The café could be made to rotate much faster, he said. The café construction team, to which an uncle of his had belonged, had tinkered with the mechanism while work was in progress. They got the time for a revolution down to eleven seconds before they were caught. Since then a cotter pin had prevented anyone from getting up to similar tricks. Rapid revolutions consumed a lot of electricity and were dangerous into the bargain. Besides, people inside the café felt sick and lurched around like sailors in a gale.

You expect me to believe that? Marie had said. It's the honest truth, the technician replied with an equivocal smile. That proves what children men are, said Marie. The two of them burst out laughing, and Jonas had dragged her away.

He went into the control booth. To his surprise, he found the cotter pin in place. Having satisfied himself that he wasn't putting the lift out of action by mistake or overdoing the revolutions like the technician's uncle, he set the regulator at 26 and switched on.

Without looking down, he made his way out onto the terrace and leant against the parapet, beneath which a grille projected from the wall. It was supposed to prevent spectacular suicides.

Wind buffeted his face. The sun was low in the sky. It was so dazzling he shut his eyes for a while. When he opened them again and looked down, he took an involuntary step backwards.

What had impelled him to come up here? The view? Memories of Marie?

Or hadn't he come of his own free will at all? Was he like a hamster on a treadwheel? Were his actions determined by someone else?

Had he died and gone to hell?

He drained the bottle of lemonade, drew back his arm and hurled it into the depths. It took a long time to fall, then hit the ground without a sound.

Inside the café he sat down at the table he associated with memories of his visits with Marie. He re-read all the text messages from her stored in his mobile. *I'm just overhead, only a few kilometres above you. – Licking an ice-cream cornet and thinking of you. :-) – Please FMH – You are terrible! * hic * :-) – I love love love love you.*

He shut his eyes and tried to send her a telepathic message. *I'm alive, are you there?*

He pictured her face, her cheeks, her clear-eyed gaze. Her lovely dark hair. Her lips with their slight downward curve at the corners.

It was difficult. Her image dissolved and faded. He could hear her voice in his head, but it sounded like an echo. He'd already forgotten her smell.

In the Internet area he booted up a computer and inserted some euros, propping his chin on his fists. While the view of the city slowly changed before his eyes, he allowed his thoughts to run on.

Perhaps he had to pass a test, one to which there was a correct answer. A correct response that would extricate him from his predicament. A password, an open sesame, an email to God.

www.marie.com
Page not found
www.marie.at
Page not found
www.marie.uk
Page not found

If a password of sorts existed, it ought to have some connection with himself. That seemed logical.

www.jonas.at
Page not found
www.help.at
Page not found
www.help.com
Page not found
www.god.com
Page not found

He fetched himself another bottle of lemonade and drank, looking out over the city as it slid past.

www.vienna.at
Page not found
www.world.com
Page not found

He tried to access dozens more known and invented websites, checked to see what pages had been stored and tried them too. In vain.

www.umirom.com
Page not found. Try again later or check your settings.

*

Bottle in hand, Jonas unhurriedly explored every part of the café. In the children's corner he came across some painting equipment. He had loved mucking around with paints as a child, but his parents had very soon confiscated all his brushes and crayons because he made a mess and ruined some of his mother's needlework.

His eye lighted on a white tablecloth.

He counted the tables in the café. There were a dozen or more, plus the ones on the upper floor.

He proceeded to strip them all. The upper floor yielded fourteen tablecloths, and he found a few spares in a dresser. By the time he'd finished, thirty-three squares of cloth lay spread out in front of him.

He knotted the ends together to form an oblong made up of three times eleven tablecloths. He had to push the tables and chairs aside to create enough room to work in. It was half an hour before he went and fetched the tubes of paint. He decided on black.

His name? His phone number? Just *HELP*?

He hesitated for a moment before starting to paint, then completed the job in short order. It wasn't easy because the tablecloths tended to wrinkle up. Besides, he had to gauge the letter-spacing and apply the paint thickly enough.

He used the remainder in the tubes to write his phone number on the walls, tables and floor.

The panoramic window couldn't be opened, so he blew out two panes on either side of an upright with the shotgun. The two reports were followed moments later by the tinkle of glass raining down on the terrace below. Wind came surging into the café, sweeping menus off the bare tables and rattling the glasses behind the bar.

Jonas knocked out the remaining shards of glass with the butt of his gun. He felt queasy when he stationed himself at the window holding the ends of his improvised banner. He ought to have turned off the motor, he realised. The café's rotation didn't exactly help. The wind lashed his face, making his eyes water. He felt as if he might topple into space at any moment, but he managed to tie the ends of the three outermost tablecloths firmly to the window frame. The material was thin, after all, and he felt sure the frame would hold.

Bundling up the rest of his banner, he hefted it out of the window. It hung down limply for a moment. Then the wind caught it, but the inscription was still not as clearly visible as he'd hoped.

He picked up the gun, cast a brief glance at the devastation he was leaving behind, and hurried to the control booth. Tools were readily available there because the in-house mechanics used it as their depot. A moment later he was standing beside the regulator with a hammer. Three blows sufficed to knock out the cotter pin. An alarm went off. The regulator offered little resistance as he turned it beyond the 26 mark.

A low, all-pervading hum filled the air. He couldn't see what was happening because the control booth had no windows, but the sound told him all he needed to know.

He continued to turn the regulator until it would go no further, however much pressure he applied. Then he grabbed his gun and dashed to the lift.

He made for the car without glancing up. He didn't look back until he'd driven a few hundred metres. The café was rotating with the banner fluttering from it. The inscription, legible from afar, read:

UMIROM.

6

Next morning he found a Polaroid photo tucked between the bread bin and the coffee grinder. It showed him asleep.

He couldn't remember seeing it before. When and where had it been taken? He had no idea why it should be there. The likeliest answer was that Marie had left it there, intentionally or not.

Except that he'd never owned a Polaroid camera. Nor had Marie.

*

Jonas arrived at his parents' old flat in Hollandstrasse armed with the biggest axe from the DIY store. He went round the rooms, picturing what he wanted. Dumping bulky refuse in the street outside the building wasn't a good idea because he wanted to keep the access clear. He didn't need the backyard, on the other hand, so he decided to use it as a rubbish dump.

Anything that wouldn't go through the kitchen window had to be chopped up small. To make room, he began by pitching upright chairs and other manageable objects through the window into the yard. Then he set to work on the three-piece suite. Having removed the cushions and ripped off the upholstery with the aid of a carpet knife, he began to dismember the frames. He hacked away so vigorously that the axe went through a chair leg and into the floor. He was rather more restrained after that.

It was the bookshelves' turn after the three-piece suite. Then came a massive linen cupboard, a chaise longue, a display cabinet, and a chest of drawers. His T-shirt was clinging to him by the time he tossed the last bits of debris out of the window, and he was breathing heavily.

He sat down on the floor, which was littered with shavings and sawdust, and surveyed the living room. Bare though it was, it made a warmer impression than before.

*

Jonas had stopped worrying about red lights and one-way streets long ago. He drove down the wrong side of the ring road at high speed, turned off into Babenberger Strasse, and came out on Mariahilfer Strasse.

Vienna's main shopping area had never appealed to him. He disliked hustle and bustle. When he pulled up outside a shopping centre, the only sound to be heard was the ticking under the bonnet. The only moving object in sight was a scrap of paper scudding across the asphalt at the next intersection, blown by the wind. It was hot. He made his way over to the entrance. The revolving door activated itself.

Armed with two suitcases taken from a boutique on the first floor, he rode the escalator up to a shop selling electrical goods. It was so stuffy he could hardly breathe. The sun had been beating down on the glass roof for days, and every window in the building was shut.

In the electrical shop he went behind the counter and opened his suitcases. Further along the aisle he found a digital video camera he knew how to operate. The cabinet contained eight boxed examples of the same model. Eight would be enough. He stowed them in one of the suitcases.

The tripods were harder to find. He could only lay hands on three. He put them in the second suitcase together with two small radio cassette recorders, an answerphone and some blank audio tapes and videotapes. Then he shut the suitcase and tested the weight. No problem.

In the radio section it took him some time to locate the most powerful short-wave receivers. He also helped himself to a Polaroid camera, plus another as a spare. He remembered the Polaroid films last of all.

The air was so stale he couldn't wait to leave. He stretched. He had a stiff back from carrying the suitcases around and from the hard work in his parents' former flat. It made him think of his masseuse, Frau Lindsay, who had a lisp and talked incessantly about her child.

*

He wolfed down his freezer fish and spooned some potato salad out of a jar. After cursorily rinsing the plate and the frying pan, he unpacked his cases. His flat didn't have enough wall sockets for the cameras' adapters, he saw. But he'd intended to take the tape recorders to the neighbouring flats in any case.

He forced his immediate neighbour's rickety door with ease. Having often crossed swords with him over his habit of playing music late at night, he'd expected to find himself in a bachelor pad littered with pizza cartons and CD sleeves. To his surprise, the place was empty. A ladder stood propped against the wall in one of the rooms. Beside it was a bucket with a tattered floorcloth draped over the rim.

He felt uneasy as he went from room to room. He hadn't noticed any sign of a move.

The longer he thought about it, the uneasier he became. Did this vacant flat possess some significance? Did it indicate that something crucial had escaped his attention?

He checked the other flats on his floor. Again to his surprise, few of the doors were locked. His neighbours had obviously been trusting souls. Only two doors resisted the crowbar. Behind all the others he found ordinary homes whose occupants might simply have been out shopping.

He returned to the empty flat, taking the adapters and batteries with him. There were seven wall sockets. He plugged adapters into six of them, reserving the seventh for one of the new tape recorders. The power had not been cut off; the displays came on.

He turned on the radio. With this model he should be able to pick up stations in places as distant as Turkey and Scandinavia. He selected a frequency and waited. Radioed a call for help, stated his location, spoke in German, English and French. He counted silently up to twenty, then changed frequencies and repeated his request to get in touch.

An hour of this convinced him that there was no radio traffic in Europe.

He turned on the short-wave receiver.

White noise from the BBC's World Service. From Radio Oslo, from Central Europe, from the Middle East, from Germany, from Morocco, Tunisia and Egypt. No reception, just white noise.

The sun was now so low that he had to switch on the light. He turned on the TV. Started the Love Parade video, pressing the mute button as usual. He adjusted the short-wave receiver to the Radio Vatican wavelength. White noise.

*

He awoke around midnight, having slid off the sofa and banged his knee. The TV screen was flickering, the radio hissing. It was hot inside the room.

With the shotgun in one hand and the tape recorder in the other, he went out into the passage. He listened.

Something was bothering him. Hurriedly, he turned on the landing light. He listened some more.

He padded barefoot over the cool stone floor and into the adjoining flat, shouldering the splintered door aside. He stared into the darkness ahead. Just then he thought he felt a draught.

'Hello?'

A narrow strip of light from the passage was shining on the door between the hallway and the living room. The door seemed to be ajar.

Again he felt a draught, this time on the back of his neck.

He went back into his flat and put the tape recorder down. Before going out into the passage again he peered in both directions and listened. Having locked the door behind him, he stole down the stairs holding the gun.

The light went out just as he reached the third floor.

He froze. Engulfed in darkness, all he could hear was his own irregular breathing. Seconds or minutes later – he couldn't have said which – he gradually shook off his inertia. With his back to the wall, he felt for the light switch. The bulb shed a dim glow. He remained where he was, straining his ears.

He found the street door closed. Although it could only be opened from outside with a key, he locked it. He looked out at the street through the glass panel. Not a sound. Absolute darkness.

Back on the sixth floor, he turned on all the lights in the flat next door without letting go of the gun.

He couldn't remember leaving the door between the hallway and the living room ajar. However, he didn't find anything suspicious. Everything seemed to be just as he'd left it. The windows were shut. He couldn't explain where the draught had come from.

Perhaps he'd imagined them both, the draught and the position of the door.

He fetched the tape recorder and put in a blank tape. Making a note of the time, he pressed the record button. He tiptoed out of the flat.

The neighbours on his floor had their own tape decks, so he didn't have to use the other tape recorder. He put tapes in the decks in seven other flats, started them off, and wrote down the times and flat numbers in a notebook. The tapes had a playing time of 120 minutes.

Back inside his own flat, he locked the door and rewound the video. He left the sound turned off. Then he got the remaining tape recorder ready and switched off the short-wave receiver, which was hissing and crackling to itself beside the window. After that, he stretched out on the sofa with his notebook and a glass of water. Apathetically, he watched the Berliners repeat their silent dance towards the Victory Column.

He glanced at the clock when his eyelids started to droop. Twelve thirty-one. He noted it down, then pressed the record button.

*

Another cloudless day.

Jonas loaded the video cameras and all their accessories into the Spider. He'd left the windows open overnight, so the interior wasn't as unbearably hot as usual.

During the drive he tried to contact various people by phone. Marie in England, Martina at home and at the office, the police, Radio Austria, his father.

He pictured the phone ringing in his father's flat. It stood on a small chest in the hallway, and above it hung a mirror that made you feel you were being watched while phoning. That dim hallway in which the phone was ring-ing, now, at this very moment, was usually a little cooler than the rest of the flat. Lying in that hallway were his

67

father's worn-out shoes, and hanging in the cupboard was the old-fashioned Loden jacket whose elbows his mother had darned. It smelt of metal and plastic, that hallway. Now, at this moment.

But did the phone really ring when no one was there to hear it?

*

Jonas didn't pull up outside Millennium City but drove straight in. He cruised at a walking pace past the boutiques, the bookshop, the jeweller's, the drugstore, the cafés and restaurants. All were open, as if today were a normal working day. He refrained from sounding his horn.

Looking at the snack bars, he was struck by how spick and span they were. No stale bread lying around, no rotting fruit, everything clean and tidy. Most of the city's cafés and restaurants looked the same.

He had to get out when he reached the Millennium Tower because there was no public access at ground level. Laden with his shotgun, the crowbar and the video camera plus accessories, he took the escalator. One of the lifts whisked him up to the twentieth floor, where he boarded another. The whole ascent took a minute.

The offices on the top floor were open. Jonas chose one whose picture window provided the best view of the city. He put his things down and locked the door.

When he went right up to the window, the view took his breath away. There was a drop of 200 metres. The parked cars looked minute, the litter bins and news-stands were almost unrecognisable as such.

He needn't have lugged the tripod up there, a table shoved up against the window did just as well. He stacked some books on it. As soon as he considered this makeshift base to be stable enough, he loaded the camera with a blank tape and placed it on top of the books. He adjusted it so that the lens was pointing at the city's sun-bathed roofs, checking its position on the miniature screen. Then, after jotting down the location, date and time in his note-book, he pressed the record button.

*

The other camera required a tripod. He set it up at the en-trance to St Stephen's Cathedral facing the Haas Haus, where acrobats used to show off their tricks to tourists. Spectacles of that kind left Jonas cold – in fact he'd been so afraid of being accosted by one of these artistes that he'd always hurried past them with his head down.

When everything was ready and he was about to start filming, it occurred to him that he hadn't yet been into the cathedral. St Stephen's was one of the few important build-ings in the city centre he still hadn't checked, a careless oversight. It seemed logical that anyone left alive in the city would seek refuge in its biggest church.

He opened the heavy door a crack and slipped inside. The first thing he noticed was the smell of incense, which lay heavy on his chest.

'Hello? Anyone here?'

His voice sounded feeble in the cathedral's huge, vaulted nave. He cleared his throat. He called again. The sound went echoing round the walls. He stood still until silence descended once more.

No candles were burning. The church was harshly illu-minated by some bulbs suspended at intervals from the roof. The numerous chandeliers were unlit, the high altar was almost invisible.

'Is anyone here?' he shouted.

The echo was so shrill, he decided not to call again. Instead, he walked around talking loudly to himself.

Having combed the cathedral and satisfied himself that no one else was there, he turned his attention to the altar of the Virgin Mary. It was she to whom those in need most often addressed their prayers. This was where there were most candle-ends, and where, in the old days, Jonas had seen dozens of mutual strangers praying side by side, fingering their rosaries, pressing their lips to sacred pictures and weeping. The sight had made him feel uneasy. He'd dreaded to think what personal disasters had brought the poor creatures there.

It was the young men in tears who upset him most. You sometimes saw women weeping in public, but he was appalled by the sight of men his own age giving way to their emotions in front of everyone. It pained him to be so close to them, and yet it was all he could do not to go up to them and stroke their bowed heads. Was one of their nearest and dearest sick? Had somebody left them? Had somebody died? Were they themselves terminally ill? There they knelt, those embodiments of mental anguish, with Japanese and Italian tourists taking flash pictures all around them. That's how it had seemed to him.

He surveyed the empty pews before the unlit altar. He would have liked to sit down but felt as if he was being watched. Felt as if someone was only waiting for him to do so.

With the shotgun on his shoulder, which hurt where the sling had chafed it, he tiptoed down the nave. The saintly figures in their niches looked unreal. Pallid and lacklustre. Their frozen faces reminded him of Pompeiians.

He knew from school that the bones of 12,000 people lay mouldering beneath his feet. The city's graveyard had been sited here during the Middle Ages. The graves were later opened and prisoners assigned the task of cleaning the bones and stacking them against the walls. The class had fallen very silent during this lesson, he recalled.

He stepped over a barrier to get to the high altar, where he left a message. He attached another to the Virgin Mary's altar. A search of the sacristy yielded nothing but a few empty bottles of communion wine. There was no clue to when someone had been there last.

Opposite the sacristy was the entrance to the catacombs. The next guided tour would leave at 3 p.m., according to the hour hand on a kind of parking disc. Minimum five persons.

Should he go down there? Not a particularly tempting idea. Besides, he was finding it hard to breathe. The smell of incense was overpowering.

At the exit he turned and looked back. The place was as if frozen. Deserted wooden pews harshly illuminated by little lamps. Grey stone columns. Side altars. Statues of saints with forbidding faces. High, narrow windows that admitted little sunlight.

No sound save the squeaking of his soles on the flagstones.

*

He set up more cameras in front of the parliament building, outside the Hofburg, in the Burgtheater, on the Reichsbrücke, and in a street in the Favoriten quarter. The camera in the Burgtheater he placed so that it was aimed at the pile of junk he'd left on the stage. The one on the Reichsbrücke was pointing down at the Danube. In Favoriten he filmed an intersection. Taking the remaining camera with him, he drove to Hollandstrasse.

After eating something he went back to work. It was the bedroom's turn today. As before, he began by clearing the decks. He chucked the smaller objects out of the window, flower stands, house plants, chairs, and dumped the contents of a display cabinet in some rubbish bags. By the time he'd chopped up the bedstead, he felt he'd done enough for one day. He placed the camera on the floor, made a note of the place and time and pressed the record button.

Back home he went round collecting the audio tapes.

He sat down on the sofa with a glass of fruit juice and a bag of crisps. He'd placed the tape recorder on the table beside him, where he could reach it.

The first tape came from his immediate neighbour's vacant flat. For a whole hour he listened to the silence that had reigned in the empty rooms next door. Sometimes he thought he heard sounds, but they were probably just noises he himself was making in the other flats. Or simply his imagination.

Looking out of the window, he saw that storm clouds had gathered for the first time in two weeks. He decided to save the next tape for later and bring the outdoor cameras under cover instead.

As he drove around the city, casting nervous glances at the steadily darkening sky, he remembered the spiritualist experiments he'd conducted as a part-superstitious, part-adventurous boy. They had been inspired by a half-demented neighbour, old Frau Bender, who kept him company when his mother was busy.

Frau Bender often told him about her experiences with 'the hereafter' or 'the other side'. About table-turning sessions during which the little wooden table had cavorted around the flat with her and her friends' fingers glued to the top, or about the poltergeists that plagued her family for eighteen months because she and her girlfriends had pooh-poohed their existence. Locked cupboard doors creaked open at night, tapping was heard inside walls, and window panes were scratched by unseen fingernails. Not all at the same time, though. Sometimes it was one phenomenon, sometimes another.

She had a particular passion for talking about the here-after, which had been described to her by gifted mediums of her acquaintance.

I'M STANDING HERE WITH A ROSE IN MY HAND. A THORN JUST PRICKED ME, her late mother had told her through the mouth of one such medium.

WE LIVE IN A BEAUTIFUL HOUSE WITH A GORGEOUS GARDEN, a deceased woman friend had reported.

IT'S ALL SO VAST, AND THERE ARE MANY ROOMS, said an uncle. EVERY INSIDE EMBODIES AN OUTSIDE, EVERY ABOVE A BELOW.

He was holding a hat in his hands and looking troubled, the medium had said. Did the hat possess some significance?

And then, for the hundredth time, Frau Bender disclosed that her uncle had been found lying dead with his hat on his chest. Nobody knew what he'd died of, and he himself wouldn't say. The most astonishing part of it was that no one except herself and the rest of the family had known about the hat.

Jonas had readily accepted his mother's suggestion that he go and play at Frau Bender's for an hour or two. Although his visit spooked him for days afterwards, he learnt a great many arcane and interesting things there. For instance, that a tape recorder left on at night would pick up the voices of the dead. Or that the dead sometimes became visible for a fraction of a second. On the many occasions when you thought you'd glimpsed something, a shadow or a movement, it was advisable not to discount the possibility that you'd seen a ghost. This happened quite often, said Frau Bender.

She also promised to appear to Jonas after her death and tell him what the hereafter was like. He must look out for little signs of her presence, she said. She didn't know if she would be able to appear in human form.

Frau Bender died in 1989.

He hadn't heard from her since.

A violent peal of thunder in the distance. He floored the accelerator.

With some reluctance, he glanced at the rear-view mirror. No one there. He turned his head. No one sitting in the back.

The storm broke just as he stowed the last outside camera in the boot. Not wanting to have to make another trip, he decided to collect the other cameras right away. He drove first to the Burgtheater and then to Hollandstrasse, where he closed the windows to prevent the rain, which was drumming almost horizontally against the panes, from doing any damage to the flat.

The Millennium Tower was his last stop. Gun in hand, he rode the escalator up to the entrance. He was about to board the lift when there was an ear-splitting crash. The lightning strike must have been very close. The lift door slid shut in front of his nose. He didn't press the button again. The risk of a power cut that might leave him stranded between the tenth and twentieth floors was too great.

In Nannini he made himself an espresso and took his cup over to one of the tables outside the entrance. On his right was the electrical appliances store, which occupied two floors. On his left he could see the walkways leading to other rows of shops. Immediately to his front was the down escalator with the tower looming up beyond it.

He craned his neck in an attempt to see the top of the tower. It was blurred and almost invisible. Rain spit-spattered on the glass roof that spanned the entire shopping centre.

He had often sat at one of these tables with Marie. Although the Millennium City shops didn't attract the smartest of customers, they had enjoyed shopping here.

He went back inside the café and called Marie's relations in England from the phone behind the counter. Nothing to be heard but the unfamiliar ringing tone.

If only her mobile's voicemail had cut in, he could have heard her voice. But the phone just rang and rang.

Jonas was so tired after playing the third audio tape, he fresh-
ened up by taking a cold shower. Although he'd found nothing on any of the tapes, he was too intrigued to go to bed. He
could always catch up on his sleep tomorrow.

Darkness had descended on the city long ago. The thunderstorm had ceased and the rain had moved on soon
afterwards. He had lowered the blinds. The young Berliners
were silently dancing across the TV screen.

He made himself a snack. Before returning to the sofa
with his plate, he stretched his arms and rotated his shoul
ders. A fierce pain shot from the small of his back to the nape
of his neck. He thought longingly of Frau Lindsay.

Shortly after 1 a.m. he put in tape number five. The sixth
followed an hour later. The radio alarm was displaying 3.11
a.m. as he pressed the play button for the seventh time.

By the time he had listened to that tape he was suffering
from severe overstimulation. While listening to the sixth he had
taken to pacing around the living room and doing physical exercises. It wore you down, constantly straining your ears and
hearing nothing. He couldn't rid himself of the sensation that
liquid was trickling from his ear canals. Every few minutes he
felt his ears and checked if there was any blood on his fingers.

More mechanically than deliberately, he put in the tape
that had recorded him asleep.

He went over to the window. With two fingers he parted
the slats of the blind. One or two windows were illuminated.
He recognised the one over there. It belonged to the flat he'd
visited.

Was everything there just as he'd found it?

At 4.30 a.m. he heard sounds on the tape.

7

Jonas worked for two hours, by which time the gurgling and rumbling in his stomach could be ignored no longer. He had something to eat and went back to work. He wasn't thinking of anything much.

By evening he reeked of sweat and had torn his trousers badly, but the living room and nursery were stripped of any reminders of the Kästner family. The kitchen he'd left untouched.

He walked slowly round the flat with his hands clasped behind his back. From time to time he nodded to himself. He'd never seen his old home in this state.

Back in his own flat his stomach started rumbling again. He fried himself some cod from the deep-freeze. That exhausted his supplies.

After a long bath he rubbed some ointment into his right shoulder. The weight of the shotgun sling had chafed the skin. Although he had carried the gun on his left shoulder since yesterday to relieve the pressure, he had hurt the spot while working today.

He extracted the damp washing from the machine. While he was draping it over the clothes horse, item by item, the tape recorder occasionally caught his eye. He looked away quickly.

When he had run out of chores and was already shuffling

from one foot to the other, he suddenly remembered the new answerphone. The instructions were brief and intelligible. He was able to record a message immediately.

'Hello! If you hear this, please come to the following address . . . My mobile number is . . . If you can't make it, tell me where to find you.'

He dialled his home number on his mobile and let it ring. The answerphone cut in after the fourth ring. With the mobile to his ear he heard the message in stereo:

'Hello! If you hear this, please come to the following address . . . '

Already there, he thought.

He sat down on the sofa with a glass of Marie's advocaat and watched the Love Parade again. The sun's dying rays were slanting through the half-closed blinds.

If he wanted to listen to the tape again, he knew he should do so now.

He wound the tape back, then forwards, then back again. It stopped by chance at the point where the first sound made itself heard. A faint rustle.

Minutes later he heard a murmur.

It was his own voice. It had to be. Whose, if not his? He didn't recognise it, though. Then a strange, hollow, staccato 'Hepp' issued from the loudspeakers. Then silence. Minutes later he heard some more murmuring. It went on for longer this time, like a coherent sentence.

He let the tape run on to the end, listening with his eyes shut. Nothing more.

Was it his voice?

And, if so, what was he saying?

*

The temperature had dropped. Dense grey clouds hid the sun. A stiff breeze was blowing, and he wasn't sorry. It was the same every year: he looked forward to the summer for months, only to tire of the heat after a day or two. Jonas had never been a sun-worshipper. It defeated him how people could barbecue themselves for hours on end.

In the supermarket he mechanically loaded a trolley with food, trying to remember a dream he'd had last night.

He had dreamt of a nasty little boy. Latin in appearance and dressed like a child from the 1930s, the youngster had spoken in a grown-up voice. He'd materialised in front of Jonas again and again. Menacingly, out of nowhere, radiating hostility.

Try as he might, Jonas could only recall the atmosphere, not what had actually happened. He hadn't recognised the boy.

He had never attributed any significance to his dreams in the old days. Now he kept a pencil and paper beside his bed, so he could make notes if he woke in the night. The paper was blank this morning. His only haul to date had been a sentence scribbled the night before last, but he couldn't decipher it.

At the supermarket entrance he turned and looked back. Nothing had changed. The refrigeration units of the deep-freeze and dairy cabinets were humming away. Several of the aisles were littered with debris. Here and there, a milk bottle peeped out from under the shelves. The air was cool. Cooler than in other shops.

Back home again, having stowed the frozen food in the three-star compartment and the tinned goods in the kitchen cupboard, he plugged in one of the video cameras and played a tape selected at random.

It showed the stage of the Burgtheater. There was the sound of something being zipped up. Footsteps receded. A door closed with a thud.

Then silence.

A heap of junk from the props department. A papier

mâché soldier with a business card pinned to his chest. A spotlight illuminated the scene from the top right.

Jonas kept his eyes glued to the screen. He considered fast-forwarding the tape but didn't for fear of missing something, some vital little detail.

He grew fidgety.

He fetched himself a glass of water, massaged his feet.

He had been staring at the screen for an hour, observing the immobility of inanimate objects, when he realised that history was repeating itself. He'd spent hours gazing intently at a meaningless jumble of objects once before. Years ago, at the theatre with Marie, who liked avant-garde plays. Afterwards she'd scolded him for being utterly unreceptive to anything new.

He couldn't sit still, felt as if his leg were going to sleep, itched all over, jumped up and refilled his glass. Flopped down on the sofa, squirmed around, pedalled in the air with both legs. And all without taking his eyes off the screen.

The phone rang.

He leapt over the sofa table and reached it in two seconds flat. His heart missed a beat, then started again – painfully. His chest heaved as he struggled for breath.

'Hello?'

'Lo?'

'Who's there?'

'Ere?'

'Can you hear me?'

'Ee?'

Whoever it was, he wasn't calling from Austria. The line was so poor and the voice so faint, he felt it must be an overseas call.

'Hello? Can you hear me? Do you speak German? English? Français?'

'Say?'

Something had to happen. He couldn't establish contact, didn't know if the caller could hear him at all. If not, there would soon be a click followed by the dialling tone.

'*I am alive!*' he shouted in English. '*I am in Vienna, Austria! Who are you? Is this a random call? Where are you? Do you hear me? Do you hear me?*'

'Ee?'

'*Where are you?*'

'Oo?'

He uttered a curse. He could hear himself but not the other person.

'*Vienna! Austria! Europe!*'

He couldn't bring himself to accept his failure to establish contact. An inner voice told him it was pointless, but he refused to hang up. He paused. Listened. Bellowed into the mouthpiece. Until it occurred to him that the other person might have gathered that there were problems and would call back. The connection might be better then.

'*I do not hear you! Please call again! Call again immediately!*'

He had to shut his eyes, he found it so hard to replace the receiver. He didn't reopen them right away but continued to sit on the stool with his head on his outstretched arm and his hand on the receiver.

Please call back.

Please ring.

*

Jonas drew several deep breaths and blinked.

He went into the bedroom to fetch his pencil and paper and note down the time. After a moment's hesitation he added the date: 16 July.

*

The work he'd undertaken in Hollandstrasse would have to wait. Jonas dared not leave the flat. He put off going to the shops and limited his activities to the bare essentials. He even slept on a mattress beside the phone.

He re-recorded the message on his answerphone at least three times a day. Which items of information were the most important? Name, date and mobile number, certainly, but he couldn't make up his mind about place and time. The message mustn't be too long, and it had to be comprehensible.

He grew more dissatisfied with his recordings the more often he listened to them. Doggedly, he amended their sequence again and again – just in case the phone should ring during the six or seven minutes he needed to spend in the supermarket, loading up with apple juice, toilet paper and deep-frozen cod.

Perhaps the phone call was a reward for not resigning himself to his fate and remaining active. For searching for clues.

With fresh determination, he set about assessing the video recordings. He didn't restrict himself to a single viewing of the tape from the Millennium Tower. Having failed to spot anything the first time, he rewound it and watched it again in slow motion.

For a while he thought the recorder's slow-motion function was defective. It wasn't. There was no discernible difference between a normal shot of Vienna's immobile roofs and one that showed those roofs in slow motion. Any trees that might have been bending before the wind were too few, too small and too far away for him to detect any movement.

Jonas pressed the freeze-frame button. He shut his eyes, wound the tape on, pressed the freeze-frame button again and opened his eyes.

No difference.

He shut his eyes, wound the tape on, pressed the freeze-frame button and opened his eyes.

No difference.

He wound the tape on, almost to the end, and put it into reverse. The picture wound back in time-lapse.

No difference.

*

Undeterred, he spent the next day analysing the videotape of the Favoriten intersection in the same way.

With the same result.

For hour after hour he stared at its total immobility without spotting anything unusual. The only thing that had changed was the shadows. He discovered this discrepancy when comparing a still from the beginning with a still from the end, but there was no sign of anything abnormal. The sun had moved, that was all.

The videotapes recorded outside the parliament building, St Stephen's and the Hofburg were equally uninformative. Jonas devoted several days to them. He wound them on, wound them back, glanced at the phone, dipped into a bag of crisps and wiped his salty fingers on the sofa's antimacassar. He froze and fast-forwarded, but found nothing. There was no hidden message.

When he put in the Hollandstrasse tape, the screen gave a brief flash and went dark.

He knuckled his forehead and shut his eyes. The tape had been a new one. He'd unwrapped it, put it in the camera and pressed all the right buttons. All of them! The REC symbol had lit up clearly.

He switched cameras. Nothing. The tape was blank. Blank, but not unplayed. He knew what an unplayed tape showed: it flickered. This one showed darkness.

He stroked his chin. Cocked his head. Ran his fingers through his hair.

It had to be chance, a technical fault. He was reluctant to see signs in everything.

To soothe his imagination he shot a test sequence with the same camera and another tape. He expected the playback to be blank. To his bewilderment, the reproduction was perfect.

So it had to be the tape.

He put it into the camera that had been running in Hollandstrasse, shot a few seconds' worth of film, wound it back and checked it. No complaints. A top-quality picture.

Although it was broad daylight, he lowered the blinds until all that relieved the gloom were two narrow strips of light on the carpet. With the shotgun propped up beside him, he watched the tape from beginning to end. It never came to life. There was nothing to be seen, absolutely nothing. Yet it had been recorded.

Halfway through he pressed freeze-frame and snapped the TV with the Polaroid, then waited tensely for the picture to appear.

It showed the screen as dark as it was in reality.

While looking at the photo he remembered his notion that continuous slowness could kill. If this were true, if you rubbed shoulders with eternity by performing an endless movement that culminated in immobility, what was that – reassuring or terrifying?

He aimed the camera at the screen once more. With his eye to the viewfinder, he put his finger on the shutter release and gently depressed it. He tried to reduce the pressure more and more.

The point of release, he felt, would soon be reached.

He depressed the button more slowly still. A tingling sensation took possession of his finger. Went up into his arm. His shoulder. He sensed that the point of release was approaching, but that the speed of its approach was lessening.

The tingling had now permeated his entire body. His head swam. He seemed to hear a distant whistling that must have been deafening at its source.

He had the impression that a process of some kind had begun. Various constants of perception such as space, matter, air, time, seemed to be coalescing. All were flowing into each other. Coagulating.

A sudden decision. He pressed the shutter release all the way. A click, a flash, and a thin sheet of card came purring out of the camera. He slumped back on the sofa. His sweat smelt acrid. His jaws were clamped together.

*

The last videotape had been shot on the Reichsbrücke. It showed the Danube flowing steadily past and the motionless shape of the Donauinsel, the island whose pubs had been among Jonas's favourite haunts. Only four weeks ago he had subjected himself, for Marie's sake, to the alcoholic hurly-burly of the Donauinsel Festival.

After a few minutes his eyes widened. Unconsciously, he sat up inch by inch and leant forwards as if to crawl into the TV.

An object was drifting down the river. A red bundle.

He rewound the tape. He couldn't make out what it was. It vaguely resembled a hiker's rucksack, though a rucksack would have tended to sink rather than float. A sheet of plastic seemed more likely, or a plastic container. Or a bag.

Jonas rewound the tape several times. He watched the little red blob come into view top left, grow bigger, gradually take shape, become clearly visible for a moment, and then go out of shot at the bottom of the screen. Should he drive there at once and search the shores of the Donauinsel, or watch the rest of the tape?

He stayed where he was. Sitting cross-legged on the sofa with his heart pounding, he stared avidly at the surface of the Danube. He wasn't disappointed when the tape ended without his noticing anything else out of the ordinary. Dutifully, he watched the whole tape again and conducted the usual freeze-frame and slow-rewind experiments before pocketing his car keys and picking up the gun.

The phone caught his eye as he passed it.

Oh well, he thought. It wouldn't ring now.

*

He wanted first of all to inspect the video camera's location, so he pulled up on the bridge itself. He saw, as soon as he got out, that something was different.

He walked around. Twenty paces this way, twenty paces that. The wind blowing into his face was so chilly he regretted not having worn a jacket. He turned up the collar of his shirt.

Something was wrong, he felt sure.

Roughly at the spot where he'd sited the camera, he rested his elbows on the parapet. He looked down at the Danube, which was flowing past with a subdued murmur. That sound had been drowned before, even at night, by the noise of cars and lorries crossing the bridge. But it wasn't the sound of the river that puzzled him.

He scanned the surface for the approximate course the object had followed. It had come into shot back there. What was over there? And it had floated out of shot down there. Where would it have drifted to?

He went over to the other side of the bridge. The long, narrow island stretched away to the north-west as far as he could see, lapped by the Danube on either side. There were no grilles or gratings in the river bed, no sizeable spits or inlets, so it was unlikely that the red object had lodged somewhere or been washed ashore. Nevertheless, he had to look for it.

As he stood there with his hands in his pockets, resting his stomach against the parapet, he suddenly recalled his old, long-held ambition: to be a survivor.

Jonas had often imagined what it might be like if he narrowly missed a train that later came to grief in the mountains.

He'd pictured it in every detail. The brakes failed, the train plunged over a precipice. Carriages impacted and were crushed. Shortly afterwards, aerial views of the scene were shown on TV. Paramedics tending the injured, firemen scurrying around, blue lights flashing everywhere. He saw the pictures on a TV in a shop window. Anxious friends kept phoning for reassurance. Marie wept. Even his father nearly broke down. For days afterwards, he had to explain how this dispensation of providence had come about.

Or he took an earlier flight than originally scheduled. He got to the airport in good time, so as to do some shopping and buy Marie something nice in the duty-free shop. Then it turned out that a seat was available on an earlier flight. In one variant of this fantasy he inadvertently checked in at the wrong desk but managed to obtain a seat thanks to a computer error. Every version of the same imaginary scenario culminated in the destruction of the plane on whose passenger list his name appeared. His death was announced on the news. Once again, he had to reassure grief-stricken friends. 'It's a mistake, I'm alive.' A shout at the other end of the line: 'He's alive!'

A car crash in which he climbed out of a complete write-off, uninjured save for a few scratches, with dead bodies lying all around him. A falling brick that missed him by inches and killed a total stranger. A heist in which hostages were shot, one by one, until police stormed the building and rescued him. A madman running amok. A terrorist attack. A stabbing. Mass poisoning in a restaurant.

Jonas had always wanted to brave some public peril. To win the laurels of one who had undergone some great ordeal.

To be a survivor.

To be a member of the elect.

Now he was.

*

Driving along the Donauinsel wasn't difficult, but he was afraid of missing some important detail, so he set off on foot. He soon came to the shop that hired out bicycles and mopeds. This, he remembered, was where he and Marie had rented one of those pedal-operated buggies favoured by tourists at seaside resorts in Italy.

The place wasn't locked. The keys for the mopeds were hanging on the wall, each tagged with its registration number.

He picked a dark green Vespa that would have delighted his sixteen-year-old self. His parents had no savings. The money he'd earned from his first holiday job wouldn't run to more than an ancient Puch DS 50. When he bought a second-hand Mazda at the age of twenty, he'd been only the second car-owner in the family after Uncle Reinhard.

With the shotgun clamped between his thighs, he cruised along the island's asphalted roads. Again he had the feeling that something was wrong. It wasn't just the absence of people. Something else was missing.

He got off and walked down to the water's edge, cupped his hands around his mouth.

'Hello!'

He hadn't shouted in the hope that anyone would hear him. It relieved the pressure in his chest for a moment.

'Hello!'

He kicked some pebbles along in front of him. Gravel crunched beneath his soles. He ventured too close to the water and sank in, soaking his shoes.

His quest for the red object no longer interested him. It seemed pointless, looking for a scrap of plastic that had drifted past here days ago. It wasn't a sign. It was a bit of flotsam.

The day was growing colder. Dark clouds were racing towards him, wind lashing the long grass beside the road. Jonas suddenly remembered the phone at home. He turned to go just as the first raindrops spattered his face.

8

He awoke from a nightmare. It took him a few seconds of bemusement to grasp that it was early in the morning, and that he was lying beside the phone. He sank back onto the mattress.

He had dreamt that people were streaming back into the city. He went to meet them. They straggled past him in ones and twos and small groups, like people going home after a football match.

He didn't dare ask where they'd been. They took no notice of him. He heard their voices. Heard them talking, laughing, joking together. Never closer to them than ten metres, he walked down the middle of the street. They passed him on either side. Every time he tried to attract their attention, his voice failed.

He was feeling worn out. Not only had he spent another night beside the phone, but he hadn't got around to undressing.

He checked to see if the receiver was on properly.

While looking for some pumpernickel in the bottom drawer of the kitchen cupboard, he caught his backside on the fridge. The mobile in his hip pocket took a knock. Although it was unlikely to have been damaged, he fished it out and checked. His mobile had to be preserved at all costs. He couldn't afford to lose the SIM card, at least.

No sooner had he pocketed it again than a terrible suspicion came over him. With trembling fingers he accessed the list of outgoing calls. The most recent entry was his own home number, dialled at 16.31 on 16.07.

He dashed to the phone. Trampling around on the mattress, he rummaged in a heap of paper until he discovered the note lying, clearly visible, on top of the address book.

16.42, 16 July.

*

Although he'd intended to do some work at his father's flat, he drove aimlessly around the city. He headed south along the Handelskai. When he passed the Millennium Tower he looked up. Dazzled by the sun, he swerved and braked sharply, then drove on more slowly. His heart was thumping.

He saw from afar that his banner was still revolving around the Danube Tower. He drove up to the entrance but didn't dare get out. He looked for some indication that the banner had lured someone there. High overhead, the café continued to rotate with a rhythmical hum that was drowned at regular intervals by ominous splintering sounds. It wouldn't be long, he imagined, before the whole superstructure disintegrated.

He drove across the Reichsbrücke into Lassallestrasse. A minute later he pulled up beside the Big Wheel. He made a brief tour of the area, gun in hand. It was hot. There was no wind. Not a cloud in the sky.

Satisfied that there were no nasty surprises outside, he walked past the café and into the Big Wheel's administrative offices. The control room lay beyond an inconspicuous door in the shop that sold miniature models of the Big Wheel and other tourist tat.

He looked at the console, which was the size of a school blackboard. Although the controls weren't marked, as they were in the Danube Tower, he quickly grasped that the yellow button turned the entire system's power supply on and off. He pressed it and some lights came on. An indicator started flashing. He pressed another button. The lowest gondola, which he could clearly see through a window from his place at the console, began to move.

A marker pen was lying on one of the desks. He used it to write his phone number on a computer screen. He also left a message on the door. Then he put the marker pen in his shirt pocket.

He walked to the nearest hot-dog stand, the one he'd eaten at on his last visit. He found a packet of biscuits on a shelf and breakfasted on them, never taking his eyes off the gondolas.

Should he board one?

*

He combed the amusement park on foot, turning on all the rides he could. Although he couldn't always get the controls to work, he managed to do so often enough to fill the fairground with music and movement. The din wasn't as loud as it used to be, of course. He hadn't started enough roundabouts and Flying Carpets for that. Besides, there weren't any people. If he shut his eyes, though, he could still, by a stretch of the imagination, yield to the illusion that all was as it always had been. That he was standing beside the fountain surrounded by half-drunk strangers. That he would soon buy himself some grilled corn on the cob. And that Marie would be back from Antalya tonight.

*

Jonas carried the mattress back into the bedroom and changed the sheets. The floor beside the phone needed tidying up. He stuffed the empty crisp packets and half-eaten bars of chocolate into a plastic sack, tossed the drink cans in as well and swept the floor. Last of all, he scrubbed off the rings the glasses had left on the floorboards. While doing this, he resolved not to let things slide again. He must at least keep order within his own four walls.

He set up the video camera facing the bed and turned it on. The view wasn't inclusive enough. Although he would later be able to observe every flicker of expression on his face, this videotape would be of use to him only if he could manage to lie still all night. Quite a challenge.

He zoomed out as far as he could. Still not enough. He moved the tripod back a metre and peered at the miniature screen again. This time the image was satisfactory. The whole of the bed was in shot. Not wanting another surprise, he made sure the camera and tape weren't damaged.

He was still too on edge to go to sleep, so he sat down in front of the TV with a bag of popcorn. He'd exchanged the Love Parade video for a feature film – a comedy – with the sound on. He hadn't watched a feature film since his first few days of solitude, so he hadn't heard a human voice other than his own.

At the first words of the female lead, such horror gripped him that he wanted to turn the film off. He resisted the urge and hoped it would pass.

It got worse. His throat tied itself into a knot. He got goosebumps. His hands started to tremble. His legs were so weak he couldn't stand up.

He switched off with the remote and crawled over to the video recorder on all fours. He substituted the Love Parade tape for the feature film. Crawled back. Hauled himself onto the sofa again.

Pressed 'Play'.
Turned off the sound.

*

In the night he woke up. Half dreaming, he shuffled into
the bedroom. He didn't bother brushing his teeth and was
past undressing, but he turned on the camera.

REC.

Flopped down on the bed.

⁋

On his way to Matzleinsdorf goods yard, where Machine
Park South was situated, he passed the church on the
Mariahilfer Gürtel. He read the poster on its façade as he
drove by:

There is One who loves you: Jesus Christ.

He stepped harder on the accelerator.

Apart from the Central Cemetery, Machine Park South
was Vienna's biggest walled enclosure. Jonas had never
been there before. It took him five minutes to find the
entrance. He was amazed when he rounded the corner.
He'd never seen such a concentration of heavy goods
vehicles parked at regular intervals as if about to be
photographed for an advertisement. There must have
been hundreds of them.

Many were articulated lorries. However, handling those
took a certain amount of practice, and the trailer had first
to be connected to the cab. He wanted an ordinary HGV.
A truck with some space.

He threaded his way between the vehicles, annoyed with
himself for having forgotten to put on any sun cream. He
was so afraid of getting sunburnt he interrupted his search
several times to mop his face and drink some mineral water

in the air-conditioned Spider. He took a swig, drummed on the steering wheel. Looked in the rear-view mirror.

At last he thought he'd found what he needed. A DAF of around sixty tons. Unfortunately, the key wasn't in the ignition. He didn't feel like searching the offices for it, so he plumped for a somewhat older but even bigger model, which was likewise equipped with all the indispensable extras. It had a radio, a small TV, air-conditioning, and, in the spacious sleeping place behind the driver's seat, a cooker.

His spirits rose when he started the engine. It was a long time since he'd heard anything like it. The truck had power to spare. He liked the view from the cab, too. In the Spider he seemed to be only a few centimetres above the road, whereas here he felt he was on the first floor of a house with picture windows.

The papers were in the glove compartment, as were some of the former driver's possessions. These he threw out of the window unexamined, together with two T-shirts that had been lying on the bunk.

He fetched two metal ramps from a repair shop. Then he used the marker pen from the Big Wheel office to write *Dear Jonas, 21 July. Yours, Jonas* on a notice board on the wall.

He drove over to the Spider and lowered the tailboard. Having gauged the distance between the wheels, he placed the ramps in position. The Spider was aboard the truck a minute later.

*

He parked the truck outside his father's flat. With a metallic clatter, he backed the Spider down the ramps and onto the roadway. Dutifully, he checked the flat. All was as it had been on his last visit, the smell included. The place still smelt of his father.

He looked at the phone in the hall.

Had it rung a few days ago, when he'd called and pictured it ringing? Had this phone actually been here? Had the flat been filled with the sound?

He surveyed the street through the bedroom window. The mopeds were obscured by the truck. So was the dustbin with the bottle protruding from it.

The wall clock was ticking away behind him.

He felt an urge to leave the city. For a while. To convince himself, once and for all, that he would never come across another soul anywhere. Even if he encountered no one in Berlin or Paris, he might find a way of getting to England. On the other hand, he couldn't imagine spending long in unfamiliar surroundings. He felt he had to fight for every metre, laboriously adapt to every place he came to.

Jonas had never understood how people could maintain two homes. How, in the long run, could they bear to spend a week or a month here and a week or a month there? In his new home he would think of his old home, and after a month the former would become the latter, and he wouldn't be able to find his way around when he returned. He would roam around the rooms and see things that were wrong. A wrong alarm clock, a wrong wardrobe, a wrong phone. Although the coffee cup he drank from at breakfast would belong to him, he would still find himself thinking of the cup he'd used the day before. And of where it was at that moment. In a crockery cupboard. Or an unemptied dishwasher.

The bathroom mirror in which he looked at himself after showering wouldn't show him anything different from the mirror he'd looked in the day before. Yet he would feel that something about the reflection was wrong.

He could lounge on the balcony and leaf through magazines. He could watch TV or use the vacuum cleaner or do some cooking. But he would inevitably think of his other home. Of the other balcony, the other TV, the other vacuum cleaner, the other pepper mill in the other kitchen cabinet. He would also think of the books on the shelves in his other home. Of the sentences in those unopened books and the stories those sentences conveyed to those who were able to interpret them.

And before going to sleep he would lie in bed and think of the bed in his other home, and he would wonder if he was about to go to sleep at home or had slept at home the night before.

*

Jonas connected the video camera to the TV. He lowered the blinds while the tape was rewinding, so as not to be dazzled by the setting sun. The room lay in twilit evening gloom.

He pressed 'Play'. Turned the sound up full.

He saw himself walk past the camera and flop down on the bed. He turned over on his stomach as usual. He couldn't go to sleep in any other position.

The subdued glow of the bedside light was bright enough to illuminate everything clearly. The Sleeper lay there with his eyes shut, breathing deeply and evenly.

Although Jonas wasn't one of those who looked in the mirror more than twice a day, he was familiar with his out- ward appearance and had a vague idea of the expression he usually wore. But the thought of watching himself with his features entirely relaxed made him rather nervous.

He took the mobile from his hip pocket and put it on the table so he wouldn't call himself again. He looked at the display. For once, he'd thought to lock the keypad.

After a few minutes the Sleeper turned his face away from the camera. There was a rustle as he buried his head under the pillow. Some time later it reappeared. He turned on his side. Shortly afterwards he rolled over on his back and drew a hand across his eyes.

Now and then Jonas stopped the tape and listened for sounds outside the door. He walked round the room, swinging his arms. Poured himself a glass of water. It was all he could do to start the tape again.

Twelve minutes before the tape ended the Sleeper turned over again with his face towards the camera.

*

Jonas had the fleeting impression that one eye had opened. The Sleeper was looking at the camera. Looking at it in full awareness of being filmed. Then the eye snapped shut again.

*

The second time he watched this sequence he wasn't so sure. The fourth viewing convinced him that he'd been mistaken. It made no sense in any case.

After fifty-nine minutes the Sleeper muttered a few sentences. He didn't get their meaning. He flung his arms about and turned away from the camera. The screen went black, the tape whirred. Jonas felt annoyed with himself for only putting in a one-hour tape.

He rewound it and watched the last minute in slow motion. He noticed nothing out of the ordinary. He listened to the four sentences. The second was the most intelligible. He thought he picked out three words: 'Kaiser', 'wood' and 'finish'. Not very informative.

He watched the whole tape again from the beginning.

Nearly fifty minutes went by without incident. Then came the sequence that had puzzled him the first time.

It happened again.

For a fraction of a second, the Sleeper's eye looked sharply into the camera. Without a trace of drowsiness. Then it shut.

Jonas scanned the sofa table for the remote. Didn't see it. He was holding it in his hand. It was a while before his trembling thumb pressed the stop button.

He mustn't drive himself crazy. If he wanted to, he was sure he could find some other disconcerting details on the tape. Just as he could hear imaginary noises on the audio tapes. If he wanted, he could find a dozen potential pointers to any number of things. Why had that bus driver eyed him so oddly on 1 July? What had Martina and their peculiar new colleague been whispering about at the office party? Why, on 3 July, had leaflets advertising a pizza delivery service been stuck to the door of every flat in the building except his? Why had it rained so seldom? Why, after ten hours' sleep, did he sometimes feel as if he hadn't slept a wink? Why did he think he was being watched?

He must cling at all costs to what existed. To what was definitely verifiable and beyond dispute.

He raised the blinds and opened the window. Made sure the door was locked and bolted. After checking all the rooms, he glanced into the wall cupboard.

With the shotgun beside him, he watched the whole tape again, frame by frame. When he reached the sequence that puzzled him he looked out of the window. Before coming to the muttered sentences he switched to normal play.

Those three words were all he could catch. He didn't get the impression that the Sleeper had wanted to tell him something. Nevertheless, he felt he was watching something important.

He set up two cameras in the bedroom. One he positioned a couple of metres from the bed, the other so that only the head of the bed was in shot. Although there was a risk that he would roll out of shot while asleep, he was anxious to watch his face in close-up, if only for a few minutes.

He put in two three-hour tapes.

9

He awoke with a twitchy hand. His thumb was itching. He thumped the pillow, scratched the place with his forefinger. The itch wouldn't go away.

He turned over on his side. Lying on the pillow beside him was one of Marie's T-shirts. She hadn't worn it, not even for one night. He'd changed the duvet covers after waving her taxi goodbye, but the smell of her lingered faintly.

He looked at her bathrobe hanging on a hook on the wall. At her chest of drawers, from which a pair of panties was peeping. At the stack of books on her bedside table.

*

On his way to the 5th District he ate an apple. He wasn't particularly fond of apples, or of any kind of fruit with pips or stones. His mother had forced them on him. Jonas had argued with her until her death about what was and wasn't healthy, what should and shouldn't be eaten. He took the view that what was good for one person needn't necessarily be good for another. She disputed this. In her world, everything had its allotted place. She used to ruin his summer holidays at Kanzelstein by roaming the garden with him daily and making him sample things: apples, pears, berries – even plants like sorrel. His father would shake his head at this but confined himself to sitting in his deckchair and reading a newspaper.

Just as Jonas turned into the Wienzeile he remembered that he hadn't got hold of any cardboard packing boxes, nor did he know of any nearby shop that stocked them. He thumped the steering wheel with his fist and did a U-turn. For the second time that morning he drove past the church whose poster assured him he was loved by Jesus. He sounded his horn.

The automatic doors of the DIY store on the Lerchenfelder Gürtel hummed open with a jerk. Without so much as grazing anything, he drove the Spider along the aisles. The packing boxes were right at the back of the store. He couldn't judge how many he needed, so he took a whole carload.

Before going into the flat he went for a walk down Rüdigergasse. He rang various doorbells but didn't wait for an answer. He shot out some window panes in Schönbrunner Strasse.

There were statues everywhere. Statues and statuettes, human figures, decorative gargoyles.

It had never struck him before. Almost every building was adorned with stone carvings. None of them was looking at him, but all had faces. Jutting from the oriel moulding on one house was a winged dog, on another a fat boy silently playing the flute. One wall displayed a grimacing face, another a little, bearded old man preaching to an invisible congregation. He'd never noticed any of these things before.

He took aim at the old preacher, but his arm shook. With a threatening gesture, he lowered the gun.

Just as he turned into Wehrgasse he caught sight of a post office sign. It occurred to him that he'd never searched a post office. Although he'd posted some cards that had never landed in his letterbox, he'd never thought to take a closer look at a post office.

The automatic door didn't open when he stepped in front of the sensor. He blasted it open. He gained access to the area behind the counter by doing the same to another door beyond it.

There wasn't much money in the drawers, 10,000 euros at most. The bulk of the cash was probably in a strongroom at the rear, but money wasn't his concern.

He sat down beside one of the big trolleys full of unsorted post. Picking up an envelope at random, he tore it open. A business letter demanding settlement of an unpaid bill for a consignment of materials.

The next letter was private. The shaky handwriting was that of an old woman writing to a girl named Hertha, who lived in Vienna. Hertha was urged to study hard, but not so hard that she let life pass her by. Love, Granny.

He examined the envelope. It was postmarked Hohenems.

He toured the premises. There was no indication that the staff had left in a hurry.

He felt in the pockets of a blue overall hanging on a hook in the back room. They contained some small change, matches, cigarettes, a packet of tissues, a ballpoint pen and a lottery ticket, filled in but not yet stamped.

In a woman's jacket hanging alongside there was a packet of condoms.

In a briefcase he found nothing but an unappetising sausage sandwich.

Before leaving he took his marker pen and wrote his mobile number on the window of every counter position. He trod on an alarm button. Nothing happened.

*

He packed one box after another, but it was a longer job than he'd expected. Many of the objects that passed through his hands were fraught with associations. In some cases he could only vaguely recall the circumstances surrounding a particular book or shirt. He would stand there, stroking his chin and staring into space. It usually helped to sniff the object, because its smell was more evocative than its appearance.

Moreover, sorting and packing weren't his forte. He chafed at having to wrap each china cup in newspaper, if only because he'd always disliked touching newsprint. The sound of sheets of paper rubbing together gave him goosebumps, just as Marie had been allergic to the squeak of chalk on a blackboard or the clatter of cutlery. He could read a newspaper, but any other kind of rustling sound was anathema to him.

Late that afternoon he broke into a local pub. He found something to eat in the deep-freeze and drew himself a beer. It tasted stale. He left as soon as he'd finished eating. The return trip seemed longer. His legs felt heavy.

Seeing the boxes stacked in every room, he had no inclination to go back to work that day. Half the cupboards and shelves had been emptied, after all, and there was no rush.

He lay down on the bed surrounded by rolls of sticky tape, newspapers, scissors. Unused boxes, not yet unfolded, were leaning against the wall.

He shut his eyes.

The clock was ticking on the wall. His father's smell still lingered in the air, but he no longer had the pleasurable sensation of being immersed in a vanished world. The rooms were filled with the atmosphere that precedes departure.

If he wanted to call anything in the world his own, he would have to re-create the past. Although everything in Vienna, every car, every vase, every glass was his for the taking, nothing remained that belonged to him.

He stood at the window, watching the sun sink below the skyline. It had reached its maximum height on 21 June and gone down behind a thick clump of trees on the Exelberg. Since then its setting point had been almost imperceptibly moving leftwards.

It was on an evening like this, sixteen or seventeen years ago, that Jonas had got ready for his first solo vacation. He had packed his rucksack, taken his new two-man tent from the cupboard, borrowed a crash helmet from a neighbour. The alarm clock went off at 4 a.m., but he'd been awake for a long time before that.

He'd got horribly cold during that eight-hour trip to the Mondsee in Upper Austria, having underestimated the night-time chill and dressed too lightly. But the adventure was worth it. Riding through villages in the dark. Passing houses in which people were just getting up, showering, shaving, brewing coffee or still asleep while he himself was on the road. The unfamiliar smells. Dawn in a place he'd never seen before. The solitude. The sense of romantic daring.

He lowered the blinds.

He paused outside the bedroom door. He withdrew his hand, which was already on the handle. Bending down, he peered through the keyhole.

On the opposite wall he saw the embroidery Marie's mother had given them, and beneath it the chest of drawers. On the right he glimpsed the foot of the bed.

The embroidery showed a woman standing beside a well with a shirt in her hands. A traditional farmhouse could be seen in the background. The door was done in bright red, whereas the other colours were muted. Above it was the inscription K+M+B, although Jonas couldn't read this through the keyhole.

On the chest of drawers was a ceramic fruit bowl. Beside it, leaning against a pile of books, a pair of imitation duelling pistols, a gift from his father.

He felt a slight draught on his eyeball.

He was separated from the picture of the washerwoman by a door. He was outside, yet he could see what was happening inside the deserted room. Strictly speaking, no one could look at that chest of drawers. From the room's point of view, there was no one there. It was like seeing the contents of an unopened book.

Or was he wrong? By looking through the keyhole, wasn't he crossing a line? Becoming a part of the room once more?

*

He started the tape. The whole of the bed was in shot. As he had the last time, he saw himself walk past the camera and fall into bed. Minutes later his gentle snoring issued from the loudspeakers.

While watching the Sleeper, he debated whether he ought to view the other tape in parallel. The one that showed his face in close-up. For that, of course, he would need another TV and video recorder. These could be obtained from the neighbouring flats. Now that he was comfortably stretched out on the sofa, however, he realised how weary he was after his exertions. He dropped the idea. It probably wouldn't make any difference.

The Sleeper must have been equally tired last night. He lay quite still. It was more than thirty minutes before he turned over for the first time. From one point of view, that was a good thing. His almost total inertia meant that the second camera had also kept him in shot, so he would later be able to study his changes of expression. On the other hand, this uneventfulness wasn't exactly a spur to his investigations.

His throat felt sore. No, it couldn't be. He normally

caught one cold a year at most. Surely he couldn't have caught another so soon. Better safe than sorry.

He prepared a hot toddy, scarcely taking his eyes off the screen, and made a mental note to get hold of some vitamin tablets.

The Sleeper rolled over again. He seemed to be hot, because he kicked his hairy white legs free of the bedclothes. A sigh was heard. A minute later he turned over so far that he escaped the second camera's field of view. The upper part of his body was now lying on the other side of the bed, beside the T-shirt Marie hadn't worn.

Jonas pulled a face. He'd overdone the sugar. There was a little whisky left in the saucepan. He poured it into his cup and added some more lemon juice.

After an hour and a half the Sleeper pressed Marie's pillow to his face.

That was last night, Jonas thought, and tonight will be the same. I shall lie there and sleep, and there won't be any difference.

This time he'd overdone the whisky. He laid the cup aside. The toddy had gone cold in any case.

Jonas rubbed his eyes. He sluiced his face and neck with cold water. He found an aspirin in the bathroom cabinet. It was soluble, but he let it dissolve on his tongue. It prickled.

Back in the living room he turned on all the lights. The dull glow from the TV screen was making him sleepy. He brewed himself some strong coffee.

The Sleeper slept on.

That should be me, Jonas thought. That should be me.

*

Two hours and fifty-eight minutes after the beginning of the tape, the Sleeper's eyes half opened. He rolled around. Stood up. Strode towards the wall with a purposeful air.

Bumped into it.

Still with his eyes half open, he explored the wall with his hands as if wanting to get into it. He concentrated on a particular spot, neither reaching up nor bending down, applying pressure with his palms as if trying to squeeze into the masonry. He even braced his shoulder against it.

There the tape ended.

*

Never before had Jonas darted so quickly from one room to another. He examined the bedroom wall in vain. No sign of an opening, no secret door. Just an ordinary wall.

His fatigue had vanished. He quickly resumed his place in front of the screen and rewound the tape.

The Sleeper opened his eyes like someone roused by a noise or by lying in an uncomfortable position. He squirmed around. Threw off the bedclothes and stood up. He seemed impervious to reality. Like a man in a dream, he groped his way over to the wall and began his exertions. He made no sound, nor did he ever look at the camera.

Jonas looked at his hands. His fingernails were chalky.

He went into the next room again. Lay down on the bed and looked at the wall. Taking the same route as the Sleeper, he tottered over to the spot with his arms extended and pushed. Braced his shoulder against the wall.

He looked round. Nothing had changed. It was his bedroom.

He watched the second tape in fast-forward. There was nothing of interest on it, as he'd expected. After an hour the Sleeper rolled out of shot. None of the mysterious happenings at the end had been recorded.

With great reluctance, he set up a camera for the night. He didn't bother with the close-up camera. He drank the rest of his cold toddy.

10

Jonas blinked. The bedside light was dazzling him. He groped for the switch, turned it out and opened his eyes. Twenty to twelve. The other duvet was lying on the floor with the overturned tripod and camera beneath it. He had no particular wish to speculate on the significance of this, so he left everything lying there and made himself some breakfast.

Before going into the bathroom he put a blank audio tape into the tape recorder and pressed the record button. He turned the machine so that it faced away from the bathroom. Then he showered, cleaned his teeth and shaved with care.

He got dressed in the living room. The display on the microwave said 12.30. The tape had been running for twenty minutes.

Standing right in front of the tape recorder's built-in microphone, he said:

'Hello, Jonas.'

He counted up to five with his eyes shut.

'Good to speak with you. How are you?'

Three, four, five.

'Feeling rested? Tense?'

He spoke for nearly three-quarters of an hour, doing his best to forget what he'd just said. A click indicated that the tape had run out. He rewound it. Meantime, he finished getting dressed.

He dialled his mobile number on the landline. It rang, and he answered it. Placing the land-line receiver on the floor with the tape recorder just in front of it, he pressed the play button. Then he put a second tape recorder beside it, put in a tape and pressed the record button. With the gun over his right shoulder and the mobile in his other hand, he left the flat.

He cruised through Döbling, driving along streets he'd never visited before. He kept the mobile pressed to his ear for fear of missing something. He steered and changed gear with his other hand. It occurred to him that he was violating a road traffic regulation. At first this idea merely amused him. But it set him thinking about a more fundamental point.

If he really was all on his own, he was free to lay down a new penal code. Laws remained in force until new ones were agreed upon by the majority. If he constituted the majority, he could discard an entire social system. Being sovereign, he could theoretically exempt theft and murder from prosecution, or, on the other hand, prohibit painting. In Austria, the disparagement of religious doctrines was punishable by up to six months' imprisonment. He could annul that law or increase its severity. Aggravated theft rendered a person liable to up to three years' imprisonment, in contrast to non-aggravated theft, the relevant sum being 2000 euros or more. He could change that.

He could even decree that everyone had to go for one hour's walk a day while listening to folk music on a Walkman. He could invest stupidities of all kinds with constitutional status. He could choose another form of government. Indeed, devise a new one. Although the system in which he lived was really anarchy, democracy and dictatorship all in one.

'Hello, Jonas.'

He nearly collided with a dustbin standing beside the road.

'Good to speak with you. How are you?'

'As well as can be expected, thanks.'

'Feeling rested? Tense?'

It was himself he was hearing. He had spoken those words an hour ago, and now they were happening, happening again. At this moment they were becoming something that was happening, that was having an actual effect on the present.

'Rested, not tense,' he muttered.

He was struck by the difference between the voice in his ear and the one he heard inside himself. The one in his ear sounded higher pitched and less agreeable.

'It's twelve thirty-two by my watch. What time do you have?'

'Thirteen fifty-five,' he replied, glancing at the dashboard.

He remembered how he'd knelt in front of the tape recorder in his living room and spoken those words into the microphone. He saw himself fiddling with the ring on his finger, studying the pattern on his coffee cup, turning up his trouser leg. He recalled what he'd been thinking when he'd spoken those words. That was then, this was now. And yet one was connected with the other.

'Turn left at the next intersection, then sharp right. Then take the second turning on the left. Stop outside the second building on the right-hand side of the street.'

The instructions took him to a small street in Oberdöbling. His taskmaster had underestimated his speed, so Jonas spent a minute drumming on the steering wheel and shuffling around on his seat.

'Now get out, taking the gun with you, and lock the car. Go to the building. If there are several floors, your objective is the ground-floor apartment. You won't need your crowbar, get in through a window. If it means a bit of a climb, so be it. Be athletic!'

He was standing outside a suburban house. A notice on the gate warned intruders of a savage dog. It was locked. He climbed over it and went up to the house. An Audi was parked outside the garage. The house was adorned with window boxes. The stretches of grass flanking the gravel path had been mown quite recently.

The nameplate beside the door read: *Councillor Bosch*.

'Mind the broken glass! Now go into the kitchen.'

'Easy!'

He peered through the window but couldn't spot an alarm system. He smashed the pane with the butt of the shotgun. Glass rained down on the floor. There really wasn't a burglar alarm. Having quickly knocked out the remaining glass, he climbed in.

'Open the fridge. If you find an unopened bottle of mineral water in there, drink it!'

'Don't badger me!'

One door led to the bathroom, another to a boxroom, the third to the basement stairs. The fourth was the right one. Breathlessly, he opened the fridge, which was encased in beechwood. He really did find a bottle of mineral water, and it was unopened. He drank it.

While awaiting fresh instructions he surveyed his surroundings. The furniture was bulky and traditional. On the wall was a poster of Dalí's *Soft Watches*, already affected by heat and steam from the stove.

He found the combination puzzling. The nature and quality of the decor suggested elderly occupants, whereas the poster belonged in a student's digs. The owners' offspring had probably insisted on this stylistic clash.

Beside the poster was a tear-off calendar. The top sheet said 3 July. Beneath the date was the motto of the day:

The truth knows its own value. (Herbert Rosendorfer)

He tore off the sheet and pocketed it.

'Now look for a ballpoint and a piece of paper.'

'Will a pencil do?'

He found a ballpoint in one of the drawers. There was a notepad on the kitchen table. The top sheet had a shopping list written on it. He folded it over and shut his eyes, humming a tune and trying to think of nothing.

'Write down the first word that comes into your head.'

Fruit, he wrote.

Great, he thought. I'm sitting in some stranger's kitchen, writing 'Fruit'.

'Put the piece of paper in your pocket. Now look round the place. Keep your eyes open. It's better to look twice than miss something.'

Jonas marvelled at the banality of his taskmaster's pearls of wisdom. He'd spent the whole time trying to remain on his own side of the line. Trying to avoid thinking of what he'd recorded on tape so as not to anticipate what was coming. Now he briefly stepped across the line. He thought hard, but he couldn't recall having spoken the last sentence. He returned to his own side. Made his mind as much of a blank as possible.

In the living room he came across a sort of ancient Egyptian statue. He didn't know much about the history of art, so he couldn't say exactly what it was. It appeared to be the figure of a woman, possibly a life-sized effigy of Nefertiti. The face was expressionless and rather forbidding. With its massive head and voluminous, veil-like hairstyle, it reminded him more of a black rap singer on MTV. He wondered who could have installed such a thing in their living room. He'd never had any clients with taste like that.

He toured all the rooms, talking into his mobile as he went. He reported on the decor of the master bedroom, the rugs in the hallway, the empty birdcage, the aquarium in

111

whose softly gurgling water no fish swam. He described
the contents of the wardrobes. He counted the files in the
study, fingered a heavy ashtray made of some unfamiliar
material. He rummaged in drawers. He went down into
the basement and paid a visit to the garage, which reeked
overpoweringly of petrol.

Just as he was leaving a girl's bedroom, which wasn't
particularly clean and tidy, the voice in his ear said:

'Did you see that?'

He came to a halt and looked back over his shoulder.

'There was something there, did you notice? You
caught a glimpse of it.'

He hadn't seen a thing.

'It was there for a moment.'

An inner voice warned him not to go back into the
room. The voice in his ear urged him to do so. He hesitated. Shut his eyes, rested his hand on the handle and
slowly pushed it down. The pressure of his hand eased a
little, so little that although he knew it was happening he
didn't feel it. He pushed the handle ever more slowly.

He was gripped by a sensation that time was freezing
beneath his hand. The brass handle felt soft. It seemed to
be melting into its surroundings. Neither hot nor cold, it
had no temperature at all. Without hearing a sound, he felt
he was being subjected to a thunderous din that had material substance and emanated from no particular direction. At the same time, he became aware that he consisted
of nothing more than the movement his hand was performing at that moment.

He let go, breathing heavily and staring at the door.

'But don't bring it home with you,' said the voice in his
ear.

*

He spent the rest of the day packing boxes like an automaton. Apart from one short break, during which he grilled some sausages in the pub as he had the day before, he worked until early evening.

It wasn't the incident in the house that disturbed him. What weighed on his mind was the potential significance of the overturned video camera. Did it have some connection with the Sleeper's odd behaviour? Would it be worth investigating that wall? Should he break it open?

Having taped up the last box, he surveyed the empty cupboards and shelves. There weren't as many as there had been. Where were the possessions they'd lived with in Hollandstrasse? Had they all been thrown away? Where was the picture that had so engrossed him as a child whenever he passed it in the hall?

Now that he came to think of it, there were other things he missed. The red photo album. The ship in the bottle. The linocut. The chessboard.

He either carried or dragged the boxes out into the street, depending on how heavy they were. When they were all loaded, he sat down wearily on the tailboard. Leaning back on his hands, he looked up. Windows were open here and there. The statues projecting from the walls stared forbiddingly over his head. The sky was a flawless, merciless blue.

*

The cellar stairs were narrow. Cobwebs clung to every nook and cranny, dusty skeins dangled from the ceiling. The plaster on the grimy walls was flaking off. Jonas shivered. Although he descended the stairs at a crouch, he hit his head twice. In a panic, he ran a hand over his face and forehead in case something nasty had stuck to them.

Pinned to the cellar door was an old damaged sign

113

vividly illustrating the dangers of rat poison. There were four panes of glass in the upper part of the door, one of them broken. The passage beyond lay in darkness. Jonas's nose was assailed by a smell of mildewed wood.

He raised his shotgun and kicked the door open. Singing at the top of his voice, he quickly turned the light on.

It was a communal cellar divided into separate sections by timber partitions a hand's-breadth clear of the floor and ceiling. There were no floorboards, just hard-packed earth studded with stones the size of a man's fist.

Although Jonas had never been down here before, he identified his father's compartment at once. He recognised, protruding into the passage from between two wooden slats, the hand-carved walking stick his father had used when walking in the woods at Kanzelstein. He hadn't carved it himself. It was the work of a toothless old peasant who was versed in that craft. Jonas had fetched fresh cow's milk from his farmstead every morning. He'd been scared of him, but one day the old man had called him over and presented him with a little carved walking stick of his own. Jonas could still remember what it looked like after all these years. He had proudly strutted around with it and worshipped the taciturn old peasant from then on.

He made sure that he was alone, and that the dimly lit compartments around him held no unpleasant surprises. Coming from one of them was a smell of paraffin so strong that he buried his nose in his shirtsleeve. One of the tanks in which the occupants stored paraffin for their stoves must have sprung a leak. But there was no danger as long as he didn't strike a light.

He took his father's bunch of keys from his pocket. The second key fitted. Jonas paused and listened before entering the compartment. The muffled, intermittent dripping of a tap could be heard. The dusty electric bulb on the wall was flickering. It was chilly.

114

With a cry of encouragement, he opened the door. And recoiled.

Most of his father's compartment was filled with the boxes he'd just loaded into the truck.

He turned on the spot with his gun at the ready. The barrel knocked some bowls and saucepans off a shelf and sent them crashing to the floor. He cowered down, peered into the passage through the slats and strained his ears. Nothing to be heard but the defective tap.

Turning back to the boxes, he stared wide-eyed at the firm's imprint.

Until he realised that they were different. Similar, but not identical. The longer he looked, the more clearly he saw that the two batches of boxes bore only a vague resemblance in shape and colour.

He tore one open and took out a bunch of photographs. He opened another. Nothing but photographs. A third. Documents and more photographs. The fourth contained books. So did the next three, which were the only ones he could get at without having to do a lot of rearranging.

He came across familiar objects everywhere. Rolled up and leaning against the wall in one corner was the map of the world from his parents' bedroom, which had so often sent his thoughts on their travels. The globe perched on top of a stack of boxes had served him as a desk lamp when he was a boy. His father's binoculars were lying on a rickety shelf with his hiking boots beside them. As a child Jonas had marvelled at their huge size.

He must have been blind. He had stowed and packed and arranged things without noticing that half of their household effects were missing.

It was surprising, nonetheless, that his father had kept these objects in the cellar. He could understand it in the case of the walking stick, and the globe needn't have stood around in the living room. But he couldn't fathom why his father had left the books and photographs to moulder away in the cellar.

The light went out.

He counted up to thirty, breathing deeply.

Gripping the shotgun in both hands, he groped his way back to the exit. A penetrating smell of grain filled his nostrils. Presumably, one of the compartments contained a small batch of the stuff with which older folk still, in spite of everything, liked to insulate their windows in winter.

*

He replaced the receiver and rewound the tapes. On one he wrote 'EMPTY', on the other 'Bosch residence, 23 July'.

With an apple in one hand, he searched the stack of camera boxes, which he'd been too lazy to dispose of, for the relevant documents. He wasn't methodical enough. Chewing hurriedly, he finished the apple and threw the core out of the window. He wiped his fingers on his trouser leg. They felt sticky, so he rinsed them under the tap and went on searching the empty boxes. Then it occurred to him that he'd thrown the instructions into the wastepaper basket.

His assumption was correct: the cameras were equipped with timers, like coffee machines or electric heaters. As long as you put in a powerful enough battery, you could programme them to start recording up to seventy-two hours ahead.

He found a portion of fish in the deep-freeze compartment. He heated it up and ate it with some mixed-bean salad straight from the jar, which wasn't a good combination. He washed up, then watched the sun go down with the mobile in his hand.

*You are terrible. * hic * :-) I love love love love you.*

Where was she at this moment? In England? Was she looking at the sun too?

This sun?

Perhaps he wasn't the only person going through this nightmare. Perhaps everyone had suddenly found themselves alone. Perhaps they, too, were stumbling through a deserted world, and the spell would be broken if two people who belonged together turned up at the same spot simultaneously. That would mean he must go looking for Marie and run the risk of missing her because she, in her world, would be doing her utmost to get to him. It would be wiser to wait here.

Besides, this theory was utter nonsense. So, probably, was every idea he'd so far entertained about the events that had overtaken him.

He picked up the duvet and tossed it onto the bed. He righted the tripod with the camera on it. Removing the tape, he put it in the camera connected to the TV in the living room. Then he ran himself a bath.

The water was hot. Floating in front of him was a mound of foam resembling a kneeling elephant. He could clearly make out its rump, legs, ears and trunk. He blew. The elephant drifted away a little. He blew again. A hole appeared in the elephant's cheek.

He recalled a story told him as a child by his mother, who had a liking for moral tales.

A little girl sits weeping in a forest. A fairy appears and asks why. The girl explains that she has smashed her father's collection of china and is afraid he'll punish her. The fairy gives her a reel of thread. If she tugs at it, time will pass more quickly. A few centimetres equals a few days, so she must be careful. If she wants to avoid being scolded and beaten, however, she should make use of the reel of thread.

Although dubious at first, the little girl decides she has nothing to lose and gives the reel of thread a tug. The next moment she's on her way home from school for the summer holidays, which are still several weeks ahead. 'That's good,' she says. 'I've escaped a beating.'

The little girl finds a scar on her knee whose origin mystifies her. She also sees some slowly fading weals on her backside when looking at her reflection in the mirror.

From then on she often gives the reel of thread a tug. So often that she's old before she knows it. She sits sobbing beneath a weeping willow in the forest where it all began. The fairy reappears, whereupon the old maid bemoans the fact that she has frittered her life away by using up too much thread. She should still be young, but she's already old.

The fairy raises an admonitory finger – and reverses the whole process. The girl finds herself sitting in the forest, young once more but no longer afraid of being punished. She walks home singing and accepts her beating gladly.

To Jonas's mother the moral of the story was beyond dispute: you must face up to everything, misfortune included. Misfortune, above all, makes people what they are. To Jonas himself the story's inherent truth was nothing like as clear-cut. If his mother's argument held good, everyone would undergo operations without an anaesthetic. As for the girl's premature ageing, he couldn't see that as a miscalculation on her part. What a terrible life the poor little thing must have led, to have tugged at her reel of thread so often!

His mother, his father and his schoolteacher, who also told the story on one occasion, all seemed to find the little girl's conduct plain stupid. Fancy throwing away her life just to avoid a few minutes' unpleasantness! It never occurred to anyone that she might, after all, have done the right thing. Jonas found it quite understandable. Having been through hell on earth, she had every right to tug at her thread. Now, in old age, she was simply viewing the past through rose-tinted spectacles, like all old people. She would have been in for a nasty surprise if she'd begun again from the beginning.

His mother had never understood that line of thought.

The bathwater was lukewarm, the elephant had dissolved.

Jonas pulled on his bathrobe without rinsing himself off. In the fridge he found three bananas whose skins were already dark brown. He peeled them, mashed them up in a bowl and added a pinch of brown sugar. Sat down in front of the TV. Ate.

*

The Sleeper walked past the camera, got into bed and pulled up the covers.

He started snoring.

Jonas remembered how often Marie had complained of his snoring. He rasped away half the night, she said. She could hardly sleep a wink. He disputed this. Everybody denied snoring. Although they couldn't possibly know what they did while asleep.

The Sleeper turned over. Went on snoring.

Jonas peered through the blinds. The window in the flat he'd visited some weeks ago was still illuminated. He took a swig of orange juice and raised his glass to it. Massaged his face.

The Sleeper sat up. Without opening his eyes, he grabbed the other duvet and flung it at the camera. The screen went dark.

*

Jonas rewound and pressed 'Play'.

The tape had been running for an hour and fifty-one minutes when the Sleeper crawled out from under the bedclothes. His eyes remained shut. His features were relaxed. But Jonas couldn't shake off the feeling that he knew exactly what he was doing. That the Sleeper was constantly aware of his actions, and that he himself was seeing something without seeing what mattered. Watching an occurrence he didn't understand, but which possessed some underlying significance.

Three, four, five times the Sleeper sat up, took hold of the duvet, put his right foot on the floor and threw it.

Jonas went into the next room. He looked at the bed, got into it. Sat up, took hold of the duvet and threw it.

He felt nothing. He might have been doing it for the first time. No sense of anything strange. A duvet. He threw it. But why?

He went over to the wall and inspected the spot the Sleeper had thrown his weight against. He rapped it with his knuckles. A dull sound. No cavity.

He leant against the wall and deliberated, his hands buried in the sleeves of the towelling bathrobe and his arms folded on his chest.

The Sleeper's behaviour was odd. Was there something behind it? Hadn't he often walked in his sleep as a child? Wasn't it understandable that he should have reverted to that habit in this exceptional situation? Perhaps his sleeping self had occasionally undertaken similar strange excursions earlier on, unnoticed by Marie.

Someone in the living room uttered a cry.

He froze, convulsed less with terror than with astonishment and disbelief. With a feeling of impotence in the face of a new law of nature, one he didn't understand and had no defence against.

Another cry rang out.

Jonas went into the next room.

At first he couldn't work out where the cries were coming from.

From the TV. The screen was dark.

Shrill cries suggestive of fear and pain, as if coming from someone who was being tortured. As if that some-one's body were being briefly stuck with pins and then allowed a few seconds' respite.

Another cry. It was loud and piercing. There was no humour in it. Just the sound of terrible happenings.

He fast-forwarded. Cries. He wound the tape on some more. Cries. He fast-forwarded to the end of the tape. Hoarse breathing, groans, occasional cries.

He rewound the tape to where the Sleeper got up and hurled the duvet at the camera. He studied his face, trying to discover some clue to what lay ahead. Nothing to be seen. The Sleeper hurled the duvet, the camera fell over, the screen went dark.

Dark, not black. He noticed that now. The tape had wound on, but blindly. Having seen the screen go dark, he'd automatically dismissed the possibility that recording had continued.

The first cry rang out ten minutes after the camera fell over. No sounds of any kind could be heard before that. No footsteps. No knocking. No strange voices.

Then, after ten minutes, that first cry. The scream of someone being skewered with an iron spike. It was a sudden cry, more of terror than of pain.

Jonas dashed into the bedroom and stripped off his bathrobe. He turned in front of the mirror, contorted his body, lifted his feet and inspected the soles. His joints creaked. He couldn't see a thing. No cuts, no stitches, no burns. Not even a bruise.

He went right up to the glass and stuck out his tongue.

It wasn't furred. No visible injuries. He pulled his lower lids down. His eyes were bloodshot.

*

He sat down on the sofa and treated himself to a few minutes of the Love Parade's silent cavortings. He ate some ice cream. Poured himself a whisky. Only a small one, though. He had to remain sober, clear-headed.

He got the camera ready for the night. In his agitation he'd forgotten how to set the timer. He was too tired to re-read the instructions. He contented himself with a normal three-hour recording.

He tried the front door. It was locked.

11

The camera was in its place.

He looked around. Nothing seemed to have changed.

He threw off the duvet. No injuries.

He went over to the mirror. His face, too, looked un-marked.

*

Jonas was already well-acquainted with the DIY store in Adalbert-Stifter-Strasse. He drove the Spider down the aisle until it became too narrow, then went looking on foot. He found a torch and some industrial gloves right away. The furniture trolley took longer. He strode briskly round the silent store. It was half an hour before he thought of look-ing in the stock room. There were dozens of trolleys in there. He loaded one into the boot.

He drove back and forth across the 20th District, steered the car along the narrow streets of the Karmeliter quarter in the 2nd, crossed over to the 3rd, performed a U-turn in Landstrasse and combed the 2nd again. That, he figured, was where he was likeliest to find what he was looking for.

He could generally tell, without getting out of the car, whether a machine beside the kerb was unsuitable.

A Vespa wouldn't do, nor would a Maxi or even a Honda Goldwing. He wanted a 1960s Puch DS, 50 cc, top speed forty k.p.h.

He spotted one in Nestroygasse, but the key was missing. Another was parked in Franz-Hochedlinger-Gasse. Again no key. Someone in Lilienbrunngasse had also been a fan of ancient mopeds. No key.

He called in at Hollandstrasse and looked round the flat. Nothing had changed. He looked into the backyard through the bedroom window. It was like a rubbish dump.

He suddenly remembered what he had dreamt of last night.

The dream had consisted of a single image. A bound skeleton lay on its back on the ground. Both feet in a single oversized leather boot. It was being slowly dragged across a field by a lasso tied to the saddle of a horse whose head could not be seen. Only the rider's legs were visible.

The image stood before him quite distinctly. A skeleton with a stout rope wrapped around its ribcage, the horse dragging it along. The feet in the boot. The skeleton's slow progress across the grass.

*

He was driving along Obere Augartenstrasse when he spotted another one. Exactly what he was looking for. A DS 50 with the key in it. Pale blue, like the one he himself had owned. He estimated its date of manufacture at 1968 or 1969.

He turned on the fuel tap, climbed aboard and trod on the kick-starter. At first he gave too little throttle, then too much. The engine sprang to life at the third attempt, sounding far louder than he'd expected. Although he wobbled for the first few yards, he had the moped under control by the time he drove through the gates into the Augarten.

It was a peculiar sensation, riding along the park's dusty paths on a DS. At sixteen he'd worn a visored crash helmet and had never felt the wind on his face, or not to this extent. Nor had the sound of the engine ever punctured such a silence.

On the long, tree-lined straight that ran past the park café he opened the throttle as far as it would go. The speedometer read forty k.p.h., but the moped was doing at least sixty-five. Its owner had been more skilful at souping up an engine than Jonas had been in his day. His one good idea had been to remove the exhaust mufflers, which had had no appreciable effect on the moped's speed but had made it sound much louder.

After circling the anti-aircraft tower he left the paths and veered off across the grass. He avoided the areas with tall hedges. Jonas didn't care for hedges. Particularly when they were trimmed with excessive care. And it was still clear that these had been. Trees, shrubs, hedges – all had been neatly pruned and clipped.

*

I'm just overhead – only a few kilometres above you.

*

Jonas made his way into the café. After he'd checked the rather small premises, he brewed himself a coffee and took it out into the garden.

Although the Augarten had never appealed to him much, he'd sat here several times. With Marie, whom he'd had to accompany to a series of al fresco film shows on summer evenings. Shuffling around on his chair and yawning furtively, he had gone there for Marie's sake, drunk beer or tea, eaten at the multicultural buffet and been plagued by mosquitoes. They seldom bit him, but the sound of them had more than once driven him to distraction.

He had waited for Marie here at the café, 100 yards from the cinema and the buffet, which operated only during the film season. He'd watched cheeky sparrows land on tables and peck at titbits. Shooed away wasps and scowled at old ladies' yapping poodles. But he hadn't been really annoyed because he knew that, any moment now, Marie would prop her bike against one of the chestnut trees, sit down beside him with a smile and tell him about her days on the beach at Antalya.

He rode the moped to the Brigittenauer embankment. The cars in the area had no ignition keys in them, he knew. He fetched Marie's bicycle from the cellar and pedalled back to the Spider within five minutes. He was in pretty good shape. Then, nagged by the feeling that he'd been wasting time, he drove off to work in Hollandstrasse.

He lunched at a pub in Pressgasse noted for its 150-year-old bar. He rubbed out the food and drink prices on the blackboard and wrote *Jonas, 24 July* on it in chalk.

*

Taking the torch and shotgun with him, Jonas made his way down into the cellar. He turned on the torch and the cellar light in quick succession.

'Anyone there?' he called in a deep voice.

The tap gurgled.

Warily, he approached his father's compartment with the gun held out in front of him and the torch clamped against the barrel. The biting smell of oil and insulating stuff filled his nostrils as before. He might be mistaken, but the smell seemed to have intensified in the last twenty-four hours.

Why was the compartment door open? Had he forgotten to shut it?

He remembered that the cellar light had gone out, and that he'd groped his way to the stairs without a second thought. So the open door was probably all right.

He hung the torch on a hook at head height so that it would light up the whole compartment when the time-switch's fifteen minutes were up. Before putting the shotgun in a corner he glanced over his shoulder.

'Hello?'

The tap went 'ping', the cellar light flickered. The skeins of dust and cobwebs around the bulb trembled in a draught.

He took a handful of photos out of the first box. Black-and-white snapshots, they looked as if they dated from the 1950s. His parents in the countryside. On walking tours. At home. At work parties. His mother in witch's get-up, his father as a sheikh. Many were stuck together as if fruit juice had been spilt on them.

A photo from the next box was of Jonas himself. Five or six years old, he was dressed up as a cowboy, complete with charcoal moustache. Standing round him and grinning at the camera were three more youngsters in fancy dress. One of them, who had lost his upper front teeth, was brandishing a sword and laughing. Jonas remembered him. Robert and he had been at nursery school together, so the snapshot must be thirty years old.

A few more photos from the nursery school era. Some with his mother. Fewer with his father. Most of the latter lacked a head or a pair of legs. His mother had been no photographer.

A picture of him on his first day at school. In colour, but faded. He was clutching a satchel not much smaller than himself.

The light in the passage went out.

He straightened up. Half facing the passage, he listened, then shook his head. If he heard any noises from now on, he would ignore them. They were nothing, meant nothing.

A snapshot of himself cuddling a tiger cub and wearing a forced smile. A seaside holiday.

He still remembered the annual holidays at North Italian resorts on the Adriatic. The whole family had had to get up in the middle of the night because the coach left at 3 a.m. He pictured the wall clock's hands showing half past twelve and vividly recalled the sense of adventure and happiness with which he had packed his little checked rucksack.

They were driven to the bus station by a friend of his father who owned a car. Seaside holidays were a communal venture involving the entire family. That was why, when they got there, he said hello to Uncle Richard and Aunt Olga, Uncle Reinhard and Aunt Lena, whom he recognised by their voices in the darkness. Cigarettes glowed, somebody blew their nose, ring-pull cans of beer snapped open, strangers took bets on when the coach would be ready to leave.

The journey. The voices of the other passengers, some of whom snored. The rustle of paper. It gradually grew lighter and he could make out faces.

A stop at a picnic area in unfamiliar surroundings. Grassy hills glistening with dew. Birds twittering. Glaring light and deep, foreign voices in the toilets. The driver, who had introduced himself as Herr Fuchs, cracked jokes with him. He liked Herr Fuchs. Herr Fuchs was taking them to a place where everything smelt different, where the sun shone differently, where the sky seemed a little denser and the air more treacly.

Those two weeks at the seaside were wonderful. He adored the waves, the seashells, the sand, the hotel meals and glasses of fruit juice. He was allowed to go for a ride in a pedalo. He made friends with youngsters from other countries. Like all the other tourist kids, he was photographed on the corso with a tiger cub in his arms. He was presented with toy pistols and helicopters. It was fun, going on holiday with the whole family. No one was bad-tempered, no one argued, and at night they lingered so long over their Lambrusco that even he didn't have to go to bed too early. They were glorious, those holidays. Yet his fond-est memory was of the few hours prior to departure. The holidays were lovely, but not as lovely as his sense of an-ticipation, the feeling that anything might happen.

Jonas had passed Herr Fuchs on the way to school a few months later. He said hello, but there was no response. No friendly smile. Herr Fuchs hadn't recognised him.

*

His stomach tensed as he inserted the videotape.

The Sleeper walked past the camera, got into bed and went to sleep.

Since when had he gone to sleep so easily? In the old days he often used to stare into the darkness for an hour, tossing and turning so violently that he woke Marie. Then she too would get up and drink some warm milk or bathe her feet or count sheep. These days he lay down and passed out as though anaesthetised.

The Sleeper turned over. Jonas poured himself some grapefruit juice, staring absently at the sell-by date on the carton. He tipped some pistachio nuts into a bowl and put it on the sofa table. Then he took the camera's operating instructions from the lower shelf.

They weren't complicated. Turn a switch to 'A', press a button and key in the required start time. So he wouldn't have to look it up again, he briefly noted the programming procedure on the back of a stray envelope.

'What a restless night we're having,' he remarked to the screen as the Sleeper turned over for the third time.

129

Jonas took a swig of juice and sat back. He put his feet up on the table, knocking over the bowl of pistachio nuts. His immediate impulse was to pick them up, but he made a dismissive gesture instead. He rubbed his shoulder, which was sore from carrying the gun around.

The Sleeper sat up. He covered his face with his hands. Then, standing with his back to the camera, he raised his arms. His outstretched forefingers were pointing to his temples.

He remained standing like that.

Until the tape ran out.

Jonas needed a pee, but he felt as if he'd become part of the sofa. He couldn't even reach for his glass. He rewound the tape with the remote, which felt like a lead weight in his hand. Watched the back of the Sleeper's head a second time. A third.

He had an urge to throw all the cameras out of the window. All that stopped him was the realisation that this would change nothing. It would merely destroy any chance he had of understanding his predicament.

There was an answer, there had to be. The outside world was a big place. He was just himself. He might never be able to find the answer outside, but he must look for the one within himself. And go on looking.

Gradually, he regained control over his limbs.

He went straight into the bedroom without a detour to the toilet and put in a new tape. He set the alarm. It was nine o'clock. Tonight he had no need to use the timer.

He pressed the record button. He went to the toilet, then into the bathroom, where he brushed his teeth and took a shower. Naked, he walked past the softly humming video camera and wrapped himself in the duvet. He hadn't dried himself thoroughly. The sheet beneath him became damp.

The camera's steady hum carried to his ears. He was tired. But his thoughts were racing.

12

The alarm clock beeped from somewhere far away. It was an exasperating sound that gradually penetrated his consciousness. Jonas groped for the clock on either side of him. His fingers closed on thin air. He opened his eyes.

He was lying on the bare floor of the kitchen-cum-living-room.

He was cold. No bedclothes. A glance at the display on the microwave informed him that it was 3 a.m. He had set the alarm clock for that hour. Its monotonous beeping continued to fill the flat.

He went into the bedroom. His duvet was lying on the bed. Thrown back, as if he'd just gone to the bathroom. The camera was on its tripod, the floor strewn with dirty clothes. He brought his fist down on the alarm clock, silencing it at last.

He looked at his naked form in the bedroom mirror. For a moment he thought he'd shrunk.

He turned and leant against the wall, frowning up at the ceiling. All he could remember were the thoughts and mental images that had passed through his mind just before he fell asleep. He couldn't account for his presence in the living room.

*

While riding out of Vienna on the rattling DS, heading west, he was reminded of the night he'd set off in the same direction eighteen years ago. It had been just as dark and cold. But pairs of headlights had regularly zoomed past him. Today, the roads were deserted. All he'd had with him then was a rucksack on his back, no pump-action shotgun. And his head had been protected by a crash helmet.

He zipped up his leather jacket. Why hadn't he put on a scarf? He well remembered how wretchedly cold he'd been throughout that first trip, and he didn't want to repeat everything to the last detail.

The moon was huge.

He'd never seen it so big. A perfect, luminous orb so close overhead it looked almost menacing. As if it had drawn closer to the earth.

He didn't look up any more.

The moped purred along at a constant speed. His old machine had almost come to a stop on hills. This one managed every incline with no obvious loss of speed. Its former owner had tinkered with the engine so much that any police check would have resulted in an instant ban.

He leant into the bends, impressed by the rate at which the DS sped downhill. His eyes were watering so much he had to put on his old ski goggles.

Whenever he came to a long descent he disengaged the clutch and switched off the ignition. Coasted silently through the darkness. He removed the two woolly hats he was wearing against the cold. All he could hear was the whistle of the wind. The headlight functioned only when the engine was running, so the road ahead lay in darkness. He only abandoned these escapades when he almost missed a bend and narrowly avoided ending up on the verge.

By the time he got to St Pölten his fingers were so numb with cold it took him several attempts to remove the petrol cap. He wanted to relax in the warm over a cup of coffee.

Instead, he drank a bottle of mineral water in the filling station shop and pocketed some chewing gum and a bar of chocolate. On the magazine rack he saw newspapers which dated from 3 July. The freezer cabinet was humming away, a defective neon tube flickering at the back of the shop. It was just as chilly inside.

I've ridden along this road before, he told himself when he was back on the moped. The person who rode along it was me.

He thought of the youth he'd been eighteen years ago. He didn't recognise himself. Your cells renewed themselves completely every seven years, so it was said. That meant you became a new person every seven years, physiologically speaking. Although your mental development didn't create you anew, it changed you to such an extent that you could happily call yourself another person after so many years.

In that case, what was an 'I'? The 'I' he used to be was still himself.

Here he was again. On a moped like this one, on the same asphalt. With the same trees and houses all around, the same road signs and place names. His eyes had seen them all before. They were his eyes, even though they had renewed themselves twice in the meantime. That apple tree beside the road had stood there last time. He'd seen it. Now he was passing it again – zooming past it! He couldn't see the tree in the darkness, but it was there, its image crystal-clear in his mind's eye.

Many past experiences seemed so fresh and immediate he felt they couldn't possibly have happened ten or fifteen years ago. It was as if time curved back on itself, so that events separated by years were suddenly mere days apart. As if time possessed a spatial constant capable of being seen and felt.

The sky was getting lighter.

Something had changed in the last few minutes, something to do with himself. His teeth were chattering, he noticed.

*

Just beyond Melk, where the countryside ahead opened out, he approached a building he felt he'd seen before. From a distance it looked in need of renovation. Some plasterwork was missing. That, too, seemed familiar. The place held some significance for him.

It was a substantial building with a spacious car park in front of it. The only car parked there was an eggshell-blue Mercedes dating from the 1970s.

Jonas tipped the moped on to its stand beside the car. He peered through a side window. Lying on the fur-upholstered passenger seat were a box of raspberry sweets and a can of beer. An air-freshener dangled from the rear-view mirror. The ashtray had been pulled out, but all it contained were coins.

He went looking for the entrance, waddling like a duck because his limbs were so stiff and painful. He came to a halt and massaged his thighs, which also helped to restore the circulation in his numb fingers. The fields beyond the building were swathed in early-morning mist. The tarpaulin covering a woodpile rustled in the wind.

Above the entrance was a sign that read: Snackbar Landler-Pröll. The name was unfamiliar to him.

He unslung the shotgun and took off his rucksack. There was something wrong here. He knew for sure that Steyr had been his first stop, and he felt just as certain that he'd never come this way since. So how did he know this establishment? Was he just imagining it?

He also found it puzzling that the entrance faced away from the road. There was no sign beside the road, either.

The door wasn't locked. Lying in the passage beyond was an untidy jumble of slippers and mud-encrusted walking shoes. He could just make out a taproom through the frosted glass of the door on his left. Some stairs on the right looked as if they led to the proprietor's private quarters.

'Anyone there?'

The taproom door creaked open. He stamped his feet, cleared his throat. Paused on the threshold. Nothing to be heard but the occasional sound of wind nudging the windows.

He turned on the lights, naked bulbs suspended from the ceiling. They shed a harsh glare. He turned them off again. By now, the morning sun was bathing the room in an unreal halflight sufficient for him to find his way around.

The restaurant was neat and tidy. Bronze ashtrays on tables with gingham cloths, every table adorned with a vase of dried flowers, banquettes with decorative, embroidered cushions. A wall clock was showing the wrong time. The newspaper on top of the pile beside the espresso machine was dated 3 July.

He knew this place. Or at least, one that resembled it.

He abandoned his plan to reproduce the original trip and not to stop until he got to Steyr. He turned on the espresso machine. In the fridge he found some eggs and bacon. He heated a frying pan.

After washing his meal down with fruit juice and coffee, he tried the old radio above the serving counter. White noise. He turned it off again. He wiped off the writing on the bill of fare, took a piece of chalk and wrote: *Jonas, 25 July*.

Then he stomped up the wooden stairs. As expected, they led to a private apartment. He saw jackets hanging in a wardrobe, more shoes, empty wine bottles.

'Hooo!' he called harshly. 'Hooo!'

A cramped kitchen with a clock ticking on the wall. The floor was sticky; his shoes made a sucking sound with every step.

He went into the next room. A bedroom. The single bed unmade, a pair of underpants lying on the floor.

Another room, evidently used as a storage room. Cluttered with stepladders, beer crates, paint pots, brushes, sacks of cement, a vacuum cleaner, old newspapers, toilet rolls, oily gloves, a mattress with a hole in it. It was only after a while that he noticed all the floors were uncarpeted. He was standing on bare concrete.

There was a coffee mug on the window sill, half full. He sniffed it. Water, or possibly some kind of hard liquor whose alcohol content had evaporated.

The living room, equally untidy. The air was damp, the temperature several degrees lower than in the other rooms. He looked around for something that might explain it. There were still-lifes and landscapes on the walls. Hanging above the TV were some antlers. All the furniture was red, he noticed. A red sofa, a cupboard lined with red velvet, a carmine red carpet. Even the old wooden table had red legs as well as a red cloth draped over it.

He climbed the stairs to the attic. They creaked. The door at the top, a thin sheet of hammer-finished metal, was unlocked.

Enveloped in cool, fresh air, he thought at first that a window must be open. Then he saw the broken panes.

In the middle of the room stood a kitchen chair with the back missing. Dangling from a beam above it was a noose.

*

Jonas got hold of a small tent and a sleeping mat in Attersee-Ort, then drove to the Mondsee. After straying down two farm tracks by mistake, he found the spot where he'd camped in the old days. Thirty metres from the shore of the lake and formerly covered with scrub, it now formed part of a public bathing place. Jonas dumped his kit and reconnoitred the area on the moped.

Modern times had arrived. The lido consisted of a tree-fringed expanse of grass the size of a football pitch. In addition to changing cubicles and toilets, it boasted open-air showers, a children's playground, boats for hire and a refreshment kiosk. The terrace of an inn lay invitingly on the far side of the car park.

He started to put up the tent. The instructions were incomprehensible. Wearily, he staggered around the grass with diagrams and poles, but he got it up in the end and tossed the mat inside. He deposited the rest of his kit beside the entrance. Then he sank onto the grass.

He wasn't wearing a watch. The sun was high, it had to be past midday. He peeled off his T-shirt and removed his shoes and socks. Gazed out across the lake.

It was nice here. Trees rustling in the breeze. Lush green grass. Shrubs dotted along the shore. The surface of the lake glittering in the sunlight. Distant mountains rising into a deep blue sky. For all that, he had to force himself to realise that he was enjoying a magnificent view. Perhaps he was short of sleep.

He recalled an idea he'd often toyed with in the old days, one to which he'd surrendered in a variety of forms, especially in idyllic spots like this. It was that some historical figure, Goethe for instance, could not see what Jonas himself was seeing. Because he no longer existed.

There had been days like this in times gone by. Goethe had roamed the fields, seen the sun, admired the mountains and bathed in the lake when there was no Jonas, yet to Goethe they had all been there in the present. Perhaps Goethe had thought of his successors. Perhaps he had pictured the changes to come. Goethe had experienced a day like this one, and Jonas hadn't existed. The day had dawned nonetheless, Jonas or no Jonas. And now Jonas was experiencing this day, but without Goethe. Goethe had gone. Or rather, he wasn't there any more, just as Jonas hadn't been there in Goethe's day. Jonas was now seeing what Goethe had seen, the scenery and the sun, and it made no difference to the lake or the air whether Goethe was there or not. The scenery was the same. The day was the same. And all would be the same in 100 years' time. But without Jonas.

That was what had bothered him: the idea that there would be days without him, days perceived without him. Scenery and sunlight and ripples on the lake, but no Jonas. Someone else would see them and reflect that others had stood there in earlier times. That someone might even think of Jonas. Of his perceptions, just as Jonas had thought of Goethe. And then Jonas pictured the day, 100 years hence, that would go by without his perceiving it.

But now?

Would someone perceive this day in 100 years' time? Would someone roam the countryside thinking of Goethe and Jonas? Or would the day be a day without observation, a day that simply existed? If so, would it still be a day? Was there anything more nonsensical than such a day? What would the *Mona Lisa* be on such a day?

All this had existed millions of years ago. It might have looked different. That mountain might have been a hill or even a hole in the ground and the lake a peak, but no matter. It had existed, and no one had seen it.

*

Jonas took a tube of sun cream from his rucksack and rubbed some in. Then he stretched out on a towel in front of the tent and shut his eyes. His eyelids twitched nervously.

Half asleep, he listened to the rustle of leaves mingling with the sibilant sound of canvas caressed by the wind and the murmur of wavelets breaking on the shore. From time to time he sat up with a start, imagining that he'd heard a birdcall. He peered in all directions, blinking in the sunlight, then lay down again on his stomach.

Later he thought he heard the voices of hikers enthusing about the view and calling to their children. Although he knew he was imagining it, he could see their rucksacks and checked shirts, the children's lederhosen, the grey stockings and long-laced hiking boots.

He crawled out of the sunlight and into the tent.

It was late afternoon by the time he felt he'd caught up on his sleep. He had a snack at the pub. On the return trip he passed an Opel with Hungarian number plates. There were towels and inflatable mattresses lying on the rear seat. He topped up his sun cream back at the tent, then walked down to the boatman's landing stage.

Various types of craft were moored there. He gave a pedalo a shove with his foot. It thudded into the boat alongside. The water gurgled beneath their keels. Each had a few inches of rainwater in the bottom with leaves and empty cigarette packets floating in it.

All he saw at first were pedalos. When he boarded the nearest one he lost his balance and nearly fell in. Standing up with one foot on the driver's seat and the other on the passenger's, he looked around for alternatives. That was how he spotted the electric motorboat. The key was hanging on a hook in the boatman's hut.

Operating it was simple. He set a switch to '1', turned the steering wheel in the direction he wanted to go, and the boat went humming out across the lake.

The boatman's hut and the kiosk beside it became smaller and smaller. His tent on the grass was just a pale speck. The mountains on the other side of the lake drew nearer. Silently, the boat cut a foaming furrow in the water.

Roughly in the middle of the lake he switched off. He hoped the motor would start again. The shore might be too far away to swim to, and he didn't want to have to try.

Jonas wondered how deep the lake was at this spot. He pictured the water draining away in an instant, as if by magic. A wonderful, fascinating new landscape would be revealed just before the motorboat plunged downwards, a landscape no human eyes had ever seen before.

In a compartment beside the driver's seat, in addition to a first-aid kit, he found a dusty pair of women's sunglasses. He wiped them and put them on. The sun glinted on the rippling surface of the water. The boat bobbed gently, then lay still. Far away, on the shore opposite his bathing place, he could make out some cars parked beneath a steep rock face. A cloud slid across the sun.

*

The cold woke him.

He sat up. He rubbed his arms and shoulders. He was wheezing, and his teeth were chattering.

Dawn was breaking. Naked except for his underpants, Jonas was sitting on the grass ten metres from the tent in which he'd gone to sleep the night before. The grass was wet with dew, the sky overcast. The trees were wreathed in mist.

The tent flap was open.

He circled the tent at a safe distance. The sides were fluttering in the breeze, the rear wall was sagging outwards. Although there didn't appear to be anyone inside, he hesitated.

He was so cold he groaned out loud. He'd got undressed because he was too hot in the sleeping bag. That was still inside the tent. At least, he assumed it was. His clothes were lying beside him, as was the shotgun. He'd taken it into the tent with him last night, he felt sure.

He put on his T-shirt and trousers, socks and boots. He pulled on the jumper, pushing his head through the neck quickly.

He went over to the moped. Noticed at once that the fuel tap was open. That meant the machine wouldn't start until he'd stamped on the kick-starter ten or fifteen times – if he was lucky. He'd sometimes forgotten to turn off the tap as a youngster.

He scanned the area for tracks. Nothing. No strange footprints or tyre marks, no trampled grass. He looked up at the sky. The weather had changed abruptly. The air was so damp it might have been late autumn. The mist hovering overhead seemed to be getting steadily thicker.

'Hello?'

He called in the direction of the car park, then across the stretch of grass. He ran down to the water's edge and shouted across the lake at the top of his voice.

'Hooo!'

No echo. The mist swallowed every sound.

Jonas couldn't make out the opposite shore. He kicked a pebble into the water. It sank with a dull splash. Irresolutely, he trudged along beneath the trees lining the shore. He looked over at the tent, at the boatman's hut with the flag flying from its roof. Out across the lake. It started to drizzle. At first he thought it was mist droplets, but then he noticed that the rain was growing heavier. He glanced at the boatman's hut again. The landing stage was scarcely visible. The mist was steadily blanketing everything.

Not taking his eyes off the tent for a second, he started to repack the rucksack. The underside was wet. He cursed aloud. His other jumper was right at the bottom, worse luck. The moisture had seeped through into it. He wondered where the moisture had come from. It couldn't have come from the morning dew and the rain alone, and he hadn't spilt anything.

He sniffed the sweater. It smelt of nothing in particular.

By the time he mounted the moped the mist had swallowed up the trees along the shore. The restaurant couldn't be seen any more either. The dim shape in the car park was, he thought, the Opel from which he'd taken the inflatable mattress.

He pounded at the kick-starter until his forehead was streaming with cold sweat. The engine was flooded with petrol. He bounced so madly up and down that he toppled over sideways, taking the moped with him. He righted the machine and tried again. The rain grew heavier still. The tyres slipped on the sodden grass. Mist engulfed him. Rain was beating down on the tent a few metres away. He was no longer able to see what lay beyond it. He mopped his face.

While doggedly trying to kick-start the moped, with his heart beating ever more violently, he debated what to do. All that came to mind was the Opel, but he hadn't noticed a key in the ignition. He considered pushing the moped up a slope, then coasting down and putting it in gear. There was a chance the engine would catch. But he couldn't think of a suitable spot. Although the grassy expanse sloped down to the water's edge, the gradient was far too slight.

The engine roared into life at last. Overcome with delight and gratitude, he hurriedly revved it in neutral. It sounded robust and reliable. Even so, he kept his hand on the throttle in case it died again. Buckling on his rucksack required some acrobatics. He slung the shotgun on, feeling a stab of pain as his shoulder took the full weight of it.

He peered through the rain in all directions, wondering if he'd left anything behind. All that remained was the tent with the sleeping bag inside, but even that was barely visible now.

He rode twenty metres in the direction of the changing cubicles, then turned. The tent was invisible now. He had to follow his tyre tracks.

Cautiously, he opened the throttle. The rear tyre spun, then gripped. He put on speed, saw the tent and headed for it.

The impact made surprisingly little noise. Tent pegs were wrenched out of the ground and flew through the air. One corner of the roof got tangled up in the footrest and was dragged along for several metres. It was all Jonas could do to keep the moped upright on the slippery grass. Once he had it under control, he braked to a halt.

He peered over his shoulder. The mist was so thick, he couldn't see the tent at all. Even his tyre tracks were being blotted out by the rain, so swiftly that they seemed to dissolve before his very eyes. He wiped his face on the sleeve of his jacket, catching a whiff of wet leather as he did so.

He rode back. The tent wasn't there. He cruised around but failed to find anything. His exact location escaped him. As he remembered it, the boatman's hut must be behind him, the car park on his right and his vanished tent somewhere on the left. He made for the car park. To his surprise, the changing cubicles loomed up ahead. At least he now knew where he was. He found the car park without difficulty, but he couldn't see the Opel. He followed the painted arrows on the asphalt that led to the main road.

Tucking his head in and arching his back, he rode away from the lido at a reassuringly steady speed. He had the feeling that a hand might grab him from behind at any moment. The sensation subsided as the mist thinned. Before long the trees beside the road became visible, and so, eventually, did the flower-bedecked boarding houses he passed.

He debated whether to raid one of them for a change of clothes, perhaps even for a raincoat. He was badly in need of a hot shower. Soon, if he wasn't to catch cold. But something prompted him to keep going.

In Attersee-Ort he made his way into a modest little café in a side street. He didn't park the moped outside but wheeled it into the café and propped it against a plush-covered banquette. If someone was really pursuing him, that would cover his tracks.

He made himself some tea and took the steaming cup over to the window. He concealed himself from view behind a curtain. Blowing on his cup, he stared out at the puddle that extended the full width of the street, its surface whipped into foam by the rain, which hadn't eased. He could hardly feel his nose and ears. He was soaked to his underpants. The damp patch on the carpet beneath him gradually widened. He was shivering, but he didn't stir from where he was.

He made himself another cup of tea and looked for something to eat in the cramped back room that seemed to have been used as a kitchen. He found some tins and heated up the contents of two of them in a not particularly clean saucepan, which he stood on a portable hotplate. He ate greedily. As soon as he'd finished he took up his place at the window again.

It was midday by the clock beside the glass cabinet when he roused himself. The door marked 'Toilets' led to a flight of stairs. The flat above was unlocked. He went in search of some suitable clothing, but the occupant had evidently been a single woman. He came downstairs empty-handed.

After leaving a message and the date on the menu board he emerged from the café, kick-started the moped and rode it out onto the main road. Rain spattered his face. He looked left, looked right. No movement. Just raindrops drilling the puddles.

In the local sports shop, more to protect himself from

the rain than anything else, he got himself a crash helmet. He also put on an all-enveloping waterproof cape of transparent plastic, not that this repaired the damage already done. He was tempted to break into some other flat and get rid of his wet clothes, but his urge to leave the area was stronger.

Jonas had experienced lonely days like this before. Days of incessant rain and unseasonal cold. Mist hovered over the fields, roads and houses and nobody ventured out who didn't have to. He had loved such days, when he lay in the warm in front of the TV, hating it when some cruel stroke of fate drove him out into the street. But in this part of the world, with its mountains, severe-looking conifers and deserted hotels and children's playgrounds, he felt as if the landscape were trying to grab him. And if he didn't hurry, he'd never escape.

He rode along the main road at top speed. He was so desperately cold, he tried to distract himself by reciting all the nursery rhymes he could remember. Before long, however, reciting them wasn't enough and he started to sing and shout. He was shivering so much the words often stuck in his throat, and his voice was reduced to a croak. He bounced rhythmically up and down on the saddle. He felt feverish.

He reached Attnang-Puchheim in this fashion. Dashed into the first building he came to, a block of flats. All the doors were locked. He tried a detached house. No luck there either. Dripping wet, he threw his weight against the locked front door. It was solidly constructed and the lock was new.

Although the windows were quite high off the ground, he raised the shotgun and prepared to blow out a pane. Just then he noticed a small, windowless house across the street. Ignoring the puddles, he ran over to it. The door was round the back.

He tried the handle. It opened. He muttered a thank-you.

Without looking left or right, he hurried into the bathroom and turned on the hot tap. Then he peeled off his clothes. They were so sodden they landed on the tiled floor with a loud smack. He wrapped himself in a bath towel, hoping there were some men's clothes in the house.

A gloomy house. There were windows only on the north side, overlooking a weed-infested garden. He turned on all the lights he passed, many of which didn't work.

With the sound of running water coming from the bathroom, he turned the kitchen upside down in search of tea bags. He rummaged in all the cupboards and emptied out the drawers onto the floor, but all he found were useless things like cinnamon, vanilla essence, cocoa and ground almonds. The biggest shelf was crammed with cake tins. The occupants of the house seemed to have lived on a diet of cakes and pastries.

On a shelf that had escaped his notice at first he found a packet of soup cubes. Although he would have preferred tea, he put some water on to boil and crumbled five cubes into the saucepan.

A mountain of foam awaited him in the bathtub. He turned off the tap and put the saucepan of soup on a damp flannel on the edge of the bath. Then he threw off the towel and got in. The water was so hot he gritted his teeth.

He stared up at the ceiling.

Foam hissed and crackled all around him.

Bending his knees, he slid beneath the water, ran his fingers through his hair a few times and surfaced again. He opened his eyes at once and looked in all directions, shook the water out of his ears and listened. Nothing. He lay back.

He had loved having baths as a child. The Hollandstrasse flat had no bathtub, just a shower, so it was a treat he could only enjoy at Uncle Reinhard and Aunt Lena's. He used to sit in their gleaming white tub, listening to the sound of his aunt clearing the table and sniffing the various soaps and bath cubes. He was familiar with them all. He even recognised the disintegrating labels on the shampoo bottles and regarded them as friends. But what delighted him most of all was the foam. The millions of tiny bubbles that seemed to twinkle in countless colours. That was the loveliest sight he'd ever seen. He still remembered paying little attention to the plastic ducks and boats and staring dreamily at the foam instead, filled with a mysterious wish: this, he thought, was how the Christkind ought to look when bringing the presents at Christmas.

*

The man who had lived here was short and stout.

Jonas surveyed his reflection in the mirror on the door of the wardrobe from which he'd taken the former occupant's shirt and Sunday-best trousers. The trousers hung loose about his hips but ended a few inches above his ankles. He couldn't find a belt anywhere, so he secured them around his waist with some black sticky tape. They felt scratchy, as did the shirt, and both garments smelt of old twigs.

In the dimly lit hallway he walked along the rows of pictures that he hadn't spared a glance until now. None of them was bigger than an exercise book, and the smallest ones were the size of a postcard. Some words had been scrawled on the wallpaper beneath each of the inappropriately massive frames, evidently their respective titles. Like the pictures themselves, they were incomprehensible at first sight. A dark mass was entitled *Liver*. A double-barrelled shotgun of some indeterminate material was *Lung*. Two crossed sticks *Autumn*. Beneath the face of a man who looked familiar to Jonas were the words *Floor Meat*.

Among these works of art was a board with keys on hooks. One of them looked like an ignition key. It briefly occurred to Jonas that, if he wanted to preserve the spirit of this venture, he would have to ride back to Vienna on the DS. He tapped his forehead. The whole trip had been a diabolical idea, and it was time he acknowledged the fact.

Beneath an umbrella that gave off a scent of the forest, he walked along the line of cars parked outside in the street. After trying the key three times without success, he wondered if there wasn't some quicker way. What sort of car would a man like the owner of this house have driven? Would he have owned a Volkswagen or a Fiat? Definitely not. Men who lived like this plump, dwarfish individual drove cars that were either small and compact or big and comfortable.

He looked all around. A Mercedes caught his eye, but it was too new a model. A 220 Diesel from the 1970s would have fitted the picture.

A dark, unobtrusive off-road vehicle. Not too big, with four-wheel drive.

He hurried across the street. The key fitted. The engine started immediately. He turned the heating up full and adjusted the control so it blew on his feet. He would have to drive barefoot. The slippers he'd put on were four sizes too small and his own shoes were full of water.

Leaving the engine running, he went back to fetch his things. He was interested to know whose guest he had been, so he looked for a nameplate on the door. When he couldn't find one he rummaged in the waste-paper sack for invoices, receipts or letters. There were none. The house contained no clue to its owner's identity.

13

Jonas looked first at the camera. It was still standing there.

He blinked and rubbed his eyes. Tried to collect his thoughts. He'd fallen into bed after his long trip without putting in a tape, but he wasn't sorry.

His throat was sore. It hurt him to swallow.

He shut his eyes and turned over.

*

He made his way downstairs and went to the supermarket. There he stowed some cartons of fruit juice and long-life milk in a shopping bag, together with a marble cake vacuum-sealed in transparent plastic, 'Use by end October'. His stomach muscles clenched when he read the date. End October. Would he still be roaming this deserted city at the end of October? What would happen in the meantime? What after that?

What in December?

In January?

Jonas got into the Spider and drove to the city centre. He rattled the doors of various cafés. They were all locked. He didn't find one open until he came to Himmelpfortgasse.

While the espresso machine was hissing away behind him, he cut some slices of marble cake and poured himself a glass of orange juice.

End October.

January. February.

March. April. May. September.

He stared at the untouched cake, knowing that he wouldn't be able to get any of it down.

He made himself a second cup of coffee. There was a newspaper on the counter. He picked it up and, for the hundredth time, skimmed the news reports for 3 July. He only sipped his espresso. Once he thought he heard a sound coming from the basement, where the toilets were. He took a few steps towards the stairs and listened. Nothing more to be heard.

In a chemist's not far from the café he looked for some aspirin and vitamin tablets. He took twice the recommended number of drops from a bottle of echinacea. Sucking a throat pastille, he strolled back to the car and drove slowly to Stephansplatz, where he perched on the Spider's roof.

Scattered clouds were drifting across the sky. A wind was blowing. A foretaste of autumn? No, impossible, not in July. Just a temporary depression. Autumn wasn't till October. End October.

And then would come November. December. January. Thirty days plus thirty-one and another thirty-one. Ninety-two days between the beginning of November and the end of January, and he would have to live through twenty-four hours in each. And through the days and hours before and after them. All by himself.

He rubbed his bare arms, looking at the Haas Haus. He'd never been inside. He'd meant to take Marie to eat at Do & Co, but they'd never got round to it.

He gazed across the deserted square, eyeing the statues that projected from the walls wherever he looked. Fantasy figures, musicians, dwarfs, gargoyles. And, on St Stephen's Cathedral, saints. They all stared mutely over his head.

He had the impression that the statues were multiplying. As if there had been fewer of them the day he made the video. Buildings all over the city seemed to be sprouting more and more of them.

*

The photographic shops in the city centre, which weren't as numerous as he'd assumed, yielded eight video cameras of his preferred model. He also loaded five tripods into the car. Then he drove to Mariahilfer Strasse by way of the Burgring and stopped outside each photographic shop. After that he tried the Neubaugürtel.

He was feeling limp. More than once he had doubts about the point of this expedition or was tempted at least to postpone it until a better day. His nose was running, his throat sore, his head muzzy. But he wasn't ill enough to go to bed. Besides, absurd though it was, he felt he oughtn't to waste any time. Although he had all the time in the world and didn't really have to do a thing, he was feeling restless. And since he'd left the Mondsee, he was feeling more restless than ever.

By afternoon the car was so full all he could see in the rear-view mirror were boxes. There were twenty video cameras and twenty-six tripods. Added to the ones at home, that made just short of thirty cameras ready for use. They ought to be sufficient.

*

Jonas gave the flat a quick once-over to see if all was well. Without putting on his industrial gloves, he took the torch and shotgun and went down to the cellar. He noticed no changes there either.

He felt in a box at random. Instead of the photographs he'd expected, his fingers dug into something soft and fluffy. He recoiled with a start, then shone the torch inside the box. It was a soft toy he'd never seen before. A dirty green teddy bear with its left eye missing and its right ear nibbled away. A string protruded from its backside. Jonas pulled it. A tune started playing.

He shuddered, transfixed by the sound, and listened to it in frozen silence. Ding, dang, dong. A soft, tinkly little tune. Then it ended, and his fingers automatically gave the string another tug.

Out of the blue, he was hit by the realisation that this had been *his* musical box. This was the melody that had lulled him to sleep as a baby. Now he remembered the song. His infant self had heard it every night. He didn't know it any more, but part of the melody had stayed with him longer than most things:

La-le-lu, only the man in the moon's watching you.

Suddenly the fever hit him.

It happened instantaneously. His head swam. He clutched his brow, noticing as he did so that billows of heat were surging through him. His legs threatened to give way at any moment. This was serious. He would never make it back home. Even getting out of the cellar would be something.

With a movement of almost infinite slowness, he stuffed the musical teddy bear under his T-shirt. He was vaguely aware of the danger this movement put him in. He concentrated on keeping the movement going, continuing it, ignoring the sound that was swelling to a roar in the distance.

He tucked the T-shirt into his waistband and turned round. Leaning on the shotgun, with the torch dangling from his wrist by its cord, he tottered step by step to the exit. The billows of heat gained strength. He was breathing through his mouth. After a couple of steps he paused to catch his breath.

He reached the stairway somehow, but his knees gave way on the second step. He crouched down, supporting himself on his hands. Ignoring the dirt and cobwebs, he rested his head against the wall. It felt pleasantly cool.

The light on the stairs went out. Now all that illuminated the stairwell were a few faint rays of sunlight coming through a small window on the half landing. It was a moment or two before he managed to turn on the torch. A bright dot of light flitted across the stone floor.

Feeling marginally better, he forced himself to stand up. Everything went round and round. His heart was thudding.

He hauled himself up on the handrail step by step, trying to reassure the panic-stricken voice inside him. He wasn't going to die. There would be no point in it. It wouldn't be a heart attack on the stairs that carried him off.

He tried hard to ignore his brief, but recurrent, missing heartbeats as he tottered upstairs to the flat. He'd stopped thinking about anything at all. He put one foot in front of the other, breathing in, breathing out, pausing to rest, moving on.

Water, he thought, when he'd locked the front door behind him. He needed a drink.

He found an aspirin in his trouser pocket. The packet was dirty and crumpled. It hadn't come from the chemist's in Himmelpfortgasse, so he'd probably been carrying it around for quite a while. His other medication was in the car. It might as well have been on another continent.

He dissolved the aspirin in some water and drank it.

He found two empty lemonade bottles. He rinsed them out, filled them with water and set off on the long trek to the bedroom, taking them with him. The shotgun he left in the hallway. It was too heavy.

He wasn't greeted by the ticking of the wall clock, which was already packed. Pale patches of wallpaper marked the places where shelves had been. The bed was stripped. The sheets had been used to protect the crockery that lay in boxes in the truck outside. He would have to manage without any bedclothes. It was summer, after all.

He lay down on the bare mattress. Almost simultaneously, he started shivering again. He'd made a mistake, he realised. Instead of toiling upstairs to the flat, he should have got into the car and turned on the heater.

He shivered himself to sleep. When he surfaced again, not knowing if he'd slept for ten minutes or three hours, his teeth were chattering violently. His arm twitched convulsively and thumped the wall. The bedstead contained a second mattress. He dragged it out and put it over himself.

Jonas submerged once more. His mind drew involuntary patterns and lines. Geometrical figures loomed up before him. Rectangles. Hexagons. Dodecagons. It was his laborious task to draw straight lines inside them. Not with a pencil, but with a look that left an instantaneous track behind it. He also had to discover the central point in a field of tension that held each geometrical figure together on the one hand, and, on the other, was rendered intangible by magnetism. Magnetism appeared to be the strongest power on earth. Confronted by an endless succession of new shapes, he had to draw lines and locate points inside them all. As if that were not enough, the two activities steadily merged without his being able to grasp how.

*

The bedside light was on. It was dark outside. Jonas took a drink of water. It hurt when he swallowed. He had to force himself. He drank half the bottle. Sank back on the mattress.

The shivering had let up. He felt his forehead. He was running a very high temperature. He turned over on his

154

stomach. The mattress smelt of his father.

He no longer had to deal with hexagons and dodecagons, but with shapes that defied his comprehension.
He knew he was dreaming but couldn't find a way out. He
was still being forced to draw lines and look for central
magnetic points. Shape after shape appeared to him. He
drew line after line, located point after point. He awoke
for just long enough to turn over. He saw the shapes bor-
ing into him but couldn't fend them off. They were there.
They were everywhere. When one appeared, the next was
already lying in wait.

*

Jonas finished off the bottle of water around midnight. He
felt sure he'd heard noises in the living room a short while
before. Huge ball-bearings rolling across the floor. A door
closing. A table being shifted. He had a sudden vision of
Frau Bender. It occurred to him that she'd never been inside
this flat. He would have liked to get up and look.

*

He was cold. The air smelt foul and he was terribly cold.
He heard a voice. Opened one eye. It was almost totally
dark. Coming from a tiny window was a ray of light just
bright enough to reveal that dawn was breaking. His eye
closed again.

The smell was familiar.

He massaged his arms. Everything hurt. He had the
feeling he was lying on stones. Again he heard a voice, even
heard footsteps quite close at hand. He opened his eyes,
which gradually grew accustomed to the gloom. He saw a
wooden fence. Protruding from between the uprights was
a walking stick decorated with carvings.

He really was lying on stones. Beaten earth and stones.

From close at hand came the sound of voices and the chink of glasses. A door slammed, the sounds ceased. Soon afterwards the door creaked open again. A woman's voice said something. The door closed, silence fell.

He stood up and made for the source of the sounds.

He got there at exactly the right moment. Standing in the middle of a dark passage, he heard the door creak open again just beside him. A man called out something that sounded like a toast. Cheerful laughter rang out in the background. There must have been dozens of people there. A shrill female voice joined the man's in a lively conversation. Then the glasses chinked once more.

Although he was standing nearby, he couldn't see a thing. Neither the door, nor the woman, nor the man.

The door closed. He positioned himself at precisely the right spot: on the threshold. Nothing.

The door creaked open. He felt a faint draught on his face, heard a babble of voices. Somebody tapped a glass and cleared his throat. Silence fell. The door closed again.

'Hello?'

*

When he awoke around noon he couldn't breathe through his nose. His throat was raw and his thirst seemed unquenchable. But the fever, he sensed at once, had left him.

He pushed the mattress off him, sat up and drained the second bottle of water without putting it down. In the kitchen he found some rusks. Although he wasn't in pain, he didn't want to subject his organism to unnecessary strain. He blew his nose.

The fresh air made him feel dizzy when he emerged into the street. He leant against the wall, holding his head. The sun was shining and a gentle breeze was blowing. The depression had moved on.

He got into the passenger seat, lowered the sun visor and examined his face in the vanity mirror. His cheeks were pale and blotchy. He put out his tongue. It was thickly furred.

He cupped an assortment of pills in his hand and tossed them into his mouth, put his head back and dripped some echinacea straight onto his tongue. Leaning back against the headrest, he stared at the dashboard. His legs were very weak, he could feel, but he no longer had a temperature.

He debated how to spend the day. He didn't want to lounge around idly. He couldn't watch films because they upset him, couldn't read because any form of reading matter seemed superfluous and unimportant. If he opted for a day's bedrest, he'd do nothing but stare at the ceiling.

On his way back to the flat he suddenly, without thinking, made for the stairs that led down to the cellar. He raised the shotgun.

'Anyone there?'

He pushed the door open with the gun barrel, turned on the light and paused.

The tap was still dripping.

He went inside. A cool draught stroked his cheeks. The smell of insulating stuff was still as pervasive. He buried his nose in his shirtsleeve.

Halfway along the passage he stopped short.

'Hello? Anyone there?'

He lowered the gun. His musical box came to mind.

*

Although he carried no more than five boxed video cameras at any one time, shuffling along like an old man, he broke out in a sweat on the way from the car to the lift. He pressed the button with his free little finger. When the door slid open, he added the boxes to the others already inside. The lift was too small to take them all at the same time, so he had to make two journeys.

He sprawled on the sofa, breathing hoarsely through his mouth. As soon as he'd recovered he squeezed some menthol gel up his nose, straight from the tube. It stung, but he could breathe freely soon afterwards.

He unpacked. Twenty cameras and twenty-six tripods had to be removed from their bubble wrap, twenty battery packs inserted in the charger and connected to the mains. He was also conscientious enough to recharge the old batteries he'd obtained from the shopping centre, including those in the cameras in front of the bed and next to the TV.

Should he watch the tape of the night before his departure for the Mondsee? He still had no idea why he'd woken up in the living room that morning. Perhaps the tape would enlighten him. On the other hand, he wasn't sure it was something he was looking forward to. He removed the tape from the bedroom camera and put it on one side.

He spread some liver pâté on a slice of pumpernickel. He didn't like it, but he could sense how short of energy he was. He made himself another slice and followed it up with an apple and a few drops of echinacea washed down with some vitamin-enriched fruit juice.

He looked at the musical box, which he'd put beside the phone. He could remember the tune it played, but not the one-eyed, one-eared bear itself.

He pulled the string and the tune played. It was as if he were touching something that no longer existed. As if he were seeing some long-extinguished heavenly body whose light was reaching him only now.

*

He spent several hours playing a computer game, breaking off just long enough to hang up the washing. By evening he was feeling tired but better than he had that morning. He blew his nose, gargled with camomile tea and took an aspirin.

The batteries were fully charged. He collected them together and put them on the sofa with the rest of his equipment. He pushed a battery into its holder and put a tape in the deck, then screwed the camera to a tripod. When he'd got two cameras ready, he took them into the empty flat next door. He unfolded the tripods and set them up side by side.

When he was finished he surveyed the semicircle of cameras confronting him in the spacious living room. Most of their lenses were trained on him. There were so many of them it seemed unreal. He felt they were crowding around him like extraterrestrial dwarfs at feeding time.

*

The Sleeper was tossing and turning as usual. An occasional snore could be heard.

Jonas wondered how to stay awake. It was almost midnight. He put the thermometer under his armpit.

How should he spend tomorrow? He was still too weak to load the furniture into the truck. He would look for suitable flats in which to set up the cameras, restricting himself to buildings with lifts.

The Sleeper threw off the duvet.

Jonas leant forwards. Without taking his eyes off the screen, he felt for his teacup. The thermometer beeped but he took no notice. He couldn't understand what he was seeing.

The Sleeper was wearing a hood.

Jonas hadn't looked as closely before. Now he noticed

that the Sleeper's head was enveloped in a black hood pierced with little holes for the eyes, nose and mouth.

The Sleeper was sitting upright on the edge of the bed. Motionless, supporting himself on his hands. He seemed to be staring at the camera. The lighting wasn't strong enough to reveal the eyes in the midst of the black material.

He just sat there. Unmoving.

In some sinister, unspoken manner, his rigid pose conveyed scorn and defiance. It was a silent challenge.

Jonas couldn't look at that black mask for long. He felt he was staring into a void. Unable to endure its emptiness, he averted his gaze.

Then he looked back at that black head, that hole of a face.

He went into the bathroom and cleaned his teeth. Paced up and down, humming to himself. Returned to the TV.

Black head, motionless body.

The Sleeper was sitting there like a dead man.

Little by little, as if in slow motion, he raised his right arm. Extended his forefinger. Pointed at the camera.

Froze.

14

Was there really no chance of getting to England?

That was the first thought that occurred to him when he woke up. Would it be possible to get from the Continent to the British Isles?

Images took shape in his mind's eye. Motorboats. Sailing ships. Yachts. Helicopters. With him on board.

He sat up in bed and looked round hurriedly. The camera was in its place and had clearly been recording. The room had undergone no noticeable changes. He went over to the mirror and pulled up his T-shirt, turning this way and that. He nearly dislocated his shoulder in an attempt to look at his back. He also checked the soles of his feet. He stuck out his chin and his tongue.

Before making breakfast he explored the whole flat in search of the unexpected. Nothing suspicious came to light.

He was feeling fresher than he had the previous day. His nose wasn't blocked up any more, his throat wasn't sore and he'd almost stopped coughing. This swift recovery surprised him. His immune system seemed to be functioning well.

During breakfast scenes from last night's dream came back to him in quick succession. He reached for a notepad and pencil so as to record them, at least in rough outline.

He had entered a cavern suffused with a dark red glow. Visibility was restricted to a few metres. There were people around him, but they didn't see him and he couldn't communicate with them. The cavern led past a cube-shaped rock thirty metres high. The passage around the cube was two metres wide.

He climbed a rope ladder to the plateau overhead. The roof of the cavern was some seven metres above him. Fixed to it were the spotlights that gave off the dull red glow.

He saw three bodies lying on the plateau. A young couple on one side, a young man on the other. He recognised all three. He'd gone to school with them. They must have been dead for years, because they looked awful. Although they were skeletons, they had faces. Contorted faces and twisted limbs. Their mouths were open. Their eyes bulging. But they were skeletons.

The man lying by himself was Marc, whom he had sat beside in school for four years. The face wasn't his, though. Jonas knew the face but couldn't remember whose it was.

The policemen and paramedics he passed still didn't speak to him, nor was he able to address a word to them. In some mysterious, non-verbal manner he learnt that the trio had died from rat poison, possibly self-administered. The strychnine had brought about dreadful convulsions and an agonising death.

It was warm on top of this rocky cube imprisoned in a cavern. Warm and still. All that occasionally broke the silence was a sound like wind ruffling a sheet of plastic.

And there were the corpses.

The faces of the dead were suddenly right in front of him. The next moment, he couldn't see them any more.

All this had some bearing on himself, Jonas realised. It held some hidden significance. *Rat poison*, cavern, he jotted down. *Laura, Robert, Marc dead. Not Marc's face. Convulsions, decay. Silence. Red glow. A tower. Suspect a wolf walled up in the rock face. Behind it the ultimate horror.*

*

At the far end of the block he found a fifth-floor flat he thought would be suitable. The view from the balcony was absolutely ideal; he could even set up two cameras there. He wrote down the address and marked the spot on his street map.

He allocated another two cameras to the Heiligenstädter Brücke. One would film the Brigittenauer embankment while the other, on the other side, would take in the bridge itself and the exit road to the Heiligenstädter embankment. If he set up one camera on the Döblinger Steg, filming the bridge, and another pointing in the opposite direction, he would not only cover the entire area but get some attractive shots, and up to this spot he would have to make use of only one stranger's flat.

Spittelauer embankment, Rossauer embankment, Franz-Josefs-Kai, Schwedenplatz. Parking the car on the tramlines, he marked the thirteenth camera on his plan. That meant it was time to turn his attention to the other side of the canal.

He spun round at lightning speed.

The leaves of the trees beside the hot-dog stands were rustling in the breeze.

The square, a motionless expanse. The windows of the chemist's, unlit. The ice-cream parlour. The steps leading down to the underground station. Rotenturmstrasse.

He turned on the spot. Not a movement anywhere. He could have sworn he'd heard a sound he couldn't identify. A sound of human origin.

He pretended to scribble something on his notepad. Head down, eyes swivelling in both directions until they ached, he watched and waited to see if the sound was repeated. Again he spun round.

Nothing.

He drove across the Danube Canal. Camera No. 14 he reserved for the Schwedenbrücke and Obere Donaustrasse intersection. At the corner of Untere Augartenstrasse he explored a building in search of another elevated camera position. He found two unlocked flats and chose the upper one. It was almost bare of furniture, and the sound of his footsteps on the old parquet floors echoed around the rooms.

His route took him from Obere Donaustrasse to Gaussplatz and from there into Klosterneuburger Strasse, which came out on the Brigittenauer embankment. The last camera but one would film the intersection of Klosterneuburger Strasse and Adalbert-Stifter-Strasse from the north. The last was also camera No. 1. He would set it up on the Brigittenauer embankment, fifty metres past his front door in the direction of Heiligenstädter Brücke.

Jonas shut his notepad. He was hungry. He took a few steps towards the entrance. Turned once more.

Something was making him feel uneasy.

He got into the car and locked the doors.

*

While driving along he noticed that a door was open. He backed up. It was the entrance to the Gasthaus Haas in Margaretenstrasse.

'Come outside!'

He waited for a minute. Meanwhile, he memorised the layout of the street.

He went inside and searched the premises cautiously. He remembered having eaten there once with Marie. Years ago. The restaurant was jam-packed and the food nothing special. Their meal had been spoilt by the people at the next table. A bunch of drunken racegoers with lots of gold around their necks and wrists, they had loudly debated the chances of various horses and tried to outdo each other in name-dropping.

A friend who was interested in canine science had once explained to Jonas why so many small dogs will attack far more powerful members of the same species despite the risks involved. It was all down to breeding. Having once belonged to a far bigger breed, they hadn't yet got it into their heads that they no longer measured ninety centimetres from shoulder to paw. In a sense, small dogs believed themselves to be the same size as their opponents and flew at their throats regardless.

Jonas hadn't gathered whether this theory was based on scientific research or just a leg-pull on his friend's part, but one thing he *had* grasped: Austrians were exactly like those dogs.

As he walked through the hall-cleared flat he had an urge to start work again. He was feeling better, so there was no reason why not.

He fetched the trolley from the truck and began with some lighter pieces. A linen chest, a standard lamp, the last remaining bookcase. He made rapid progress. Although sweating, he wasn't breathing much faster than usual. Clothes horse, TV, sofa table, bedside table all disappeared into the truck one by one. All that remained in the end were the bed and the wardrobe.

Jonas eyed the wardrobe, leaning against the wall with his arms folded. It held a lot of associations for him. He knew how the left-hand door creaked when it was opened, a whining sound that went through the whole scale, from high to low. He knew how it smelt inside. Of leather and clean linen. Of his parents, his father. For years he had lain on the sofa beside this wardrobe when ill because his mother didn't want to go into the bedroom to bring him tea and rusks. Traces of that period must surely be visible.

There was an energy-saving bulb in the ceiling light. It was too dim to reveal much. Jonas fetched the torch and shone it on the side of the wardrobe. He could clearly make out some numbers and letters scratched on the pale wood with the tip of a penknife.

8.4.1977. Tummy-ache. Mummy's new hat. Yellow. 22.11.1978. 23.11.1978. 4.3.1979. Flu. Tea. Given a model of Fittipaldi's car. 12.6.1979. 13.6.1979. 15.6.1979. 21.2.1980. Ski jumping.

There were a dozen more dates, some with comments, many unexplained. He was surprised his father hadn't got rid of these inscriptions. Perhaps he hadn't noticed them or hadn't wanted the expense of restoration. His father had never liked spending money.

Jonas tried to think himself into the skin of the boy he'd been then.

He was lying there. Feeling bored. He wasn't allowed to read because reading strained your eyes. He wasn't allowed to watch TV because the set emitted rays to which a sick child should not be exposed. He was lying there with his Lego set and his marbles and his pocket knife and other things to be concealed from his mother's gaze. He had to occupy himself, so he often played rafts, a game that came to his rescue even on rainy afternoons when he was well. The raft was an upturned table. Or, if he was lying beside the wardrobe with a temperature, the sofa itself.

He was adrift on the high seas. It was warm and sunny. He was bound for exciting places where he would have adventures and make friends with great, heroic figures. But he needed provisions for the voyage. So he found excuses for creeping around the flat, pinched chewing gum, caramels and biscuits from the sweets drawer, begged slices of bread, filched bottles of lemonade from under his mother's nose. Laden with this haul, he returned to the raft and put to sea again.

It was still as warm and sunny, but the raft was tossing around on the waves. He had to clutch his possessions to him to prevent them from becoming soaked with spray.

America was a long way off, however, and his stores were still insufficient, so he landed once more. He needed books and comics, plus some paper and a pencil to write and draw with. He needed more clothes. He needed various useful things to be found in his father's drawers. A compass. A pair of binoculars. A pack of cards with which to win money from villainous opponents. A knife with which to defend himself. He must also take a gift for Sandokan, the Tiger of Malaysia, to seal their friendship. He could barter his mother's string of pearls with the natives.

He needed all kinds of things, and he wasn't satisfied with his equipment until there was barely room for himself on the sofa and he was hemmed in on all sides by blankets and ladles and clothes pegs. It thrilled him through and through to think that he'd accumulated all he needed in order to survive. He needed no outside help. He had everything

Then his mother appeared to see how he was getting on. She was astonished that he'd managed to get together so many forbidden items in such a short time. Some of them, after much argument, he was allowed to keep. Then the raft put to sea again, lightened of one or two treasures by Blackbeard.

Jonas gave the wardrobe a shake. It scarcely moved. Manhandling it outside would be quite a business. He would have to turn the thing over because it stood on feet and couldn't be loaded onto the trolley in an upright position.

8.04.1977. Tummy-ache.

On 8 April nearly thirty years ago he'd lain beside this wardrobe suffering from a stomach-ache. He had no recollection of that day or his discomfort. But these clumsy letters and numerals were his handiwork. He'd been feeling ill even at the moment when he was scratching that T, that U, that M. He, Jonas. That had been him. And he'd had no inkling of what was to come. No inkling of the exams he would sit later on, of his first girlfriend, of his moped, of leaving school and starting to earn a living. Or of Marie. He had changed, grown up, become an entirely different person. But this writing was still here. When he looked at these marks he was looking at frozen time.

On 4 March 1979 he'd had flu and been made to drink lots of tea, which he disliked in those days. Tito was still alive in Yugoslavia, Carter was president of the United States, Brezhnev ruled Russia, and he was lying beside this wardrobe with flu, not knowing what it signified that Carter was in office or that Tito would soon be dead. He had been preoccupied with his new model car, a black one with the number 1 on the side, and Brezhnev didn't exist for him.

When he'd carved these letters the doomed crew of *Challenger* were still alive, the Pope was new in his job and had no idea that Ali Agca would shoot him, and the Falklands War hadn't started. When he'd written this he hadn't known what was to come. Nor had anyone else.

*

The rattle of the trolley wheels on the stone floor echoed round the building. He paused to listen. He recalled the feeling he'd had on the Brigittenauer embankment. The feeling that something was wrong. And the sensation of being watched outside the Gasthaus Haas. Leaving the trolley and wardrobe where they were, he went out into the street.

'Hello?'

He sounded the truck's horn in short, sharp bursts. Peered in all directions. Looked up at the windows.

'Come outside! At once!'

He waited for a few minutes. Pretended to be lost in thought, sauntered around with his hands in his pockets, whistling softly to himself. Every now and then he turned and stood stock-still, looking and listening.

Then he went back to work. He trundled the trolley outside, and soon afterwards the wardrobe was on board the truck. That only left the bed, but he'd done enough for today.

*

Something about the narrow cellar passage puzzled him. He stopped and looked around. Nothing caught his eye. He gave himself time to collect his thoughts, but he couldn't think what it was.

He went to his father's compartment, cleared his throat in a deep voice and wrenched the door open so roughly it crashed back against the wall. He gave a harsh laugh, looked over his shoulder and shook his fist.

A snapshot of himself with Frau Bender. He was sitting on her lap with one arm around her waist, laughing. She was smoking a cigarette. On the table in front of her, a glass of wine with the bottle and a vase of wilting flowers beside it.

He couldn't remember her drinking. A child wouldn't have noticed such a thing, presumably, but it didn't fit in with the image he still had of her. She lived on in his memory as a friendly, well-groomed old lady. Far from looking friendly, the woman in the photograph was glaring at the camera. Frau Bender didn't look very well-groomed, either – quite unlike his idea of a lady. She looked like a slovenly old hag. All the same, he'd been fond of her then and he still was.

Hello, old girl, he thought. So remote.

While studying this dusty snapshot of his parents' former neighbour he recalled her favourite pastime: dangling a weight over photographs, preferably those dating from the war, to see if the people in them were still alive. Meanwhile, she would reminisce to Jonas about the people in question.

He shut his eyes and pressed his forefinger against the bridge of his nose, trying to remember. If the weight swung to and fro it meant *alive*, if it moved in a circle, *dead*. Or was it the other way round? No, that was right.

Jonas slipped off the ring Marie had given him and opened the catch of the silver chain he wore around his neck. He threaded the ring onto it and tried to close the catch again. His trembling fingers made this difficult, but he finally succeeded.

Having improvised a table out of a stack of boxes, he turned on the torch and hung it on a hook. Then he placed the photograph on the topmost box and dangled the chain and ring over his face in the picture. His arm was too unsteady, so he had to support it.

The ring hung motionless.

It started to swing slightly.

The swinging increased.

The ring swung to and fro in a straight line.

Jonas looked around. He went out into the passage. In the light of his torch, a thick skein of dust cast a restless shadow on the wall. The tap was dripping incessantly. The air smelt strongly of the insulating material, but the smell of oil had disappeared altogether.

'Come on out now,' he called gently.

He waited a moment before going back into the compartment. He stretched out his hand again, this time over Frau Bender's face. He rested his elbow on the carton and supported his forearm with his free hand.

The ring hung motionless over the photo. Then it started to shake, to swing. The swinging increased. It moved in a circle. A definite circle.

How often Frau Bender had done the same thing. How often she had sat over photos of people and pronounced them dead. And now he was doing it over a picture of her, and she was beside him no longer. She'd been dead for fifteen years or more.

He reached into a box and brought out a handful of snaps. Himself with a school satchel. With a scooter. In a field with a badminton racket. With some playmates.

He studied the last picture. Four boys, one of them himself, playing in the backyard now filled with the Kästner family's junk. Some sticks shoved in the ground, a little coloured ball, in the background a plastic tub of water with objects floating in it.

Jonas placed the photo on his makeshift table. He held out his arm and dangled the ring over his face. It started to swing evenly, back and forth. He held the ring over one of the boys, Leonhard.

He stared at the chain.

The light in the passage went out, leaving the box dimly illuminated by his torch. He shut his eyes and forced himself to remain calm.

The ring didn't stir.

He withdrew his hand and shook his arm to relax it. Removing the torch from the hook, he picked up his gun and stomped out into the passage.

'Hey!' he called. 'Hey, hey, hey!'

He switched on the passage light and turned on the

171

spot. After standing there for several seconds, he went back into the compartment.

He repeated the experiment. Over himself the ring swung to and fro. Over Leonhard, nothing.

He dangled the ring over the third boy and waited, trying to remember his name.

The ring didn't move.

What nonsense it all is, he thought.

He fiddled with the catch, intending to remove the ring from the chain. Then, on impulse, he put out his arm again and held the ring over the picture of the fourth boy, Ingo.

It quivered and started to swing.

To move in a circle.

He repeated all four experiments. Over himself the ring swung to and fro, over Ingo it moved in a circle, over Leonhard and the nameless boy it remained motionless.

He pushed the photograph aside and reached for the pile he'd left on the edge of his table of boxes.

Himself in the backyard in bathing trunks. Himself with a trophy he certainly hadn't won. Himself with two ski poles. Himself in front of an enormous Coca-Cola hoarding. Himself with his mother outside his primary school.

He laid the photo down, stretched out his arm and dangled the ring over his own picture.

The ring briefly moved in a circle, probably because he hadn't kept his arm steady enough, then went back into the usual pendulum motion.

He held it over his mother's face.

It hung motionless, then moved in a circle.

Photos of himself with his mother, of himself with a football, of himself with a tomahawk and feathered headdress. Of his mother on her own, of his mother in hiking gear. Of his grandmother, who had died in 1982. Of two men he didn't remember.

He held the ring over them. It moved in a circle both times, just as it had over his grandmother's picture.

Photos of Kanzelstein. Himself with his mother in the garden, picking sorrel. Himself in a field with bow and arrow. Himself at the wheel of Uncle Reinhard's VW Beetle. Himself at the ping-pong table, which came up to his chest.

Finally, a photo of himself with a man whose head had been cropped by the upper margin of the picture. He laid it down on the table.

Above his own face the ring swung to and fro.

Above the picture of the man beside him it remained motionless.

That might have been because the head wasn't shown. Hurriedly, Jonas looked through the pile until he found a photo that showed his father's face as well. He repeated the experiment.

The ring didn't move.

*

Hungry and exhausted, Jonas flopped down on the mattress and draped the ragged blanket he'd fetched from the truck over his feet. He hadn't noticed the time, and it was already dark. He had avoided being outside after dark ever since his trip to the Mondsee. In view of the feeling of uneasiness that had come over him on the Brigittenauer embankment, he had no desire to go home at this hour.

He cleared his throat. The sound echoed around the empty flat.

'Yes, yes,' he said aloud, and turned on his side.

Lying within reach on the floor, which was littered with scraps of paper and crumpled balls of sticky tape, was a box of photographs he'd brought up from the cellar.

He took out a batch of them. They hadn't been sorted. Photos from different decades were mixed up together. Ten snaps displayed five different locations, two black-and-white photos followed three in colour, and the next pictures dated from the late 1950s. In one he was tugging at the bars of his playpen, in the next he was being confirmed.

He studied a photograph of himself taken a week after his birth, according to the inscription on the back. He was lying, wrapped in a blanket, on his parents' bed. The bed he was lying on at that very moment. Only his head and hands were visible.

That bald creature was him.

That was his nose.

Those were his ears.

That pinched little face was his.

He peered at the tiny hands. He held his right hand in front of his face and looked at the right hand in the picture.

It was the same hand.

The hand he could see in the photo would learn to write, first with a pencil, then with a fountain pen. Nearly thirty years ago the hand in front of his face had learnt to write, first with a pencil, then with a fountain pen. The hand in the photo would stroke the cats that wandered over from their next-door neighbour in Kanzelstein, take hold of the old wood-carver's ornamental walking stick, play cards. The hand in front of his face had stroked the cats in Kanzelstein, taken hold of that walking stick and played cards. The little hand in the photo would some day design interiors with a ruler and compasses, type on a computer keyboard, light someone's cigarette. The hand in front of his face had signed contracts, moved chessmen, sliced onions with a kitchen knife.

The hand in the photo would grow, grow, grow.

The hand in front of his face had grown.

He kicked off the blanket and went to the window. The street lights weren't on. He had to press his forehead and nose against the pane to make out the shapes outside.

The Spider was parked in the street with the truck in front of it. The tailboard was down. It hadn't looked like rain.

He tiptoed back to the bed. The carpet felt rough beneath his feet.

15

Jonas sat up with a start and looked round. To his relief, he discovered that everything wasn't red.

Extricating his feet from the ragged blanket, he sank back on the mattress. He stared at the opposite wall. A pale rectangle marked the spot where he'd removed a water-colour. He blinked and rubbed his eyes. They made another circuit of the room. All the colours were normal.

He couldn't remember the dream in detail. Only that he'd been striding through a big building in which everything, walls and floors and objects, was a rich, luminous red. The various shades of red differed only slightly, creating the impression that things were dissolving and merging into one another. He had wandered through this building, in which no sound could be heard, encountering nothing but colour, the colour red. It even dictated the shape of things.

*

He threw the mattresses out of the window. The first row of slats he wrenched out of the bedstead offered considerable resistance. The second proved less difficult. He trundled both into the street on the trolley and stowed them in the back of the truck beside the mattresses. Taking the handsaw he'd obtained from the DIY store, he set to work on the bedstead itself. It took him nearly an hour, but then it was done. He stacked the pieces of the bed on the trolley, wheeled them outside and loaded them into the truck.

He made a final tour of inspection. The kitchen cabinets were unfamiliar, they hadn't been in his parents' home, so they stayed where they were. Likewise the kitchen stove, fridge and bench. He'd cleared out all the other possessions. Last of all he took the box of photographs and put it in the Spider's boot.

He perched on the rear end of the truck and looked up at the sky. He had a sense of déjà vu. It was as if the few open windows had only just been opened. The stone figures projecting from the walls seemed to be watching him. One in particular, a knight in chain mail brandishing a sword from behind a shield emblazoned with a fish, was regarding him with scorn. All this he'd experienced before.

Moments later everything was normal again. The windows had long been open. The statues were merely statues. The swordsman stared down with indifference.

Jonas swung round.

He clambered onto the roof of the cab and looked up and down the street. Nothing had changed in the last four weeks. Not the smallest detail. The piece of plastic over the bicycle saddle still fluttered in every breath of wind. The bottle still protruded from the dustbin. The mopeds were still in their usual places.

He swung round again.

He fetched some paper and sticky tape from the cab, together with the marker pen which he'd got from he couldn't remember where. He stuck a note on the door of the building, where anyone coming back would see it at once.

Come home. Jonas.

After a moment's thought he attached another sheet of paper bearing the same message to the inside of the door as well.

Jonas drove the truck back to Hollandstrasse. Under a blistering sun he cycled back to Rüdigergasse, where he picked up the Spider and drove it to the Brigittenauer embankment. He had a headache. He blamed it on the sawdust he must have inhaled when dismembering the bed, but it might also have been the heat.

It occurred to him, as he removed the photos from the Spider, that he'd forgotten to clear out the cellar. That annoyed him. He hadn't wanted to set foot in the Rüdigergasse flat again. Now he would have to go back there tomorrow.

He opened the front door and listened. Closed it behind him and locked it. Stood there, straining his ears and peering round. Everything looked as it had when he left the building the day before. When he opened and closed the door, flyers went fluttering across the floor. Lying in the corner was a toy that had belonged to a neighbour's Alsatian, a well-chewed tennis ball. The lift was on the ground floor, the air laden with the musty smell of damp plaster.

Cautiously, he opened the door of his flat. He searched all the rooms, then locked the door. He put the shotgun down and tossed the photos onto the sofa. He didn't feel he'd been imagining things the day before. Something had been different from usual. Although appearances were against it and indicated an overactive imagination.

When he shampooed his hair he avoided shutting his eyes until the foam made them smart. He held his face under the shower and wiped the foam away with nervous little movements. His heart beat faster.

For some time now, Jonas had had to contend with an uninvited guest whenever he closed his eyes in the shower. The beast came into his mind on this occasion too. Walking upright on two legs, it was a shaggy creature over two metres tall, a cross between a wolf and a bear, and he knew that its fur concealed something far more intimidating. Every time he shut his eyes he felt overcome with fear of this creature, which came prancing up and threatened him. It moved much faster than a man – faster, too, than any animal he knew. It bounded in, rattled the door of the shower cubicle and tried to pounce on him. But it never got that far because he opened his eyes just in time.

Hearing a rustling sound in the corner, Jonas looked round, yelled and dashed out into the passage. With shampoo in his hair and foam over his naked body, he stood peering back into the bathroom.

'Oh, no you don't! Ha, ha!'

He dried himself on a towel from the cupboard in the bedroom. But what about all that shampoo in his hair? He paced irresolutely to and fro between the kitchen sink and the shoe cupboard in the passage without crossing the bathroom threshold.

He was being silly. A rustling sound. That was all. And the wolf-bear creature existed only in his imagination. He could take a shower with his eyes shut, no trouble. No one was threatening him.

The door was locked.

The windows were closed.

No one was hiding in the wardrobe or lurking under the bed.

No one was clinging to the ceiling.

He went back into the cubicle and turned on the tap, held his head under the shower. Shut his eyes.

He guffawed. 'Hey! Ha, ha! There! You see? I told you! Hallelujah!'

*

It was getting dark outside when he sat down on the living-room floor, wrapped in a bathrobe, and rested his back

179

against the sofa. He smelt of shower gel and was feeling refreshed.

He put the photos on the carpet in front of him.

Ingo Lüscher.

He'd been trying the whole time, at the back of his mind, to recall the full name of the boy above whom the ring had moved in a circle. He had also been pondering the name of the unknown boy. At least he'd remembered Ingo's surname. They'd teased him, saying he shared the name of a Swiss downhill skier, which had naturally annoyed a patriotic sports fan like Ingo. Jonas hadn't seen him since primary school. He hadn't lost sight of Leonhard, on the other hand, until they were put in different classes when they started secondary school.

His thoughts strayed back to his pendulum experiments in the cellar. In principle, he considered such things nonsense, although he had to admit that the results were remarkable. Had he influenced the pendulum without meaning to? His mother was dead and his father had disappeared. He knew this, so he couldn't dismiss the possibility that his subconscious had guided the chain.

He opened the catch, threaded the ring back onto the chain and dangled it over the first snap he came to. It was one of himself trailing a tennis racket far too big for him across a stretch of grass.

The ring hung motionless.

Started to swing.

Started to move in a circle.

Jonas let out an oath and rubbed his arm. He repeated the experiment. With the same result.

He found a picture of his mother. The ring moved in a circle above her this time too. Above his father, on the other hand, it started to swing after remaining motionless for some time. Above Leonhard it moved in a circle, above Ingo it swung gently to and fro, above the unidentified boy it didn't move at all. The next time he held the ring above a photo of himself it hung motionless above the box with the crumpled corners.

He was getting inconsistent results.

They were the results he'd expected of such hocus-pocus before he tried it out in the cellar. He ought to be glad. It was a graphic demonstration of how meaningless his experiments at Rüdigergasse had been. But he was more confused than ever.

He hurried into the bedroom and pulled Marie's shoe-box of photos from under the wardrobe. They were recent pictures taken with a single-lens reflex camera, none more than four years old. Most were of Jonas himself. In summer in bathing trunks and flippers, in winter in anorak, bobble hat and boots. He pushed them aside.

Photos showing him with Marie. They were taken from too far away. He put them to one side.

A large close-up of Marie's face, one he wasn't familiar with.

He held his breath. He was seeing her for the first time since she'd planted a kiss on his lips on the morning of 3 July and run, stumbling, out of the door because the taxi was waiting. He'd often thought of her since then and pictured her face, but he'd never seen it.

She was smiling at him. He looked into her blue eyes, which were observing him with a mixture of derision and affection. Her expression seemed to say: Don't worry, it'll all come right in the end.

That was how she'd been, how he'd known her, how he'd fallen in love with her at a friend's birthday party. That look was her. So optimistic. Challenging, endearing, smart. And brave. Don't. Worry. Everything's. Fine.

Her hair.

Jonas recalled the last time he'd stroked it. He imagined the feel of it, imagined holding her close. Resting his chin on her head, inhaling her fragrance. Feeling her body against his.

Hearing her voice.

He saw her doing her hair in the bathroom, wrapped in a towel and looking over her shoulder as she told him the latest gossip from work. Standing at the stove frying her Catalonian courgettes, which were always a bit overseasoned. Swearing at CDs that had been put in the wrong sleeves. Slurping hot milk and honey on the sofa at night and commenting on what was on TV. Lying there, when he tiptoed into the bedroom two hours after her. With the book that had slipped from her hand beside her and one arm draped over her eyes to shield them from the bedside light.

For years he had taken all this for granted. It was simply the way things were: Marie was at his side, where he could hear, smell, feel her. Whenever she went away she returned a few days later and lay beside him once more. It had been the most natural thing in the world.

Not any more, though. Now he merely came across an odd stocking of hers, or picked up a bottle of nail varnish, or discovered one of her blouses hiding at the bottom of the laundry basket.

He went into the kitchen and pictured her standing there, clattering saucepans and drinking white wine.

Don't worry.

Everything's fine.

Jonas lay down on the floor beside the sofa with her photo in front of him. He twisted the ring between his fingers, feeling cold and nauseous.

He flung the chain aside.

After a while he stretched out his arm as if the ring were still in his hand. He swung an imaginary pendulum to and fro, then pulled back his arm.

He opened the window and breathed deeply.

He took the photo back into the next room and tossed it into the shoebox without looking at it again. Removing the tape from the camera in the bedroom, he put it in the one connected to the TV and rewound it.

He looked out of the window. Many of the lights that had been on for the first few weeks had gone out. If it went on like this, he would soon be looking out into darkness. And if he didn't like that, he could always call in at selected flats during the day and turn on all the lights. That would enable him to postpone the night when darkness would take over. It would come in the end, though.

The window of the flat he'd visited after that nightmare was still lit up. On the other hand, many of the street lights that were on now had been off for the first few days. In other streets the lights came on one night and were off the next. Many thoroughfares were unlit every night, one of them being the Brigittenauer embankment.

Jonas shut the window. When he glanced at the blue TV screen, his stomach clenched. He had programmed the video camera with the timer. He might well have to listen to the Sleeper snoring for three whole hours. Equally, he might see something else.

Snoring would be preferable.

He went into the kitchen and drank a glass of port. He felt like another but put the bottle away. He emptied the dishwasher, although there wasn't much in it. The cardboard boxes containing the video cameras had already been flattened. He gathered them up, dumped them in a neighbouring flat and locked the door again.

Never mind, he thought, as he reached for the remote.

*

The Sleeper lay there, staring at the camera.

Jonas couldn't see what time it was because the alarm

183

clock had fallen over. He'd forgotten what time he'd set the timer for: 1 a.m., he seemed to recall.

The Sleeper was lying on the edge of the bed, on his side, with his head propped on his hand. Hoodless this time, he was staring intently at the camera. Now and then he blinked, but mechanically and without averting his gaze. His face remained immobile. He didn't move an arm or a leg, nor did he toss and turn. He simply lay there, looking at the camera.

After ten minutes Jonas felt he couldn't stand that piercing gaze any longer. He didn't understand how anyone could lie there like a statue for so long. Without scratching, without sniffing, without clearing his throat or adjusting his position.

After a quarter of an hour he took to shielding his eyes like a cinemagoer when some gruesome scene is being shown. Occasionally he peeped at the screen through his fingers, only to see the same thing.

The Sleeper.

Staring at him.

Jonas couldn't interpret the look in those eyes. He saw no hint of kindliness or friendliness. Nothing that might have inspired confidence or conveyed intimacy. But he also saw no anger or hatred. Not even dislike. The expression was one of cool, calm condescension and a sort of emptiness that clearly related to himself. It became so intense that he noticed he was displaying signs of mounting hysteria.

He drank some more port, nibbled crisps and peanuts, did a crossword puzzle. The Sleeper continued to look at him. He refilled his glass, fetched himself an apple, did some exercises. The Sleeper was still looking at him. He dashed to the bathroom and threw up. And returned to meet the Sleeper's unwavering gaze.

The tape ran out after three hours two minutes. The screen went dark for a moment, then switched to the pale blue of the AV channel.

184

Jonas roamed around the flat. He examined some marks on the fridge. He sniffed door handles and shone his torch behind cupboards, where it wouldn't have surprised him to find letters. He tapped on the wall the Sleeper had tried to squeeze into.

He put a new tape in the bedroom camera, looking at the bed as he did so. That was where the Sleeper had been lying. And staring at him. Less than forty-eight hours ago.

He lay down, adopting the same position as the Sleeper, and looked at the camera. Although it wasn't recording, a shiver ran down his spine.

'Hi there,' he tried to say, but dizziness overcame him. He had the feeling that the objects around him were growing smaller and more compact. Everything was happening infinitely slowly. He opened his mouth to scream. Heard a noise. Felt as if he could actually touch the speed at which he was pursing his lips. When he fell out of bed and felt the floor beneath him without hearing the noise, when everything seemed normal again, he was filled with a sense of gratitude that immediately gave way to exhaustion.

16

He didn't know the painting he was looking at. It depicted two men dwarfed by some windmills in the background and holding a big dog on a leash. A colourful picture. He'd never seen it before. The radio alarm clock on the bedside table was as unfamiliar to him as the bedside table itself and the old-fashioned bedside light, which he mechanically turned off.

The TV wasn't his, nor were the curtains and desk. Nor was the bed. It wasn't his bedroom, his home. Nothing here belonged to him except for the shoes beside the bed. He had no idea where he was or how he had got there.

The room had no personal touches at all. The TV was small and shabby, the bedding stiff as cardboard, the wardrobe empty. Lying on the window sill was a bible. A hotel room?

Jonas slipped his shoes on, jumped up and looked out of the window. A stretch of woodland met his eyes.

He tried the door. It was locked. The key was attached to a metal tag. It clattered against the lock as he rattled the handle. He unlocked the door and opened it a crack, looked left. A musty-smelling passage. He hesitated before opening the door wider and peering round the doorpost to the right. At the end of the passage he made out some stairs.

His door had a '9' on it. He'd guessed rightly. On the way to the stairs he passed some other rooms. He tried the door handles, but all the doors were locked.

He went down the stairs and walked along a passage to a door at the end. Beyond it lay another passage. The walls were decorated with children's drawings. The inscription beneath a sun with ears read: *Nadja Vuksits, aged 6, from Kofidisch*. A piece of cheese with smiling faces instead of holes was by Günther Lipke from Dresden, a kind of vacuum cleaner by Marcel Neville from Stuttgart, a farmhand wielding a scythe by Albin Egger from Lienz. The last picture, which had been painted by Daniel from Vienna, Jonas identified with difficulty as a sausage firing a bullet.

He turned the corner and nearly bumped into a reception desk. The drawer beneath it was open. On the receptionist's chair was an open folder containing postage stamps. Lying on the floor, lit by the greenish glow from some neon tubes on the ceiling, were two glossy postcards.

The automatic door whirred open. Hitching up his trousers by the belt, Jonas went outside. His hunch was confirmed: he was in Grossram. He'd woken up in a motel room in the motorway service area.

Either someone else was responsible for this, or he himself was. But that he simply couldn't believe.

It was cold and windy. Jonas, who was in his shirtsleeves, shivered and rubbed his arms. He lifted the flap of the letterbox next to the entrance and peered inside, but it was too dark to see anything.

The Spider was in the car park. He took the keys from his trouser pocket and opened the boot. The shotgun wasn't there, but he hadn't expected it to be. He removed the crowbar.

The letterbox didn't have many good leverage points. He began by trying to force the flap the postman opened with a key, but the tip of the crowbar kept slipping out of the crack. Eventually he lost patience and inserted it in the mouth of the letterbox itself. Bracing his chest against the crowbar, he leant on it with all his weight. There was a crack, the crowbar gave way beneath him, and he fell flat on his stomach.

He swore, rubbing his elbows, and looked up. The top of the letterbox had broken off.

He fished out envelope after envelope, postcard after postcard, careful not to cut himself on the jagged metal. He read most of the postcards. Letters he opened, skimmed their contents and tossed away. The wind blew them over to the filling station, behind whose windows lights were burning dimly.

6 July, Grossram service area.

He stared at the card in his hand. He had written these words not knowing what lay ahead of him. This G with a flourish, he'd written it without having any idea how things were in Freilassing, Villach or Domzale. Twenty-five days ago he'd posted this card in the hope that it would be collected. This letterbox had been spattered with rain and scorched by the sun, but no postman had come to clear it. What he'd written had been imprisoned in the dark for over three weeks. In solitude.

He tossed the crowbar into the boot and started the engine, but he didn't drive off right away. His hands tightened on the steering wheel.

What had happened the last time he sat here?

When had he sat here last?

Who had sat here last?

Either someone else.

Or himself.

*

Although he noticed nothing unusual outside the block of flats on the Brigittenauer embankment, he was warier than

188

normal. When the lift door opened he hid round the corner until he heard it close again. He only got in the second time. On the seventh floor he leapt out so as to catch any potential enemy off guard. He realised how stupid he was being, but it always helped him over the difficult moment of decision. The sense that he was being active, attacking, gave him some feeling of assurance.

The shotgun was leaning against the wardrobe. 'Morning,' he greeted it. He cocked it. The noise sounded good.

He glanced into the toilet and the bathroom. Went into the kitchen and looked round. All was as it had been. The glasses on the sofa table, the dishwasher open, the video camera beside the TV. The smell, too, hadn't changed.

The change in the bedroom he spotted immediately.

A knife was sticking into the wall.

Protruding from the wall at the spot the Sleeper had thrown his weight against it in that recording was the hilt of a knife that looked familiar. Jonas examined it. It was his father's knife. He tugged at it. It refused to give. He wiggled it. The knife didn't move a single millimetre.

Jonas looked more closely. The blade was embedded, up to the hilt, in the concrete wall.

He took hold of the handle and tugged with both hands. They slid off. He dried them on his shirt, wiped the handle and tried again. No effect whatever.

How could anyone drive a knife so deep into a concrete wall that it couldn't be pulled out?

He looked at the camera.

*

Jonas boiled some water. Leaving the herbal tea to brew, he cleaned his teeth in the living room. Doing it at the basin in the bathroom would have meant turning his back on the door.

He looked out of the window while the electric toothbrush was humming against his teeth. The clouds had moved on. It might be a good day to set up the cameras.

In the bedroom he leant against the doorpost and eyed the knife embedded in the wall. Perhaps it was a message. An order to go into buildings and search them thoroughly, to get to the bottom of things. The Sleeper wasn't evil, he was just a well-meaning prankster.

He emptied his trouser pockets but found nothing that hadn't been in them the day before.

Opening the freezer drawer, he took out the goose he'd got from the supermarket, which he planned to cook for dinner. He put it in a big bowl to thaw and made sure the casserole was clean.

He carried his herbal tea over to the sofa table, then went to get some sheets of cardboard, a pair of scissors and a pencil. He cut the cardboard into rectangles the size of visiting cards. Without giving any thought to the wording, which he promptly forgot, he wrote on them in quick succession. After a while he counted them. There were thirty. He put them in his pocket.

*

The tripods clattered together behind him as he pulled up. After a reassuring glance at his notebook he got out, taking two cameras with him.

The flat smelt bad. He held his breath until he was standing on the balcony, then set up the cameras as planned. One was looking down at the embankment road, the other in the direction of the Heiligenstädter Brücke. He'd left his watch at home, so he took out his mobile. It was midday. He checked the times on the camera displays. They tallied. Having estimated how long he would take to set up twenty-six cameras, he programmed these two to start recording at 3 p.m.

He made faster progress than he'd expected. By half past twelve he was setting everything up at Rossau Barracks, at a quarter to one he was driving back over the Danube Canal, and shortly before half past one he was outside his block of flats. He had over an hour to spare, and he was hungry. He wondered what to do. His goose wouldn't be ready till late that evening.

*

The canteen of the Brigittenauer swimming baths smelt of rancid fat and stale tobacco smoke. Jonas looked in vain for a window overlooking the street, so that he could air the place. He put the contents of two tins in the microwave.

While eating he leafed through a 3 July edition of the *Kronen Zeitung*. Stale breadcrumbs crackled between the pages, many of which were spotted with gravy. The crossword puzzle was half completed, the five mistakes in the picture puzzle had been marked with a cross. In other respects this edition didn't differ from the ones he'd come across in other places. An article on the Pope on the foreign news page, rumours of a cabinet reshuffle in the home news section. The TV pages carried a profile of a popular presenter. He had read all these pieces dozens of times without discovering any allusion to unusual events.

As he read the article on the Pope he couldn't help remembering a prophecy that had appeared in various magazines and programmes since the end of the 1970s, sometimes seriously, mostly ironically: that the present Pope would be the last but one. This prediction had scared Jonas even as a boy. He had tried to work out what it meant. Would the world come to an end? Would a nuclear war break out? Later on, as an adult, he'd speculated that the Catholic Church might undergo a fundamental reform and dispense with an elected leader. He had to try and remember if the prediction had come true.

It hadn't.

He was convinced that St Peter's Square in Rome looked no different from the Heldenplatz in Vienna or the Bahnhofsplatz in Salzburg or the main square in Domzale.

Jonas pushed the empty plate away and drained his glass of water. He looked down through the window at the indoor pool. The muffled, regular lapping of water reached his ears. The last time he'd been here was with Marie. That was where they'd swum together, down there.

He wiped his lips on a paper napkin, then wrote *Jonas, 31 July* on the menu board.

*

At 2.55 p.m. he parked the Spider in the middle of the Stifterstrasse–Brigittenauer embankment intersection. He wanted to be on the move by the time he came into shot. So as not to be filmed as he set off, he had programmed the camera at this intersection to start recording at two minutes past three. A window of two minutes would be enough.

He ambled round the car with his hands in his pockets, kicked the tyres, leant against the bonnet. A strong wind was blowing. Above his head, an unsecured window hit the wall beside it with a crash. He looked up at the sky. Clouds had gathered once more, but they were far enough away, hopefully, for him to collect the cameras in good time. As long as the wind didn't blow them over.

2.57 p.m. He got into the car and dialled his home number.

The answerphone cut in.

2.58 p.m. He dialled Marie's mobile number.

Nothing.

2.59 p.m. He dialled a twenty-digit made-up number.

Number unobtainable.

3 p.m. He floored the accelerator.

Between Döblinger Steg and the Heiligenstädter Brücke he reached a speed of over 120 k.p.h. He had to brake hard to make it round the bend leading to the bridge. Tyres screaming, he raced down to the Heiligenstädter embankment. He accelerated, changed gear, accelerated, changed gear, accelerated, changed gear. Although he had to concentrate on the road, he caught a glimpse of the camera as he roared beneath it a split-second later.

The speedometer was reading 170 as he passed the Friedensbrücke and 200 just before Rossau Barracks. The buildings beside the road were just blurred shapes. They loomed up and were there, but he'd left them behind before he could take them in.

On the Schottenring he had to slow down to avoid skidding off the bend and ending up in the Danube Canal. He headed for Schwedenplatz at 140, braked at the last moment and raced across the bridge. His heart was pumping the blood so furiously through his body he started to suffer from a stabbing pain behind the eyes. His stomach tied itself in knots, his arms twitched. Sweat was streaming down his face, and he only breathed by fits and starts.

More bends here, so ease off, was the message sent him by the rational part of his subconscious.

He trod on the accelerator and changed up.

Twice he nearly lost control of the car. He felt he was seeing everything in slow motion. Yet he felt nothing. It wasn't until he got the car back on track that something inside him seemed to snap. Desperately, he put his foot down even harder. He was perfectly aware that he'd crossed a line, but he was powerless. He could only watch, eager to see what he would do next.

He had thoroughly familiarised himself with the place where the embankment road and Obere Donaustrasse diverged. If he wanted to avoid crashing at the Gaussplatz roundabout, he shouldn't be doing more than 100 k.p.h. at the intersection before it. He glanced at the speedometer as he passed the traffic lights. 120.

For a second he kept his foot hard down. Then he stamped on the brake pedal with all his might. According to the driving course he'd completed during his national service, the pedal had to be pumped, in other words, depressed and released alternately. Centrifugal force and muscular cramp prevented him from bending his leg. The Spider grazed a parked car and skidded. Jonas wrenched at the wheel. He felt a violent impact and heard a crash. The car went into a spin.

*

He mopped his face.

Looked left and right.

Coughed. Put on the handbrake. Released his seat belt. Pressed the central locking button. He tried to get out, but the door was jammed.

Leaning forwards, he found he'd come to rest on the roundabout's tramlines. The clock on the dashboard was showing twelve minutes past three.

His fingers trembled as he scratched a dried gravy stain off his trousers. He put his seat belt on again and drove down Klosterneuburger Strasse.

As he passed the Brigittenauer swimming baths he decided to do the whole circuit again. He accelerated away, but he failed to reach the speeds he'd managed on his first tour. It wasn't the car's fault. His testosterone level had dropped and he was feeling dazed. Going too fast had lost its charm for him. He found 100 k.p.h. enough.

After rounding the Danube Canal between Heiligenstadt and the city centre for a second time, driving at a more moderate speed, he set about collecting the cameras, which he'd numbered so he wouldn't get the tapes mixed up later on. When he got out on the Brigittenauer embankment in order to collect the two cameras from the balcony of the flat, he stumbled. But for a rubbish skip, which he clung to in the nick of time, he would have fallen over.

He circled the Spider. The nearside tail light was smashed and the offside rear bodywork dented. The front of the car had suffered the worst damage. Part of the bonnet had been torn off and the headlights were shuttered.

He dragged himself to the entrance on legs like cotton wool and took the lift up. He didn't bother to inspect the cameras, just pressed the stop button and turned them off.

*

It occurred to him, as he lifted the dripping goose out of the bowl and put it down on the work surface, that his airbag hadn't inflated after the crash. He wasn't sure he remembered all the details correctly, but the state of the car said it all. The impact must have been considerable. The airbag should have inflated.

Product recall campaign, he thought. He couldn't help laughing.

He got out some salt, pepper, tarragon and other herbs, chopped some vegetables, rinsed the casserole dish and preheated the oven. Then he dismembered the goose with poultry shears. It hadn't thawed out completely, so he had to use a lot of force. He slit open the stomach and cut off the wings. Jonas wasn't a very skilful cook, and before long the work surface was a scene of devastation.

He stared at the drumsticks. The wings. The parson's nose.

He stared into the maw.

He surveyed the carcass in front of him.

Dashed to the toilet and vomited.

After cleaning his teeth and washing his face, he took a big shopping bag from the hall cupboard. Without looking too closely, he swept the bits of goose off the work surface and into the bag, which he tossed into a neighbouring flat.

He switched off the oven. The chopped vegetables caught his eye. He took a carrot and put it in his mouth. He felt tired. As if he hadn't slept for days.

He sank onto the sofa. He would have liked to check the door. He tried to remember. He was pretty sure he'd locked it.

So limp. So tired.

*

He surfaced abruptly from a welter of confused, unpleasant images. It was after 7 p.m. He sprang to his feet. He mustn't sleep, he had things to do.

While packing he floated around the flat like a sleepwalker. If he needed two things that were lying side by side he would pick up one and leave the other. He went back as soon as he noticed his oversight, only to think of something else and leave it lying there again.

Even so, he was ready in half an hour. His needs were few, after all. T-shirts, underpants, fruit juice, fruit and vegetables, blank tapes, cables and leads. He went into the deserted flat next door, where he'd dumped the cameras after his drive. He selected five of them and removed the tapes, which he marked with the numbers of their respective cameras.

While driving to Hollandstrasse he remembered the dream he'd had that afternoon. It had had no plot. Again and again half a head or a mouth had appeared. An open mouth, its most notable feature being that it was toothless, with cigarette butts embedded in the gums where teeth should have been. That gaping mouth, with its uniform rows of cigarette butts, had appeared to him again and again. Nothing was said. There had been a cool, empty feeling about things.

The truck was standing outside. Jonas pulled up a few metres beyond it, where the Spider wouldn't get in his way. He put two cameras in his bag and slung it over his shoulder.

It was stuffy inside his parents' former flat. His footsteps echoed as he walked across the old parquet floor to the windows and opened each in turn.

Fresh, warm evening air flooded into the room. He perched on the window sill and looked out. The truck was blocking his view of the street. It didn't bother him. He was filled with a feeling of familiarity. This was where he had stood as a small child, a box under his feet so he could look out at the street. That hole in the window flashing, that drain in the gutter, the colour of the roadway — all were familiar to him.

He got to his feet again. No time to lose.

In the hallway he laid some planks down on the short staircase that led to the ground-floor flats, making a ramp for the trolley. Having wheeled the two halves of the bedstead up it, he leant them against the wall.

He wouldn't be able to put the bed up again without technical aids of some kind. He could try to glue them together again, it was true, but they probably wouldn't support his weight. So he went and fetched some blocks of wood from the truck, blocks he'd obtained from a building site specifically for the purpose. Outside in the street he glanced anxiously at the sky. It would soon be getting dark.

He arranged the blocks on the floor. They were of different heights. He went outside again and returned with a box of books. The first three volumes he took out were valuable, he even remembered their former position in the mahogany bookcase. The next half dozen were Second World War tomes his father had collected after his mother's death. They were dispensable.

He balanced two of them on the smallest block and distributed the rest, then checked the height. He switched two around, checked again, picked out a slender volume he didn't need and added it to one of the supports. Now they were equal in height.

He wheeled in the first half of the bed, his mother's side. Carefully, he tipped the bulky frame over and lowered it until the edge came to rest plumb in the centre of the supports. He did the same with the other half of the bedstead. That done, he fetched the mattresses and laid them down on top.

Gingerly at first, then more confidently, he rested his weight on the bed. When it didn't collapse as he'd expected, he pulled off his shoes and stretched out on the mattresses.

Job done. Night could fall. He wouldn't be faced with a choice between braving the darkness on the drive home to his flat on the Brigittenauer embankment and sleeping on the floor here.

Although he was feeling faint with hunger and the light was steadily fading, he worked on. One piece of furniture after another was wheeled in and placed in position. He wasn't as careful as he'd been when loading up. Rattles and bangs filled the air, the walls shed flakes of plaster, black streaks disfigured the wallpaper. He didn't care as long as nothing got broken. Even professional removal men scratched things.

The last load of the evening consisted of two pictures, three cameras and the TV. Jonas turned on the TV. He fancied something, he didn't know what. He untangled some leads and connected a camera to the TV. He had to press several buttons on the remote before the screen went blue, indicating it was ready.

It was dark now, but the street lights hadn't come on as he'd hoped. Hands on hips, he looked through the window at the truck. All that could be heard behind him was the faint hum of the camera, which was on stand-by.

Chocolate.

He was ravenously hungry, but what tormented him most of all was a craving for chocolate. Milk chocolate, chocolate with nuts, chocolate creams, anything, even cooking chocolate, would have done. As long as it was chocolate.

The hallway was in darkness. Shotgun in hand, he groped his way to the light switch. When the dim bulb in the ceiling came on, he cleared his throat and let out a hoarse laugh. He tried the door of the flat opposite. Locked. He tried the next one. Just as he turned the handle he realised that it was Frau Bender's former home.

'Hello?'

Jonas turned the light on. His throat tightened. He gulped. He slid along the walls like a shadow. The flat was unrecognisable. Its occupants appeared to have been young people. Photos of film stars hung on the walls. The video collection filled two cupboards. TV magazines were lying around. In one corner stood an empty terrarium.

Everything looked unfamiliar. All he remembered was the handsome parquet floor and the moulded ceilings.

He was astonished to note that Frau Bender's flat had been almost three times the size of his parents'.

He found no chocolate, only some biscuits of a kind he disliked. Then he remembered the grocer's two streets away. Jonas had often shopped at Herr Weber's as a boy. He'd even been allowed to buy things on account. The old man with the bushy eyebrows had eventually given up the business. If he remembered correctly, the shop had been acquired by an Egyptian who sold oriental specialities. Still, perhaps he'd stocked chocolate as well.

Out in the street it was a mild, windless night. Jonas peered left and right. The hairs stood up on the back of his neck as he set off through the gloom. He felt tempted to turn back, but he summoned up all his willpower and walked on.

The shop wasn't locked. There was chocolate. In addition to tinned goods and powdered soups, the establishment had sold milk, bread and sausage – all of it spoilt now, of course. The owner had dealt in almost all the basic necessities. Alcohol was the only thing Jonas couldn't find.

He put several bars of chocolate in a rusty shopping basket and added a few tins of bean soup, some peanuts and a bottle of mineral water. He also raided the shelves for a random assortment of sweets and biscuits.

The shopping basket proved a nuisance on the return trip. It was impossible to carry the thing and hold his gun at the ready at the same time. He walked slowly. Here and there a lighted window illuminated a stretch of pavement.

He couldn't shake off the notion that someone was lying in wait behind the parked cars. He paused to listen. All he heard was his own tremulous breathing.

In his imagination a woman was lurking behind that van parked on the corner. She was wearing a kind of nun's wimple, and she had no face. There she crouched, waiting for him as if she'd never moved before. As if she'd always been there. And she wasn't waiting for just anyone. She was waiting for *him*.

He had an urge to laugh, to yell, but he didn't utter a sound. He tried to run, but his legs refused to obey him. He approached the building steadily, not daring to breathe.

In the hallway he turned on the light, walked up the ramp and along the passage to the flat. He didn't look back. He went in, put the basket down and pushed the door shut with his behind. Only then did he turn round and lock it.

'Hahaha! Now we'll feast! Now we'll guzzle! Hahaha!'

He looked round the kitchen. The units and all the equipment had belonged to the Kästner family. He put a large saucepan on the stove and emptied the contents of two tins into it. His tension gradually eased as the scent of bean soup rose into the air.

After eating he took the shopping basket into the living room, where he was greeted by the hum of the camera. The bed didn't collapse this time either, when he tested its stability with his foot. He went to get a blanket and a pillow and lay down. Tearing the wrapper off a bar of milk chocolate, he thrust a couple of squares into his mouth.

He surveyed the room. Although the furniture was still far from complete, the pieces he'd so far brought in were back in their original places. The brown bookcase and the yellow one. The ancient standard lamp. The rather greasy armchair. The rocking chair with the worn arms, in which he'd sometimes felt queasy as a child. And, on the wall opposite the bed, 'Johanna', the picture of an unknown woman that had always hung there: a beautiful, dark-haired woman leaning against a stylised tree trunk and gazing into the beholder's eyes. His parents had jokingly christened her Johanna, although no one knew who had painted the picture or whom it represented. Or even where it had come from.

The undersheet was soft. It still gave off a familiar odour.

Jonas turned on his side and reached for another piece of chocolate. Tired and relaxed, he stared at the window that overlooked the street. A double window, it was so ill-fitting that old blankets had been laid on the sill between the inner and outer casements to prevent draughts in winter.

This was where he'd handed over his letter addressed to the Christkind just before Christmas.

His mother used to remind him to make out a wish list for the Christkind at the beginning of December. She never forgot to mention that he must be modest in his requests because the Christkind was too poor to be able to afford more than a thin garment. So Jonas would sit at the table with his feet dangling clear of the floor, chewing his pencil and dreaming. Would a remote-controlled jeep be too expensive for the Christkind? How about a toy racetrack? Or an electric motorboat? The most wonderful presents occurred to him, but his mother said his requests would put the Christkind in an awkward position because they couldn't all be granted.

As a result, Jonas's wish list eventually consisted of just a few small items. A new fountain pen. A packet of transfers. A rubber ball. His letter ended up on the threadbare blanket between the windows, ready to be collected by an angel on one of the following nights and delivered to the Christkind.

How would the angel manage to open the outer window?

That was the question Jonas pondered before going to sleep. He didn't want to shut his eyes and yearned to stay awake. Would the angel come tonight? Would he hear him?

His first thought on waking: I fell asleep after all. But when, when?

He ran to the window. If the envelope had disappeared, as it usually did on the second or third day, seldom on the first because angels were so busy, Jonas experienced a feeling of happiness far greater than anything he felt weeks later on Christmas Eve itself. He was delighted with his presents, and with the thought that the Christkind had been near enough in person to leave the parcels beneath the Christmas tree while he was sitting in the kitchen. His parents used to invite Uncle Reinhard and Aunt Lena, Uncle Richard and Aunt Olga to dinner. The tree was lit up with candles. Jonas would lie on the floor half-listening to the grown-ups' conversation, which had become a steady murmur by the time it reached him. He felt enveloped by the sound as he leafed through a book or examined a toy train. This was all very lovely and mysterious, but nothing compared to the miracle that had occurred a week or two earlier, when an angel had come to collect his letter during the night.

Jonas sighed and turned over. Only a few squares of chocolate were left. He put them in his mouth and crumpled up the wrapper.

Aware that he wouldn't be able to remain awake much longer, he overcame his inertia and got to his feet.

He stationed three cameras side by side, facing the bed. He looked through the lenses, adjusted their angle, put a tape in each. When everything was ready he turned his attention to the TV and the camera connected to it. Last night's tape was in his trouser pocket. He inserted it and pressed 'Play'.

*

The camera wasn't pointing at the bed, nor was it located in the bedroom. The screen displayed the shower cubicle in the bathroom. The bathroom of this flat. In Hollandstrasse.

Someone seemed to have been taking quite a long shower, a hot one. The glass sides of the cubicle were misted up and steam was rising above them, but the swoosh of the water couldn't be heard. The scene appeared to have been shot without sound.

After ten minutes Jonas began to wonder if this waste of water would go on for much longer.

Twenty minutes. He was so sleepy, he had to switch to fast-forward. Thirty minutes, forty. An hour. The bathroom door was shut, the room became more and more steamed up. The door of the shower cubicle was barely visible.

After two hours, all that could be seen on the screen was a dense grey mass.

Another fifteen minutes, and visibility rapidly improved. The bathroom door reappeared. It was open now. So was the door of the shower cubicle.

The cubicle itself was empty.

The tape ended without his having seen anyone.

Jonas turned off the TV. Warily, as if there were a direct connection between what he'd seen on the tape and what was happening at this moment, he peered into the bathroom. He looked at the rubber mat. The shower head. The soap dish projecting from the tiles. Nothing had changed.

That was impossible, though. Something had to be different. Something.

This was where what he'd seen on the tape had occurred, so it belonged to the place. But the place had sloughed it off – no vestige of the past clung to it. Just a shower cubicle. No steamed-up glass. No condensation. Just a memory. A void.

It was shortly after eleven. He programmed one camera to come on at 2.05 a.m. and another at 5.05. Then he turned on the third, undressed and got into bed.

17

He could hardly believe it when he checked the time on his mobile. It was after ten. He'd slept for eleven hours, but he didn't feel refreshed in the least.

In the kitchen he realised he'd forgotten to get any bread from the Egyptian's shop the night before. He heated up another tin. There was some coffee, but it was a sort he disliked. He made do with mineral water.

After breakfast he tidied up. He opened all the windows to ventilate the stuffy rooms and shook the bedclothes. He rewound the tapes, filling the air with their threefold hum, and put the dirty crockery in the dishwasher. While engaged in these activities and without admitting it to himself, he kept a constant watch. For changes. For pointers to something he hadn't noticed the day before.

He had a cold shower without shutting his eyes, belting out a sea shanty in which pirates were keelhauled and made to walk the plank. While he was drying himself in the living room his eye lighted on a bar of chocolate. He hesitated for a moment, then reached for it.

Within an hour he'd emptied the entire truck. Everything was inside the flat. All the chairs, all the bookcases, all the cupboards, all the boxes. Not sorted out yet, of course, but he didn't have to leave the building from now on. He could watch last night's tapes while working.

It took him just under three hours to dust all the furniture, check it for damage and shift it into position. While the Sleeper slept on the screen beside him, Jonas dusted lampshades, mended a hole in an armchair and buffed off the scratches on a cupboard, watching the TV at every opportunity.

The Sleeper seemed to have had a quiet night. He turned over now and then, but most of the time he lay still. Jonas even thought he heard an occasional snore. He wondered why he was so tired.

Between the first and second tapes he took a break. He found a ready-to-serve meal in a kitchen drawer and heated it up in a little wok. It was inedible. He added some soy sauce and other seasoning. No use. Grimly, he plunged the opener into yet another tin of bean soup.

The second tape began the way the first had ended. He fast-forwarded it. Meanwhile, he tidied things away. When he was working in the kitchen and out of sight of the TV, he switched to normal play and turned the volume up full. He also darted into the living room every couple of minutes to see if the Sleeper was still buried beneath the bedclothes. On the right stood the bed. Facing it on the left was its miniature reflection on the TV screen. He himself was lying asleep in that reflection.

The Kästner family's crockery and kitchen utensils ended up on the rubbish dump in the backyard. All he kept were some frying pans and saucepans, because he'd noticed that his father's kitchen equipment was less than ideal. He couldn't find the mug with the bear on it, the one he'd drunk from as a child. Only three of the old glasses were there. As for kitchen gadgets that required some skill, such as a pressure cooker or a coffee machine, his father appeared to have got rid of them.

He switched to fast-forward again. Whatever might eventually happen to him, it was impossible to make complete recordings of himself while asleep and watch those recordings conscientiously during the day. That would mean doing nothing but sleeping and watching himself sleeping. He wouldn't be able to do a thing, he would be tied to the cameras.

Towards the end of the second tape, when the Sleeper was still lying motionless under the bedclothes, Jonas felt he'd been taken for a fool. His movements became more sluggish. He slammed cupboard doors and stuffed clothes into drawers regardless of whether or not he was creasing them. Until, among a pile of books, he discovered some old comics that had escaped his notice while packing.

Jonas liked comics. Even as an adult he had bought the occasional Mort & Phil comic without blushing. There was even one in the toilet at his flat on the Brigittenauer embankment. But these were special. He leafed through them as if they were much sought-after rarities, examining every dog-eared, jam-stained page. He must have been twelve, or fourteen at most, the last time he'd held this comic in his hand. Twenty years had gone by since he'd cut the slice of bread whose butter and jam had smeared this page. This comic had languished unopened on a shelf for two whole decades. He'd finished reading it one day, put it away and forgotten all about it. And he hadn't had a clue how long it would be before he saw this picture, this speech balloon, again. He was seeing them again only now.

A marginal note scrawled in a childish hand: *Funny!*

He had written that. He didn't know why, only that he'd written it, that it was twenty years ago, and that he'd still known so little at the time. That this 'Funny!' had been written by a boy who knew nothing about girls, who would later study physics and aspire to become a teacher or academic, who was interested in football and may have had some maths homework to do. And that the person who had rediscovered this comic was wondering why he hadn't come across it before. The comic. And the memory.

He glanced at the screen. The Sleeper wasn't stirring.

The characters on one page had been given glasses drawn with a ballpoint pen. He couldn't remember doing that.

Jonas started to read the comic in his hand. Even the first page made him grin. He read on with increasing enjoyment, casting only an occasional, mechanical glance at the TV. The absurdity of the plot, the characters, the drawings delighted him. The next time he looked at the screen it was blue. At once, he put in the third tape. The Sleeper was still asleep. He pressed the fast-forward button.

He finished the comic, laughing aloud more than once. Having read the last page he skimmed the rest of it again in a happy mood. He couldn't remember this issue. He might have been seeing and reading it for the first time. This surprised him. Once read, his children's books had always imprinted their stories and characters on his memory.

The Sleeper was sleeping. So soundly that Jonas checked to see if he'd pressed the freeze-frame button by mistake.

He arranged the books on the shelves, browsing from time to time when one aroused his interest. He glanced at the screen, looked around to see if he'd done enough to justify taking a break, then read on until his curiosity was satisfied.

Box after flattened box went sailing out into the back-yard. Pressing the freeze-frame button, he went into the bathroom to connect the washing machine and hang some hand towels on the hook beside the washbasin. Back in the living room he pressed 'Play' and set about sorting out his father's personal possessions. A few rings. His medals. His passport. Some minor souvenirs. These he put in the drawer they'd been kept in for decades. Only the knife was missing. It was stuck in the wall. He also couldn't find some photos, which might turn up in the cellar at Rüdigergasse.

The thought of the knife being irretrievable distressed him. His mood had brightened for the first time for weeks and he didn't want to sour it. He picked up another comic.

Jonas surveyed the room. He'd finished, really. A few things might benefit from a more thorough clean, but that he could do another day.

He stretched out on the bed and helped himself to some peanuts. The tape was fast forwarding, the display registered 2.30. He switched to normal play. With his head facing the TV, he turned over on his stomach and started reading. He crunched a peanut with relish.

*

Out of the corner of his eye he glimpsed movement on the screen.

The tape had been running for two hours fifty-seven minutes. The Sleeper extricated himself from the bed-clothes and sat up on the edge of the bed, a metre from where Jonas was lying. The Sleeper turned to face the camera. He looked wide awake.

Jonas sat up too. Turned up the volume. Looked at the Sleeper.

The Sleeper cocked an eyebrow.

The corner of his mouth twitched.

He shook his head.

And burst out laughing.

Louder and louder he laughed. The Sleeper's hilarity wasn't feigned. He seemed to be genuinely amused by something. He laughed and laughed, fighting for breath and trying to pull himself together, only to bellow with laughter once more. Just before the tape ran out he regained his composure and stared straight at the camera.

Jonas had never seen anyone stare so fixedly, least of all himself. It was a look of such determination that he found it overwhelming.

The screen went blue.

*

Jonas stretched out his arms and legs. He stared up at the ceiling.

The ceiling he'd stared at twenty years ago. And three weeks ago.

He had lain here as a child and thought about himself. About the self that was synonymous with the life in which each individual was imprisoned. If you were born with a club foot you retained it all your life. If your hair fell out you could wear a wig, but you were well aware you were bald and couldn't escape that fate. If all your teeth had been pulled out you would never again be able to chew with your own teeth for the rest of your days. If you suffered from a disability you had to resign yourself to it. You had to come to terms with anything you couldn't change, and most things couldn't be changed. A weak heart, a sensitive stomach, a deformed spine – they formed the individual, they were yourself, a part of life. And you were trapped in that life and would never know what it was like or what it meant to be someone else. Nothing could convey to you what another person felt on waking up or eating or making love. You could never know what life felt like without a backache or without belching after meals. Your life was a cage.

He had lain there and yearned to be a comic book character. He didn't want to be the Jonas he was in the body he inhabited. He wanted to be the Jonas who was also Mort or Phil, or both of them, or at least a friend of theirs. He wanted to live in their reality, under the rules and natural laws that governed their world. They were forever being beaten up, having accidents, jumping off skyscrapers, getting burnt, dismembered or devoured, exploding or being hurled through space to distant planets. But explosions didn't kill them and severed hands could be sewn on again. They got hurt, admittedly, but the pain had gone in the next picture. They had a whale of a time. Being them must be fun.

They didn't die, either.

The ceiling. To be that, nor Jonas. To be suspended, year after year, above a room in which people came and went. Some would disappear and others take their place, but he would remain suspended up there. Time would trickle on. He wouldn't care.

To be a pebble by the sea. To hear the roar of the waves. Or not to hear it. To lie on the shore for centuries and then be tossed into the sea by some little girl, only to be washed up again after hundreds more years have gone by. Washed up on the shore. On seashells embedded in sand.

To be a tree. When it was planted, Henry I, or IV, or VI ruled, and then came a Leopold or a Charles. The tree had stood in a field with the sun shining down on it. It had bidden the sun farewell at dusk, when the dew started to fall. Reunited in the morning, the tree and the sun couldn't have cared less whether someone named Shakespeare was alive or some queen was beheaded 1,000 kilometres away. A peasant had come and lopped off some branches, and the peasant had a son, and the son had a son of his own, but the tree continued to stand there. It was still young, pain-free, fearless. Napoleon became emperor, but the tree didn't budge. Napoleon came past and bivouacked in its shade, but the tree didn't care. Kaiser Wilhelm had come and touched the tree later on, unaware that Napoleon had done the same, but the tree cared as little about Napoleon and Wilhelm as it did about the great-grandson of the great-grandson of the first peasant who had come and pruned its shoots.

To be a tree like that one, a tree that had stood in the field at the outbreak of the First and Second World Wars, in the sixties, eighties and nineties. One that was standing there now, caressed by the wind.

*

The sun was twinkling through the blinds. Jonas locked the door behind him and searched the flat, leaving his shotgun beside the hall cupboard. No one appeared to have been there. The knife was still embedded in the wall. He tugged at it without success.

He made himself something to eat and drank a grappa. Leaning out of the window, he savoured the sun's rays with his eyes shut.

Eight o'clock. He felt tired but couldn't afford to go to sleep, there was so much to do.

He removed the tapes from the cameras in the flat next door and numbered them. Clasping tapes 1–26 to his chest, he returned to his own flat, pushed a blank video into the recorder and put tape 1 in the camera.

The Spider came into shot, travelling at full speed. It raced along the Brigittenauer embankment, heading straight for the camera. The roar of the engine was so deafening as it drove past he turned the volume down.

The din subsided to a distant hum. Moments later silence fell.

The screen showed the deserted embankment.

No sign of movement anywhere.

He wound the tape on. Three, eight, twelve minutes. Then pressed the play button. Again he saw the deserted embankment. He waited. Another few minutes, and the sound of a rapidly approaching car could be heard. The Spider came into shot once more. It raced towards the camera, its battered bonnet clearly visible. And roared past.

The street lay there, deserted once more. The branches of the trees lining the embankment stirred gently in the wind.

Jonas rewound the tape. He pressed the play button on the camera and the record button on the recorder. Just as the car sped out of shot, he stopped recording. He removed tape 1 and put in tape 2, which showed the route from the balcony. He pressed the red button. Again he stopped recording just as the Spider went out of shot.

The third tape, which came from the other balcony camera, had filmed the Heiligenstädter Brücke. He had to rewind it twice to catch the precise moment when the car came into shot. The Spider crossed the canal and disappeared. Jonas stopped recording and left the tape in the camera running.

He looked at the deserted bridge.

No one had ever seen what he was seeing. The bridge railings, the waters of the Danube Canal. The street, the winking traffic lights. At just after 3 p.m. on that particular day. It had been recorded with no one nearby. This recording had been made by a machine with no human witnesses around. Any enjoyment to be derived from the process had been confined to the machine itself and its subjects. The deserted street. The traffic lights. The bushes. Otherwise: no one.

But these images proved that those minutes had elapsed. They had come and gone. If he went there now, he would encounter a different bridge at a different time from the one he was seeing. Yet it had existed, even though he hadn't been present.

He put in tape 4, followed by 5, 6 and 7. He made rapid progress. From time to time he got up to refill his glass, make a snack or simply stretch his legs. He never took long, but it was dark outside by the time he played the tape showing Gaussplatz.

The Spider grazed a parked car and went into a skid. It rammed a car on the opposite side of the street, then skidded back across the roadway and collided with a van. The impact was so violent, Jonas stared at the screen transfixed. The Spider cannoned off the van and out onto the roundabout, where it spun several times on its own axis and finally came to rest.

For a minute nothing happened. Another minute went by. And another. Then the driver got out, went round to the back of the car and opened the boot. After looking for something, he sat behind the wheel again.

Three minutes later the car drove on.

Jonas still hadn't transferred this sequence to the video recorder. He rewound the tape, but he didn't press the record button even then. He watched the accident in disbelief, saw the driver get out and look around to see if he was being observed, then go to the back of the car. Why had he done that? What was he looking for in the boot?

And why couldn't he, Jonas, remember all this?

The tape came to an end at half past eleven. He still hadn't watched the second circuit. Maybe he would catch up with it another time. One circuit would suffice for the present. He would watch it when he got a chance.

Jonas roamed the flat, glass in hand, thinking how many years he'd lived there. He made sure the front door was locked. Read Marie's text messages on his mobile. Flexed his stiff shoulders. Contemplated the knife in the bedroom wall.

Catching sight of his eyes in the mirror as he cleaned his teeth, he gave a start and looked down while the humming electric toothbrush whipped the toothpaste into foam. He spat it out and rinsed his mouth.

Back in the bedroom once more, he gripped the hilt of the knife and tugged with all his might. It didn't move a single millimetre.

He examined the carpet on his knees. It seemed to him that the carpet beneath the knife was a little cleaner than the surrounding area.

He took the vacuum cleaner from the bedroom cupboard, where the unwieldy contraption was kept for lack of space. Removing the bag, he went into the bathroom and emptied its contents into the bathtub. A cloud of dust went up. He coughed, one hand shielding his face and the other probing the wad of compressed fluff. He soon came across some white powder.

Plaster dust.

18

Perhaps order was the key.

He rubbed his eyes, trying to fix the thought in his mind. Order. Changing as little as possible and, wherever possible, re-creating the original state of affairs.

He blinked. He'd had a dream, a bad dream. About what?

He looked at the wall. The knife had gone. He sat up abruptly. The camera, the shotgun, the computer, all were in their proper places. But the knife had disappeared.

He scanned the floor while trying to button his shirt with trembling fingers. Nothing. He went into the living room. No knife.

His head was aching badly. He took two aspirins and breakfasted on some marble cake straight from the plastic wrapping. It tasted artificial. He washed it down with orange juice. The memory of his dream came back to him.

He was in a room full of undersized pieces of furniture that looked as if they'd shrunk or been made for midgets. Seated in an armchair facing him was a body without a head. It didn't move.

Jonas stared at the headless man. He thought he was dead until one of his hands moved. So, soon afterwards, did his arm. Jonas muttered something unintelligible. The headless man made a dismissive gesture. Jonas noticed that the place between his shoulders from which the neck would have emerged was dark with a white circle in the middle.

Without knowing or understanding what he was saying, Jonas addressed the headless man once more. The upper part of the headless man's torso moved stiffly, as if he meant to turn and look sideways or over his shoulder. He was wearing jeans and a lumberjack shirt, the top two buttons undone to reveal a chest covered with curly grey hair. Jonas said something. Then the headless man started to rock in his chair. Back and forth, back and forth he went, much faster than normal strength and agility would have permitted.

Laying aside his slice of cake, Jonas drained his glass and jotted down the outline of the dream in his notebook.

*

All he could find in the tool drawer was a small hammer suitable at best for knocking picture hooks into a plywood partition. He looked in the box beneath the bathroom washbasin, where he kept tools when he was too lazy to take them downstairs. Empty.

He took the lift down. His compartment in the cellar smelt of cold rubber. The toolbox containing the bigger tools was behind the Toyota's winter tyres.

Jonas swung the sledgehammer experimentally. That would do the trick. He got out of the cellar quickly and ran back up the stairs. From below came more and more noises he didn't like the sound of. He was imagining them, of course. But he didn't want to expose himself to them for too long.

He stood in front of the wall. For a moment he debated whether it wouldn't be better to abandon the whole idea. Then he raised the sledgehammer and swung it with all his might. It struck the very spot where the knife had been embedded. There was a dull thud. Flakes of plaster rained down.

He took a second swing. This time the sledgehammer made a big dent in the wall. Red brick dust trickled from it.

Bricks in a building made of reinforced concrete?

He swung at the wall again and again. The hole grew bigger. Before long it was the size of the mirror-fronted cabinet over the bathroom basin. Now, whenever the sledgehammer landed on the edges of the hole, it bounced off them.

He explored the cavity with his hands. This part of the wall really did consist of brittle old brickwork, whereas the surrounding area, which was impervious to the sledge-hammer, was concrete.

His fingers felt something wedged between two bricks.

Carefully, he knocked them out. A piece of plastic. He yanked at it, but it seemed to be deeply embedded.

There was so much debris on the floor by now that he had to fetch a broom and sweep it up. Deeper and deeper into the wall he went. He didn't like the look of the thing he was tugging at, so he slipped on a pair of rubber gloves. The dust was making him cough.

Having exposed a substantial area with one hard blow, he gave the object another tug. With a jerk, it came away in his hand. Holding it gingerly, he took it through to the bathtub.

Jonas examined his find closely before turning on the tap. He wanted to make sure that the grey film adhering to the surface was ordinary dust, not powdered potassium or magnesium, substances that gave off an inflammable gas when in contact with water. It might even be some kind of explosive that detonated under similar circumstances. He would simply have to risk it.

Using the shower head, he washed off the dust and dirt that clung to the object. It was indeed made of plastic. It looked like a raincoat. He mopped his brow and used the same cloth to dry the object. Then he picked it up and spread it out.

It wasn't a raincoat. It was an inflatable doll. Although, on closer inspection, it lacked the orifices that would have identified it as a sex toy.

*

Jonas deposited the two suitcases beside the Spider. He circled the car, closely examining the bodywork. He could now understand why the front had been so badly damaged. After a crash like that, it was a miracle the car still went.

He inspected the boot very closely before loading the suitcases. It was empty save for the first-aid kit and the crowbar. What he had been doing in there after the collision remained a mystery.

He checked the number of kilometres on the clock, comparing the numerals with those he had recorded in his notebook the day before. They tallied.

At his parents' flat he discovered he was short of space. The cupboard he'd kept his clothes in as a boy had ended up on a rubbish tip years ago. He would have to dump the unopened suitcases in his former nursery until he found the time to get hold of an additional wardrobe, which he would also put in there. The living room was now as it had been in his childhood, and any extraneous piece of furniture would spoil its appearance.

He vaguely remembered that they'd stored a lot of things in the attic because there were no storage spaces in the basement. He hadn't been up there since he was a boy.

He fetched the bunch of keys left behind by the Kästner family, together with the torch and the shotgun. There was no lift, but he was scarcely out of breath by the time he reached the fifth floor. At least he was still reasonably fit.

The heavy door creaked open. A cold current of air rushed out at him. The light switch was so thick with dust and cobwebs that he guessed he must be the attic's first visitor for years. He surveyed it by the light of the naked bulb suspended from a beam.

There were no separate compartments. Numbers scrawled in whitewash on three-metre-high beams indicated that the space beneath each belonged to a particular flat. In one corner lay a bicycle frame without its tyres and chain, and not far from it a heap of sacks filled with plaster. Some broken slats were leaning against the wall in another corner. He also spotted a tubeless TV.

On the floor beneath the number of his parents' flat stood a heavy chest. Jonas knew at once that it had belonged to his father, not the Kästners. There was nothing to indicate this, no nameplate or label. Nor did he recognise it. But it was his father's beyond a doubt.

When he went to open the chest, he found that it had no lock or handles.

He examined every side, getting his hands dirty in the process. He patted off the dust on his trouser legs and pulled a face. Then he gave up.

He went downstairs again. At least the attic would have enough room for the boxes. Before carrying them up there, however, he wanted to inspect their contents. For the moment, he dumped them in one of the neighbouring flats.

It struck him that he could simply leave them there. It was cleaner and he wouldn't have so far to go if he needed something. But he stuck to his original plan: to restore order and maintain it. Those boxes didn't belong in his parents' flat. They had no business there, only in the space reserved for them in the attic.

*

The wind had got up again. Dozens of rustling plastic and paper bags, which must have escaped from one of the vegetable stalls in the Karmelitermarkt, were scudding across the square. Jonas got a speck of dust in his eye. It started to water.

He made himself a quick snack in an inviting-looking pub, then walked on through the streets. This district had undergone many changes since his boyhood. Most of the shops and restaurants were unfamiliar to him. He felt in his pocket for one of the little cards he'd written on. It bore the word 'Blue'. That was no help. He looked around but couldn't see anything that colour.

The wind was so strong it nudged him in the back. He kept on breaking into an involuntary trot. He turned to look. Just the wind, nothing more. He walked on, only to swing round again.

The street was deserted. No suspicious movement, no sound. Just the slithering of paper and scraps of refuse being blown along the street by the wind.

In Nestroygasse he looked at his watch. Not even six yet. He had plenty of time

*

The front door wasn't locked. He called, waited a few moments, then ventured inside.

A low hum was coming from behind the door on his left. He raised his shotgun and kicked the handle. The door burst open. He fired, cocked the gun and fired again. Waited a moment, then yelled and dashed into the room.

It was empty.

He was standing in a pellet-riddled bathroom, and the sound he'd heard was the gas boiler heating up the water. Catching sight of his reflection in the mirror above the washbasin, he quickly averted his gaze.

The floorboards creaked as he made his way around the flat. From the bathroom into the hallway. From the hallway to the kitchen. Back into the hallway and from there into the living room. The place was dark, like most old flats. He turned some lights on.

He searched various drawers for notes, letters and similar documents. All he found were bills.

The bedroom curtains were drawn. He saw the framed photograph on the wall as soon as he turned on the light. A boy of about ten with an expressionless face. Ingo. For a moment he thought the boy was smiling. Something else puzzled him, but he couldn't put his finger on it.

'Anyone there?' His voice cracked.

There were some photo albums on a shelf in the living room. He pulled one out and flicked through it without putting his gun down.

Photos dating from the seventies. Colour prints as poor as the ones he'd found at Rüdigergasse. The same haircuts, the same trousers, the same shirt collars, the same little cars.

All at once it went dark outside. He ran to the window. The shotgun fell over with a crash behind him. But it was only a storm cloud passing across the sun.

He had to sit down. Absently, he glanced at photo after photo. He felt close to tears. His heartbeat steadied, but only gradually.

In one of the photos he recognised himself.

He turned over the page. Snaps of himself and Ingo. More of the same on the next page. He couldn't recall being on such close terms with Ingo. He'd been here only once, so he couldn't think when or where these pictures had been taken. The backgrounds offered no clue.

A page torn from a newspaper fell out of one of the albums and onto his lap. It was foxed and faded and folded in the middle. Most of it was filled with death notices.

Our Ingo. In his tenth year. Tragic accident. Sorely missed.

Shaken, he laid the album aside. Then he remembered the framed photograph. He went back into the bedroom. This time he noticed what had escaped him before: it had a black border.

He was almost as thrown by his former playmate's death as he was by the fact that he hadn't learnt of it until twenty-five years after the event. They'd only had anything to do with one another in primary school. To him, Ingo Lüscher had been alive throughout these years – in fact he'd sometimes wondered what had become of the fair-haired lad from the neighbourhood. Little had been said about the accident, it seemed. His parents couldn't have known Ingo's, or they would have mentioned it.

How had it happened?

He made another search of the drawers in the living room. He shook the photograph albums, but only a couple of loose prints fell out. He looked for a computer, but the Lüschers didn't seem to have gone in for modern technology. There wasn't even a TV.

The folder was in the bedside table. It contained press cuttings. Accident: child killed. Motorbike knocks boy down: dead.

He read every article. What one omitted, the other mentioned, and he soon managed to form an idea of what had happened. Ingo had evidently run out into the street while playing, and the motorcyclist had been unable to avoid him. The rear-view mirror had broken the boy's neck.

Killed by a rear-view mirror. Jonas had never heard of such a thing before.

He paced around the flat in a turmoil. A collision with a motorbike had caused the boy's death. Thirty-year-old Ingo didn't exist because of ten-year-old Ingo's accident. The thirty-year-old might have escaped injury. He could have protected the ten-year-old, but the ten-year-old had been unable to protect the thirty-year-old.

The same person. One a boy, the other an adult. The latter didn't exist because the former had had an accident. A rear-view mirror, which mightn't have done much to the adult, had broken the boy's neck.

Jonas pictured thirty-year-old Ingo standing on the other side of the street and watching the motorbike knock down his ten-year-old self, knowing that he would never exist. Did the two of them speak to each other? Did the ten-year-old apologise to the thirty-year-old? Did the latter console the former by saying it was an accident for which he bore no blame?

And Jonas himself? What if a car had killed him? Or a disease? Or even a murderer? Then he wouldn't have existed at twenty or thirty, nor would he exist at forty or eighty.

Or would he? Would the older Jonases have existed? Somehow, somewhere? In some unfulfilled form?

*

He parked the truck outside his block of flats. The embankment road was as deserted as ever. The Danube Canal gurgled softly past. Nothing seemed to have changed.

Once inside the flat he packed the clothes belonging to the dwarf from Attnang-Puchheim in his holdall and took a last look round. The inflatable doll was lying in the bathtub where he'd left it. The sack filled with debris from the wall was bursting at the seams. He tied up the neck and heaved it out of the window. He enjoyed watching it fly through the air. It landed with a crash on the roof of a car.

He thought for a moment. Yes, that was the lot.

He was worried there wouldn't be room for the 4WD, but the tailboard shut even after he'd driven it up the ramp and stopped a good two metres short of the Spider, which he'd loaded aboard the truck in Hollandstrasse. There was even some room to spare.

He found a filling station near the Augarten. While diesel was flowing into the tank he explored the shop. He'd already skimmed every newspaper and magazine on the shelves. The shop also stocked a wide range of soft toys, personalised coffee mugs, sunglasses and models of St Stephen's Cathedral, as well as drinks and chocolate bars. Jonas filled one plastic bag with a random assortment of snacks and tossed some cans of lemonade into another.

On a revolving stand, in addition to products for cleaning car windows and polishing bodywork, were some Day-Glo nameplates of the kind truck drivers liked to display behind their windscreens. Albert headed the list, followed by Alfons and Anton. Out of curiosity he looked for J. To his surprise he found a couple of Jonases sandwiched between Johann and Josef. He took one and put it behind the truck's windscreen.

*

Although it wasn't dark yet, he got the cameras ready for the night. He was tired, and he wanted to make an early start. Besides, he hoped that if he watched last night's tape before sunset, it wouldn't prey on his mind so much.

Jonas locked the door and shut all the windows. He looked out at Hollandstrasse. The truck was parked outside the building next door, so as not to obstruct his view. No movement was visible. Standing close to the window pane, he thumbed his nose and stuck his tongue out.

*

The bed was empty.

No sign of the Sleeper.

The knife was embedded in the wall.

Jonas wondered when the recording had been made. He couldn't remember what time he'd set it for, and, as so often, the alarm clock was lying face down on the bed although he'd turned it to face the camera.

He was about to fast-forward when he heard a sound coming from the TV. It was a long-drawn-out, high-pitched wail. So high-pitched it could well have been made by a human voice, but also by a musical instrument.

Eeee!

Angrily, he jumped out of bed and darted across the room. Either he was hearing a ghost, or someone was making fun of his fear of ghosts.

Eeee!

He was tempted to switch off, but his desire to know what would happen next proved too strong. He got back under the bedclothes. For a while he turned his back on the screen, but that was even more unendurable. He looked again. No one to be seen.

Eeee!

'Very funny,' he called out. His voice was hoarse. He cleared his throat. 'Oh yes. Yes, well. Oh. Yes, yes.'

Should he fast-forward? He might miss some message. It wasn't beyond the bounds of possibility that the sound would lead to something.

Eeee!

He immersed himself in a comic. This enabled him to push the wailing sound to the back of his mind sufficiently for him to let the tape run on. He even grinned at some drawing now and then, but he more than once had to start a page again from scratch.

Music?

Where was the music coming from?

He turned off the sound. Listened. The wall clock was ticking away.

He turned up the volume again. Wailing. But there was something else, something softer. A kind of tune.

He listened, but he couldn't hear it any longer.

Eeee!

'And the same to you!'

It was getting dark. Assailed by toothache and a fit of conscience, Jonas pushed away the box of chocolates he'd been eating, there were hardly any left in any case, and pressed the pause button. Then he went to the bathroom and cleaned his teeth. On the way back he noticed that the kitchen was in darkness. He turned on the light.

All he saw at first was someone's back coming into shot. The figure turned round. It was the Sleeper.

Wide-eyed, Jonas watched the Sleeper go over to the wall and grip the hilt of the knife, staring defiantly at the camera. He pulled it out with ease.

The Sleeper walked towards the camera until his head almost filled the screen. He stepped forwards, his eyes and nose becoming visible in extreme close-up, then stepped back again and winked in a strangely endearing manner. The only thing Jonas didn't care for was the way he brandished the knife near his throat.

Having nodded as though in confirmation of something, the Sleeper moved out of shot.

19

Although it was only first light, Jonas padded barefoot across the creaking floorboards to his clothes, which were draped over a chair. He peered out of the window. Some rubbish skips were standing on the other side of the street, just visible in outline. The street looked as it did on a normal Sunday morning, when the last of the night owls had come home and everyone was asleep. He had always liked this time of day. Everything became easier when the darkness receded. It was appropriate that murderers should be strapped into the electric chair or sent to the gas chamber a minute after midnight, Jonas thought, because there was no more hopeless time than the middle of the night.

He had some breakfast and packed the camera. When the sun came up he said: 'Goodbye, have a nice time!'

He not only locked the front door behind him, he sealed it with sticky tape. No one would be able to get in without his knowing.

*

While driving along the motorway he pondered on the latest videotape.

How had the Sleeper pulled the knife out of the wall with no effort when he himself had failed to do so several times? True, the Sleeper wasn't in bed when the tape started. He could have messed around with the wall and the blade beforehand. But how? The wall was undamaged.

Where the motorway had three lanes, Jonas drove in the middle. Where there were two he kept to the right. He sounded the horn from time to time. Its powerful blare gave him a feeling of security. He'd switched on the driver's transceiver, which was emitting a soft hiss. So was the radio.

In Linz he looked for the pub where he'd eaten during the thunderstorm. He spent some time cruising around the district where he thought it was, but he couldn't even find the chemist's he'd raided for cold cures. He gave up and drove back to the main road. Finding the car showroom was all that mattered.

The Toyota was standing outside, just as he'd left it. Although it didn't appear to have rained for quite a while, the car was quite clean. The air was evidently less dirty than it used to be.

'Hello, you,' he said, and drummed on the roof.

He'd never felt sentimental about the Toyota before. But now it was *his* car, the one he'd owned in the old days. The Spider would never be that for the same reason that Jonas never got himself any new clothes. No new shirts or shoes, because he couldn't have regarded them as his property. What had belonged to him before 4 July belonged to him now. He would never get any richer.

He backed the 4WD and the Spider off the truck. The Toyota started first time. He drove it aboard. Although the Spider had been smaller, there was still room for the 4WD.

*

He left the motorway at Laakirchen. The road to Attnang-Puchheim was well signposted, but the house he'd slept in was considerably harder to find. Not having expected to return, he hadn't bothered to memorise the route. Eventually he recalled that the house with the few windows had been near the station. That narrowed it down. Five minutes later he spotted the DS standing beside the kerb.

Jonas trod on the kick-starter and the engine fired. He let the moped putter away for a while. Then he pushed it up the ramp and into the truck and secured it to the side. He counted backwards. It was almost incredible but true: he'd been here only a week ago. It felt like months.

Whether or not he'd turned off all the lights before leaving the house, he had to turn them on again now. Going into the bedroom with the bundle of clothes under his arm, he caught sight of his approaching figure in the wardrobe mirror and dropped his gaze. He put the shirt and trousers back where they belonged.

'Thanks for these.'

He left the room without looking back and headed, stiff-backed, for the front door. He wanted to walk faster, but something held him back. He paid no attention to the curious pictures in the hallway and replaced the car key on its hook.

Just then it struck him that there was

one

more

picture

than last time.

He shut the front door behind him and made his way along the narrow path to the street with marionette-like movements. Nothing in the world could have persuaded him to set foot in that house again

He wasn't mistaken. One of those pictures hadn't been there a week ago. Which one, he didn't know, but there had been seven. Now there were eight.

230

No, he must have miscounted. That was the only explanation. He'd been tired and agitated and soaked to the skin. His memory was playing tricks.

*

On the way to Salzburg he felt hungry. He opened the bag of sweets lying on the bunk behind him and drank some lemonade. The weather was deteriorating. Just before the Mondsee exit he drove into a violent rainstorm. Memories of his last visit were not pleasant and he didn't want to stop, but at the last moment he braked and swerved off down the exit road. The truck's big wiper blades were whipping back and forth across the windscreen, the cab was warm and he had plenty to eat and drink. He felt almost snug. His shotgun was lying beside him. Nothing bad could happen.

There was a crash as he drove through the lido gate. The signboard above the entrance went flying, but he didn't feel the slightest jolt.

The car park roads were narrow and separated by strips of grass enclosed by low walls. Ignoring the rows of saplings he was mowing down, he made straight for the stretch of grass beside the lake. With malicious glee he rammed the Hungarian car, which was still there. He put his foot right down. A metal barrier hurtled through the air. He giggled. The grass was slippery. He braked so as not to plunge the truck into the lake.

Keeping well clear of the water's edge, he reconnoitred the area without getting out, without even stopping. Rain was drumming on the roof of the cab with such violence that he had no need of the inner voice warning him not to get out.

No trace of his tent. Jonas turned and drove as far as the changing cubicles, then back to the car park, which was strewn with branches and debris. He lowered the driver's window and put his arm out into the rain. Levelling his forefinger at an invisible passer-by, he yelled some garbled sentences, the content of which he himself didn't understand.

*

Finding the Salzburg Marriott presented no problem, in part because it had stopped raining. When he got out in front of the hotel he was both alarmed and exultant.

He couldn't hear any music.

The CD of the Mozart symphonies, the one that had been meant to attract people to the scene, had evidently been turned off. Or had turned itself off. Or there'd been a short circuit.

Had someone been here? Was someone here?

He would know soon.

Soon.

Shotgun at the ready, he entered the lobby. The notes on the door and the reception desk had both disappeared, but a video camera had been set up in the middle of the passage, its lens trained on the entrance.

'Who's that?' he shouted.

He fired at a lampshade, which exploded in a shower of glass. The sound of the shot continued to echo for several seconds. Without knowing why, he ran out into the street and looked around. No one in sight. He drew a deep breath.

Step by step, hugging the walls and taking cover behind columns, he ventured back into the hotel. He couldn't stop gulping.

He reached the video camera. No lights were on in the corridor beyond it, which led to the restaurant. Jonas raised the gun, intending to fire into the gloom. He tried to cock the weapon, but it jammed. He flung it away. The missing knife crossed his mind.

'What's the matter, eh? What's the matter? Come on, don't be shy!'

He yelled the words at the darkness. All around, everything was quiet.

'Hang on! I'll be back in a minute!'

He grabbed the camera and dashed outside. Tossing it onto the bunk complete with its tripod, he locked the doors of the cab and drove off.

He pulled into the next service area. There was a TV in the café. He looked at the video camera. It was the model he used himself.

He went and fetched a lead from the truck. Having connected the camera to the TV, he raided the drinks shelf. His toothache was coming back.

He started the tape.

*

A man on a station platform wearing the blue uniform of the Austrian State Railway. Whistle in mouth, he was pumping his bat up and down as though signalling to an engine driver.

It was night-time. A train was standing alongside the platform. The uniformed man blew a shrill blast on his whistle and gesticulated in an incomprehensible manner. As if the train were about to pull out, he ran along beside it and leapt aboard. Recovering his balance, or so it seemed, he disappeared inside the carriage. The scene was so perfectly staged, Jonas had the momentary impression that the train was moving.

He looked more closely, his head swimming. The train was stationary.

A blue sign in the background read: HALLEIN.

The uniformed man did not reappear. A few minutes later, without any footsteps being heard, the tape ran out.

*

Jonas pocketed the tape and replaced the camera and lead in the truck. He acted as if nothing out of the ordinary had happened. Whistling a tune with his hands in his pockets, he sauntered across the car park to the filling station and back. He looked round surreptitiously. Nobody seemed to be watching him, no sign of anyone near him. He was surrounded only by the wind.

*

He felt defenceless without the shotgun. When he passed the station building in Hallein and gained access to the platform by a side entrance, he behaved as if his leg were hurting. He hobbled along, clutching his knee and groaning.

"Oh, ouch! Arrgh!"

Nothing. Nothing spectacular, anyway. According to the noticeboard, the train standing at the platform was bound for Bischofshofen. Jonas got in. Coughing and calling out, he searched each carriage and compartment in turn. The train smelt of stale tobacco smoke and damp.

At the end of the train he jumped out onto the platform again. He was so bewildered, he forgot to limp.

The automatic door that led to the booking hall whirred aside. He sprang back. Motionless, he stared out into the concourse. The door slid shut again. He stepped forward and it opened once more.

Dangling from the roof of the booking hall were eleven ropes with greatcoats attached to them. They looked like hanged men. Only the bodies were missing.

A twelfth was lying on the ground. The rope had snapped.

His legs were numb by the time he hurried back to the truck. He was breathing heavily. The stitch in his side was growing more painful by the second. Now and then he heard himself cry out. His voice sounded hoarse and strange.

*

Jonas got to Kapfenberg late in the afternoon. He still had time, so he drank a coffee in the garden of a café in the main square. He relaxed and stretched his legs, looking around like a visitor checking out his holiday resort. He had passed through Kapfenberg in the train a few times. Apart from that, he hadn't been there since he was a boy.

He went in search of a gun shop. After walking around fruitlessly for half an hour, he went into a phone booth and consulted the directory. There was a gun shop on his route. He returned to the truck.

The shop catered exclusively for sportsmen. He couldn't see a pump-action, and there weren't even any ordinary small-bore shotguns on display. On the other hand, he couldn't complain of the selection of sporting rifles. He helped himself to a Steyr 96 – he seemed to recall reading about its ease of operation somewhere – and filled his pockets with ammunition. Then left the shop in double-quick time. He had to get there before sunset at all costs.

From Krieglach onwards he followed the map. He hadn't been there for twenty years. Besides, never having driven there himself, he'd paid little attention to the route.

Beyond Krieglach the road began to wind and climb. Just as he began to worry that the truck would be too wide for the steadily narrowing road, he came to an intersection. After that the road widened again.

Jonas had estimated that his destination would come into view after half an hour, but forty minutes went by before he thought he recognised a particular bend in the road. He had a feeling his goal lay just beyond it, and this time he wasn't mistaken. Almost obscured by the long grass bordering the road was a wooden sign welcoming him to Kanzelstein. The sign was unfamiliar, but not the view that met his eyes when he rounded the long bend. On the left stood the inn run by Herr and Frau Löhneberger, which only attracted customers from the surrounding villages on Sundays. On the right was the holiday house. Between these two buildings the strip of asphalt petered out into a narrow, dusty track that disappeared into the forest. This was as far as you could go, at least by car. Jonas had found it surprising, even as a boy, that a village could consist of only two buildings, the more so since one of them was occupied only at certain times of the year: at Christmas, New Year and Easter, and during the summer.

Where it came from he didn't know, but the sight of the two lonely buildings filled him with a vague sense of dread. It was as if something was wrong with the place. As if something had been waiting for him and had hidden itself just before he arrived.

That was nonsense, though.

His ears popped. He pinched his nose and breathed out with his lips compressed to equalise the pressure. Kanzelstein was 900 metres above sea level. 'The healthiest altitude of all,' his mother had never failed to mention when they got there, ignoring the look of impatience on his father's face.

Jonas sounded his horn. Once he had satisfied himself that a light flashing in one of the windows of the inn was just the reflection of the sun, he jumped down from the cab. He breathed deeply. The air smelt of forest scents and grass. A pleasant aroma, but fainter than he'd expected.

Parked outside the holiday house was a brightly painted Volkswagen Beetle, and beside it a motorbike. Jonas checked the number plates. The holidaymakers came from Saxony. He peered into the car but could see nothing of importance.

With the rifle under his arm he plodded along the path to the garden gate in front of the holiday house. His heart was beating faster. He couldn't help reflecting, at every step, how often he'd trodden this path, but as an entirely different person leading an entirely different life. Twenty or more years had gone by. The surrounding fields, the forest looming darkly beyond the house, he'd seen them all as a boy. He remembered the house well. Did the house remember him? He had eaten meals, watched TV and slept within its walls. That lay far in the past, but to him it was all still valid.

The front door wasn't locked. That came as no surprise to him. The locals never locked their doors for fear of being thought needlessly suspicious. His parents had also observed this convention and given him many an uneasy night as a child.

There were two rooms on the ground floor: a storeroom and the games room. He glanced inside. The ping-pong table was still there. He even remembered the view from the window.

The first floor was approached by a winding, creaking flight of stairs. There Jonas was confronted by five doors. Three led to bedrooms, the fourth to the bathroom, the fifth to the kitchen-cum-living-room. He went into the first bedroom. The bed had not been made, nor had the suitcase on the table been unpacked. It contained clothes, toilet articles and books. The room smelt stuffy. He opened the window and looked back down the road he'd come by.

In the second bedroom, whose window faced the Löhnebergers' inn, the bed was made up but had not been slept in. An alarm clock was ticking on the rickety bedside table. Startled, Jonas picked it up, but it was a battery-powered model.

He looked around the room once more. The red-and-white-checked bedspread. The faux baroque wooden panelling. The crucifix in the corner. He himself had never slept in this room. It had usually been allocated to Uncle Reinhard and Aunt Lena.

The last and largest bedroom was a regular dormitory. The balcony blinds were lowered. They rose with a familiar rumble when he pulled them up. He looked at the décor. The room resembled a hospital ward. Six single beds stood facing one another in two rows of three. At the foot of each iron bedstead was a bar of the kind a patient's medical record might have hung from. Jonas tapped the metal with his fingernails. He and his parents had slept in this room several times.

He went out onto the balcony and rested his hands on the balustrade. The wood beneath his fingers was warm. In many places it was encrusted with blobs of bird shit the rain had failed to wash off.

The forest stretched away below him. Mountains and hills, wooded slopes and alpine pastures were visible on the skyline. He remembered this view well. This was where his father had sat in a deck chair with his crossword puzzle, and where he himself had hidden from his mother when she wanted to show him something in the garden. They both stood firm to begin with, but his father had sent him downstairs when her voice became steadily shriller.

From the living room he looked out at the garden. The redcurrant bushes were still there. The vine arbour, the benches, the crude wooden table on which they'd played cards, the garden fence, the fruit trees, the rabbit hutch, all were still there. The grass needed cutting and the fence needed repairing, but in other respects the garden was in reasonable condition.

The view triggered a memory. He had dreamt of this garden some years ago. Here among the apple trees he'd seen a man-sized badger cavorting on two legs. The creature, whose face looked like Grandpa Petz from the children's TV programme, came prancing across the garden in a series of strangely rhythmical movements. It bobbed up and down instead of swaying to and fro. After a while, Jonas joined in. He was frightened of the huge beast, which was twice his size, but it showed no hostility towards him. They had danced together, and he'd felt good.

Having carried his gear into the room whose bed had been slept in, he stripped off the duvet cover and sheet and fetched some clean ones from the biggest bedroom. By the time he'd finished he had to turn on the light. He was growing jittery.

He made sure everything that mattered was inside the house, then noted down the truck's kilometre reading and locked it. Passing the old skittle alley, he headed for the entrance to the inn. The decrepit Fiat in the car park must have belonged to the Löhnebergers.

The doorbell tinkled as the door closed behind him. He recognised the sound. The bell had been there in the old days. He waited. Nothing stirred.

A second door led to the bar and restaurant. Jonas wasted no time on reminiscences. He simmered a packet of peas from the freezer, adding some wine and stock cubes to improve their flavour, if only marginally.

Should he climb the stairs to the Löhnebergers' private quarters? He'd never been up there before. A glance out of the window reminded him that the sun was already low in the sky. He put two bottles of beer in a plastic bag.

*

All seemed peaceful.

Jonas strolled through the garden, combing the long grass with his fingers. He picked some redcurrants. They tasted insipid. He spat them out. Behind the house he came to the door of the wood cellar. He'd forgotten about that.

Still standing in the middle of the cellar, which was lit only by such sunlight as could penetrate the little window above the woodpile, was the big tree stump used as a chopping block. The cellar was another of the places where Jonas had hidden from his garden-obsessed mother. He'd used his pocket knife to carve little figures out of blocks of wood, some of them quite successful, and had left a sizeable collection of them behind at the end of the holidays. Although he hadn't liked sitting in this gloomy vault, he preferred the company of spiders and beetles to that of his overzealous mother.

He peered at the corner behind the door. Looked away, looked again. There were some tools there. A spade, a hoe, a broom. And a walking stick.

He looked more closely, then picked up the walking stick. It was decorated with carvings.

Jonas took it outside for a better look. He recognised the carvings. No doubt about it. It was the stick the old man had given him.

He went inside the house. Luckily, he found the key in a little box beside the front door, which he locked behind him. He thought for a moment, then put the key in his pocket. Having opened a bottle of beer, he sat down in the living room and examined the walking stick.

Twenty years.

This walking stick was unlike the bench he was sitting on, or the bed on which he would later lie down, or that wooden chest over there. Twenty years ago it had been his property, and in a certain sense it had never stopped being that. It had stood in its grimy corner, ignored by everyone.

On twenty separate occasions, people nearby had celebrated the last day of the year and let off fireworks, but the walking stick had continued to stand propped against the wall of the wood cellar, unconcerned by Christmas and New Year and visitors singing. Now Jonas had returned and the walking stick still belonged to him.

Much had changed since the last time he saw it. He had left school and done his national service, had girlfriends and lost his mother. He had grown up and started on a life of his own. The Jonas who had last touched this stick had been a child, an entirely different person. Yet not so different, for if Jonas searched his inner self the self he found was the same as the one he remembered. Twenty years ago, when he'd said 'I' with this stick in his hand, he'd meant the same person as he was today. He, Jonas, was that person. He couldn't escape. Would always be that person. Whatever happened. Never anyone else. Not Martin. Not Peter. Not Richard. Only himself.

*

Jonas couldn't bear to watch the night at its work. The blinds came rattling down as he lowered them. He connected the camera to the TV and put in last night's tape.

He saw himself walk past the camera and get into bed.

After an hour the Sleeper tossed around for the first time.

After two hours he turned over on his side.

He continued to sleep in that position until the tape ran out.

Nothing, absolutely nothing had happened. Jonas switched off. Midnight. He was thirsty. He'd polished off the second bottle of beer a long time ago. All he could find in his bag of snacks from the filling station was a packet of pumpernickel, some chocolate bars and some cans of lemonade. He wanted beer.

He made his way out onto the landing, tapping the wall with his knuckles as he went. He turned off the light and peered out of the window. The darkness outside was impenetrable. Clouds had blotted out the stars. There was no moon. He sensed rather than saw the track that led past the skittle alley to the inn.

Uncle Reinhard had wanted to make a bet with him one night: Jonas was to go and get a bottle of lemonade from the inn. All by himself and without a torch, he was to sally forth into the darkness and buy a bottle from the Löhnebergers, who were serving some late customers. The banknote Uncle Reinhard produced from his pocket made Jonas stare wide-eyed and made his parents quietly groan.

Nothing to it, they all said briskly. There was a light above the inn door. It was only really dark near the skittle alley. He was chicken if he didn't go. No fuss now, just get it over with quickly.

No, he said.

Uncle Reinhard came closer, waving the banknote under his nose. They were downstairs, just inside the front door. Jonas looked at the path that led past the skittle alley, looked at each grown-up in turn.

No, he repeated.

And that was that, even though his mother was gesticulating and pulling angry faces behind Uncle Reinhard's back. Uncle Reinhard had laughed and patted him on the shoulder. Jonas would soon discover that ghosts didn't exist, he said. His parents had turned away and hardly spoken to him for the next two days.

'Don't kid yourself,' Jonas said, vainly scanning the darkness for some recognisable shapes at least.

He turned his head abruptly. He couldn't get rid of the feeling that sooner or later, when he looked over his shoulder like that, the wolf-bear would be standing there. It would be there, and he would have known it would appear.

Leaving the rifle behind, he went downstairs. He opened the front door and stepped out onto the weather-worn flagstones of the forecourt.

It was cold. And pitch-black. No wind, no crickets chirping, no sound save the grating of pebbles on the flag-stones beneath his feet. He couldn't get used to the absence of sounds made by living creatures. Wasps, bees and flies could be annoying. He had cursed their persistent hum-ming and buzzing a thousand times. The barking of dogs had sometimes struck him as a diabolical nuisance, and even some birdsong was strident rather than easy on the ear. But he would have preferred the whine of a mosquito to the relentless silence prevailing here. Even, perhaps, the roar of a prowling lion.

He had to go, he knew.

'Well, this is it.'

He pretended to be holding something in his hand as if shielding it from view. Meanwhile, he ran through the forthcoming excursion in his mind's eye. He pictured him-self opening the garden gate, making his way past the skit-tle alley and, finally, reaching the inn's terrace. He would open the door, turn on the lights, get two bottles of beer from the bar, turn out the lights and return by the same route.

'Really nice,' he muttered, scratching his palm with a fingernail.

In thirty seconds he would set off. In five minutes at most he would be back. In five minutes' time he would be holding two bottles. He would also have proved something. Five minutes were bearable, they were a mere nothing. He could count off the seconds and think of something else.

His legs felt numb. He stood motionless on the flag-stones with the open door behind him. Minutes went by.

So he was wrong. He'd been mistaken when he'd thought it would all be over in five minutes. He'd been destined to set off a few minutes later. The time he'd thought would mark the end of his ordeal was really its beginning.

He concentrated on making his mind a blank and setting off.

He thought of nothing, thought of nothing, thought of nothing. And then set off.

He bumped into the garden gate. Opened it. Stumbled through the darkness. Groped his way along the wooden wall of the skittle alley.

A crunch of gravel beneath his feet announced that he'd reached the car park. He glimpsed the terrace and hurried on. I'll kill you, he thought.

The bell tinkled. He didn't think he could bear it. His hand felt for the light switch. He screwed up his eyes, then cautiously opened them and looked round. Don't think, carry on.

'Good evening, I've come for some beer!'

He turned on all the lights, laughing harshly, and helped himself to two bottles of beer. Without turning off the lights he made his way back across the terrace to the car park. The glow from the inn windows was enough for him to see where he was going. But he could also see where the light ended and the sea of darkness awaited him.

When he plunged into the gloom he felt he wouldn't make it. He would start thinking again any minute. And that would be that.

He broke into a run. Tripped and recovered his balance at the last moment. Kicked the garden gate open. Bounded across the threshold, slammed the front door and locked it. Slid to the floor with his back against it, a cold bottle of beer in either hand.

At 2 a.m. he was lying in bed, checking to see how much of the second bottle was left. The camera was facing the bed, but he hadn't started it yet. He did so and turned over on his side.

He awoke and peered at the alarm clock. It was 3 a.m. He must have fallen asleep at once.

The camera was humming.

He thought he could hear other sounds overhead. Creaking footsteps, an iron ball rolling across the floor. At the same time, he was in no doubt that those sounds were all in his imagination.

He couldn't help reflecting that the camera was filming him at that moment. Him, not the Sleeper. Would he spot the difference when he watched the tape? Would he remember?

His bladder was bursting. He threw off the bedclothes. As he passed the camera he waved, gave a twisted grin and said: 'It's me, not the Sleeper!'

He padded barefoot along the passage to the bathroom. On the way back he gave the camera another wave. He patted the dust off the soles of his feet before getting into bed. Then pulled the bedclothes over his ears.

20

He blinked at the camera. It hadn't been moved. Nor, it seemed, had anything else.

It was 4 August. A month had gone by. At this hour four weeks ago he'd been waiting in vain for a bus. That was how it had begun.

He opened the shutters. A sunny day. Not a branch or blade of grass was stirring. He got dressed. He felt the notebook in his pocket. He opened it at the first blank page and wrote:

I wonder where you'll be on 4 September and how you're doing. And how you've been doing in the previous four weeks. Jonas, 4 August, Kanzelstein. Standing at the bedroom table, dressed, tired.

He looked at the picture on the wall. To judge by the battered frame and faded colours, it was quite old. It depicted a lone sheep in a field. The animal was dolled up in jeans and a red sweater. It wore socks on its feet and, on its head, a hat cocked at a rakish angle. This curious sight reminded him of his dream.

He'd been looking out of the window of his flat on the Brigittenauer embankment. A bird landed on the arm of a chair standing on a balcony that his flat didn't have. He was delighted to see the bird. A living creature at last!

All at once the bird's head changed, becoming broader
and more elongated. Its expression was mean and angry,
as if Jonas were to blame for all that was happening to it.
Under his intent gaze the bird underwent another transformation. It developed a hedgehog's head and its body
grew bigger. Jonas was now confronted by a hedgehog's
head on the body of a millipede one and a half metres long.
The millipede curled up and scratched its face, which meta-
morphosed into that of a man. The human millipede
gasped, its tongue protruding as if it were being throttled.
Its countless little legs were flailing madly, and pink foam
oozed from its nostrils.

The head changed yet again. It turned into that of an
eagle and a dog in quick succession. Neither the eagle nor
the dog looked the way they should have looked. All these
creatures gazed at him. The look in their eyes told him that
they knew him of old. And that he knew them.

*

He breakfasted on pumpernickel and instant coffee. Then
he opened all the windows and prowled around the house.

He spent quite a while gazing out over the countryside
from the south-facing balcony. Its dimensions puzzled him.
Everything looked smaller and more cramped than he remembered. The balcony itself, for instance. It had once
been a terrace spacious enough to play football on. Now he
was standing on an ordinary balcony some four metres
long and one-and-a-half wide. It was the same with the garden. He could have walked from end to end in well under
a minute. He used to think of the Löhnebergers' inn as a really big establishment. Now he saw that the open space
outside could accommodate no more than four cars parked
side by side. Yesterday he'd counted the tables in the bar.
There were six.

As for the view from the balcony, in his imagination it had stretched for hundreds of kilometres. He now discovered that he could see little further than the next valley. His eye was brought up short by a range of hills no more than twenty kilometres away. The only really sizeable feature was the forest behind the house, which marked the extent of the property.

In the games room he recognised the cupboard in which the table-tennis bats and balls and a spare net were kept. He examined its wooden sides for inscriptions and messages. He took out a bat and began to play against himself. He hit the ball high, to give himself time to get to the other end and return the shot. The sound of the ball striking the table top went echoing round the almost empty room.

This was where his father had taught him to play. At first Jonas had made the mistake of standing too near the table, which exasperated his father. 'No, back! Further back!' he would yell, and he'd been known to hurl his bat at the net when annoyed with his incorrigible pupil. Jonas's mother and Aunt Lena didn't enjoy playing table tennis, and his father was no match for Uncle Reinhard.

The handle of the bat had lost some of its plastic coating. Jonas's hand stuck to it. He tossed it back into the cupboard, took out another and gave it an experimental swing, turning it over in his hand. It looked familiar.

He eyed the bat with a touch of emotion. He had always picked it in the old days because he preferred its black surface and ribbed handle. Now he couldn't see any appreciable difference between this bat and the others.

Here. This was the place. His father had stood over there, he himself on this side.

He flexed his knees to re-create a child's-eye view of the table and leapt to and fro as if diving for the ball.

His bat. His walking stick, too. From a time that was long gone. That would never come back. A time he could never re-enter, never use again.

*

Early that afternoon Jonas cooked himself some lunch at the inn. A plateful of noodles and potatoes from the larder he'd discovered behind an inconspicuous door. He ate a lot and drew himself a beer. It tasted and smelt bad. He poured it away and opened a bottle instead.

He sat down on the terrace with the bottle and a fleece belonging to the landlord tied round his waist by the arms. He had also put on a frayed old peasant hat he had found hanging on a hook. The sun was scorching hot, but a strong wind was blowing. He finished off the bottle. Then he thought of the transceiver. He went inside and spent half an hour looking for it until he was satisfied it had gone.

It had been there that Christmas nearly twenty-five years ago, but it hadn't been working. They were snowed in, the roads were impassable, and then it happened: Leo the waiter, who was helping out over the holidays, gashed his hand chopping wood. Although the wound wasn't thought to be too serious, it became infected. They couldn't call a doctor because all the phone lines had been brought down by avalanches. To everyone's alarm, Leo was confined to bed with blood poisoning. They were afraid he would die.

Jonas happened to hear about the defective transceiver. The grown-ups, who thought he wanted to play some game or show off, gave him sidelong, pitying looks when he asked to see it. One look at the relay circuit, however, and Jonas realised that he really could be of help. He had drawn so many circuit diagrams in physics, an optional subject he was studying at school, that he asked for a length of copper wire and a soldering iron.

A few minutes later, with his heart thumping, he gestured grandly at the transceiver and announced that it was working again. They all thought at first that he was joking. In fact his father showed signs of wanting to chuck him out of the window, transceiver and all. Jonas turned it on. As soon as the landlord heard it crackling he dashed over and sent an SOS. The helicopter that flew Leo to hospital landed two hours later.

Frau Löhneberger wept. Herr Löhneberger slapped Jonas on the back, stood him an ice cream, and invited the whole family to a meal on the house. Jonas thought he would be in for more praise and more ice creams, but the incident wasn't mentioned again after a day or two. Nor was any further reference made to a reporter who had wanted to put something about it in the local paper.

*

Once in the forest, Jonas put on the fleece and zipped it up. It didn't seem to have rained here for some time. Little puffs of dust arose at every step he took up the path to the alpine hut. He recalled wearing a hood as a boy, for fear of ticks, which he wrongly believed to lurk in trees. Now, even one of those revolting little creatures would have been a comfort to him.

He thought he remembered which way to go. To his surprise, however, nothing looked familiar. It wasn't until he reached the hut from which he'd collected milk, and where he'd been presented with the walking stick, that images came to life in his mind's eye.

One summer holiday he was allowed to bring a school-friend whose parents had naturally, at his father's insistence, been expected to pay for their son's board and lodging. Jonas had decided to invite Leonhard. And it was with Leonhard, he now remembered, that he'd been up here one day. They had prowled around the hut like two Redskins planning to raid a ranch. Then, when the grizzled old giant of a man appeared in his doorway, the raiders' courage had suddenly deserted them. They had bidden the trapper a sheepish good morning and vanished into the undergrowth.

Jonas surveyed the mountainside, rifle over shoulder and peasant hat on head. He rested for a minute or two. Should he break into the hut? No, he didn't feel hungry or thirsty, so he left the clearing and started climbing again.

Nothing looked familiar to him.

Now and then he heard a crack, like someone stepping on a fallen branch. He froze, listening.

Jonas suppressed his mounting alarm. There was no need to be scared, he'd proved that last night. No one was after him. The sounds he was hearing sprang from his overheated imagination or were chance natural phenomena. Twigs snapping by themselves, perhaps. He was alone.

'You aren't there either,' he said, looking over his shoulder. He repeated the words and laughed aloud despite himself, as if he'd cracked a joke.

His mobile was showing half past five. The battery was nearly flat. There was no dialling tone, he noticed. That worried him, but why? Who would he have called? All the same, it was like a warning that he'd strayed too far. He turned back.

And lengthened his stride.

Something was welling up inside him. Growing stronger.

To take his mind off it he recalled how, as a boy, he'd gone looking for Attila's grave in these woods. He'd heard tell of it. According to legend, the king of the Huns had died while marching through Austria and been buried in a forest. Any hummock might conceal his tomb, and if Jonas found the spot it would make him rich and famous. He had also combed these woods with Leonhard. Every time they had come to a sizeable mound of earth they'd looked at each other and discussed its chances like experts. When out by himself he had only searched the edge of the forest within sight of the holiday house or the inn.

The path was so overgrown with bracken, he kept tripping over hidden stones. Twice the rifle dug him hard in the side, knocking the breath out of him. He was annoyed he'd taken it with him, for all the use it had been.

As if he'd bumped into a wall, he stopped short. It took him a long moment to realise what he'd just heard: a bell. A cowbell.

There – there it went again, over to his left.

'Wait! Now you'll see something!' he yelled.

Holding his rifle in front of his chest, he dashed in the direction he thought the sound had come from. To his bewilderment, the third clang seemed to come from even further to his left. He changed direction. He gave no thought to what he would find and what he would do when he found it. He simply ran on.

The sixth time the bell clanged, he felt unsure whether he was heading towards it or away from it.

'Hooo!'

No answer. The bell, too, remained silent.

He looked around. A geocaching tree caught his eye. Something told him he was on the right track. He hurried past the tree and squeezed through some bushes. Beyond them he came out in a small clearing with a lone birch tree standing in the middle.

The bell was hanging from one of its branches.

He scanned the area before going over to it. It was suspended on a surprisingly thin length of cord. The metal rims were flecked with rust, but there was no indication of how long the bell had been there or who had hung it up. It clanged whenever the wind blew, that was the only certainty.

It occurred to Jonas how the bell might have got there, but that theory was too unpleasant to be credited.

He looked for the route he had come by. Having ventured too far, he needed to get his bearings again. It wasn't long before he thought he knew where he was and where he would come upon a path. He set off in that direction. Ten minutes later, when he had merely strayed even deeper into the forest, he was overcome by the feeling he'd had before.

'Well, Attila, coming to get me?'

He tried to give the words a hint of mockery, but his voice sounded feebler than he'd intended.

He looked back. Dense forest. He didn't even know which direction he'd come from.

He ploughed straight on. On and on. You had to look for fixed points, enlist the help of the sun or the stars, that's what he'd been taught as a boy. But he'd never got lost before, and he'd forgotten how you made sure of going straight ahead instead of in a circle.

After another hour he thought he recognised a particular spot. However, he couldn't decide whether he'd passed this way before or after he heard the cowbell. Or even twenty years ago.

It surprised him how quickly the light was fading.

Ahead of him was a small clearing overgrown with knee-high bracken and hazel bushes. The trunks of the surrounding beech trees were thickly coated with moss. The air smelt of mushrooms, but there were none to be seen.

He hadn't noticed it while on the move, but as he stood there, lost in thought, it struck him how cold it was getting. Mechanically, he rubbed his arms, chest and thighs. He took a few steps. His legs were leaden and his back ached. He was thirsty.

In the middle of the clearing he sat down. Visible overhead was a rectangular patch of blue sky tinged with red.

At that moment, he knew the wolf-bear would appear tonight. He would hear crackling sounds, then footsteps. And then the beast would burst through the bushes over there and pounce on him. Huge, unstoppable, impersonal. Invincible.

'No, please don't,' he whispered feebly, tears springing to his eyes.

The darkness frightened him even more than the increasing cold. The battery in his mobile was flat, so he didn't know what time it was. It couldn't be much after seven. He had obviously strayed deep into the forest.

He took one of the little cards from his pocket.

Shout loudly!, it read.

The fact that chance had dealt him a suitable instruction raised his hopes. He got to his feet, the better to shout.

'Hello! I'm here! Over here! Help!'

He turned and shouted again in the opposite direction. He didn't dare shoot because he'd left the bag of cartridges behind on the old chest. Although he didn't think he would have to fight off something or someone in the immediate future, the feel of the smooth wooden butt reassured him. At least he wasn't completely defenceless.

But . . . What if nobody came?

What if he couldn't find his way back?

He peered in all directions. He shut his eyes and listened to his inner self. Was this how it would end? Ashes to ashes, dust to dust?

He tried hard to make his mind a blank. Took deep breaths, imagined himself elsewhere. Some place where there were no goosebumps, no hunger and no suspicious rustling sounds. With Marie. In bed with Marie, thigh to thigh. Feeling her softness, her warmth. Feeling her breath on his face and the pressure of her hands. Inhaling her scent, hearing the faint grunt as she turned over without losing contact with him.

He wasn't alone. She was with him. He always had her with him if he chose. All at once, she was far nearer to him than three or four weeks ago, when he thought he'd lost her.

He was feeling better. His fear had dwindled to a growl in the background. He was calm. Tomorrow morning he would find his way back. He would go home. And then he would go looking for Marie. He mustn't fall asleep, that was all.

He opened his eyes.

It was dark.

*

It must have been about midnight when the stiffness in his arms and legs became unbearable. He tossed the rifle into the grass and sat down.

His thoughts had stopped obeying him hours ago. They drifted, took on colour, lost it again. Enveloped him, were enveloped. The wolf-bear appeared in them, he couldn't chase it away. The creature radiated a savage power and determination that tormented him until, without his doing anything, it disappeared and he was filled with a mysterious warmth and cheerfulness. He felt tempted to get up and go on looking for the way back, but the knowledge that he would soon be governed by other emotions restrained him.

He looked up. Convinced that he was being stared at by someone seated almost within arm's reach but invisible to him. At the same time, he noticed that his eyelids took longer to blink than they should. Alarmed, he reached for the gun. It seemed two or even three times further away than it had been. He couldn't see his hand, but he sensed that its progress towards the gun was becoming steadily, inexorably slower. He lowered his head and shook off his hat. He wasn't moving at all, he felt. Listening to the rustle of the trees, he noticed that every sound consisted of many individual notes, and that these, in their turn, were made up of acoustic particles.

He didn't know how he managed to snap out of this. His willpower proved stronger than his inertia. He jumped up, levelled the rifle – and waited to see what he would do next.

He laughed.

To his own surprise.

*

3 a.m. Possibly 2 a.m., possibly half past three. He didn't dare go to sleep. Although his joints were aching and red rings were dancing before his eyes. Every sound the night wind struck from the trees echoed in his head. Trying to keep reality and imagination apart, he looked around. He pretended he was having problems with his shoelaces or the zip of the landlord's fleece, just so he could scoff and swear aloud.

Whenever he had thought about God and death, the same image had always recurred: that of the body from which all derived and to which all returned. He had doubted the Church's teachings. God wasn't one, he was everyone. What other people called God, he saw as a principle in the form of a body. A principle that sent everyone off to live and then report back. God was a body that sent off human beings, possibly animals and plants as well, or even stones, raindrops and light, to acquaint themselves with everything that went to make up life. Returning to the body at the end of their existence, they shared their experiences with God and absorbed those of other people. That way, they all learnt what it was like to be an arable farmer in Switzerland or a motor mechanic in Karachi. A teacher in Mombasa or a whore in Brisbane. Or an Austrian adviser on interior decoration. What it was like to be a waterlily, a stork, a frog, a gazelle in the rain, a honey bee in springtime or a bird. A woman in heat, or a man. A success, a failure. Fat or slim, robust or frail. A murderer or a victim of murder. A rock. An earthworm. A stream. A puff of wind.

Living life in order to return and bestow that life on others. That had been his notion of God. And now he wondered if the disappearance of all life meant that God and the others had no interest in his life. That his life was redundant.

6 a.m. He sensed the dawn before he saw it. It didn't come in its usual form, as a kind of resurrection or liberation. It was merely cold. As soon as it was light enough for him to avoid bumping into trees, he got to his feet. His teeth were chattering, the dew-sodden shirt and trousers clinging to his body.

He spent the first hour trying to get his bearings, following false trails, looking out for landmarks. All he saw was a monotonous alternation of bushes and undergrowth, glades and dense forest. None of it looked familiar.

Later he came to a broad clearing. There he remained until the sun had driven the cold from his bones. His thirst, which was steadily intensifying, made him move on. No longer centred on his stomach, his hunger had induced a feeling of general weakness. His dearest wish was to lie down and go to sleep.

From then on he proceeded haphazardly. He consulted the cards in his pocket, but their only injunctions were *Red Cat* and *Botticelli*. He trudged on with his head down. Until a sound came to his ears, a liquid sound. It came from his right.

He didn't make a dash for it at once; he looked in all directions. No one was watching him. No would-be practical joker.

He set off to his right. His ears hadn't deceived him, the gurgling sound grew louder. He fought his way through the undergrowth, ripped his trousers on a bramble bush that scratched his hands and arms as well. Then he saw the stream. Clear, cold water. He drank until his belly almost burst and rolled over on his back, panting.

Images arose before him. Of the office, of his father, of home. Of Marie. Of earlier years, when he'd had a different hairstyle. Of a younger Jonas with all kinds of interests. Flirting with Inge in the park, arguing heatedly with friends in cafés, counting empty beer bottles in the kitchen the morning after. As an adolescent in front of the brightly lit windows of sex shops. As a boy on a pushbike, smiling as only children smile.

He clenched his fists and punched the ground. No, he would find his way out of this forest.

He got up and patted his trousers down, then followed the course of the stream. For one thing, because he didn't want to die of thirst; for another, because streams usually led somewhere, quite often to houses.

He took the easiest route. Sometimes the stream narrowed and he leapt across it, hoping that it wouldn't become a trickle and peter out. Sometimes it sank into the ground, but he always found the spot where it re-emerged into the light. He shook his fist.

'Hahaha, we'll soon see!'

He no longer felt tired and hungry. He walked on and on until the forest suddenly ended. He found himself standing on a slab of rock over which the stream plunged, almost inaudibly, into the depths.

Before him lay a broad expanse of open countryside. To his front, separated from him by a deep gorge, he could

258

make out a small village. It took him a while to identify the dark specks he saw in the surrounding fields as bales of hay. He counted a dozen houses and as many outbuildings. There was no sign of life. He estimated that the village was ten kilometres away, possibly fifteen.

Immediately in front of him was a drop of at least 100 metres. A precipitous wall of rock, and no path leading down into the valley.

He couldn't account for it, because he felt sure he'd never been there, but the distant village looked familiar.

He turned left. Keeping to the edge of the plateau, he walked until the village had long disappeared from view. He encountered no road, no track, no fence or signpost, not even a notice put up by the Forestry Commission or the Alpine Association.

Worried that he was getting further and further away from Kanzelstein and the surrounding villages, he retraced his steps. Three hours later he was back at the place where the stream plunged down the gorge. Having drunk his fill, he leapt across it with contemptuous ease. He looked over at the village. It was as lifeless as before.

Something about this panorama alarmed him. Ignoring it, Jonas walked on. He pulled his hat brim down with his left hand to avoid having to see the village out of the corner of his eye. He felt like shouting something. But he was too weak.

*

In a big clearing he waited for darkness to come. He had no illusions about his fate. He even felt vaguely thankful that it was happening like this, here, where he preserved at least an inkling of what had been, and that he hadn't ended his life in a lift immobilised between two floors.

And yet . . . Something within him could not believe that this was the end.

He took a card from his pocket.

Sleep, he read.

He crumpled it between his fingers.

*

Jonas had often thought about death. He managed to banish the thought of that dark, looming wall for months at a time, but then it recurred day and night. What was death? A joke you understood only after the event? Was it good, evil? And how would it strike him down? Cruelly or mercifully? Would a blood vessel in his skull burst? Would pain rob him of his reason? Would he feel a stab in the chest or be felled by a stroke? Would his guts churn? Would he vomit for fear of what lay ahead? Would he be knifed by a madman, so that he still had time to grasp what was happening to him? Would he be tormented by some disease, fall from the sky in a plane, drive into a brick wall? Would it be: Five . . . four . . . three . . . two . . . one . . . zero? Or: Five, four, three, two, one, zero? Or: fivefourthreetwoonezero?

Or would he grow old and die in his asleep?

And was there someone who already knew this?

And was it all preordained, or could he still do something about it?

Whatever happened, he'd told himself, there would be people who thought of him and reflected on the fact that he'd died in such and such a manner, not another. On the fact that he'd always wondered how it would happen, and now they knew. Who wondered how they themselves would die some day.

But it wouldn't be like that. No one would ever reflect on his death. No one would ever know how he'd died.

Had Amundsen wondered the same thing adrift on his ice floe, or struggling in the water, or afloat on the wing of his plane, or wherever it had happened? Or had he assumed that his body would be found? But they never did find it, Roald. You simply disappeared.

He could hardly see his hand before his face, but he didn't reach for the rifle lying beside him in the grass. He stretched out on his back and stared into the darkness.

What lay in store for him, he had wondered, transition or extinction?

Whatever his destination, he had always wanted his final thought to be of love. Love as a word. Love as a condition. Love as a principle. Love was to be his final thought and ultimate emotion. A yes, not a no, regardless of whether he was only being transported elsewhere or coming to a full stop. He had always hoped he would manage to think of it. Of love.

21

Jonas awoke, roused by the cold and the drops of moisture on his face. He opened his eyes without grasping where he was. Then it dawned on him that he was in the forest, and that it had started to rain. It was daylight, the sun no more than a pale glimmer in a mass of grey cloud. He shut his eyes again and didn't move.

Some inner voice urged him to his feet. Without thinking, he set off in a particular direction. Leaning on the rifle, he trudged up slopes, scrambled over fences, stumbled across muddy hollows. He passed a barn but didn't stop. He felt he mustn't diverge from his route. As if through a veil, he realised that the rain was lashing his body. His sense of time had deserted him completely. He might have been on the move for one hour or four – he didn't know.

A valley opened out in front of him. Some buildings came into view. The inn was the first one he recognised. All he felt was the wind and rain on his skin. No sense of relief.

*

He opened his eyes. There were no trees to be seen nearby. He wasn't in the forest, he was lying in front of the garden fence.

He stood up and looked down at himself. His clothes were in tatters, his forearms covered with thin red scratches, his fingernails as black as a motor mechanic's, and he'd lost his hat. Still, he seemed to be largely unscathed. He wasn't in pain, either.

The garden gate squeaked. He noticed, as he walked up the gravel path to the front door, that he'd left the rifle behind. Instinctively, he clenched his fists.

'Hooo!'

His voice went echoing round the house.

He stuck his head into the storeroom, the games room. Nothing had changed. He dashed into all the bedrooms. Nothing seemed to have been touched.

He avoided looking at his reflection in the bathroom mirror, but one brief glance was enough: there was something written on his forehead.

The glass felt smooth and cool beneath his fingers as he locked eyes with the face in the mirror. The inscription on his forehead was in mirror writing, so he read it the right way round:

MUDJAS!

Jonas had no idea what Mudjas meant.

He peered at the word more closely. It seemed to have been written with a marker pen, and he felt sure he knew which one. He would find it outside in the cab of his truck.

He stared at the reflected letters.

Perhaps he's real and I'm the reflection?

Without removing the fingers of his left hand from the glass, he used his right hand to wash his face. At first he tried soap. When the letters merely faded a little, he resorted to a scrubbing brush lying on the floor, which had presumably been used for scouring the tiles. He held it under the hot tap, then scrubbed his forehead.

Having showered without thinking of the wolf-bear, he threw his torn clothes into the dustbin and changed into

263

some clean ones. He couldn't help reflecting, when his gaze fell on the things in his suitcase, that the last time he'd stood there, looking into the suitcase, he hadn't known what lay ahead. He hadn't known that he would be lost in the forest for two days. And this suitcase had lain on the table the whole time. It hadn't moved, just waited. Had been neither looked at nor touched.

*

In the inn kitchen he plugged his mobile into the charger. He was surprised to see that it was already 4 p.m. by the digital clock on the stove. The rain had stopped, but clouds were scudding across the sky and the sun was invisible.

While the saucepan of water for the beans was rattling away on the hob, Jonas went in search of things he remembered. All the electrical appliances in the kitchen were new, like the TV, which was connected to a satellite dish on the roof. A soup tureen on a shelf looked familiar. He took it down and turned it round in his hands. It was almost deep and wide enough for him to have stuck his head in it.

He picked up a blue beer mug inscribed *Lotta*. He hadn't thought of Lotta once since he'd been here, oddly enough, although he'd often helped the crippled maidservant to feed the hens. This had evidently been her personal mug. She was a beer drinker, he remembered.

He made another leisurely tour of the building. Occasionally he would touch some object, shut his eyes and commit the moment to memory. Days or weeks hence, perhaps months, he would shut his eyes and picture himself touching this lamp or that bottle opener. He would remember what he had thought and felt at the time. And that bygone moment was now. Right now.

He made sure all the windows were closed. He took a wooden-handled spoon from the taproom as a souvenir and stowed some beer in a plastic bag. Leaning against the old wood-burning stove, he ate the beans salted and tossed in garlic. He washed up. The bell over the door tinkled one more time. Then he was standing on the terrace.

He knew he would never return.

*

Jonas took the walking stick to the wood cellar and put it back behind the door. He contemplated it for a while, then gave it a nod and went outside.

He locked the front door of the holiday house and barricaded it with an armchair from the games room, fully aware that this was less a safety measure than an aid to preserving the illusion that he hadn't entirely lost the initiative.

Then he sat down on the chest in the living room and drank some beer.

He had played cards and Memory over there.

He had sat on that bench and listened to the grown-ups talking over their wine.

He had hidden in this chest when playing hide-and-seek with Uncle Reinhard.

He added the empty bottle to the collection behind the door and helped himself to another. Fetching the camera from the bedroom, he turned it on and wound the tape back. While plugging in the leads he remembered a dream he must have had at some stage in the last forty-eight hours.

They were walking across a big field. He, Marie and hundreds of other people. He spoke to no one and no one spoke to him. In fact, he didn't even see the others' faces. They were there, though, all around him.

A monster was coming. It was rumoured to have been seen on that hillside over there. Several people claimed, wordlessly, that it was in an orchard on the far side of the valley. From time to time a rumbling sound could be heard, followed by a crash that shook the ground like an explosive charge. That was it, they said. It was roaming around and hunting people down.

Then he saw it. The creature had a hump like a camel, but it was far broader and heavier, and it walked semierect. Protruding from its back were two stunted wings. Over three metres tall, it went trampling across a lovely orchard. People were running away from it, screaming in panic. Most frightening of all was the way the ground shook. Those tremors indicated how huge and dangerous the creature was.

Jonas was standing some twenty metres away. The winged bear was hunting people, and with a speed that didn't seem possible, given its immense bulk.

But no, the worst thing wasn't its appearance and the tremors, as he'd initially thought. It was the fact that this creature actually existed. That it was rampaging around in defiance of all he'd thought possible.

Winged bear, he wrote in his notebook. *1500 kg. No voice. Rampaging, close.*

He glanced through his notes on other dreams. Many referred to animals or creatures resembling animals. That surprised him. Animals had never been important to him. Although he respected them as fellow inhabitants of the planet, it had never occurred to him to acquire a pet.

Something about his entries puzzled him, but he couldn't identify it. He read them over again and again. At last it dawned on him.

His handwriting.

It seemed to have undergone an almost imperceptible change. The letters sloped a little further to the left than before and he pressed harder when he wrote. What this signified, he didn't know.

He was feeling heavy with fatigue.

He opened the window overlooking the garden. Nothing to be heard but the wind. He secured the bar and lowered the blinds.

Then he tiptoed into the dormitory and locked the balcony door, securing the wooden bars there too. Having checked the other windows, he locked the door leading to the ground floor and removed the key.

He pressed the camera's play button and sat down on the wooden chest.

*

He saw himself walk past the camera and get beneath the covers. Before long he heard regular breathing. The Sleeper lay there without moving.

Jonas stared at the screen. Although the beer was taking the edge off his agitation, he kept glancing over his shoulder at the big old dining table. The eight chairs. The three-legged stool. The wood-burning stove.

The Sleeper got out of bed, waved at the camera and said: 'It's me, not the Sleeper!'

Jonas heard a door opening, footsteps receding. A minute later the toilet was flushed. He saw himself give the camera another wave and get beneath the covers.

He rewound the tape. It wasn't the Sleeper he looked at during the minutes before he got up and went to the toilet. It was himself, he was awake and ruminating. He got up, went to the toilet and got into bed again. And he looked no different from the Sleeper.

He let the tape run on. The Sleeper was snoring, one arm over his eyes as if dazzled by the light. He turned over twice before the tape ended. Nothing else happened.

*

He took the camera back into the bedroom and inserted a new tape. Then he got undressed and went to the bathroom to clean his teeth. He didn't turn his back on the door for an instant, nor did he look in the mirror.

His last thoughts before going to sleep were of Marie. They had often been apart. The only time it had troubled him was when she'd spent a few days in Australia between flights. They were so far apart that synchronicity was impossible. When he looked up at the sun, he couldn't picture her doing likewise at exactly the same moment. That was the hardest thing. Although far apart, they should at least have been able to lock eyes in space. He had consoled himself by imagining that the sun, on its journey westwards, was conveying a look from her to him.

Had they locked eyes in the sky today?

22

England. The idea came to him while driving, when his mind had been blank for minutes on end. He now had a plan. Or an idea, at least. An idea of how to get to England.

He wanted to be home by early that afternoon, and he made it. With a final hiss of its air brakes, the truck pulled up outside the building next door. Then silence fell.

He tore the strips of sticky tape off the door of his flat. It felt cool inside. He opened all the windows to let the warm air flood in. He went round the flat, opening cupboards and drawers, singing and yodelling and whistling. He talked about his trip, putting in incidents that hadn't occurred, but he said nothing about his adventure in the forest or the toothache that was troubling him more and more.

He heated up the last two tins of bean soup. Then, taking the rifle with him, he backed the Toyota out of the truck.

*

The items on display at the gun shop were dusty. Other than that, nothing had changed since his last visit. Taking a pump-action shotgun from the cabinet, he loaded it, went out into the street and fired in the air. It functioned perfectly. He went back into the shop and stocked up with ammunition.

He drove at random through the city centre. Occasionally he stopped and turned off the engine. He sat there, gazing at some familiar or unfamiliar building, drumming on the wheel or looking through the text messages on his mobile.

I'm just overhead.

He dialled her number. It rang. Five times, ten times. He wondered for the hundredth time why her recorded message didn't cut in. The sound of her voice might have made it easier for him to reach a decision. On the other hand, he couldn't discount the possibility that he might have reacted to it as he did to music or films. With shock, in other words.

His eye fell on the two guns on the passenger seat. An idea came to him.

From force of habit, Jonas looked in the rear-view mirror as he drove off. He caught a momentary glimpse of his eyes – *his* eyes. He wrenched the mirror off the windscreen and hurled it out of the window.

There was no sign that anyone had been at Rüdigergasse either. The slip of paper he'd left on the door was still there. He didn't go inside the flat itself. With his new shotgun at the ready and the rifle slung across his back, he went down to the cellar. The shot-riddled door was standing ajar. He turned on the light.

The tap was dripping.

He stole along the passage. His father's compartment was empty save for a few boxes. He unslung the rifle and propped it against the wall, stepped back and looked at it leaning, all by itself, against the grimy brickwork.

He had no idea why he did this. It simply pleased him to think that this gun would stand here for all eternity. The rifle that had been slumbering in a cabinet in Kapfenberg until four days ago had spent a long time, certainly weeks, possibly months, in that gun shop. Now it was here. Perhaps it was pining for its former surroundings, perhaps its former neighbours in that shop in Kapfenberg were missing it too. It used to be there, now it was here. That was the way of the world.

'Goodbye,' Jonas said softly as he left the cellar.

*

He went into a nearby pub and defrosted a frozen meal. Meanwhile, he wandered round the bar.

The people in the newspaper lying on the bar had been given black beards with a ballpoint. Many of their heads had sprouted horns and some of their backsides were adorned with curly tails. Several of the advertisements had been ringed in pencil, all of them for sexual contacts. The five mistakes in the picture puzzle hadn't been marked.

Long practice enabled him to spot the differences between the two pictures at a glance. They showed a pair of prison inmates. One was fat and mournful-looking. The other was so thin he'd just squeezed through the bars of their cell and was grinning at his new-found freedom. The mistakes in the right-hand picture were as follows: (1) A finger missing from the fat man's hand; (2) Five bars over the window instead of four; (3) A criss-cross scar on the thin man's cheek; (4) The fat man's extra double chin; and (5) A high heel protruding from one of the thin man's shoes.

Laying the paper aside, he ate, then looked for the menu board. It was half hidden behind the espresso machine. He was about to wipe it clean with a cloth when he stopped short. Instead of a list of 'Today's Specials' it bore a face drawn in chalk. The draughtsman had been no artist, of

271

course, and the face on the blackboard could have belonged to any number of people. And yet. That prominent chin, that close-cropped hair, that nose. Many men had a chin and hair and a nose like that, but the face on the blackboard displayed no feature that Jonas himself did not possess. It was him.

*

Jonas was still so flummoxed, he nearly drove into a bollard. Looking up, he discovered that he'd strayed down a dead end in the 1st District. He put the car into reverse. The next side street was the Graben. He turned right. A minute later he pulled up in front of St Stephen's.

The cathedral door was closed. He had to exert all his strength to open it.

'Anyone there?'

The echoes of his voice sounded strange. He called again, louder this time. Without uttering another sound, he continued to stand in the vestibule for two, three, five minutes.

Silence lay heavy over the pews. The smell of incense was fainter than last time. One or two lights seemed to have failed. The nave was gloomier.

He nodded to left and right as he walked on.

The sacred figures projecting from the walls were more aloof and forbidding in appearance than ever. Neither the sculptures nor the paintings looked at him. They stared vacantly into space.

Puzzled by something that had caught his eye, he bent down to examine St Joseph's plinth. A little coloured transfer was stuck to the stone. The height at which it had been applied suggested that it had been secretly left there by a child. It showed an old fighter plane. The caption read: *FX Messerschmitt.*

He sat down on a pew. Wearily, not knowing why he'd come, he surveyed his surroundings.

The pews were old and creaky. How old? A hundred years old, three hundred? Only fifty? Had war widows knelt here? Revolutionaries?

'Anyone there?' he called.

'There-ere!' came the echo.

He started to walk round again. In St Barbara's Chapel he visited the meditation room reserved, so a notice board informed him, only for the use of those wishing to pray. Turning round, he passed another notice advertising guided tours of the catacombs. He walked on and came to the lift that took visitors up the North Tower. He pressed the button. Nothing happened. He tugged at the door and a light came on inside.

Hesitantly, he went into the lift. The door closed. The upholstered interior resembled a padded cell. A notice on the wall read, in English: *Please put your rucksack down.* It made him think of England and what lay ahead of him as soon as he'd rested for a while. He pressed the button. His stomach gave a lurch.

He held his breath without realising it. Up and up he went. The lift should have got there long ago. He looked for a stop button. There wasn't one.

The lift came to a stop. Jonas got out quickly. The sunlight was dazzling. He put on his sunglasses and set off along the narrow walkway. The view was obscured by grilles intended to thwart potential suicides. A flight of steps led up to the Pummerin, a very big and heavy bell, which was hidden behind another grille. He inspected the bell but found it unimpressive.

On the viewing platform he took a breather. He stretched, rubbed his face, yawned, kicked some pebbles at the parapet. The wind was refreshing. Looking around, lost in thought, he paid no proper attention to the view until something caught his eye.

A telescope had been installed for the benefit of tourists. He inserted a coin in the slot and swivelled it to the north-east. The Danube Tower. The restaurant had stopped revolving and his banner was hanging limp. It must have happened during his absence. A short circuit, presumably.

It didn't really matter. The word he'd dreamt of and written on the tablecloths had been a red herring. He hadn't come across UMIROM again, at least.

Cupping his hands around his mouth, he shouted 'Umirom!' and laughed.

He looked at the panorama for a while longer. He saw the slowly revolving Big Wheel. The Danube Tower. The Millennium Tower. He saw UNO City and factory chimneys. He saw the Spittelau incineration plant, the Caloric Power Station. He saw churches and museums. Most of those places he had never visited. Although a small capital city, Vienna was still too big for anyone to become familiar with all of it.

The ride down was even more unpleasant. What alarmed Jonas more than being shut in was the thought that the brakes might fail and the lift plunge seventy metres. Once at the bottom he hurried to get out.

While descending the steps to the catacombs he tried to recall what he'd learnt about them during his school-days or on previous visits. It wasn't much. There were two parts, he remembered. The older catacombs dated from the fourteenth century, the newer from the eighteenth. The older part, which contained the Cardinal's Crypt, lay beneath the cathedral, the newer extended a little way beyond its walls. After serving as Vienna's municipal cemetery during the Middle Ages, the catacombs had been abandoned for lack of space.

'Hello?'

He came to a small chamber containing pews and brightly lit by lamps in every corner. A trail of candle-wax droplets led across the floor. He followed it.

He had to turn on the light in every chamber. If he failed to find the switch at once, he coughed and laughed. As soon as the ceiling light came on, he ventured further. Occasionally he paused. Nothing to be heard but his own rapid breathing.

He entered a narrow passage lined with clay vessels. The temperature here was noticeably lower than in the other chambers. Jonas couldn't explain this phenomenon. The chambers weren't separated from each other by doors, just stone sills.

He took three steps back into the chamber he'd just come from. Warmer.

Three steps forward. Colder. Far colder.

Something told him to turn back.

A faint glow was coming from a side chamber at the end of the passage. Jonas felt sure he hadn't turned the light on. He wondered exactly where he was. Probably near the high altar. Still beneath the cathedral, anyway.

'Hello!'

He remembered how it had been in the forest. How quickly he'd lost his bearings. This was no forest, true, but he didn't feel like fumbling his way around the catacombs of St Stephen's Cathedral. He knew his way back from here. If he went any further, that could change fast.

The light in the side chamber seemed to flicker.

'Come over!'

'Over,' called the echo, and died abruptly.

He took a card from his trouser pocket.

Sleep, it read.

He laughed derisively. Taking the whole bunch of cards from his pocket, he shuffled them thoroughly and withdrew another.

Sleep, it read.

I don't believe it, he thought.

He shuffled the cards again. Just as he was about to pick one, the truth hit him like a slap in the face. The third card he withdrew read *Sleep*. So did the fourth. And the fifth, sixth and seventh.

Sleep.

All thirty cards read *Sleep*.

He dropped them on the floor. Blindly, he dashed back through the musty subterranean chambers, up the steps to the exit, and out into the cathedral square. He felt in his pocket for the ignition key but failed to find it immediately. At last he got the engine started. The car gave a jerk as he drove off.

*

Jonas took the external lift to the top floor of Steffl's department store in Kärntnerstrasse. He wasn't so scared this one would crash, perhaps because it was a glass-encased, panoramic lift. Although aware of how high above the ground he was, he could see what was happening. That made the ride more acceptable.

He mixed himself a cocktail behind the counter of the Sky Bar. Should he put some music on? He removed a CD from its sleeve but replaced it in case it upset his equilibrium.

He sat down on the terrace. From there he had a thoroughly familiar view of the city centre. In front of him loomed St Stephen's, bronze roofs gleaming in the light of the setting sun.

He had often been to this bar with Marie. The sight of its stylish clientele made her dream of a time when she herself would be rich and leisured, and she enthused about the white wines served there. Jonas had no time for Vienna's smart young things, nor could he share her enthusiasm for wine, which he didn't drink. But it had filled him with quiet self-assurance to sit here with her early in the afternoon, when the place was sparsely filled and she was off on a trip the next day. To sit quietly on the wooden deck, listening to the muted sounds of the city and gazing at the ancient cathedral. To reach across the table and stroke each other's arm in silence from time to time. Those had been moments of great intimacy.

Jonas took a sip of his cocktail. He'd made it far too strong. He tasted again, grimaced and went to get a bottle of mineral water.

As he gazed across at the cathedral's bell tower, he experienced a sudden hankering to be a child again. To be plied with jam sandwiches and fruit juice. To play in the street and come home dirty and be scolded for tearing his trousers. To be plonked in a bath and put to bed by his parents. To be careless and carefree. To have no responsibility for himself or anyone else. Above all, though, he wanted a jam sandwich.

He stared at the blackened walls of the cathedral. Over there, down below ground near the altar, was something extraordinary, he felt sure. It might not be dangerous. But it was something he didn't understand.

And now his cards were down there. Many with the inscription face upwards, others not. *Sleep*, they said in his handwriting. Almost his handwriting. If he never went down there again they would continue to lie there until they crumbled away to dust. No one would ever read them, but there they would lie, enjoining sleep. Stone walls. A musty odour. And, when the last light had gone out, total darkness.

*

Jonas got home before dusk. He locked the door and checked all the windows. The clock on the bedroom wall was ticking steadily. A mellow sound.

He went into the kitchen. Once the coffee machine had stopped hissing, he poured himself a cup.

He had got all he needed from a stationer's. He cut the sheet of thin card into equal rectangles, and wrote on them in thick ballpoint. As before, he tried to think of nothing, to make his mind a blank and write by instinct. He succeeded so well, that when he surfaced from the timeless void he momentarily wondered where he was and what he was doing there. When he awoke from his trance he had the feeling that something was wrong. After a few moments' thought, he realised what it was. He had run out of blank cards.

Although his cheek was throbbing dully, he couldn't resist the temptation to put a box of chocolates on the empty side of the bed. He set up the camera and put in last night's tape, then sat down cross-legged on the mattress with his back against the wall. Defiantly, he opened the box of chocolates.

He was about to start the tape when it occurred to him that he might get chocolate on his shirt, and besides, he would be more comfortable in pyjamas. So he got undressed, trying to ignore the worsening ache in his upper jaw.

*

Jonas saw himself walk past the camera and get into bed. He tossed and turned for a minute or two. Then the movements beneath the bedclothes diminished and became more infrequent. After a while, faint snores could be heard.

Jonas removed the screw top of a liqueur bottle, a miniature, and drank a toast to the screen.

The Sleeper was asleep.

Jonas put a chocolate in his mouth. Moments later he

bit so hard on the nut inside it he felt as if a knife had been driven through his skull. Trembling, he clenched his fists and waited for the pain to subside. When he could open his eyes again he threw the box of chocolates into the bin. He wiped away his tears with the ball of his thumb and took a painkiller.

The Sleeper got up. As he passed the camera he waved. 'It's me, not the Sleeper,' he said with a smile.

'What *is* this?' Jonas exclaimed.

He searched his jacket pockets for the first tape he'd recorded at Kanzelstein. Meanwhile, he saw himself give the camera another wave and get back into bed.

'Damn it!'

If he'd got the tapes mixed up, where had the other one – the one he'd recorded last night – got to? He'd felt sure he would find it in his jacket.

He looked in his holdall. The tape was right at the bottom. He read the inscription. *Kanzelstein 1*.

He stopped the tape in the camera and took it out. *Kanzelstein 2*.

He rewound it.

He saw himself get out of bed. As he passed the camera he waved. 'It's me, not the Sleeper,' he said with a smile.

Those eyes.

He rewound the tape.

He saw himself get out of bed, go over to the camera and wave, smiling. 'It's me, not the Sleeper.'

That smile.

That look.

He rewound the tape again and pressed freeze-frame.

He gazed into the Sleeper's unblinking eyes.

23

It was midday by the wall clock. Jonas swung both feet out of bed at the same time. His neck was stiff, his right leg ached. The throbbing in his cheek, on the other hand, was a familiar sensation. He wondered whether to take another painkiller.

Why had he slept so long? What had happened during the night to knock him out for twelve whole hours and leave him feeling not refreshed, but as exhausted as if he'd just done a hard day's work?

He looked for the camera.

It wasn't there.

'Easy!' He raised his hands defensively. 'Just a minute . . .'

He stared at the floor, tugging at a strand of hair and trying to think. His mind was a total blank. He looked up.

The camera had disappeared.

He checked the front door. Locked from the inside. He examined the windows. Nothing. He shone his torch under the bed, opened cupboards and drawers. He even inspected the bedroom ceiling, the bin, the cistern in the toilet.

Over breakfast he tried to remember what he'd done before going to bed. He'd put in a new tape and programmed the camera to start recording at 3 a.m. Then he'd cleaned his teeth. In despair, for want of any better idea, he'd wrapped his face in a tea towel against the toothache. He had got into bed at midnight or thereabouts.

The tea towel! That had disappeared too.

He put the coffee cup down and looked at his hands. They were his hands. This was him.

'It's you,' he said.

*

He kept an eye open for the camera on the way to the chemist's. It wouldn't have surprised him to find it on the roof of a car or in the middle of an intersection, possibly surrounded by bunches of flowers. But he didn't see it anywhere.

He took two Parkemeds and pocketed the rest of the box. They'd always been effective against toothache in the past. He couldn't understand why they hadn't worked last night.

His jaw was throbbing badly. If he applied pressure to the relevant spot, even gently, the pain shot through his neck.

He felt tempted to look in a mirror and see if his face was swollen. But it was out of the question. He felt both cheeks at the same time. He couldn't make up his mind. Possibly, yes. Yes, maybe.

*

When the pain had eased he set off on foot for the city centre. On the Salztorbrücke he leant against the parapet. The wind blew specks of dust into his eyes. He looked down at the canal, blinking. The water seemed cleaner than before.

Leaning against the balustrade with arms outspread, he surveyed the waterfront promenade, which was strewn with empty cigarette packets, trampled beer cans, plastic cartons and scraps of paper. He used to stroll here in summer with Marie, eating ice cream. Sometimes they would decide to have dinner at the Greek restaurant beside the canal. Dusk brought out the mosquitoes. They never bit Jonas. But no matter how many incense candles Marie burnt or how much insect repellent she used, she would wake up the next morning covered in dozens of red bumps.

He swung round.

No one was there.

The Danube Canal gurgled softly past below him.

He walked on. His toothache was returning. He felt his cheek. It was definitely swollen now.

In the kitchen of a restaurant on the Franz-Josef-Kai he discovered a number of deep-frozen meals and heated one up in a frying pan. Although he ate cautiously, he caught his bad tooth on the fork. Transfixed with pain, he didn't let out a yell until several seconds later, when the searing, throbbing pain was already subsiding.

Parked in Marc-Aurel-Strasse was a Mercedes with a black box behind the windscreen. Sat Nav. The key was in the ignition. Jonas started the engine and turned on the system.

'Hello,' droned a robotic female voice.

After irresolutely scrolling through the user menu, Jonas selected Mariahilfer Strasse and keyed in the number of the shopping centre.

'Turn left in fifty metres,' said the computerised voice. At the same time, the screen displayed a 50 and an arrow pointing left.

Jonas turned left at the next intersection. The voice broke in once more and the display indicated that he should take another left turn after seventy-five metres. He obeyed. Five minutes later he was outside the shopping centre.

He got some swimming goggles from the sports shop

and the other things he needed from the stationer's. On the bonnet of the Mercedes he cut out two cardboard blinkers for the goggles. Before sticking them on he painted the plastic eyepieces black, all but a narrow slit.

He checked the visibility. It ought to be sufficient to avoid collisions. Next, he put the goggles on. He selected a street at random from the Sat Nav's list and keyed in a number without looking.

'The specified address does not exist.'

Jonas removed the goggles. He had selected 948 Zieglergasse. Where house numbers were concerned, it was evidently advisable to key in no more than two digits.

He put the goggles on and tried again, entering just one digit for the house number.

'Turn left in 150 metres,' said the computer.

Jonas soon lost his bearings. He had left the ring road behind, but he wasn't sure where he had turned off. He concentrated on not grazing the kerb and stopped worrying about what street he was in.

Hovering several hundred kilometres above him at that moment, a satellite was sending radio messages to the gadget in front of his nose. Although he knew better, Jonas visualised it as a sphere bristling with aerials on every side. But whatever form the satellite took, he could be certain that it was high overhead in an orbit around the earth, and that no one could see it. It was up there all on its own, transmitting information.

Jonas pictured the sphere hurtling through space. He pictured its surroundings. How the blue planet was revolving beneath it. The way it favoured the earth with a glance. All this quite on its own, unseen by human eyes. But that it was happening was beyond a doubt. The proof was in the robotic voice that instructed him to take the next street on the right and informed him that his destination was the third building on the left.

His toothache was becoming more and more painful. He didn't feel like making any more reconnaissance trips. He squeezed a Parkemed out of its blister pack. It stuck in his throat. He stopped at a kiosk and took a can of fizzy lemonade. Washed the tablet down.

*

He parked the Mercedes outside Steffl's department store. While riding up in the panoramic lift he waved in all directions, the back of his hand facing out. He made himself some camomile tea and sat down at the same table as the day before. His glass of mineral water was standing there untouched. In front of him loomed the spire of St Stephen's. The sky was blue and cloudless.

The pain eased after a while. Although his cheek continued to throb, he was so glad to be pain-free he started rocking to and fro on his chair, skimming one beer mat after another over the railings, watching them sail into the depths.

Of all the tapes he had watched in recent weeks, last night's was probably the most mysterious. It was almost identical to the one he'd recorded three days earlier. Two tapes existed, so his suspicion that he might have pressed the play button instead of the record button was unfounded. Besides, there were three minor differences: first, the Sleeper's gaze; secondly, the wink; and, thirdly, the voice. The Sleeper's gaze was more piercing than Jonas had ever seen it, either in the mirror or in videos and photographs. He also remembered, quite distinctly, that he hadn't winked at the camera the first night.

What had the Sleeper meant by that? Was it just a joke? Some kind of mockery?

He felt himself losing consciousness, lapsing swiftly into sleep. Absurd, colourful images took shape in his mind's eye. They made no sense, yet he grasped that they followed some clear-cut pattern.

He came to with a start and peered in all directions, then jumped to his feet and made a tentative search of the whole establishment. There was no one there. No one to be seen, at least. But he couldn't shake off the feeling that someone had been there. That was a familiar sensation, though. Imagination, nothing more.

He returned to the terrace. The sun had disappeared from view. He couldn't see it any more, only its rays gleaming on the roofs below.

Whether anyone apart from himself still existed, in South America or Poland, Greenland or the Antarctic, was a question of the same order as the one that used to be asked about the existence of extraterrestrials in the old days.

Jonas had never been seriously interested in theories about the existence of intelligent life far from the earth. The facts were fascinating enough. When a robot landed on Mars, he, Jonas, seated at his computers in the office and at home, had contributed to NASA's servers crashing. Eager to see the first pictures taken of the red planet, he had clicked on the browser's 'Go' button every few seconds. What he eventually got to see was not particularly spectacular. He even thought that Mars resembled Croatia. But it fascinated him beyond measure that those pictures existed, that a man-made device should be taking them on such a distant heavenly body.

He pictured the probe in flight. Pictured it speeding silently through space. Unloading the capsule containing the robot. Pictured the capsule entering the atmosphere and drifting down on parachutes. Pictured it landing.

No one had seen the robot land, no one. Yet the landing had taken place. Millions of kilometres beyond the range of any human eye, a robot was trundling across an expanse of red sand.

Jonas had imagined being there and watching the robot's arrival. He had imagined being the robot himself, remote from all that was known to humankind through its own observation. He had imagined how distant the earth now seemed, together with everyone he knew. With all that was familiar to him. Yet he was alive, capable of living unobserved by anyone.

Then, returning to earth, he had thought of the robot. How was it feeling, all by itself on Mars? Was it wondering what was happening back home? Was it experiencing something like loneliness? Rejoining the robot in his imagination, Jonas had surveyed its surroundings. A red, stony desert. No footprints in the sand.

The robot was still there now, at this very moment. Even as Jonas replaced his empty glass on the bar, a robot was slumbering on Mars.

*

Back at the flat he took another painkiller. Three Parkemeds were the maximum daily dose, but he wouldn't worry about that if it came to it.

He was feeling shattered. He did some knee-bends and dunked his head in cold water, wondering if he ought to lie down. The missing video camera crossed his mind. He had a feeling he would see it again. If so, he would probably be in for an unpleasant surprise.

He lay down on the bed, lay there doing nothing, trying to ignore every sound. The next time he checked the time it was half past nine. The street was in darkness.

He forced himself to eat something for fear the painkiller wouldn't work. Then he took another. Although his tooth wasn't hurting at the moment, he was anxious to keep the pain at bay for as long as possible. His cheek was throbbing.

He felt his forehead. He probably had a temperature, but he didn't feel like getting the thermometer and finding out for sure. He fetched himself a beer from the fridge. What would he do if it didn't stop?

24

Jonas awoke with a taste of blood in his mouth. He was feeling simultaneously drunk and hung over, and his head seemed to be floating above him.

Opening his eyes, he ran his tongue over the row of teeth in his upper jaw. The tooth that had tortured him yesterday had been replaced by an enormous, yawning gap. It wasn't just the bad tooth that was missing; its immediate neighbours had gone too. The taste of blood intensified when he put pressure on the gum.

He simply lay there for a while. The images that swam through his head were too potent and feverish to be pinned down. Questions, again and again: When? How?

He sat up. It was midday. The pillow was sodden with blood. The camera was standing where he had set it up before going to sleep. The bedroom displayed no noticeable changes. He felt his cheek. It was swollen.

He staggered and almost fell when climbing into his trousers. What was the matter with him? He felt as if he'd been on a bender.

There were some half-obliterated spots of blood on the edge of the bath. The waste bin contained nothing that hadn't been there the previous day, and he noticed nothing out of the ordinary in the kitchen. Feeling dizzy, he sat down and tried to collect his thoughts, work out what was happening to him. He was completely drunk, no doubt about it.

He cocked his shotgun and went out into the street. The Mercedes was parked behind the Toyota, the Toyota behind the truck. The kilometre readings of all three vehicles were the same as they had been the night before.

When he went to rewind the tape he found that it had disappeared. He looked everywhere. It had gone.

He unearthed a box of Diclofenac in the medicine cabinet. The accompanying leaflet stated that it was anti-inflammatory and analgesic. It was inadvisable to take more than three tablets a day. He squeezed two out of their blister pack and washed them down with tap water, then followed them up with an Alka-Seltzer. It was years since he'd had such a hangover. He changed the pillow case and got back into bed.

Two hours later his raw gum began to ache again. He took another two Diclofenac, then heated up a tin of beef stew. He was more than once on the point of hurling his plate into the backyard, but he forced himself to eat everything up.

He buried his face in his hands after swallowing the last mouthful and gave an involuntary belch, sweating and panting in his efforts to keep the food down. He remained like that for several minutes. Then he felt better.

He fished a card out of his pocket.

Get out, it read.

*

Jonas drove through the streets wearing his blinkered ski goggles, which were a tight fit. He tried to distract himself as he followed the instructions of the computerised voice, so as not to register the route he was taking.

All at once he wondered if he was awake. He wasn't sure that what he was thinking and feeling at this moment was real. Was he really here? This steering wheel, this accelerator, this gear lever, were they a part of reality? This brightness he saw through the slit in the goggles, was it the real world?

He heard a scraping sound. The car went jolting over the kerb. He braked and drove on more slowly. He felt tempted to tear off the goggles but resisted the impulse.

'Turn right at the next intersection.'

A beep. He turned right and accelerated away.

He had read somewhere that your eyes initially saw everything inverted by 180 degrees. That they transmitted an upside-down image of the world to the brain. But because the brain knew that people didn't walk around on their heads and mountains were broader at the base than the summit, it turned the image round. Your eyes deceived you, in a sense, and your brain acted as a corrective. Whether true or not, this posed an important question: how could he be certain that what his eyes were seeing was genuinely there?

He was really just a lump of flesh groping its way through the world. His knowledge of that world derived mainly from his eyes. They enabled him to get his bearings, make decisions, avoid collisions. But nothing and no one could guarantee that they told him the truth. Colour blindness was just one harmless example of this potential untruthfulness. The world could look like this or differently. To him it existed in only one possible form, the one allowed by his eyes. His self was a blind thing in a cage. It was all that his skin contained. His eyes formed part of this – or not, as the case might be.

The disembodied voice announced that he had reached the required destination. He pulled off his goggles.

The suburbs. Some outlying district, at all events. Expensive cars parked alongside garden fences. Detached houses with satellite dishes, balconies with ornamental plants. Jonas saw a broken branch lying in the roadway at the next intersection.

The street looked familiar. He checked the address. Something flashed through his mind, but he couldn't pin it down. It wasn't until he got out that the memory resurfaced: the suburban house he was standing outside was only 100 metres from the one he'd searched weeks ago. The one to which he'd been directed by his own phone messages, and in which he'd shied away from entering a particular room.

He read the name on the garden gate: *Dr August Lom*. He rang the bell, lifted the latch. The gate swung open with a rattling sound.

Jonas had a momentary vision of a shaggy beast cavorting around the garden on the far side of the house, its long tongue slapping each ear in turn as it lashed to and fro. The creature was only waiting for him to dare to go in.

Outside the front door, on which a wreath woven from sprigs of fir was hanging, he unslung his shotgun, listening intently. He cocked the weapon and concentrated.

Something told him that he'd reached a dead end.

He tried the door. Locked. He smashed a window. The burglar alarm went off. He registered it for a second, no longer, then it receded into the background. The moment his feet touched the carpet in the hallway, he heard nothing, smelt nothing. He set off.

A room. Furniture, a TV, pictures.

Another room. More furniture. House plants. Strangely, puzzlingly untidy.

The next room. Gym mats, a punchball, a home trainer.

And the next. Shower, bathtub, clothes horse.

He searched the place with a firm gaze and brisk movements, turned off the burglar alarm, tramped across carpeted floors, felt things, went down into the basement and up into the attic. Now and then a lucid part of his brain warned him to retract his hand or turn on his heel.

By the time he was back outside and gradually coming to his senses, he felt convinced that nothing in the house could be of any help to him. And that was all he'd wanted to know.

He smelt of sweat, he noticed as he got back into the car. It was the acrid smell he gave off when very tense. That annoyed him. There was no need to be scared, he'd proved it that night at Kanzelstein.

He was briefly tempted to put on the blinkered goggles and go back inside. Without his gun, what's more.

'No way,' he said, and turned the car.

*

He was gazing at the cathedral from the terrace of the Sky Bar. His coffee cup stood untouched on the table beside him. Without really thinking, he swallowed two Diclofenac. Something was bothering him. It was minutes before he realised that they'd stuck in his throat. He washed them down with some water.

He wandered around the terrace, flapping his arms for warmth. Spat over the balustrade and saw the spittle splash-land on the canopy below.

Good. The time had come. He must leave. Preferably today. That was asking too much, but he might have completed all his preparations by tomorrow.

By a conservative estimate, at least a third of the world lay beyond his reach. He could drive to Berlin, Paris, Prague or Moscow. He could inspect the Great Wall of China. The route to the Saudi Arabian oilfields lay open to him. He could visit Base Camp below Mount Everest if he could get used to the altitude and raise enough energy for a two-week trek on foot. What he could never get to was America. And Australia. And the Antarctic.

With a feeling of envy, he recalled his youthful dream. At some stage in his life, he had promised himself, he would stand amid the ice and touch the signpost reading *Geographic South Pole*. However he got there, whether with a traditional expedition of the kind that was seldom undertaken these days and would probably not accept him, or whether he landed in a chartered Russian military machine, he wanted to touch that signpost, shut his eyes and think of home. Of Marie doing the shopping at that moment, of his father playing chess in the park, of Martina rejecting a design at the office. Of the alarm clock ticking away in his flat. Unnoticed, because there was nobody there. It didn't matter to the alarm clock whether Jonas was at the South Pole or in the kitchen next door. He wasn't there. The alarm clock was all on its own.

To touch that signpost in a white wilderness. Not to go for a walk or a short trip by car, but to be fifteen hours by air from civilisation. That had been his dream. To go as far south as possible, to indulge his yearning for far-off places.

He would never see the Pole.

Jonas sat down again and put his feet up on the balustrade. He scanned the roofs below. How old were those houses? A century-and-a-half? Three centuries? And how many people had lived in them? The world changed little – the world he knew, at any rate. But it changed constantly and lastingly. Someone was born every second, someone died every second.

Austria. What was Austria? The people who lived there. The death of someone meant no essential change. Not, at least, from the country's point of view, only from that of the person in question. And of their relations. Austria didn't change much when someone died. But if you compared the Austria of a few weeks ago with Austria a century ago, you could hardly claim there had been no change. No one who had lived in those houses was still alive. All were dead. All had departed one by one. A big difference from their angle, none from that of the country.

'Austria.' 'Germany.' 'The United States.' 'France.'

People lived in houses they'd inherited and walked streets paved by others long before them. Then they got into bed and died, as they had to. To make room for another 'Austria'.

Everyone dies for himself alone. Statistics, fellow citizens, community, us, TV, football stadium, newspaper. Everyone read a certain writer in the paper. When he died, everyone read what his successor wrote. They all thought, ah, that's that guy, he writes this and that. And when *he* died they'd say, ah, a new guy, he writes this. They'd go home, still a part of the whole. Lie in bed and die, and suddenly no longer be part of the whole. No longer members of the Alpine Association or the Academy of Sciences or the Union of Journalists or the local football club. No longer customers of the best hairdresser in town or patients of that nice lady doctor. No longer fellow citizens, just 'the dead'.

It made a difference to the people who had disappeared. Or did it? Did it make a difference only to him, the one left behind?

*

Jonas emptied the back of the truck completely. He swept and scrubbed the interior until the metal floor and sides had almost regained their original colour. Then he lined the floor with self-adhesive, non-slip carpet tiles.

He trundled a three-piece suite and an additional sofa out of a furniture store on the Lerchenfelder Gürtel and manhandled them into the back of the truck. To these he added a massive coffee table, a scroll-fronted TV cabinet containing a TV and a video recorder, two standard lamps with broad bases, and an additional armchair. He put throws and cushions on the sofa and a bound stack of Mort & Phil comics beside it. He pushed a fridge up against the side and plugged the lead into a transformer he'd got from Machine

Park South. He also took two generators.

He filled the fridge with mineral water, fruit juice, beer, lemonade, pickled gherkins and other things that tasted better chilled. Beside it he stacked crates of long-life milk, tinned food, vacuum-packed pumpernickel, biscuits, bags of flour and similar stuff, not forgetting such extras as salt, pepper and sugar, oil and vinegar.

More crates were needed. One for cutlery and crockery, another for batteries, a camping stove and cartridges, and several for the cameras he fetched from the Brigittenauer embankment. He unscrewed the tripods and laid them down wherever there was room on the floor. He stacked six-packs of mineral water along the sides.

He checked the stability of his load. Anything that threatened to fall over he secured with tape.

He chained the DS to the vertical load bars. To the horizontal bars on the opposite side he secured a Kawasaki Ninja with only 400 metres on the clock, which he wheeled straight out of the dealer's showroom and onto the hoist. Last of all, having filled the Toyota's tank as well, he drove it on board. He might have measured the available space with a ruler, it fitted so perfectly.

*

Jonas put his plate in the dishwasher and turned on the light. He went over to the window. The sun had sunk below the rooftops, the clouds were glowing in various shades of red. He cast a last glance at the truck standing ready below, then shut the window.

He had a feeling that the journey ahead of him was the prelude to a final act. Everything seemed so clear all of a sudden. Tomorrow he would set off in search of Marie. Then he would return here with or without her. Probably without her.

25

At Linz he made a special detour from the motorway to visit the Spider. He climbed through the shattered glass door into the car showroom. The Spider was where it had come to rest, the kilometre reading unchanged.

Jonas got in behind the wheel. He touched the gear lever, touched the heating, air-conditioning and warning-light controls, depressed the pedals. He shut his eyes and cast his mind back.

It was strange. Having thought he would never regard this car as his property, he now recalled the trips he'd made in it. He remembered what it was like to be the Jonas who had sat here and driven this sports car around Vienna.

He recalled the day he'd brought the Spider back here. He had loaded up the Toyota, never thinking he would return. And the Spider had stood here on its own all this time. While he was elsewhere.

He wrenched his eyes open and smacked his forehead with the flat of his hand. If he continued to sit here he would fall asleep in no time. He had woken up so exhausted this morning, he'd kept the truck to the middle lane for fear of nodding off.

He sounded the horn as he drove away and gave the Spider a final wave.

A good opportunity to set up the next camera presented itself just beyond Passau. Jutting out from the dilapidated walls of a road maintenance depot was an overhanging roof, beneath which sacks of salt were stored for protection in winter. He set up the camera beneath this with the lens trained on the direction he'd come from and programmed it to start recording at 4 p.m. the next day.

He read the kilometre mark on a post in the ground and recorded it in his notebook, then added the figure 3 and drew a circle round it. The 2 above it referred to a car park near Amstetten, the 1 to a sign between Vienna and St Pölten. Those first two cameras were in the open. He hoped it wouldn't rain before he returned. If it did, at least the tapes should be intact.

He emptied a bottle of water over his head and drank a can of some energy drink that claimed to contain as much caffeine as nine cups of espresso.

The air was cool, the temperature well below what he was accustomed to in Vienna. Fields of maize stretched away on all sides. A tractor stood abandoned on a farm track.

'Hello!'

He walked across the carriageway and climbed over the crash barrier. No parked cars. No sign of life. Nothing.

'Hello!'

Although he shouted as loudly as he could, his voice sounded feeble out here. The moment he stopped, it was as if no man-made sound had been heard here for an eternity.

*

He had lunch at a service area near Regensburg. The café yielded some onions, noodles and potatoes, fortunately, so he didn't need to touch his stores. After eating he wrote *Jonas, 10 August* on one of the menu boards.

He set up the fourth camera beside the filling station. He noted down its location, then programmed the tape for 4 p.m. the next day and filled up with diesel. In the shop he spotted a coffee mug with his name on it. He stowed it in a bag, together with some cold drinks.

He was dog-tired. His eyes were smarting, his jaw ached, and his back felt as if he'd been lugging sacks of cement around for days. When he got in behind the wheel he almost gave in to the lure of the bunk behind his seat. If he went to sleep now, however, he would have to drive too far tomorrow, and he didn't want to be pressed for time.

The next cameras he set up near Nuremberg, one before the exit road and one beyond. The seventh he stationed at the exit road to Ansbach, the eighth at Schwäbisch Hall. Despite the possibility of rain, he left the ninth in the middle of the carriageway near Heilbronn. The tenth, too, was simply left on the asphalt just short of Heidelberg, unprotected and without a tripod.

Half dreaming, he drove through tracts of countryside he'd never seen before. They failed to arouse his interest. Sometimes he was aware of the luxuriant scenery, the dense forests and lush meadows and friendly little houses near the motorway. Sometimes he seemed to be driving through an interminable wasteland, a bleak grey wilderness of ramshackle barns and scorched fields, unsightly factories and power stations. It was all the same to him. With precise, unvarying movements he set up his cameras and got back into the truck.

*

At Saarbrücken he could go no further. His target for the day had been Rheims, which would have meant a comfortable drive the next day. Even so, he'd driven far enough not to have to worry about getting there by 4 p.m.

He parked in the middle lane. Taking last night's tape with him, he made his way round to the back of the truck. His legs were so weak, he couldn't clamber aboard and had to use the remote control. The humming hoist carried him up.

He inserted the tape and dug out some biscuits and a bar of chocolate. Although the wound left by the extractions wasn't hurting, he took two Diclofenac. He sank onto the sofa with a sigh of relief.

He shut his eyes. He meant to do so for only a moment, but it was an effort to open them again. They were smarting with tiredness.

He turned on the TV and selected the AV channel. The screen turned blue. Everything was ready, but he hesitated to start the tape. Something was bothering him.

He looked around but couldn't put his finger on it. He sat up and had another look.

It was the rear entrance. He couldn't see it because the Toyota was in the way. The tailboard had been left open to admit daylight, but he couldn't relax like this. He turned on every available light and pressed the remote control. For a moment he thought he was falling forwards, but it was really the tailboard folding up towards him.

*

A bare room. No furniture, not even a window. White walls, white floor. Everything was white.

The naked figure on the floor was also white. White and so motionless it was a minute before Jonas realised he wasn't looking at an empty room. He didn't look more closely until he detected movement. Gradually, he began to make out shapes. An elbow, a knee, the head.

After ten minutes the figure stood up and walked around. It was covered from head to foot in white paint, or possibly dressed in a white leotard. Its hair was invisible, creating an impression of baldness. Everything was white: eyebrows, lips, ears, hands. It walked around the room in a seemingly aimless fashion, as if lost in thought or waiting for something.

Without a sound.

Over half an hour went by. Then the figure slowly turned to face the camera. When it raised its head, Jonas saw its eyes for the first time. Their appearance fascinated him. They were clearly wearing contact lenses, because no irises or pupils could be seen. The figure stared at the camera with two white orbs. Motionless. For minutes on end. Tensely.

At length it raised its arm and tapped the lens with the knuckle of its forefinger. It looked as if it were tapping its way out of the TV screen.

It tapped and tapped again. Mutely, white orbs staring, it continued to tap the screen.

Somehow, Jonas managed to operate the remote. He meant to switch off, but he pressed fast-forward instead. The tape ended after an hour.

*

Fresh air streamed into the stuffy interior when Jonas opened the tailboard. He drew several deep breaths, then picked up a pair of binoculars and jumped down onto the roadway. He spent a long time scanning the area with the binoculars clamped to his eyes.

Lifeless clusters of houses, abandoned cars up to their hub caps in mud. A scarecrow in an overgrown field, broomstick arms extended. Scattered clouds drifting across the sky. The only sound was that of his footsteps on the brittle asphalt.

In the cab he made a note of the truck's kilometre reading and locked himself in. Without setting up a camera or getting undressed, he flopped down on the bunk and, with a final effort, pulled a blanket over himself. His eyelids felt like sandpaper.

Saarbrücken, 10 August, he thought. Now for some sleep. Tomorrow I'll drive on. Everything's OK. Everything's fine.

Calm down, he told himself.

The motorway. Cars drove along motorways. Sitting in the cars were the people who drove them, their shoes planted firmly on the gas pedals. Those shoes contained feet. Austrian feet. German feet. Serbian feet. Feet had toes. Toes had nails. That was the motorway.

Stop thinking, he told himself.

His face sank ever deeper into the decrepit mattress, which smelt of a stranger's sweat, as if someone were pinning him down.

He turned over, wondering why sleep wouldn't come.

He heard noises he couldn't identify. For a while he got the impression that someone was rolling marbles across the roof of the cab. Then he thought he heard something creeping around the truck. He was past moving. The blanket had slipped off. He felt cold.

*

He leant over the driver's seat and peered through the windscreen, blinking. A red sun was edging above the hills on the skyline. Lying on the road in front of him was an object.

A camera.

He felt as if he hadn't slept at all. Half senseless with fatigue, he climbed down from the cab. A dream from last night flashed through his mind, so he must have nodded off at least.

He made one circuit of the truck, swaying like a drunk. There was no one to be seen. He picked up the camera and climbed quickly back into the cab.

It struck him after a while that he was sitting limply in the driver's seat, staring at the road. What was he doing there? He ought to be in the back – he wanted to watch the tape.

The camera. He examined it. All his cameras had been numbered since his video trip in the Spider. He checked. It bore the number of the one that had disappeared some days ago.

Something told him he would do better to leave here, not get out again to watch the tape. He locked the doors and helped himself to a can of juice from the glove compartment. Then he drove off.

The dream came back to him.

The images were clearer this time. He was standing in the bathroom of his flat on the Brigittenauer embankment. He could see in the mirror that his face, or rather his entire head, was undergoing a transformation. He acquired a different creature's head every second. One moment he would be standing there with a bear's head, the next with the head of a vulture, a dog, a pig, a stag, a housefly, a bull, a rat. Each metamorphosis took only the blink of an eye to complete. Head followed head in swift succession.

*

Jonas set up the eleventh camera on the road near Metz and programmed it for 4 p.m., like the others. He had breakfast in the back with his feet comfortably propped on the sofa table. The powdered coffee, which he drank from the new mug bearing his name, tasted bitter. The peach compote, on the other hand, he ate with gusto. It was a brand he'd often had as a child. The taste of it was on his tongue the moment he spotted the tin in the supermarket.

Still chewing, he jumped up and squeezed his way along the side of the truck to the driver's door of the Toyota. He checked the clock. It read thirty kilometres more than the day before.

His weariness returned with unexpected intensity. He mustn't sleep now, not for anything. He poured cold water over his head, soaking his shirt. Icy shivers ran down his spine. He did some exercises to stimulate his circulation and shook a few coffee bonbons into his palm. Instead of sucking them, he washed them down with an energy drink.

*

The unknown video was in black and white. It showed a hilly landscape clothed in woods and vineyards, but without any roads. The camera panned to a woman's face and zoomed in. The face came nearer and nearer.

Something in his brain refused to understand, so it was several seconds before he grasped the significance of what he was seeing. He leapt to his feet and stared at the screen transfixed.

The woman on the screen was his mother.

The camera lingered on her face for some moments, then panned left to someone else.

His grandmother.

Her lips moved silently, as if she were speaking to him. As if the distance the words had to cover were too great.

Jonas wrenched out the lead that connected the TV to the camera. As he hurried to the rear of the truck, squeezing between the Toyota and the Kawasaki, he gashed his arm on a projecting piece of metal and felt a fleeting stab of pain. Still holding the camera as if it might explode, he hurled it as far as he could into the maize field beside the road.

Shuffling impatiently from foot to foot, he watched the tailboard close with agonising slowness. Then he shot the bolt and jumped into the cab.

*

He drove as if he'd turned on an autopilot. His mind was unavailable. Now and then he registered some feature of the world outside. He noticed abrupt changes in weather conditions, but they didn't affect him, they were like something seen on TV. He read place names: Rheims, St Quentin, Arras. They meant nothing to him. It was a new smell that brought him back to the present. The air was heavy with salt. He would soon be at the coast.

This realisation seemed to cheer Jonas and remind him of why he was here. He had banished the videotape to the nethermost region of his consciousness. He was hungry, he noticed. Not knowing whether he would come to another service area, he pulled up on the hard shoulder in the shade of some tall weeping willows. The sun was high in the sky. It was sweltering.

While applying a dressing to the gash in his arm, he ruefully contemplated the devastation brought about by his hurried departure. The butter was on the floor, likewise the bowl containing the rest of the peach compote. Bits of peach were scattered all over the three-piece suite. The upholstery was stained with spilt coffee, that was the worst thing. Jonas got busy with a swab. After that he lit the camping stove and heated up two tins of stew.

As usual, his tiredness returned after he'd eaten. It was only one o'clock. He couldn't afford to take a nap.

He rinsed the plate and saucepan with mineral water beside the road. The empty tins he tossed into the ditch. He'd already got into the cab when he thumped the

304

steering wheel, climbed out again and retrieved the tins, which he shoved under the Toyota for the time being.

He took the next exit road. Thereafter he followed the map. It was up-to-date and accurate, and he had no trouble finding his way. At 2 p.m. he pulled up not far from the yawning mouth of the Channel Tunnel.

He wasted no thought on Calais, which once he would have liked to visit. He couldn't imagine driving through a sizeable town, not now. As few buildings as possible and as few things that were big and overwhelming, that was what he wanted.

He began his preparations at once. He wheeled the DS down onto the unmade-up road that ran along the fence enclosing the railway tracks. Armed with crowbar and wire-cutters, he went in search of a way through it. He found one after a few hundred metres: a gate used by construction workers for delivering building materials, and it was open. He took the crowbar and wire-cutters back to the truck.

He debated what to take in his rucksack. Food and drink, certainly, and cartridges for the shotgun. A torch, matches, a knife, some string. But were a raincoat and a spare pair of shoes indispensable items of equipment? Maps and first-aid dressings were more important. And ought he to take an extra can of petrol, or could he be sure of finding another vehicle on the other side?

It was half past three when he fastened the straps of the rucksack. He went and sat in the back of the truck, where he was at least shielded from direct sunlight, if not from the heat. His fingers felt for something to occupy themselves with. He longed to shut his eyes for a little, but he knew he wouldn't open them again for hours if he did.

He took out his mobile. The network display showed *Orange*, so he could, in theory, have phoned even from here.

He skimmed through his stored text messages. All were from Marie and one was several years old. Jonas had anxiously preserved it every time he changed mobiles. It was her first declaration of love. She'd written it, because she'd been too shy to come out with it during their most recent conversation, even though everything had already been said or hinted at. They'd intended to see in the New Year together, but Marie's sister had been taken ill and she'd had to fly to England unexpectedly. Her message was timed at exactly 0.00.

Approaching, he thought.

At one minute to four he climbed onto the roof of the cab. He followed the second hand on his watch. At 4 p.m. precisely he spread out his arms.

Now.

At this moment almost a dozen cameras were coming to life, filming a landscape that existed for them alone. That stretch of motorway near Heilbronn, that car park at Amstetten. They existed purely for themselves at this moment, but he would witness it. This selfsame moment was occurring throughout the world. He was capturing it in eleven different places. Now.

And this one. Now.

In a few days, possibly weeks, he would watch the films of Nuremberg and Regensburg and Passau and reflect that he'd been standing on top of the truck at that moment. That he had set off afterwards, and that at the moment recorded fifteen minutes later he would already be below ground. On his way to England.

*

He kept to the strip between the tracks. This was a smooth expanse of concrete, fortunately, so he didn't have to ride over any sleepers. The tunnel was wide for the first hundred metres. Then the walls gradually converged. His headlight illuminated the tube in front of him. The clatter of the engine was amplified by the confined space, and he soon regretted not having worn a helmet. He didn't even have a handkerchief he could have torn up for ear plugs.

He was so tired he kept throttling back in alarm, under the impression that he'd spotted some obstacle ahead. He also fancied he saw pictures, faces, figures on the walls on either side of him.

'Hooo!'

He was bound for England, he really was. He had to say it aloud to make himself believe it. He was really on his way.

'Hooo! I'm coming!'

He rode flat out, undeterred by the fact that he could hardly keep his weary eyes open and was having to screw them up against the headwind. All fear had left him.

He was the wolf-bear.

Nothing could stop him now. He would surmount every obstacle. He was afraid of no one. He was on his predestined way.

You're close to collapse, said someone at his elbow.

Startled, he gave the handlebars a jerk. His front tyre grazed a rail. He managed to regain his balance in the nick of time and throttled back. He would have to lie down for a sleep as soon as he got to the other side, even if only in a field in pouring rain.

And then an obstacle really did loom up ahead.

He mistook it for an optical illusion at first, but as he drew nearer the reflection of his headlight in the tail lights banished all doubt. It was a train.

He dismounted but left the engine running so he could see. He rested his hand on one of the buffers of the rear-most carriage.

Jonas was now so bemused with fatigue, he considered

pursuing his journey on the roof of the train. Then it occurred to him that he couldn't get a moped up there for one thing, and, for another, that there simply wasn't room on the roof for a moped rider.

He checked the sides. The train and the wall of the tunnel were forty centimetres apart at most.

A moped wouldn't go through.

Only a man on foot.

*

He was halfway along the tunnel, he estimated. That meant a fifteen-kilometre walk with a torch in his hand and legs that could scarcely carry him.

He set off. One step, one metre after another, with a beam of light ahead of him. Descriptions of wartime experiences surfaced in his mind. People were capable of walking in their sleep. Perhaps he was asleep already. Without realising it.

Marie.

'Hooo,' he tried to call, but he wasn't up to producing more than a hoarse, uncontrolled whisper.

Hearing a noise behind him, he stopped short and shone the torch. Nothing, just rails.

The next few steps were an immense effort. Mountaineers must feel like this just before reaching the summit, he reflected. One step a minute. Or perhaps not a minute, only seconds. Perhaps he was walking at a normal speed. He'd lost his sense of time.

Again he thought he'd heard something. It sounded as if someone were walking along the tunnel in the same direction, fifty metres behind him.

The third time he heard the noise it didn't seem to come from behind, nor was its source ahead of him. It was inside his head.

The decision to lie down wasn't a conscious one. His knees buckled and the ground came up to meet him. He lay there, arms outstretched.

*

Unrelieved darkness. Jonas opened his eyes wide. Blackness.

He hadn't known such darkness existed. Utter darkness, without a speck of light. It was so all-embracing, he had an urge to sink his teeth into it.

He felt for the torch. He'd put it down beside his head, but it wasn't there. He felt for the rucksack but couldn't find that either.

He sat up and collected his thoughts. The rucksack had been on his back when he went to sleep. Now it was gone, like the torch. Not only would he have to manage without his supplies, he would have to proceed in total darkness.

He wondered what time it was. His watch was an analogue model without a light.

He got to his feet.

Despite his fatigue, he set off at a trot. He felt that if he stopped again it would be the end. Something would suddenly be there. It was there already, he could sense it. The moment he lay down it would descend on him.

He had a sudden vision of the hundred or more metres of seawater above his head. He managed to brush it aside, but it soon recurred. He thought of something else. The vision returned. Himself inside a concrete tube with a gigantic mass of water overhead.

This is an ordinary tunnel.

It doesn't matter what's above the tunnel, sand or granite or water.

Jonas paused to listen. He thought he could hear water dripping, even hissing under pressure. At the same time, he had the feeling that something was robbing him of breath, as if the oxygen in the tunnel were being sucked out. Or displaced by something else.

He walked on, half supporting himself with one hand against the side of the tunnel.

He felt more and more afraid of noise. He feared an explosion might go off right beside his head and burst his eardrums.

There's no explosion down here. Everything is quiet.

He had the feeling that he should have reached the end of the tunnel by now. Could he have turned around in his sleep? Could he be going in the wrong direction?

Or had he woken up somewhere else? Did the tunnel he was in lead nowhere? Would he walk on for ever?

'Hey! Hello! Hey!'

Think of something pleasant.

His most enjoyable daydreams in the old days had transported him to distant lands. He had pictured himself standing on a seaside promenade, glass in hand, gazing out to sea. It didn't matter to him whether he'd travelled there by car or in the chandelier-hung stateroom of a luxury liner. In his imagination he could smell the salt air and feel the sun caressing his skin. No worries, no more responsibility for others or himself. All he had to do was be at peace with himself and enjoy the sea.

Or he transplanted himself to the Antarctic, where it was never, in his imagination, unpleasantly cold. He trekked across the eternal ice beneath a blazing sun. He reached the South Pole, hugged some bearded scientists who were spending the winter at the research station there, and touched the signpost, thinking at that moment of his home.

Whenever things were bad in the old days, whenever he was suffering from personal unhappiness or professional dissatisfaction, he would dream himself into the distance.

He'd wanted to know as little as possible about it in the past few weeks. Distance meant loss of control. And you didn't plunge into some reckless venture when you sensed that everything was slipping through your fingers.

As he did right now.

He was mad, completely round the bend. Stumbling along in pitch-darkness. What did he think he was . . .

Think of the Antarctic.

He saw ice-clad mountains, blue and white. The ice across which he was hauling his rucksack was white, an infinity of whiteness. The sky above him was blue.

He had once seen a TV documentary in which scientists extracted a cylinder of Antarctic ice from a depth of one kilometre. The piece of ice they brought up was meant to help them understand climate change. Jonas was less fascinated by the climatic outlook than by the cylinder itself.

A piece of ice half a metre long and ten centimetres in diameter. Until a few minutes earlier, buried under millions of cubic metres of ice. Exposed to the light of day for the first time for – yes, since when? – a hundred thousand years. Frozen an eternity ago, this water had bidden the world a gradual farewell. Ten centimetres below the surface. Fifty. Two metres. Ten. And what a long time had elapsed between the day it left the surface and the one on which it reached a depth of ten metres. Jonas could scarcely imagine such a lapse of time, but it was a mere click of the fingers compared to the interval between ten metres and a kilometre.

Now it was there, that piece of ice. It was seeing the sun once more.

Hello, sun, here I am again. How've you been?

What was going on inside it? Did it realise what was happening? Was it pleased? Worried? Thinking of the time it began its descent? Comparing one time with another?

He had to think of the ice still down below, the immediate

neighbours of the fragment that had been brought to the surface. Were they missing it? Envying it? Feeling sorry for it? And he had to think as well of the other ice two or three kilometres down. How it had got there. Whether it would regain the surface and when, and what the earth would look like when it did. What it was thinking and feeling down there in the dark.

Jonas thought he heard a sound. A distant roar.

He stopped. No, no mistake. The sound of rushing water was coming from up ahead.

He turned and ran, tripped and fell headlong, felt a sharp pain in his knee.

It seemed to him, as he lay there, that the track sloped gently downwards. Immediately afterwards he had the opposite impression. He stood up and took a few steps, but he couldn't tell whether he was walking uphill or down. He seemed to be going downhill one moment and uphill the next, but he noticed that steps taken in the original direction were more of an effort.

He walked on. The roar increased in volume. His feet were splashing through water. The sound grew steadily louder. A clap of thunder rent the air. Seconds later he was standing in the open.

It was night. Lightning zigzagged overhead, followed almost simultaneously by fierce growls of thunder. Rain came pelting down on his head. The gusts of wind were so strong they almost blew him over. No lights on anywhere.

He quit the railway track in a hurry despite the storm. Before long he found an open gate in the fence. He turned left, where he thought he'd find buildings sooner. He might just as well have gone in the opposite direction. It was pitch-dark and he had no idea where he was going. He hoped he wouldn't plunge straight into the sea, whose breaking waves he thought he could hear between claps of thunder.

He was walking across a field of long grass. A flash of lightning glinted on something a few metres away. A motorbike. The sides of the tent beyond it were ballooning in the wind.

Beneath the awning Jonas stumbled over wet rucksacks, trampled on shoes, caught his foot on a stone that was weighing down a mat. His fingers were trembling so much with cold and exhaustion, it took him a while to open the flap. He crawled inside but only zipped up the mosquito net so as to be able to see out.

He explored the interior by touch. His fingers found a sleeping bag. A small pillow. An alarm clock. Another sleeping bag. Beneath the second pillow was a torch. He turned it on. At that moment an all-enveloping clap of thunder rent the air. Startled, he dropped the torch.

He felt he must sleep very soon.

He retrieved the torch and shone it round the interior. In one corner were some tins of food and a camping stove. On the opposite side of the tent was a Discman with a stack of CDs beside it. In the corner near the entrance he found some toilet articles: razor, shaving cream, skin cream, a box of contact lenses, soap, toothbrushes. Lying between the rucksacks was a Bosnian newspaper dated 28 June and a sex magazine.

Jonas had a feeling that someone or something was nearby. Imagination, he told himself.

He turned off the torch. In the dark he stripped off his sodden clothes, unzipped the mosquito net and wrung them out beneath the awning. His shirt, trousers and socks he deposited on the other side of the tent and crawled, naked, into one of the sleeping bags. The other he used as a blanket. He turned his head and looked at the entrance, shivering.

While listening to the storm he wondered if there was higher ground nearby, or if he should be prepared for a lightning strike. Moments later the interior of the tent was lit up, bright as day, by an electric flash. He shut his eyes and made his mind a blank. The ensuing clap of thunder came several seconds later than he'd expected.

He tossed and turned, teeth chattering, but he couldn't relax. The thunderstorm gradually receded, but rain continued to lash the roof of the tent, soaking the field and churning up the puddles that had formed. The wind tugged so hard at the tent poles, Jonas more than once expected to be buried beneath folds of sodden canvas.

Was that someone running his hand over the tent's outer skin? Were those footsteps he could hear? He sat up and peered out. Amorphous darkness. He couldn't even see the motorbike.

'Get lost!'

No footsteps. Only the wind.

Jonas lay down again.

He was lapsing into sleep. Everything was drifting away.

Voices? Could he hear voices?

Footsteps?

Who was coming?

26

He awoke because it was hot and stuffy. At first he didn't recognise his surroundings. Then he realised that he was lying inside the tent and the sun had warmed it up.

He felt his trousers. They were still damp. He picked up his clothes and tossed them out of the tent without giving them a thought. Taking the camping stove and two tins with him, he went outside.

The sky was cloudless, but a stiff, cool breeze was blowing. The grass beneath his bare feet was still wet. He looked round. There were no buildings in sight.

From one of the rucksacks the campers had left beneath the awning he took a pair of trousers – he had to roll up the bottoms – and a T-shirt too tight for him across the shoulders. He also pulled on a jumper. The socks he found were too small, so he cut off the toes with a knife. The sandals were also too small, but they would do at a pinch.

He strolled around while the contents of the tins were heating up in a saucepan on the stove. Fifty metres away was a clump of trees. He sauntered in that direction, then thought for a moment and walked back. Something was bothering him.

He examined the motorbike.

Both tyres were flat.

He took a closer look at them.

They'd been slashed.

*

Jonas set off in search of some village or town. His eyelids kept drooping. He was so tired, he felt tempted to sink to the ground, out here in the open, and pillow his head on his hands.

He'd been walking for a good hour when he came to a house. A car was parked outside. The key wasn't in the ignition, but the front door was unlocked.

Beyond it lay a dim passage, *'Hello?'* he called in English. *'Somebody at home?'*

'Of course not,' he answered himself politely.

Without dwelling on the noises in the house, a dark old cottage full of creaking beams, Jonas looked round the rooms in search of the car keys. He quickly averted his gaze whenever he caught sight of a mirror. Sometimes, when he glimpsed himself moving in a mirror on a wall or a wardrobe door, it looked in those gloomy rooms as if someone were standing behind him. Hemming him in, even. When that happened he lashed out with his arms but didn't move from the spot, hard though he found it not to.

He discovered the keys in the pocket of a pair of jeans. Stuck to them was a wad of chewing gum. Despite himself, Jonas almost threw up. He didn't know why.

*

He drove, unconscious of the passage of time and heedless of the countryside gliding past. When he came to a road sign he looked up at it, made sure he was still heading in the right direction, and slumped behind the wheel again. His mind was a blank, save for the images that flooded into his head unbidden and vanished as quickly as they had come. They left no impression behind. He was empty. Wholly intent on staying awake.

He managed to skirt London to the north. As soon as he felt satisfied he was clear of the city, he pulled up in the middle of the motorway, folded the seat back and closed his eyes.

*

4 a.m. He lowered the window. It was cold and damp outside. An unpleasant smell hung in the air, like burnt horn or molten rubber. All that broke the silence was the sound of his fingernails scratching the door panel. At this hour he would normally have heard birds twittering.

When he tried to drive off the car wouldn't budge. Then it gave a sudden lurch and sent up a shower of red and yellow sparks, accompanied by a metallic screech.

He got out and shone the torch over the area immediately around the car. And then he directed it at the wheels.

All four tyres had been removed. The vehicle was standing on its bare hubs.

Some way from the car he came upon a smouldering mound he recognised as the remains of his tyres. A blackened tyre lever was jutting from.

There was no other car in sight. It was a long way to the next service area, and he didn't know how far it was to the next exit road. He would have to leg it back to the last one, he supposed.

He stared irresolutely, first at the evil-smelling bonfire, then at the car. He was feeling devoid of energy. It had cost him an immense effort to get this far, and it would cost him an even greater effort to get to Smalltown and back. Such a soul-destroying thing to happen.

With his hands buried in his pockets, he set off in the direction he'd come from.

When he sighted a secondary road and, beyond it, a village, he scrambled down the motorway embankment. At around 6 a.m. he found a car with the key in the ignition. He debated whether to eat somewhere. First, however, he wanted to get further north. He didn't like being so near London. It was deserted, he felt sure. He would only get lost in that vast metropolis and achieve nothing.

Jonas didn't exceed 120 k.p.h. He would have liked to go faster, but he didn't dare. Whatever it was, the tyre incident or a premonition, he felt he would expose himself to danger needlessly if he put his foot down too hard.

8 a.m. 9. 11. 2 p.m. The place names he saw on signs were familiar to him mainly from his childhood, when he was still interested in football and used to read newspaper reports about the English championship. Luton, Northampton, Coventry, Birmingham, West Bromwich, Wolverhampton, Stoke – the names of deserted towns and cities. They didn't matter to him. All that mattered to him was the remaining distance to Scotland. Smalltown was less than five kilometres from the border.

Liverpool.

He'd taken an interest in Liverpool as a boy. Not much, because he didn't like the football club. And not because Liverpool was the home of the Beatles. But the name had such a peculiar ring to it. There were words that seemed to change as you looked at them or said them aloud, words whose meaning seemed to disappear before your eyes. There were dead words and live ones. Liverpool was alive. Li-ver-pool. Lovely. A lovely word. Like, for example, space, when it meant the universe. *Space*. So apt. So lovely.

England, Scotland: ordinary words. Ger-ma-ny: an ordinary word. But Italy, that was a word with soul and music.

This had nothing to do with his liking for the country, it was the word itself. Italy was the country with the loveliest name, followed by Peru, Chile, Iran, Afghanistan, Mexico. If you read the words Ireland or Finland, nothing happened. Read the word Italy, and you sensed a kind of softness. It was a mellow, supple name. Eire and Suomi sounded much better than Ireland and Finland.

Jonas had often noticed that a word could drive you crazy if you read it several times in succession. You started to wonder if it was spelt wrong. Any word, nothing extraordinary, such as 'flicker'. F. L. I. C. K. E. R. Fli-cker. Flick. Flick-er. Every word had something unfathomable about it. It was as if it were a fake that bore no relation to what it denoted.

Mouth.

Foot.

Neck.

Hand.

Jonas. Jo-nas.

He had always found it hard to read his name and believe that it indicated him. The name Jonas, written down on a sheet of paper. Those lines, those letters, signified that person. Person – another of those words. Per-son. Perrr-son. Prrrrr.

Just beyond Bolton, it was late afternoon by now, he folded the seat back, but not before he'd got out to make sure there was no tyre lever in the boot and he had no knife with him. He locked himself in.

*

It was dark when he opened his eyes. He was sitting in the car, but his surroundings seemed to have changed.

3 a.m. The air smelt of rain. Jonas was cold, but not hungry or thirsty. He turned on the interior light. He

rubbed his face. It felt greasy. A piece of spaghetti was stuck to the ball of his thumb. From the taste in his mouth, he might just have polished off a rare steak. His breath reeked of . . . What was it? Wine. The smell revolted him. He felt in his pockets. No chewing gum. Nothing that might have taken away the taste in his mouth.

He turned the key in the ignition. The car wouldn't start. The fuel gauge stood at zero.

He got out. The ground was wet. It was drizzling. Some distance away he caught sight of a lighted window. While walking towards it he was surprised to see the silhouette of an aircraft. Beyond it he made out another, and another. Was he dreaming? He went over and touched the landing gear. The tyres were real enough.

He had an urge to call out, 'Hooo!', but didn't dare.

The closer he got to the lighted window, the more mystified he became. Where was he? An airfield or airport, that was obvious, but where? Bolton? Liverpool?

He slowed his pace, looking up at the window. It seemed to be an office window. He thought he could see some pot plants behind the blinds, which were half lowered.

He wasn't sure if what was waiting for him up there was entirely good.

He turned round. No one there. Nothing to be seen in the gloom, not even vague shapes, and he had only a rough idea of where he'd left the car.

It wasn't that he'd sensed someone nearby. On the contrary, he'd never felt so remote from everything in his life. Even so, he thought it better to change his location, so he ran for fifty metres, silently zigzagging like a hare. This brought him to a building with a big sign on the side.

Exeter Airport.

Exeter? Surely not? He knew the city by name because special products were manufactured there for the processing of wood for furniture-making. Although he'd never been there, he knew roughly where it was: far to the south and almost on the coast.

A whole day's driving wasted.

He belched involuntarily, reeking of wine.

Quite suddenly, his legs started to tremble. He felt weary, infinitely weary. His one remaining wish was to stretch out and go to sleep. He was so eager to escape from the profound inertia that filled him, it didn't matter to him at this moment that he might once more put himself at the mercy of a process he couldn't understand, still less control. He longed to rest, to lie down and sleep. But not here on the rain-soaked asphalt. Somewhere comfortable, or at least soft. Not cold, anyway.

Like a blind man, with one hand held out in front of him, he tottered back to the car.

*

He awoke just before 7 a.m. Although he didn't feel fully rested, his tiredness was less tormenting.

He wrote *Jonas, 14 August* on a slip of paper. Before putting it behind the windscreen he looked at the letters he'd written. Jonas. That was him, Jo-nas. And 14 August, that was today. This 14 August would never recur. It was a one-time occurrence, so the memory of it would be unique. The fact that there had been other days bearing this date, a 14 August in 1900, another in 1930, others in 1950, 1955, 1960, 1980, was a human simplification, a lie. No day ever recurred. None. And no one day resembled another, whether or not people lived through it. The wind blew north, the wind blew south. The rain rained on this stone, not that. This leaf fell, that branch snapped, this cloud drifted across the sky.

Jonas had to find himself another car. After walking for an hour he came across an old Fiat whose rear seat was covered with soft toys in plastic wrappings. Beer cans lay scattered around it, some full, some empty. The taste of raw meat still lingered on his tongue. He rinsed his mouth out.

A locket was dangling on a chain from the rear-view mirror. He opened it. It contained two photographs. One was of a smiling young woman, and concealed beneath it was one of the Virgin Mary.

*

Jonas took the exit road to Bristol, fighting off a renewed urge to sleep. Several times he pulled up, walked around for a bit and performed some exercises. He never stopped for long. The wind was so strong it almost blew him off his feet. He felt he oughtn't to stray too far from the car.

Midday came and went, but he drove on. He didn't want to go to sleep, he wanted to drive on. On and on.

Liverpool.

The mysterious videotape came to mind. The one on which he'd seen his mother and grandmother. He didn't want to think about it, but the images forced themselves on him. He saw the old woman's waxen face, saw how she seemed to be talking to him soundlessly.

Preston.

Lancaster.

Only 150 kilometres to the Scottish border. He couldn't go on, though. He knew it would be a mistake to go to sleep, but every fibre of his being cried out for rest. He couldn't steer straight any more.

He pulled up and lowered the driver's window, shouted something and drove on.

He didn't know how much further he'd gone when he noticed that his left eye was shut. His right eyelid, too, was almost beyond control, and his chin was propped on the steering wheel. He wondered where he was going.

Where was he going? Why was he in this car?

He had to sleep.

*

Jonas opened his eyes, but everything was still dark. He tried to get his bearings, couldn't even remember going to sleep. His last memory had been of the motorway, the monotonous grey ribbon ahead of him.

He straightened up with a jerk and hit his head, let out a yell and sank back, rubbing his forehead.

His voice had sounded hollow. Where was he? He seemed to be holding a knife in his hand. He checked with the other hand. Yes, it was a hunting knife or something similar.

He found he couldn't turn round, he was hemmed in on all sides. He could barely move, there was no room. His legs were bent, his body was doubled over.

Where was he?

'Hey!' he shouted.

He thumped the wall with his fist. Just a dull thud, no echo.

'Hey! What is this?'

He braced both forearms against the obstruction above him, but it didn't move.

A coffin.

He was in a coffin.

He hammered on the walls of his prison and shouted. His voice sounded muffled, horribly muffled. Something seemed to explode inside his head. He saw colours he hadn't known existed. Inexplicable images danced in front of his eyes, mingled with sounds. A penetrating smell of glue filled the box he lay in. He lashed out with his feet.

Another wall, Before long, his feet and fingertips felt as if they were on fire.

Was a fire being lit under him? Was he being roasted in a vessel of some kind?

He thought of Marie.

He thought of the Antarctic. Of the signpost at the South Pole. He tried to send his mind there. No matter where he was, no matter what was happening, the Antarctic existed, the signpost existed. A little in his head but entirely so in reality. It would be there even when he himself was no more.

'This can't be happening!' he shouted. 'Help! Help!'

Mouth open wide, he positively wrenched the air into his lungs. He realised he was hyperventilating but couldn't help it. He was wasting precious oxygen, that was no less clear to him.

At that moment, halfway through a violent intake of breath, time suddenly slowed. His breathing lost its spasmodic quality, he noticed, and all became calm and steady. He lay quite still. As the second's duration of a breath expanded to an eternity, he heard a swelling roar.

'No!' said someone, possibly Jonas himself, and he surfaced once more.

He ran a hand over his sweaty face.

And tried hard to think. If the Sleeper alone was responsible for all that had happened in the last few days, this was mere shadow-boxing. No one could shut himself up in a coffin and bury it. If the Sleeper had incarcerated himself, there must be a way out.

He kicked and pushed. To no avail.

How long would he take to use up all the oxygen in such a confined space? Two hours? Half a day? What would happen to him? He would become sleepy, then confused. He would probably be unconscious by the time he died of suffocation.

Sleepy? He was sleepy already. Utterly exhausted.

*

He opened his eyes. Total darkness.

His limbs ached with tension and from lying on a hard surface. His feet had gone to sleep. His hand was clutching the handle of the knife.

He had no idea how long he'd been asleep, it might have been ten minutes or four hours, but he still found it hard to keep his eyes open. This indicated that he hadn't slept for long. Besides, he hadn't suffocated. A space as confined as this couldn't contain enough oxygen to last him many hours, that much was certain.

Unless there was some hidden source of air.

Unless things weren't as they appeared.

The knife in his hand . . . A friendly invitation? More of a prop in a comedy, perhaps? The Sleeper certainly wouldn't entomb himself of his own free will.

Or would he?

No, he must have overlooked something.

He investigated his prison once more. There was no scope for movement on the side his head was resting against, nor on the opposite side. He tapped the wall on his right. No form of aperture or lock – or, if there was, he couldn't find it.

It was different on the other side. The left-hand wall felt the hardest. Above all, though, it wasn't the same all over. There were cracks in it.

Laboriously, he switched the knife from his right hand to his left and began to probe these cracks. The wall didn't seem to be a proper wall, it consisted of two overlapping metal cylinders. He dug and probed away in the hope of finding a gap. The blade snapped, leaving him with the useless hilt in his hand.

He fought back his feeling of resignation. This was a game.

He ran his fingers over the upper cylinder. There! Between the cylinder and the roof was a gap just big enough to admit his fingertips. He exerted pressure on the metal and pulled. The cylinder moved almost imperceptibly. Gripping it further down, he pulled some more. Once again he felt a slight movement.

Painstakingly, little by little, he shook the cylinder free from between the roof and its counterpart below. This brought more and more of his body beneath the massive metal component. He tried not to think about this.

He slid the cylinder over himself, panting hard. Once he had distributed the weight of the load better, he could breathe. He managed to raise the lower cylinder and squeeze beneath it. This created enough room on the right for the first cylinder. He rolled the second one over himself and, after much pushing and pulling, placed it on top of the first.

On the left, where he now had some elbow room, he felt something soft and rounded: an expanse of cloth. When he applied pressure with his fist, it sank in.

That was when it dawned on him.

His hand felt for the crack and found it. Felt for the catch and found that too. Pulled it and, at the same time, gave the cloth-covered wall a push. The seat folded forwards. He crawled out of the boot and onto the back seat of the car.

It was night. Stars were twinkling overhead. He seemed to be in the middle of a field. No road or track ahead of him. He looked to his right. Saw the tent but failed to catch on right away. It didn't dawn on him where he was until he recognised the motorbike with the slashed tyres.

*

At dawn Jonas stopped at a filling station and heated up the contents of two tins on a squalid gas stove in the back room. He drank some coffee and drove on.

He was so tired he kept nodding off. On one occasion he would have hit the crash barrier if he hadn't yanked at the wheel at the last moment. Undeterred, he drove flat out, racking his brains for some way out of this trap. Nothing occurred to him. His only recourse was to keep trying, to keep heading for Scotland and hope that he would get there before sleep overcame him.

Pills were a possibility, but where to get them? How was he to know which ones to take?

He drove on, jaws aching, eyes watering. His joints felt as if they were filled with foam. His legs were two numb stilts.

The M25. Watford. Luton. Northampton.

At Coventry he was so overcome with fatigue, he wondered what time of day it was. He saw the sun but didn't know whether it was climbing or declining towards the horizon. He felt feverish. His cheeks were burning, his hands trembling so badly, he couldn't open the ring-pull on a can of lemonade.

He was trapped in a limbo in which he dreamt and drove, dreamt and saw, dreamt and acted. He perceived sounds and images. He smelt the sea. He read signs that were transformed an instant later into scraps of memory, into dreams, into songs that were sung in his ear. Many of these dreams he retained for a while, wrestling with them or doubting their existence. Other, more abstract ones were of such short duration he doubted he'd had them at all.

Spacey Suite.

He thought he'd read the words, but they turned into a building under construction by workmen. The walls melted, dissolved, engulfed him. 'I've nothing to do with this,' said his inner voice. Feeling constricted for a moment, he coughed up some crystalline bubbles and breathed freely once more.

He dreamt he was climbing a flight of stairs, many hundreds of them, higher and higher. Then it seemed to him that, instead of dreaming it, he was recalling a dream, or an actual event from minutes or hours or years before. The effort of deciding which was right almost tore him apart.

'Don't you believe me?' said his grandmother.

She was standing in front of him, speaking. Her lips didn't move.

'Stop that,' said his mother's voice. He couldn't see her and didn't know who she was talking to.

He saw the sun complete its day's trajectory within a few seconds. Again and again it appeared on the horizon, glided across the sky, one two three four five, and sank in the west, leaving night behind it. Then it reappeared, only to speed on its way again and vanish. Night. Night lingered. It lingered and did its work.

*

He was roused by the cold and the whistle of the wind. He opened his eyes, expecting to see a road. Instead, he was flying. Or hovering in the air with an immense open space in front of him. He was at least fifty metres above the ground. Below and ahead of him glistened the sea.

After a few seconds he realised that he wasn't flying or hovering; he was on board a ship, an enormous liner lying at anchor in a big harbour. He had no time to reflect on this, however, because another realisation hit him.

He was sitting in a wheelchair, unable to move his legs. Draped over his knees was a rug of the kind seen in films when paraplegics are taken out for an airing.

He made another attempt to move his legs. They didn't move a single millimetre. He could wriggle and flex his toes at will, but that was all.

The wind was blowing a gale. He shivered. At the same time he was hot inside. He was too appalled by his crippled state to speak or think. Before long his mood changed. Horror gave way to dejection and dejection to fury.

Never to be able to walk again.

The fact that, being paralysed, he would probably never leave this ship, let alone reach the Scottish border or return to Vienna, came home to him in all its implications. What shocked him most of all, however, was that something irreversible had happened to him. Something would never again be as it had been. In their heart of hearts, everyone itched to commit some irrevocable act. Like pushing some inoffensive stranger in front of a train. Or jerking the steering wheel while driving at 180 k.p.h. Or throwing a friend's pet dog out of a sixth-floor window. You didn't have to be a murderer or a suicide to experience that urge. Just a human being.

And now it had happened to him. Something that divided life into before and after. In a way, this wheelchair meant something even worse than waking up in a world emptied of its inhabitants. Because it affected him directly. His body, his last frontier.

He gazed out to sea. Far below him, waves were breaking against the ship's side with a monotonous, resounding crash. The wind carried the sound upwards, set a canvas awning fluttering, caused some tackle nearby to vibrate.

'Yes.'

He had to clear his throat.

'Yes, yes, that's the way it is.'

*

Could a paraplegic really move his toes?

Could he really feel his thigh when he slapped it?

He tugged at the rug. It was so firmly pinned beneath him, freeing it was quite an effort. At last, with a sudden jerk, he pulled it off his lap.

And saw that his legs were tightly secured to the chair with insulating tape.

There was something shiny beneath his feet: a snapped-off knife blade. Performing painful contortions, Jonas managed to bend down and pick it up. He cut his bonds. The blood streamed back into his legs so violently he cried out.

It was several minutes before his limbs felt somewhat less numb. He stood up, holding on to the back of the chair. Dragging his left leg, which had gone to sleep, he hobbled into the cabin.

He'd never seen such a luxurious suite in any hotel, let alone on board ship: fine wood and leather, lights everywhere, comfortable armchairs, an outsize plasma screen on the wall. An elegant spiral staircase leading to an upper deck.

Some notepaper was lying on the bureau. Jonas looked at the letterhead: *Queen Mary 2*.

*

Southampton docks were the biggest Jonas had ever seen. Their size meant he very soon found a car with the key in the ignition.

He drove slowly through the deserted streets in search of a bookshop. At one point his route was blocked by a truck, but he didn't dare get out to investigate. He felt he was negotiating a minefield. Although this English seaport seemed no more menacing and mysterious than any other deserted city, he found its lifelessness unpleasant, far more so than that of Vienna, where he was at least familiar with the streets.

A bookshop at last. He got out. A binbag full of empty wine bottles was lying on the pavement. He picked it up and hurled it blindly at some shop windows, hunched his shoulders and performed a clumsy dance, giving an impression of a drunken hooligan.

The door of the bookshop was open. A spacious two-storeyed establishment, it was lined from floor to ceiling with bookshelves. Aluminium ladders were leaning against them. The musty interior smelt of paper, of books.

He found the reference section after fifteen minutes and a pharmacopoeia after another ten. Then came the hardest part of his task. He didn't even know the German term for what he was looking for. There had to be some remedy for sleeping sickness. Sleeping sickness was also known as narcolepsy. So he looked up Narcolepsy. Nothing under that heading. Narcolon, Narcolute and Narcolyte were the first terms that appeared on the relevant page.

The nature and effect of those drugs were described in detail, and Jonas had to devote some time and effort to each entry before he could be sure that none of them would be of help. They were soporifics, not sleep inhibitors. But what would a drug against sleeping sickness be called? Antinarco? Narcostop? He bit his lip and went on turning the pages.

Although it wasn't midday yet, he could already feel tiredness stealing over him. This spurred him on. What he was doing now he should have done yesterday or the day before. If he allowed things to get to a stage where the Sleeper merely woke him up for brief periods in random locations before sleep overcame him once more, he would be . . .

Lost.

Yes, lost.

No, he was lost already. If the Sleeper gained complete control over him, he would be something other than that. What would he be then?

Conscious that he was staring into space, he straightened up again.

*

That afternoon he found it. He turned the page on impulse. At first he thought he was mistaken, believing that his clouded brain was merely misrepresenting what he was reading. But he checked and checked again until he was satisfied that, according to the pharmacopoeia, the drug Umirome contained various stimulants such as ephedrine and was one of the most effective remedies for sleeping sickness available.

*

A nearby chemist's stocked Umirome. Jonas took a bag and filled it with boxes of the stuff, ten of them with sixteen tablets in each. If need be, he would take every last one.

There was a fridge in the back room. Jonas looked for some mineral water, but all it contained, apart from a slab of butter and a piece of vacuum-packed steak, were some two dozen cans of beer. He shrugged his shoulders and cracked a can. Modern drugs were OK with alcohol. Besides, gastric discomfort or mild inebriation were the least of his concerns. He swallowed a tablet and put the box in his pocket.

Maximum daily dose: two tablets.

He fished out the box again and took another.

27

It was the motorway that seemed to move while Jonas
stayed where he was. His car made no sound, the white
lines glided past and the scenery changed, but he might
have been stationary.

The tyreless car flashed past him. He raised his arm
stiffly, unable to wave, then turned and watched it grow
smaller. When he turned back again he noticed that the
countryside was moving past far more slowly. He put his
foot back on the accelerator and everything went back to
how it had been before.

Shortly before it got dark he stopped near Northampton for some food. He searched the kitchen of a pub, but
all he found was a rock-hard loaf, some rancid bacon and
several eggs he didn't dare to eat. As he turned to go he
caught sight of some tins on a shelf. Without bothering to
check what was in them, he tipped the contents of two of
them into a saucepan.

*

It was dark. He was driving, he realised. He seemed to be
getting used to the effects of the drug. Its effects and side
effects. He was alert and lucid, without a trace of fatigue.
His heart was racing, his forehead permanently moist with

sweat. When he wiped the film away it reappeared within ten seconds. Before long the wiping became just a habit.

His powers of perception were gradually returning. He knew that he was going north, that night had fallen and he'd been driving for hours. He knew he'd stopped near Northampton and had something to eat. On the other hand, he'd forgotten *what* he'd eaten and whether he'd had anything to drink, whether he'd spent long there and done anything else. But that was unimportant.

He was driving.

*

He needed a break at some stage. He pulled up in the centre lane and folded the seat back. There was no danger of his going to sleep, he wasn't sleepy. He needed to relax, that was all.

He folded his hands on his chest and shut his eyes.

They opened again.

He shut them.

They opened again.

He clamped his eyelids together. His eyes were smarting. He could feel and hear the veins throbbing in his temples.

His eyes opened yet again.

He lay there for a while, gazing with owl-like intensity at the roof of the car. Then he returned the seat to its normal position. He mopped his brow and his eyes and drove on.

*

Dawn was just visible on the horizon when he stopped at a filling station near Lancaster. He got out. It was cold. He looked on the back seat for something to put on. No luck, and the boot contained nothing but a grubby sheet of plastic.

He waited, rubbing his arms and shuffling from one foot to the other, while the petrol flowed into the tank. It was a slow business. Something was wrong with the pump. He got back in the car and closed the door, watched the needle of the fuel gauge creep across the dial.

He had a strange sensation.

He felt he'd been here before. He hadn't, of course, but he couldn't shake off the impression that' he'd seen this little filling station with the flat concrete roof once before – in a different place. It was as if someone had uprooted a place familiar to him and transplanted it here.

He peered out. Nothing. As far as he could see, nothing and no one nearby. No one had been here for the last six weeks.

A trap. This incredibly slow petrol pump: a trap intended for him. He mustn't get out again. He must get away from here.

He lowered a rear window and swung round. There was no one behind him. He leant out of the window, then recoiled. No hand came reaching into the interior. He put his head out again. Swung round again. Still no one there. No alien creature, no wolf-bear, although he'd *seen* it. In the fraction of a second he'd spent looking out of the window, something had been sitting behind him. *Sitting behind him, staring at his back.*

He reached out of the window, released the catch on the nozzle of the petrol pump and let it fall to the ground. He shut the flap without screwing the cap back on, then closed the window, climbed back onto the driver's seat and drove off.

He looked in the rear-view mirror.

No one.

He switched on the interior light and turned round.

Dirty upholstery. A crumpled cigarette packet. A CD.

He switched off the light. Looked in the rear-view mirror again.

Mopped his brow.

Listened.

*

8 a.m. Smalltown.

The sun was up, but Jonas felt it was a cinematic hoax, as if the sky were a sheet of painted canvas in a film studio. He couldn't feel the sun's rays. He couldn't feel any wind.

He looked at the building, the number on the gate, the railings in front of it. On a hoarding across the road, a young housewife was advertising some product he'd never heard of.

Without reckoning up how many he'd taken, he swallowed another tablet. Quite suddenly he wondered how he'd got here. It wasn't that he couldn't remember the journey, but everything had become so unreal. Nothing seemed real, neither the drive here, nor the car, nor his present surroundings. Those tablets. Strong.

He rested his hands on the steering wheel. You. This is you, here and now.

Smalltown. Home to Marie's sister, who had married an English sexton, and to her mother, who had moved in with her younger daughter after her husband's death. This was where Marie had spent brief vacations twice a year. Jonas had never accompanied her, pleading pressure of work. The truth was, he'd always disliked getting to know his girlfriends' parents.

This was the building. The number was right and its appearance matched Marie's description of it. A four-storeyed, brick-built block of flats on the outskirts of town.

Jonas kicked the driver's door open but didn't get out. He eyed the woman on the hoarding. She reminded him

336

of an actress he'd much admired. In the days before he acquired a video recorder he had postponed and cancelled appointments for her sake, filled with an abiding sense of gratitude for the privilege of being her contemporary.

He had often tried to imagine what it would have been like to be born in another age with other contemporaries. In the fifteenth century, or in AD 400, or in 1000 BC. In Africa or Asia. Would he have been the same person?

Chance dictated who you lived with. The waiter who served you in a restaurant, your coal merchant, your schoolteacher, your daughter-in-law. They were your contemporaries. Singers, CEOs, scientists, committee chairmen – they were the people with whom you shared the planet in your day. People living 100 years hence would be different and have other contemporaries. Even if they lived in another part of the world, contemporaries were, ultimately, something positively private. They could just as well have lived 500 years before or after you, but they were doing so now. At the same time as you. That was how Jonas had felt, simply grateful to many of his contemporaries for being alive at the same time as himself, for breathing the same air and seeing the same sunrises and sunsets. He would have liked to tell them so, too.

He had wondered, many a time, whether Marie was his predestined partner in life. Would he have met her in any event? Might they also have met ten years later, and would the outcome have been the same? Might there exist, somewhere in the world, another woman who had been predestined for him? Might he only just have missed her on some occasion? Had they been standing together in a bus? Could they even have exchanged a glance, never to see each other again? Was her name Tanya, did she live with a man named Paul, was she unhappy with him, did she have children by him, was she wondering whether there might have been someone else?

Or was there a woman living in some other age with whom he should be, or should have been, linked? Was she already dead? Had she been a contemporary of Haydn? Of Schönberg? Or was she yet to be born, and had he himself been born too soon? When debating all these possibilities, Jonas had ruled nothing out. He'd really been more interested in the question than in any possible answers.

Drawing a deep breath, he got out and went up to the entrance, where he read the list of names beside the intercom.

T. Gane / L. Sadier
P. Harvey
R. M. Hall
Rosy Labouche
Peter Kaventsmann
F. Ibañez-Talavera
Hunter Stockton
Oscar Kliuna-ai
P. Malachy

That was the name. Malachy. The name of the man Marie's sister had married. The sexton.

Jonas drew another deep breath, then pushed the door open. It didn't occur to him to look around for a weapon. Although the lobby and stairs were only dimly lit, he felt unafraid. What drove him was a mixture of longing and despair. Nothing that would have made him turn back, whatever unpleasantness he encountered.

The flat was on the second floor. He tried the handle. The door wasn't locked.

He turned the light on. The first thing he saw was a pair of shoes – hers. Almost at the same time, he remembered how they had bought them together from a shop in Judengasse. He rubbed his eyes.

When he looked up again he saw her jacket hanging from a hook in the passage. He put out his hand and stroked the material, buried his face in it, breathed in her smell.

'Hi,' he said dully.

He couldn't help thinking of the rest of her clothes. The ones in Vienna at this moment. How far away they were. Thousands of kilometres away.

It was a spacious flat. The kitchen led off the living room, the living room adjoined a bedroom, probably that of Marie's sister and her husband. The occupant of the next bedroom was clearly an elderly woman. This was apparent from various objects, but also from its tidiness and the way it smelt.

The third bedroom lay at the end of the passage. One look was enough to convince him. Marie's suitcase against the wall. Her make-up case on the chest of drawers. The slippers she took everywhere beside the bed, on which lay her nightdress. Her jeans, her blouse, her jewellery, her bra, her scent. Her mobile. Which he'd called so often. And on whose voicemail he'd left messages. The battery was flat. He didn't know her PIN number.

Having dumped the suitcase on the bed, he opened the wardrobe and drawers and packed anything that came to hand. He didn't bother to fold things any more than he worried about soiling her blouses with the soles of her shoes.

A last look around. Nothing else. He knelt on the suitcase and zipped it up.

*

He lay on her bed, his head on her pillow, her duvet over him for warmth. Her smell enveloped him. He found it odd that she seemed far more alive to him here than in the flat they'd shared. Perhaps it was because this was where she'd been last.

He heard a noise. He didn't know where it was coming from, but it didn't scare him.

*

He hadn't checked the time, so he couldn't have said how long he'd been lying there. It was after midday. He carried the suitcase out to the car and went back to see if he'd missed anything. In the wastepaper basket he found a shopping list in Marie's handwriting. He smoothed it out and put it in his pocket.

*

He drove steadily, nonchalantly. Now and then he turned his head, but not for fear that someone might be sitting behind him, just to make sure the suitcase was really there. He stopped to eat and drink and stacked some bottles of mineral water on the passenger seat. He'd been tormented since that morning by an almost unquenchable thirst, probably another side effect of the tablets. His urine, when he relieved himself, had a pinkish tinge. Shaking his head, he squeezed another tablet out of its blister pack. His shoulders were going numb.

He soon lost all conception of how long he'd been driving. Distances seemed to be relative. The motorway signs meant nothing. Having only just passed Lancaster, he came to the Coventry turn-off shortly afterwards. On the other hand, the stretch between Northampton and Luton seemed to take hours. He looked at his feet operating the pedals.

As a youngster he'd been mystified when pop and film stars committed suicide. Why kill yourself when you had everything? Why did people snuff themselves out when they had millions in the bank, consorted with other celebrities and went to bed with the most famous and desirable individuals on the planet? Because they were lonely, was the answer. Lonely and unhappy. How stupid, he'd thought. You didn't kill yourself because of that. That singer shouldn't have slit her wrists, she should have called him instead. He would have been a good friend to her. He would have listened to her, comforted her, taken her away on holiday. She would have had a better friend in him than any she could ever have found among her fellow stars. He would have taken a detached view of her problems and straightened her out. In his company she would have felt secure.

Or so he had thought. It wasn't until later that he grasped why those people had killed themselves: for the same reason as the poor and unknown. They couldn't hold on to themselves. They couldn't endure being alone with themselves and had realised that other people's company was only a palliative. That it thrust the problem into the background without solving it. Being yourself twenty-four hours a day, never anyone else, was a blessing in many cases but a curse in others.

*

At Sevenoaks, south of London, he exchanged the car for a moped big enough for him to wedge the suitcase between his legs and the handlebars. Whether he would last fifty kilometres like that was another matter, but he needed a two-wheeler. He had no wish to go through the Tunnel on foot. The light of the setting sun helped him in his quest. He hadn't wanted to make his way through Dover in the dark.

Jonas rode down the motorway at eighty to ninety k.p.h., trying every few minutes to find a more comfortable position for his legs. He drew up his knees and cautiously rested his feet on the suitcase, hung his legs over it and let his feet dangle. He even doubled up one leg and sat on it, but a relaxed position eluded him. When it got dark he wedged his legs between the suitcase and the seat and left it at that.

The headwind seemed to refresh his brain. He soon felt more clear-headed and less as if he were propelling himself along under water. He was able to reflect on what lay ahead. First through the Tunnel, then across France and Germany, collecting up the cameras. And all this on tablets, with a smouldering fuse.

He would never sleep again.

Shortly before his destination he recognised a grain silo despite the darkness. From here it was barely two kilometres to the mouth of the Tunnel. If he turned off right, however, he would get to the field where he'd spent the night.

He didn't know why, but something inside him made him turn off. His muscles automatically tensed as the beam of the moped's headlight illuminated the field ahead of him. The wind was strengthening. The silence seemed to be more natural, and that was just what Jonas found so unpleasant. But he didn't turn back. Something lured him on. At the same time, he knew that he was being irrational, that there was no good reason for this escapade.

Outside the tent he killed the engine but left the headlight on. He got off.

The motorbike with the slashed tyres. The awning. Sleeping mats lying around. An uninflated air-bed. A torn road map. Two sacks of rubbish. And the clothes he'd left here. He felt them. They were almost dry. He took off his borrowed things and put on his trousers and T-shirt. Only his shoes were past wearing. The damp had warped and shrunk the leather. He couldn't get his feet into them.

He switched off the moped's headlight, not wanting to be stranded here with a flat battery.

Although everything inside him balked at the prospect, he went inside the tent and sat down. He groped for the torch and turned it on. Two rucksacks. The tins of food. The camping stove. The Discman and CDs. The newspaper. The sex magazine.

Five days ago he'd spent the night here.

This sleeping bag had been lying here on its own for five days. And for over a month before his first visit. It would lie here on its own from now on.

Something brushed against the outside of the tent.

'Hey!'

It sounded as if someone were searching for the entrance on the wrong side. Jonas strained his eyes but could see nothing, no figure, no moving shape. He knew it was the wind, could only be the wind, but he gulped involuntarily. And coughed.

No need to be scared of anything that has a voice, he told himself.

Taking care to move steadily and smoothly, he crawled out of the tent. It was a clear night. He drew several deep breaths. Without looking round, he started the moped and rode off with one arm raised in farewell.

Never again. He would never come back here again.

This thought preoccupied him on the way to the Tunnel. The same thought continued to preoccupy him as he plunged into its dark mouth and the space around him was suddenly filled with the throaty hum of the engine. That tent, those sleeping bags, those CDs – he'd seen them for the last time, would never see them again. They were over and done with. He realised that they were arbitrarily selected, unimportant objects. To him, however, they possessed importance, if only the importance conferred on them by the fact that he remembered them better than other things. They were objects he'd touched and whose touch he could still feel. Objects he could recall as vividly as if they were right in front of him. End of story.

He squeezed between the train and the side of the tunnel. Once past the rearmost carriage, he felt around in the darkness until he grasped the handlebars of the DS. The saddle emitted its usual pneumatic hiss as he sat down on it. A well-remembered sound. He smiled.

'Hello,' he murmured.

The DS had been waiting here since he'd abandoned it. It had stood in this spot beneath the sea while he'd been in England, hearing and seeing nothing, just standing here behind the train. It had been standing here in the dark when he got to Smalltown. Standing here with these handlebars and this seat and this footrest. Click-click. With this gear change. Here. While he was far away.

And now the moped was standing at the other end of the train. It would continue to stand there for a long time. Until it rusted away and disintegrated, or until the roof of the tunnel collapsed. For many years. All alone in the dark.

Jonas wedged the suitcase between himself and the handlebars. He'd had more room on the moped, but there was enough to enable him to ride straight along a tunnel. He stepped on the kick-starter. The engine caught, the headlight came on.

'Ah,' he said softly.

*

Stars were twinkling overhead when he reached the other side, and he felt he ought to greet each one. The moon was shining, the air was mild. Silence reigned.

The truck was standing where he'd left it. He thumped the side with his fist. No sound of movement. Cautiously, he opened the tailboard and peered in. Darkness.

He crawled inside. He knew roughly where a torch was to be found. While feeling around for it he sang a marching song at the top of his voice, one his father had taught him. Whenever he couldn't remember the words he plugged the gaps with barrack-room expletives.

He turned on the torch and searched every corner of the interior, even shining a light beneath the furniture. It wouldn't have surprised him to come across an explosive charge or an acid bath, but he found nothing. Nothing that struck him as suspicious.

He wheeled the DS on board. He was about to secure it to the bars when the floor beneath his feet gave a lurch. At the same time, he heard a clatter.

He leapt out of the truck. On the ground the swaying sensation was even stronger. Feeling dizzy, he lay down.

An earthquake.

It stopped just as this occurred to him, but he went on lying there for several minutes with his arms and legs stretched out, waiting.

An earthquake. Only a minor one, but an earthquake in a world in which only one human being existed provided the latter with food for thought. Was this an ordinary natural phenomenon – part of a process that would continue for countless millions of years? Was it a displacement of tectonic plates, in other words, or was it a message?

After lying on the bare ground for ten minutes and getting his clothes wet again, he ventured back into the truck. He promptly closed the tailboard and turned on all the lights. Then he stripped off his wet things and took some trousers and a pair of shoes from a cupboard.

While changing he recalled what had been reported about another quake some years ago. That one had occurred on the sun, not the earth. Its magnitude had been estimated at 12 on the Richter scale. The most powerful quake ever recorded here on earth had reached a magnitude of 9.5. Because magnitude 12 defied the imagination, the scientists added that the sunquake had been comparable in extent to the cataclysm that would result if dynamite were laid across all five continents to a depth of one metre and detonated all at once.

A layer of dynamite one metre deep. All over the world. Detonated all at once. That was magnitude 12. It sounded colossal, but who could really imagine the devastation that would be wrought by the detonation of some 150 million cubic kilometres of dynamite?

Jonas had pictured that sunquake, yet no one had been there to witness it. The sun had quaked in solitude. At magnitude 12. Neither he nor anyone else had been there. Nobody had seen that quake, just as nobody had seen the robot land on Mars, but it had happened just the same. The sun had quaked, the robot had floated down to the surface of Mars. Those events had taken place – had exerted an influence on other things.

*

Dawn was breaking when Jonas collected the first camera at Metz. He was delighted to discover that it hadn't rained and the mechanism was still working. He rewound the tape, which appeared to have recorded something. He would have liked to watch it right away, but there was no time.

Although his eyes were smarting more and more, he drove on. He didn't bother with another tablet for the time being. He wasn't tired. The problems with which his body was contending were mechanical. His eyes. His joints. It was as if the marrow had been sucked from his bones. He swallowed a Parkemed.

He stared at the grey ribbon ahead of him. This was him, Jonas. Here on the motorway to Vienna. Homeward-bound with Marie's suitcase. And with unsolved mysteries.

He thought of his parents. Could they see him at this moment? Were they sad?

Jonas had always done this at the sight of someone in distress: thought of the parents of the person concerned and wondered how they would feel if they could see their offspring in that state.

Whenever he watched a cleaning woman at work, he wondered whether it saddened her mother that her daughter had to pursue such a menial occupation. Or when he saw the holes in the dirty socks of a wino sleeping it off on a park bench. He too had had a mother and father, and his parents must have dreamt of a different future for their son. The same applied to the workman breaking up asphalt in the street with a pneumatic drill, or to the timid young woman sitting anxiously in a doctor's waiting room, awaiting his diagnosis. Their parents weren't present, but they would be riven with pity if they could see how their offspring were faring. The concern they felt would be directed at a particular aspect of those offspring: at the child whom they'd reared, whose nappies they'd changed, whom they had taught to speak and walk, whom they had nursed through childhood ailments and accompanied to school. The child whose life they had shared from the very first day, and whom they had loved from first to last. That child was now in distress. It wasn't leading the life its parents had wanted for it.

Jonas had thought of the parents whenever he saw a small boy in a sandpit being bullied by a bigger one. Or workmen with gaunt faces and grimy fingernails and coughs, with worn-out bodies and atrophied minds. Or failures. Or those in distress, in dread, in despair. Their faces spoke of their parents' sorrow, not merely their own.

Could his own parents see him at this moment?

*

Jonas took the next tablet after collecting another camera at Saarbrücken. He could hear the roar of a waterfall that

347

existed only in his head. He looked around. He was sitting on the end of the truck with his legs dangling. The bottle of mineral water beside him had toppled over and spilled some of its contents on the asphalt. He took a swig and screwed the cap on.

He drove on, picking up more cameras as he went. Sometimes he deliberately concentrated on the difficulties that lay ahead, sometimes he allowed his thoughts to wander. This occasionally caused him to sideslip into a world he found uncomfortable, and he had to extricate himself by force – by feeding his mind with images and subjects that had proved themselves in the past. Images of an icy waste. Images of the seashore.

He drove as fast as he could. It would be hard to spot the cameras on the motorway at night, he realised, but he had to stop three times. Once to relieve himself, once because he was hungry, and once because he couldn't bear to sit in the cab any longer and felt he would go mad if he didn't get out at once and stretch his legs.

He got to Regensburg and picked up the camera there. At the service area where he'd eaten on the outward trip he strolled around the shop, eyeing the shelves full of chocolate bars and drinks, but nothing took his fancy. All he wanted to do was walk and allow his mind to wander.

He thumbed through some sports papers. Tried to fathom the content of an article in a Turkish newspaper. Played with the buttons on the lighting console. Wheeled a wire trolley filled with containers of engine oil in front of the filling station and looked at it on the CCTV screen. Planted himself in front of the camera and pulled faces. Went back to the monitor. Saw the trolley standing there.

He got back in the cab before dawn could be seen in the sky. It was so light by the time he neared Passau, fortunately, that he spotted the road maintenance depot just as he drove past it.

At the Austrian border he felt a weight lift from his shoulders. He had often felt this in the past, but only when driving in the opposite direction. Now he was almost through. Two more cameras, then on to Vienna. To complete his work.

He glanced at the suitcase lying on the bunk behind him. That had been her, the woman with whom he'd felt a part of something great. Although he hadn't needed anyone's confirmation that Marie was right for him, he could have done with such an oracle in other respects. When in his life had he been in extreme danger without realising it? The answer might have been: On 23 November 1987, when you very nearly touched a live wire. Or on 4 June 1992, when you were tempted to make some truculent remark to that uppity type in the bar but swallowed your annoyance, thereby avoiding a lethal punch up. But Jonas would have been interested in more mundane questions as well. Like: What profession should he have taken up in order to become rich? Which women would have come home with him like a shot, and where and when? Had he met Marie before their first conscious encounter without remembering it? Or: Did there exist, somewhere in the world, a woman who was looking for a man exactly like himself? Answer: Yes, Esther Kraut of such and such a street in Amsterdam. One look, and she would have pounced on you.

No, that was cheap of him. The answer would probably have been: You've already found her.

Question: Which well-known woman would have fallen in love with me if I'd done something? Answer: The painter Mary Hansen, if you'd spontaneously, without saying a word, presented her with a lucky charm in the foyer of the Hotel Orient, Brussels, on the night of 26 April 1997.

Question: Who would have become the best friend I could ever have had? Answer: Oskar Schweda, 23 Liechtensteinstrasse, Vienna 1090.

Question: How often has Marie cheated on me? Answer: Never.

Question: On whom would I have fathered the nicest children? Answer: Your masseuse, Frau Lindsay. The two of you would have produced Benjy and Anne.

Well, who knows?

He squeezed another tablet out of the pack and washed it down with some beer.

28

Jonas went round the flat. He didn't notice any changes. It looked as it had before his departure. He returned to the truck.

He sat down on the sofa and stretched his legs, then stood up again. It seemed unreal to him that his trip was over. He felt as if he'd made it years ago, as if the drive to Smalltown were something that hadn't taken place, properly speaking, but had existed within him for ever. Yet it had happened, he knew. That mug with his name on it had fallen over and he'd had to mop coffee off these pieces of furniture. But it was as if those objects had lost some of their character. The armchair in a truck parked on a motorway in France was something other than the armchair he saw here now. The TV on which he'd watched that awful video was the same as the one in the cabinet over there, but it seemed to have lost something. Importance, perhaps. Significance, magnitude. It was just a TV. And he was on the move no longer. He was back.

*

His flat smelt stuffy. He went through the rooms in silence. No one had been here. Even the inflatable doll was still lying in the bath, which was grimy with plaster and brick dust.

He set up a camera in front of the wall mirror in the bedroom. Checked the light and looked through the lens. Saw the reflection of the camera facing the mirror and his figure bending over it. Put in a tape and started filming.

He shut the door. Outside it, right in front of the key-hole, he stationed the second camera. He looked through the lens. The camera position needed adjusting. The chest of drawers with the picture of the washerwoman above it was clearly visible now. He pressed the record button.

He was just leaving when he caught sight of a videotape on top of the TV in the living room. It was the one that had recorded his circuit of the Danube Canal. He took it with him.

*

He walked through the Belvedere Gardens to stretch his legs, which were stiff after the drive. His thoughts were becoming muddled again. He slapped his face. It was still too soon for the next tablet. Better to set to work.

With the aid of a furniture trolley, he took twelve TVs from a nearby shop to the Upper Belvedere Palace. Steadily, slowly, he put them down one after the other on the gravel path. He didn't want to hurry. He never wanted to do anything quickly ever again.

He placed the fifth set on the first, the sixth on the second, the seventh on the third. The eighth went on top of the fifth, the ninth on the sixth, the tenth on the eighth, the eleventh on the tenth. The twelfth he deposited facing the rest to act as a seat. Cautiously, he sat down to see how it looked. The TVs in front of him formed a handsome sculpture.

He plugged dozens of extension leads together and connected the TVs to sockets inside the Upper Belvedere Palace. Then he turned them on. They all worked. An elevenfold hiss filled the air.

He connected the video cameras to the TVs. The screens turned blue one after another. Then he connected the cameras to mains adaptors, which he also plugged into sockets inside the palace.

It was just before half past two. He programmed all eleven cameras to switch to 'Play' at 2.45. Although he took his time, he was ready five minutes after the half-hour.

With impressive precision, all the cameras clicked on together. A moment later, the eleven screens were displaying eleven different images.

St Pölten, Regensburg, Nuremberg, Schwäbisch Hall, Heilbronn, France.

4 p.m. on 11 August eleven times over. Eleven times the same moment recorded in different parts of the world. At St Pölten clouds had gathered, at Rheims a strong wind was blowing. At Amstetten the air shimmered with heat, at Passau it was drizzling.

At precisely that moment Jonas had been standing on the roof of the cab near the mouth of the Channel Tunnel, thinking of these cameras. Of the one at Ansbach – that one there, hi! Of the one at Passau – that one there. Of the one at Saarbrücken. Of the bit of Saarbrücken he was seeing now. Of the bit of Amstetten he was seeing now.

He shut his eyes, recalling those minutes on top of the truck. He felt the roof of the cab beneath him, sensed the heat, smelt the smell. At that time

this
– he opened his eyes –
had been there.
This.
Had been
there.

And now that time was over. It existed only on these tapes. But it was there for ever, whether or not it was shown.

He switched all eleven cameras to pause.

At Hollandstrasse he sat down on the floor and unzipped the suitcase. He had packed Marie's things higgledy-piggledy, so the contents spilled out. He buried his fingers in the soft material. Pulled out one garment after another. Sniffed them. Smooth, cool blouses. Her fragrance. Her.

He weighed her mobile in his hand. There was no object he associated with her more closely. Not her keys, not her blouses, not her panties, not her lipstick, not her identity card. This phone had sent him her messages. She had taken it everywhere with her. And stored in it were the messages he'd sent her. Before and after 4 July.

And he didn't know her PIN.

He repacked everything in the suitcase and put it down beside the door.

*

He put on the blinkered goggles. The computerised voice guided him across the city. Several times he felt a jolt and heard a scraping sound.

The block of flats outside which he removed his goggles was a modern one in Krongasse, only a few streets from his father's deserted flat. It made a friendly impression. The front door was open, so he was able to leave the crowbar in the boot.

He climbed the stairs to the first floor and tried the doors. All were locked. He went up to the second floor. Door number four opened. He read the nameplate.

Ilse-Heide Brzo / Christian Vidovic

There was a draught. Windows appeared to be open on both sides of the flat. He turned left. The bedroom. Rumpled sheets. On the wall, a huge map of the world. Jonas measured the distance he'd driven on his trip to England.

It wasn't far at all. Africa was far away, Australia even further. Vienna to England was only an outing.

Smalltown. That was where he'd been. Just there.

The study. Two desks, one bearing a computer, the other a manual typewriter. Walls lined with bookshelves. Most of the titles were unfamiliar to him. One shelf held a dozen copies of each of three books. He read the titles. A chess manual, a thriller, a lifestyle adviser.

He examined the typewriter, an Olivetti Lettera 32. It amazed him that anyone had still been using such a mechanical monster. What were computers for?

He pressed some keys, saw the types hinge forward.

He put in a sheet of paper and wrote:

I'm standing here, writing this sentence.

A typewriter. The whole alphabet was there. Typed in the correct order, letters could spell out anything. Horrific novels, books on the meaning of life, erotic poems. You only needed to know the correct sequence. Letter after letter. Word. Word after word. Sentence. Sentence after sentence. Forming a whole.

He recalled what, as a boy, he had imagined foreign languages to be. It hadn't occurred to him that they could differ in vocabulary and grammar. He'd thought a particular letter in German corresponded to a particular letter in English and to other letters in French or Italian. An E in German might be a K in English, an L in German an X in French, an R in German an M in Hungarian, an S in Italian an F in Japanese.

Jonas might be Wilvt in English, Ahbug in Spanish and Elowg in Russian.

The kitchen-cum-living-room. A dining table, a range of kitchen cabinets, photographs on the wall. One was of a man and a woman with a little boy. The woman was smiling, the boy laughing. A pretty woman. Blue eyes, fine features, good figure. The boy, a slice of bread in his hand, was pointing to something. A nice-looking child. This Vidovic fellow was lucky to have such a family. He had no need to look so strained. Although smiling, he didn't seem wholly at peace with himself.

A pleasant flat. People had lived there harmoniously.

Jonas sat down on the sofa and put his feet up.

*

Most of the overhead lights in St Stephen's Cathedral had gone out. The smell of incense, on the other hand, was no fainter. Jonas walked along the aisles, looked into the sacristy, called out. His voice went echoing around the walls. The saints in their niches resolutely ignored him.

He was growing sleepy, he noticed, so he took a tablet.

His heart was thumping. He wasn't agitated. On the contrary, he was feeling relaxed and carefree. The palpitations were a side effect of the tablets. They made him feel he could remain on his feet for days longer, provided he continued to take them at regular intervals. Apart from an accelerated heartbeat, their only disadvantage was the sensation, stronger at some moments than others, that his head was being inflated.

He looked around. Grey walls. Creaky old pews. Statues.

*

Back at the Brigittenauer embankment he packed the two cameras and went round the flat once more. Whatever met his eye, he looked at it knowing he would never see it again.

He blamed his slight feeling of nausea on the tablets.

'*Goodbye*,' he said in a husky voice.

Although Jonas had looked out of his window at the *Kurier* building countless times, he'd never been inside. Having broken the door down, he searched the commissionaire's cubby hole for a plan of the building. He failed to find one, but he did find two bunches of keys, which he pocketed.

Part of the *Kurier*'s archive was in the basement, as he'd guessed. Luckily, it was the older part. Back numbers more recent than 1 January 1980 were kept elsewhere.

He walked down row after row of shelves and filing cabinets, pushing library steps aside and pulling out massive steel drawers undoubtedly capable of withstanding fire for some time. Many of the labels on the box files had faded, and he had to pull them out and check their contents to find out the date of the newspapers inside. At last he came upon the section in which newspapers from his year of birth were kept. He looked for the month, opened the relevant box file, and removed the editions that had appeared on his birthday and the day after.

'Thanks,' he said. 'Good night!'

*

He went to Hollandstrasse to fetch Marie's suitcase. His original intention had been to leave at once, but the sight of those familiar surroundings made him linger.

He roamed around touching things, shutting his eyes and remembering his parents. His childhood. Here.

He went into the next room, where he'd left the boxes he hadn't unpacked. He reached into one containing photographs and removed a handful. He also took the musical teddy bear with him.

On the way out he suddenly remembered the chest. He put the suitcase down and went upstairs.

He stared at the chest with his arms folded. Should he go and get an axe? Or should he get it over and done with and blow the cursed thing up?

He dragged it across the dirty attic floor and over to a skylight. As he did so, he thought he heard a brief clatter. He examined the chest from every side but couldn't locate the source of the sound.

He sat down on it and buried his face in his hands.

'Ah! What an idiot I am!'

He turned the chest upside down. It had been the wrong way up – there was the handle. He raised the lid. It wasn't even locked.

He saw photos, hundreds of them, together with some old wooden platters, several dirty watercolours without protective frames, a set of tobacco pipes and a small silver box with nothing in it. What galvanised him was the sight of two spools of film. They reminded him of the Super-8 camera Uncle Reinhard had given his father in the late 1970s. For some years it had often been used to film special occasions such as Christmases, birthdays and wine-drinking excursions to Wachau. In those days his father would never get into Uncle Reinhard's car without the camera.

Jonas picked up one of the spools. He felt sure the films were of family outings, of excursions to the wine district, of his mother and grandmother. The ones shot before 1982 would show his grandmother talking to the camera – in silence, because the Super-8 had no sound-recording facility. He felt positive he would find such shots. But he had absolutely no intention of making sure.

*

358

The double bed was on castors. Jonas trundled it out of the furniture store's delivery bay and into Schweighofergasse, where he gave it a shove. It coasted down to Mariahilfer Strasse and hit a parked car with a resounding crash. He pushed it on towards the ring road with his foot. Just short of Museumsplatz, where the ground dropped away, he pushed it ahead of him like a bobsleigh and, when it picked up speed, leapt aboard. He got to his knees, then his feet, and went surfing down Babenberger Strasse to the Burgring. It wasn't too easy to keep his balance.

He set up the bed in Heldenplatz, not far from the spot where he'd painted his plea for help on the ground six weeks earlier. His intention had been to obliterate the letters, but rain had already relieved him of that task. All that remained of them were four vague smudges.

He loaded the essentials for the coming night into the truck and drove it to the square. He arranged some torches round the bed at a distance of five metres and placed two TVs at its foot. These he connected to the cameras he'd filmed with that morning on the Brigittenauer embankment, likewise to the accumulator. For safety's sake he checked the output level. All was well. There wouldn't be any power failure tonight, at least.

At random intervals all over the square he distributed spotlights, aiming them at the sky because he didn't want to be directly illuminated. Before long there were so many cables snaking across the grass and concrete he kept tripping over them, especially as it was getting dark.

He placed Marie's suitcase beside the bed. He wedged the photos he'd brought from Hollandstrasse into a side pocket, together with the newspapers, to prevent them from blowing away. He fetched the pillow and blanket from the cab of the truck and tossed them onto the mattress. By now the spotlights were bathing the square in an unreal glow. It was like being in an enchanted park.

There stood the Hofburg and there the palace gate. Beyond them, the Burgring lined with trees. On the right, a monument: two basilisks grappling head to head, knee to knee, though they looked as if they were propping each other up.

In the middle of the square, his bed. He felt as if he was on a film set. Even the sky looked artificial. In this orange half light, everything seemed to have two aspects. The trees, the wrought-iron gates, the Hofburg itself, all looked natural and authentic but, at the same time, relentlessly slick.

Jonas lit the torches and started the videotapes. He stretched out on the bed, hands clasped behind his head, and gazed up at the orange-tinged night sky.

There he lay.

Untroubled by the wolf-bear.

Or by ghosts.

Untroubled.

*

Jonas swallowed another tablet, just to be on the safe side. He was lying on a bed, after all. He looked at the two TV screens. One showed a camera with the red light blinking and, in the background, part of the bed in which he'd slept for years, the other the top of a chest of drawers surmounted by some framed embroidery.

Apart from the red flashes, both pictures were without movement.

The square was silent save for the hum of the cameras and an occasional puff of wind that stirred the trees.

The very first photograph showed him as a boy with his father, half of whose head was missing, needless to say. His father had draped his left arm round Jonas's shoulders and was gripping the boy's wrists in his right hand, as if the two of them were tussling. Jonas's mouth was open, as if he were squealing.

Those hands, his father's hands. Big hands, they were. He remembered how often he'd nestled against them, those big, rough hands. He felt the roughness of that skin, the strength in those muscles. He even caught a momentary whiff of his father's smell.

Those hands in that photo had existed. Where were they now?

The picture he was seeing wasn't just a snapshot taken by his mother. What he was seeing was what his mother had seen at the instant she took it. He was seeing with his mother's eyes. Seeing what a long-dead person had seen at a particular moment many years ago.

He still had a vivid recollection of the phone call. He was sitting in his flat on the Brigittenauer embankment, into which he'd moved a short while before, doing a difficult crossword puzzle. He'd opened a can of beer and was looking forward to a quiet evening when the phone rang. His father said, with uncharacteristic bluntness: 'If you want to see her alive one more time, you'd better come at once.'

She'd been ill for ages, so they all knew it would happen. Even so, that sentence rang in his ears like a thunderclap. He dropped the ballpoint and drove to Hollandstrasse. The hospital had taken his mother home at her own request.

She was past speaking. He took her hand and squeezed it. She didn't open her eyes.

He sat down on a chair beside the bed. His father sat on the other side. He reflected that he'd been born in this room, this bed, and now it was his mother's deathbed.

It happened in the small hours. They both knew exactly when. His mother heaved a loud, stertorous sigh and fell silent. Silent and still.

It occurred to Jonas that, if people's accounts of near-death experiences were to be believed, she was hovering overhead, looking down at them. Looking down at what she was leaving behind. At herself.

He stared at the ceiling.

He waited for the medical officer to come and certify her death. He waited for the men from the Municipal Funeral Service. There was a dull thud as they were placing the corpse in the metal coffin, as if her head had struck the side. He and his father winced. The men didn't turn a hair. They were the most aloof and taciturn individuals he'd ever come across.

He helped his father with the formalities, which entailed registering the death certificate in a gloomy government office and applying for a cremation licence. Then he drove home.

Back at his flat he recalled the previous day, when she'd still been alive – when he'd still been ignorant of what was to come. He walked around, looking at various objects and thinking: the last time I saw this, she was still alive. He thought this while looking at the espresso machine, the kitchen stove, the bedside light. The newspaper, too. He went on doing the crossword puzzle, looking at the letters he'd written in the night before and remembering.

A before. And a now.

*

Towards midnight Jonas felt hungry. He daubed some slices of pumpernickel with jam in the semi-darkness of a supermarket aisle.

*

The screens were displaying their usual images. He had switched the cameras to repeat, so this was their third showing of the camera in the mirror and the room with no one in it. His back was stiff. He stretched, grimacing with pain, then lay down on the bed and took out the newspapers.

He remembered this typeface and layout. This was what the *Kurier* had looked like when he was a boy.

He read the articles in his birthday edition without really taking them in. It fascinated him to think that he was reading what people had read on the day his mother brought him into the world. This was what they had held in their hands at that time.

He perused the next day's paper even more closely. After all, it reported what had happened on his birthday. He learnt that Americans had demonstrated against the Vietnam War, that Austria was in the grip of election fever, that a drunk had driven his car into the Danube without injuring anyone, and that the open-air swimming baths had been besieged because of the glorious weather.

That had been his birthday. His first day on earth.

*

In the morning he turned off all the spotlights and dunked the torches in a bucket of water. They hissed, sending up clouds of steam. Having got hold of a video recorder from an electrical shop on the way, he connected it to a TV. He put in the tape of his drive to Schwedenplatz, which he hadn't watched after editing it.

He sat down on the bed and pressed 'Play'.

He saw the Spider coming towards him. It rounded the bend and headed towards the bridge. Drove along the Heiligenstädter embankment and past the Rossbauer Barracks to Schwedenplatz. Drove across the bridge and along

Augartenstrasse to Gaussplatz, where it had an accident.

The driver got out, walked unsteadily to the back of the car and reached into the boot. Got in again and drove on.

Jonas turned off the recorder.

*

He found himself back in the Prater. It was just before noon. He'd been for a long walk but couldn't remember it in detail. All he knew was that he'd simply set off, immersed in thoughts that had long eluded him.

He was dragging one leg, he didn't know why. He tried to walk normally. It was something of an effort, but he succeeded.

He walked across the Jesuitenwiese. He didn't know what he was doing there, but he walked on. The sun was almost directly overhead.

It occurred to him that he'd meant to revisit the pubs in which he'd left messages, so as to recall the meal and day in question, but he didn't care to do so, not now.

He felt as if he'd been in a battle. Such a violent and protracted battle it no longer mattered who had won.

He swallowed a tablet and crossed over into the Wurstelprater. At the cycle-hire depot he got into a rickshaw, one of those canopied four-wheelers tourists used to enjoy pedalling across the Prater. There was something he still had to do.

*

Pedalling steadily and rhythmically, he rode across the Central Cemetery. The spade he'd got from the cemetery's nursery clanked against the rickshaw's frame. A gentle breeze was blowing, and the sun had disappeared behind a small bank of clouds. This made the trip even pleasanter. In contrast to the hush prevailing in the city, he found the silence here soothing. At least it didn't intimidate him.

His quest for a freshly dug mound of earth took him past the graves of many famous people. Many were reminiscent of royal mausoleums. Others were plain, with nothing more than unobtrusive stone slabs bearing the names of their occupants.

It surprised him to see how many well-known people were buried here. In the case of some names, he wondered why their owners had been laid to rest among celebrities, as he'd never heard of them. Where others were concerned, he was astonished to see that they'd died only a few years ago, having been under the impression that they'd been dead for decades. In the case of still others, he was surprised he hadn't heard of their death.

He was so enjoying his leisurely progress across the cemetery, he temporarily forgot why he'd come. He recalled the frequent occasions in his childhood when he and his grandmother had travelled here by tram to tend his great-grandparents' grave. Later on he had visited his grandmother's grave with his mother. His mother had lit candles, pulled out weeds and planted flowers while he wandered around, inhaling the cemetery's characteristic scent of flowers, soil and freshly mown grass.

He'd wasted no thought on death, nor even on his dead grandmother. The sight of all the trees had aroused visions of the marvellous games he and his friends could have played in this place and how long one would take to be found in a game of hide-and-seek. When his mother summoned him to fill the watering can at the fountain, he had returned to her world with reluctance.

In a way, he'd been closer to the dead than to the living around him. The dead beneath his feet he incorporated into his daydreams as a matter of course. The grown-ups carrying their carrier bags along the paths, on the other hand, he faded out. In his imagination he'd been alone with his friends.

Did it really have to be a new grave? The soil wouldn't be that much looser.

An idea occurred to him.

*

The post-1995 records were stored in a data bank. The heavy ledgers used in previous years smelt of mildew and some of the pages were coming adrift. Jonas had to consult one of these tomes. He knew the year precisely, 1989. But he wasn't so sure of the month. He thought it was May. May or June.

His search was made more difficult by the handwriting of the officials who had recorded the location of the graves. Many entries, especially the ones written in Gothic script, were almost indecipherable, others had faded. What was more, the tablets' side effects were becoming more pronounced. His head felt as if it were in a vice and the lines were dancing before his eyes. He was determined to go on looking, however, even if he had to sit on this worn-out swivel chair for another twenty-four hours.

And then he found it. Date of death: 23 April. Date of interment: 29 April.

He hadn't been present at the time.

He wrote the coordinates of the grave on a slip of paper and replaced the ledger tidily on its shelf. The rickshaw was standing in front of the cemetery's administration building. He pedalled off, spade clattering. There was a strong scent of grass.

Bender, Ludwig 1892–1944
Bender, Juliane 1898–1989

The old woman had never mentioned a husband, but that didn't matter now. He took the spade and started digging.

After a quarter of an hour he had to get down into the pit to go on working. After an hour his hands were raw and blistered. His back ached so badly he had to keep shutting his eyes and groaning. He laboured on until, nearly two hours after his spade first bit into the ground, it struck something hard. At first he thought it was just another of the stones he'd already thrown out of the grave. To his relief, however, a little more of the coffin was revealed with each spadeful of earth he flung aside.

The lid had become dislodged. He peered through the crack. It might have been his imagination, but he thought he saw a shred of cloth with something grey inside it.

He straightened up, breathing heavily. To his surprise, he could smell nothing but earth.

Sorry, it has to be done.

He pushed the lid aside. Lying in the damp, decaying wooden box was a human skeleton clad in rags.

Hello.

That was what remained of Frau Juliane Bender. That hand had held his own when it was still clothed in flesh. He had gazed into that face when it was still a face.

Goodbye.

Jonas replaced the lid, climbed out of the grave and shovelled the soil back on top of the coffin, working steadily. He wondered if it had all been worthwhile.

Yes. Because now he knew that the dead were dead. They'd been dead before 4 July and they still were. Where the living had got to, he couldn't tell. They probably weren't below ground, and he couldn't think of anywhere else they might be. But the dead were still there. That was one certainty, at least.

But what of the dead on the earth's surface?

What of Scott in his tent in the Antarctic? The tent that had collapsed on top of him and his comrades and was probably covered by a sheet of ice. Did that count as being dead and buried? Was his body still there?

What of Amundsen? What if his remains had spent the last eighty years on an ice floe? Were they still there?

And what of all the people who had died in the mountains and never been buried? Had they disappeared like the living, or were they still there?

He no longer needed to know.

*

He made his way into St Stephen's carrying Marie's case and a folding chair. The smell of incense was as faint as it had been the last time. Only two of the overhead lights were still on.

With the case and the folding chair in either hand, Jonas set off slowly, step by step, for the lift. He turned to listen.

Silence.

He put the case and the chair in the lift and turned once more.

Silence.

*

Jonas unfolded the chair and sat down, pulling the case towards him. He looked out across the twilit city. An occasional puff of wind fanned his face.

I hope I don't catch cold, he thought.

And laughed.

He picked up a pebble and examined it. Felt the dust that stuck to it. Looked at the curves and protrusions, indentations and tiny fissures on its surface. No other pebble like this existed. Just as no two people resembled each other in every detail, so no two pebbles were exactly similar in shape, colour and weight. This pebble was unique. There was no other pebble in existence like the one his hand was holding right

now.

He tossed it over the parapet.

He knew he would never see it again. Never, even if he wanted to. He wouldn't find it even if he searched the whole of the cathedral square. Even if he found a pebble resembling the one he'd thrown away, he could never be sure he was really holding the right one in his hand. No one would be able to tell him. No certainty, only vague conjecture.

Yet he remembered holding the pebble and what it had felt like. He remembered the moment he'd held it in his hand.

*

The Sleeper came into his mind, as did something that used to bother Jonas about hand-to-hand combat. When two people fought because one was trying to throttle or knife the other, they were so close in spatial terms that little difference existed between one and the other, assailant and victim. But only spatially. They were grappling skin against skin, but one was a murderer and the other his victim. One self was attacking. The other, two millimetres away, was being killed. So near, yet so great the difference between being one or the other.

Not so where he and the Sleeper were concerned.

He started flicking tablets over the edge of the parapet.

The self. The selves of others. What of the others? What had happened to them?

Why hadn't he woken up screaming on 4 July?

He had often asked himself that question. If countless people perished simultaneously because of some natural or nuclear disaster, why hadn't he sensed it? How was it possible for so many to disappear without his receiving news of them? How could hundreds of thousands of selves meet their end without transmitting some message? How could someone chew bread or watch TV or cut his nails at precisely that moment without getting goosebumps or experiencing an electric shock? So much suffering? And no sign?

That could mean only one thing: it was the principle that counted, not the individual. Either all were doomed or none was.

Or none. So what was he doing here? Why had he woken up all alone? Was there nothing in the entire universe that wanted him?

Marie. Marie wanted him.

With her case in his hand, he climbed over the parapet. He could see the truck standing in the cathedral square far below.

He looked out over the city. He saw the Millennium Tower, the Danube Tower, the churches, the public buildings, the Big Wheel. His mouth was dry, his palms were moist. He smelt of sweat. He sat down again.

Should he do it deliberately, or would it be better to act on impulse?

He leafed through his notebook until he came to the place where he'd asked himself to think, on 4 September, of the day he'd written those words. He had jotted them down in his room at Kanzelstein on 4 August. Now it was 20 August.

He thought of 4 September. The one in two weeks' time and the one 1,000 years hence. There would be no difference between the two, or none worth mentioning. He had once read that, if humanity succeeded in exterminating itself, not a vestige of civilisation would remain after only 100 years. By 4 September in 1,000 years' time, therefore, everything in front of him would have disappeared. But, even on 4 September two weeks from now, there would be no witness left. That being so, how did the two days differ?

Marie. He could see her face. Her whole being.

He wedged the case between his legs and took the old musical teddy from his pocket. Took out Marie's mobile.

Wound up the music box,
thought of Marie,
and toppled
forwards,
slowly,
falling,
ever more slowly.

*

Jonas was already familiar with the distant but swelling sound, except that this time it seemed to be coming from within him. Within him yet remote. At the same time, he was enveloped in a glow that seemed to bear him up. He felt he was being caught hold of and embraced. He felt he could absorb everything that came his way.

A life. You were the same for only two or three years, then you had less and less in common with the person you'd been four years ago. It was like being on a suspension bridge or a tightrope high in the air. Wherever you went, the rope sagged at the point of maximum weight. One step forwards or backwards and the sag became less pronounced, and some distance away the effect of the weight upon the rope was scarcely visible. Such was time, and such was the effect of time on personality. Jonas had once come across some letters he'd written to a girlfriend but never sent. The writer was a completely different person. Another person, not another self, for that remained constant.

He saw Marie's face in front of him. It grew bigger and bigger until it settled over him, spread itself out above his head and slid into him. Was he already falling? Was he falling at all?

The uproar inside him seemed to liquefy. He could smell and taste the closeness of a sound. He saw a book coming towards him and absorbed it.

A book was written and printed, delivered to a bookshop and placed on a shelf, taken out and examined from time to time. After spending a few weeks among other books, between James and Marcel or Emma and Virginia, it was sold. Taken home by the purchaser. Read and placed on a shelf. And there it remained. Years later it might be read a second or third time. But back it would go on the shelf. Five, ten, twelve or fifteen years later it would be given away or sold, read once and placed on a shelf once more. It would be there during the day, when it was light, and in the evening when the lights went out, and at night in the dark. And at daybreak it would still be on the shelf. For five years or thirty, after which it would be resold. Or given away. That was a book: a life on a shelf that harboured life within itself.

He was falling, yet he didn't seem to be moving.

He hadn't known that time could be so sluggish.

He felt as if hundreds of helicopters were starting up all around him. He tried to clasp his head but couldn't see his hand move, it was so slow.

Dying old or young. He had often thought how tragic it was to die young. And yet, in a way, the tragic nature of an early death was diminished by the passing of time. Two men were born in the year 1900. One died in the First World War, the other lived on for twenty, thirty, fifty, eighty years. In 2000 he died too. It no longer mattered that he'd seen many more summers than the one who died young, or that he'd undergone this or that experience denied to the younger man, who had been hit by a Russian or French or German bullet. Why not? Because none of that counted any more. All those days in springtime, all those sunrises and parties, love affairs and winter landscapes were long gone. All of them.

Two people were both born in 1755. One died in 1790, the other in 1832. Forty-two years' difference in age. A great deal at the time. Two centuries later, statistics. Everything far away. Everything small.

The persistent uproar was all around him now. All around and inside him too.

He saw a tree flying towards him. He absorbed the tree. He knew the tree.

Nuclear waste was stored in the ground. Radioactive fuel rods lay buried at many points in the world. They would continue to give off radiation for 32,000 years. Jonas had often wondered what people would say about those responsible for that problem 16,000 years hence. They would think that other people living 16,000 years before them had failed to grasp the meaning of time. Thirty-two thousand years – 1,000 generations. Mystified, everyone would have to work hard to pay for what two or three or ten earlier generations had done for their own short-term benefit. Time was a juxtaposition, not a succession. Generations were neighbours. In 1,000 years' time, householders would be complaining about the retarded hooligan living in their basement and making their lives a misery.

Or so Jonas had thought. But it wouldn't come to that, not now. The fuel rods would continue to emit radiation until it had all dispersed, yet silence would have reigned on the planet for no longer than the time it took to click your fingers.

He was falling ever more slowly. His body seemed to be a part of what lay ahead, just as he was becoming a part of that moment and the owner of the uproar in and around himself.

People had spoken of heaven and hell, heaven being reserved for the good and hell for the bad. Good and evil existed on the earth, it was true. Perhaps those people had been right, perhaps heaven and hell did exist. But you didn't have to play the harp or be roasted on a spit by creatures with horns. Heaven and hell, as he had conceived of them, were subjective forms of expression for the past self. Anyone who had come to terms with himself and the world would feel better and find peace in that long, long moment of death: that was heaven. Anyone spiritually impure would consume himself with fire: that was hell.

He could see everything so clearly from up here.

Happiness was a summer's day in childhood, when the grown-ups were watching the World Cup on TV and water wings were being handed out at the swimming baths. When it was hot, and there were ice creams and lemonade, shouts and laughter.

Happiness was a winter's day on which you should have been at school but were on board the night train to Italy with your parents. Snow and mist and an imposing railway station, a comic book and a cosy compartment. Cold outside, warm within.

He saw a mirror flying towards him. He saw himself. He went into himself.

He saw the Secession building wrapped in sticky tape, the Danube Tower, the Big Wheel. He saw the bed in the middle of Heldenplatz, infinitesimally small. He saw his TV-set sculpture in the Belvedere Gardens, barely visible.

Happiness was also being pushed along in your pram as a little child. Watching the grown-ups, listening to their voices and marvelling at so many new things. Being greeted and smiled at by unfamiliar faces. Sitting there and riding along at the same time. Clutching something sweet in your hand and feeling the warmth of the sun on your legs. And, possibly, meeting another pram, a little girl with curls, being wheeled past each other and waving in the knowledge that she was the one, she was the one, the one you would come to love.